~ DREAM WITH ~

# ~JENNY~
# COLGAN

**Jenny Colgan** is the author of numerous bestselling novels, including *The Little Shop of Happy Ever After* and *Summer at Little Beach Street Bakery*, which are also published by Sphere. *Meet Me at the Cupcake Café* won the 2012 Melissa Nathan Award for Comedy Romance and was a *Sunday Times* top ten bestseller, as was *Welcome to Rosie Hopkins' Sweetshop of Dreams*, which won the RNA Romantic Novel of the Year Award 2013. Jenny was born in Scotland and has lived in London, the Netherlands, the US and France. She eventually settled on the wettest of all of these places, and currently lives just north of Edinburgh with her husband Andrew, her dog Nevil Shute and her three children: Wallace, who is twelve and likes pretending to be nineteen and not knowing what this embarrassing 'family' thing is that keeps following him about; Michael-Francis, who is ten and likes making new friends on aeroplanes; and Delphine, who is eight and is mostly raccoon as much as we can tell so far.

Things Jenny likes include: cakes; far too much *Doctor Who*; wearing Converse trainers every day so her feet are now just gigantic big flat pans; baths only slightly cooler than the surface of the sun and very, very long books, the longer the better. For more about Jenny, visit her website and her Facebook page, or follow her on Twitter @jennycolgan.

~ DREAM WITH ~

# JENNY COLGAN

## The
# Endless
# Beach

sphere

SPHERE

First published in Great Britain in 2018 by Sphere

1 3 5 7 9 10 8 6 4 2

A CIP catalogue record for this book
is available from the British Library.

ISBN 978-0-7515-6482-2

Typeset in Caslon by M Rules
Printed and bound in Great Britain by
Clays Ltd, St Ives plc

Papers used by Sphere are from well-managed forests
and other responsible sources.

Sphere
An imprint of
Little, Brown Book Group
Carmelite House
50 Victoria Embankment
London EC4Y 0DZ

An Hachette UK Company
www.hachette.co.uk

www.littlebrown.co.uk

*To my cousins Marie and Carol-Ann Wilson,*
*for their amazing work in fostering*
*babies and children*

# A Word from Jenny

Hello!

I first wrote about goings-on on the tiny Scottish island of Mure last year and had such a good time doing it I really wanted to go back. There is something very special to me about the communities in the Highlands and Islands of Scotland, where it is so very beautiful – but life can be tough up there too.

Let me quickly get you up to date from the last book, in case you haven't read it – which doesn't matter, by the way – or just so that you don't have to rack your brains remembering who is who, because I hate having to do that and I have a terrible memory for names. (I am also saying this as a get-out clause in case we meet and I forget your name!)

So: Flora MacKenzie, a paralegal in London, was sent up to the remote Scottish island of Mure – where she was raised – to help her (rather attractive and difficult) boss Joel.

Reunited with her father and three brothers, she realised how much she had missed home, and, quite to her own surprise, decided to stay and make a go of it, opening the Summer Seaside Kitchen, which sells the amazing local produce from her family farm, as well as making old recipes from her late mother's recipe book.

To absolutely everybody else's surprise, her boss, Joel, decided to relocate too, giving up his crazy rat race life for something calmer and more grounded. He and Flora are just taking their very first faltering steps into a romance.

They were both working for Colton Rogers, a US billionaire who wanted to buy up half the island, whereupon he (Rogers) fell in love with Flora's talented cheese-maker brother Fintan. With me so far? There's definitely something in the water up there (and dreadful Wi-Fi and long winters, both of which help) . . .

The other two people you need to know about are Saif and Lorna, both of whom appeared in *A Very Distant Shore*, the short book about Mure I wrote for the Quick Reads series.

Saif is a doctor – a Syrian refugee – who endured incredible hardship to make his way to Europe and was granted asylum in the UK, as long as he took his medical skills where they were most needed – the remotest parts of Britain. He has now had no news of the rest of his family for over a year. Lorna is the local primary head teacher, and Flora's best friend.

Okay, I think that is us! Oh no . . . there is one more thing. In my Rosie Hopkins series of novels, there is a baddie who is a social worker, and several social workers wrote to me to complain that they do an underfunded and undervalued job in very difficult circumstances and they didn't think the portrayal was very fair.

So I had another look at the character and decided this was a good point. I hope the social workers in this book help mitigate this, and go some way to showing a little of the genuine respect I have for the dedicated people who do this really tough job day in, day out.

Anyway, I very much hope you enjoy *The Endless Beach*, and have a wonderful day wherever you are. And if you are on holiday, one, I am very jealous as it is statistically raining where I am, and two, send me a selfie! I'm on Facebook or Twitter: @jennycolgan!

With love,

*Jenny*
x x x

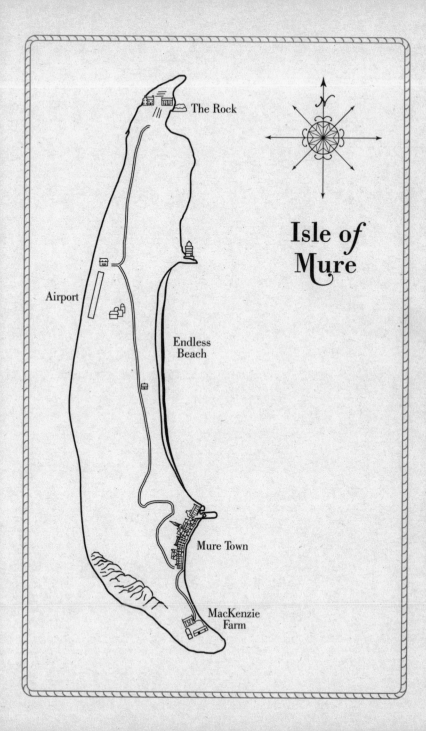

The Rock

Airport

Endless
Beach

Isle of
Mure

Mure Town

MacKenzie
Farm

# A Quick Note on Pronunciation

As well as saying 'ch' like you're about to cough something up, here's a quick guide to pronouncing some of the more traditional names that appear in this book:

**Agot** – *Ah-got*
**Eilidh** – *Ay-lay*
**Innes** – *Inn-is*
**Iona** – *Eye-oh-na*
**Isla** – *Eye-la*
**Saif** – *S-eye-eef*
**Seonaid** – *Shon-itch*
**Teàrlach** – *Cher-lach*

cynefin (n): *one's place of true belonging; the place where one feels most fully at home*

*Once upon a time there was a prince who lived in a high tower made entirely of ice. But he never noticed, as he had never seen anything else, nor been anything else, and to him, being cold was simply the way of things for he had not known anything different. He was the prince of a vast wasteland; he ruled over bears and wild things and answered to nobody.*

*And wise advisers told him to travel; to take a bride; to learn from others. But he refused, saying, 'I am comfortable here,' and eventually the tower of ice grew thick and impossible to enter and nothing grew and it could not be climbed and dragons circled the tower and it became perilous and still the prince would not leave. And many people tried to climb the tower to rescue the prince, but none succeeded. Until one day . . .*

# Chapter One

Even in early spring, Mure is pretty dark.

Flora didn't care; she loved waking up in the morning, curled up close, together in the pitch black. Joel was a very light sleeper (Flora didn't know that before he had met her, he had barely slept at all) and was generally awake by the time she rubbed her eyes, his normally tense, watchful face softening as he saw her, and she would smile, once again surprised and overwhelmed and scared by the depth of how she felt; how she trembled at the rhythm of his heartbeat.

She even loved the frostiest mornings, when she had to pull herself up to get everything going. It was different when you didn't have an hour-long commute pressed up against millions of other commuters breathing germs and pushing against you and making your life more uncomfortable than it had to be.

Instead, she would rake up the damped peat in the wood-burner in the beautiful guest cottage Joel was staying in while working for Colton Rogers, the billionaire who owned half the island. She would set the flames into life – and the room became even cosier in an instant, the flickering light from the fire throwing shadows on the whitewashed walls.

The one thing Joel had insisted on in the room was a highly expensive state-of-the-art coffee machine, and she would let him fiddle with that while he logged on to the day's work and made his customary remark about the many and varied failures of the island's internet reliability.

Flora would take her coffee, pull on an old jumper and wander to the window of the cottage, where she could sit on the top of the old oil-fired radiator, the type you get in schools but had cost Colton a fortune. Here she would stare out at the dark sea; sometimes with its white tips showing if it was going to be a breezy day; sometimes astonishingly clear, in which case, even in the morning, you could raise your eyes and see the brilliant cold stars overhead. There was no light pollution on Mure. They were bigger than Flora remembered from being a child.

She wrapped her hands round her mug and smiled. The shower started up. 'Where are you off to today?' she shouted.

Joel popped his head out the door. 'Hartford for starters,' he said. 'Via Reykjavik.'

'Can I come?'

Joel gave her a look. Work wasn't funny.

'Come on. We can make out on the plane.'

'I'm not sure . . . '

Colton had a plane he used to get in and out of Mure, and Flora was absolutely incensed that it was strictly for company business and she'd never been allowed on it. A private plane! Such a thing was unimaginable, really. Joel was impossible to tease where work was involved. Actually, he was quite difficult to tease about anything. Which worried Flora sometimes.

'I bet there is absolutely nothing the stewardesses haven't seen,' said Flora. This was undoubtedly true, but Joel was already scrolling through the *Wall Street Journal* and not really listening.

'Back two weeks Friday. Colton is consolidating literally ... well ... '

Flora wished he could talk more about his work, like he could when she was still in the law trade. It wasn't just confidentiality. He was guarded about everything.

Flora pouted. 'You'll miss the Argylls.'

'The what?'

'It's a band. They tour and they're coming to the Harbour's Rest. They're really brilliant.'

Joel shrugged. 'I don't really like music.'

Flora went up to him. Music was in the lifeblood of everyone on Mure. Before the ferries and the aeroplanes came, they'd had to make their own entertainment, and everyone joined in with enthusiasm, if not always too much talent. Flora danced well and could just about play a bodhrán if there wasn't anyone better around. Her brother Innes was a better fiddler than he let on. The only one who couldn't play anything was big Hamish; their mother had just tended to give him a pair of spoons and let him get on with it.

She put her arms around him. 'How can you not like music?' she said.

Joel blinked and looked over her shoulder. It was silly,

3

really, a small thing in the endless roundabout that had been his difficult childhood, that every new school was a new chance to get it wrong: to wear the wrong thing; to like the wrong band. The fear of doing so. His lack of ability, or so it seemed, to learn the rules. The cool bands varied so widely, it was absolutely impossible to keep track.

He had found it easier to abdicate responsibility altogether. He'd never quite made his peace with music. Never dared to find out what he liked. Never had an older sibling to point the way.

It was the same with clothes. He only wore two colours – blue and grey, impeccably sourced, from the best fabrics – not because he had taste, but because it seemed absolutely the simplest. He never had to think about it. Although he'd gone on to date enough models to learn a lot more about clothes: that was something they had been helpful for.

He glanced over at Flora. She was staring out at the sea again. Sometimes he had trouble distinguishing her from the environment of Mure. Her hair was the fronds of seaweed that lay across the pale white dunes of her shoulders; her tears the sprays of saltwater in a storm; her mouth a perfect shell. She wasn't a model – quite the opposite. She felt as grounded, as solid as the earth beneath her feet; she was an island, a village, a town, a home. He touched her gently, almost unable to believe she was his.

Flora knew this touch of his, and she could not deny it. It worried her, the way that he looked at her sometimes: as if she were something fragile, precious. She was neither of those things. She was just a normal girl, with the same

4

worries and faults as anyone else. And eventually he was going to realise this, and she was terrified about what would happen when he realised that she wasn't a selkie; that she wasn't some magical creature who'd materialised to solve everything about his life ... She was terrified what would happen when he realised she was just a normal person who worried about her weight and liked to dress very badly on Sundays ... What would happen when they had to argue about washing-up liquid? She kissed his hand gently.

'Stop looking at me like I'm a water sprite.'

He grinned. 'Well, you are to me.'

'What time's your ... ? Oh.'

She always forgot that Colton's plane left to their schedule, not an airline's.

Joel glanced at his watch. 'Now. Colton has a real bug up his ass ... I mean ... There's lots to do.'

'Don't you want breakfast?'

Joel shook his head. 'Ridiculously, they'll be serving Seaside Kitchen bread and scones on board.'

Flora smiled. '*Well*, aren't *we* fancy?' She kissed him. 'Come back soon.'

'Why, where are you going?'

'Nowhere,' said Flora, pulling him close. 'Absolutely nowhere.'

And she watched him leave without a backwards glance, and sighed.

Oddly it was only during sex that she knew, one hundred per cent, that he was there. Absolutely and completely there, with her, breath for breath, movement for movement. It was not like anything she had ever known before. She had

5

known selfish lovers and show-off lovers, and purely incompetent lovers, their potential ruined by pornography before they were barely men.

She hadn't ever known anything like this – the intensity, almost desperation – as if he were trying to fit the whole of himself inside her skin. She felt utterly known and as if she knew him perfectly. She thought about it constantly. But he was hardly ever here. And the rest of the time she wasn't any clearer about where his head was than when they'd first met.

And now, a month later, it wasn't so dark, but Joel was still away, busy on one job after another. Flora was travelling today but nowhere quite so interesting, and alas, she was back in the farmhouse.

There was something Flora felt as an adult about being closeted in the bedroom – in the single bed she grew up in, no less, with her old highland dancing trophies, dusty and still lining the wall – that made her irritable, as well as the knowledge that however early she had to get up – and it felt very, very early – her three farmworking brothers and her father would already have been up milking for an hour.

Well, not Fintan. He was the food genius of the family and spent most of his time making cheese and butter for the Seaside Kitchen and, soon they hoped, Colton's new hotel, the Rock. But the other boys – strong, dim Hamish and Innes, her eldest brother – were out, dark or light, rain or shine, and however much she tried to get her father, Eck, to slow down, he tended to head out too. When she had worked down in London as a paralegal, they had joked that she was lazy. Now that she ran an entire café single-handedly, she'd hoped to prove them wrong, but they still saw her as a lightweight, only getting up at 5 a.m.

She should move out – there were a few cottages to rent in Mure town, but the Seaside Kitchen wasn't turning over enough money for her to afford to do something as extravagant as that. She couldn't help it. They had such amazing produce here on Mure – fresh organic butter churned in their own dairies; the most astonishing cheese, made by Fintan; the best fish and shellfish from their crystal-clear waters; the rain that grew the world's sweetest grass, that fattened up the coos. But it all cost money.

She immediately worked out in her head what time it was in New York, where Joel, her boyfriend – it felt ridiculous, she realised, calling him her boyfriend – was working.

He had been her own boss, sent up with her to work on some legal business for Colton Rogers. But being her boss was only a part of it. She'd had a massive crush on him for years, since the first moment she'd set eyes on him. He, on the other hand, spent his life dating models and not noticing her. She hadn't ever thought she could get his attention. And then, finally, when they had worked together last summer, he had thawed enough to notice her: enough, in the end, to relocate his business to work with Colton on Mure.

Except of course it hadn't quite turned out like that. Colton had assigned him a guest cottage, a beautifully restored hunting lodge, while the Rock was preparing to officially open, which was taking its time. Then he'd shot off all round the world, looking after his various billionaire enterprises – which seemed to require Joel with him at all times. She'd barely seen him all winter. Right now, he was in New York. Things like setting up home – things like sitting down to have a conversation – seemed completely beyond him.

Flora had known theoretically that he was a workaholic; she'd worked for him for years. She just didn't realise what that would mean when it came to their relationship. She seemed to get the leftovers. And there wasn't much. Not even a message to indicate he was aware she was going to London today, to formally sign her leaving papers.

Flora hadn't been sure if they could keep the Seaside Kitchen going over the winter, when the tourists departed and the nights drew down so low it was never light at all, not really, and the temptation was very much to stay in bed all day with the covers over her head.

But to her surprise, the Kitchen was busy every single day. Mothers with babies; old people stopping to chat to their friends over a cheese scone; the knitting group that handled spillover Fair Isle orders and normally met in each other's kitchens who had decided to make the Seaside Kitchen their home, and Flora never got tired of watching the amazing speed and grace of gnarled old fingers producing the beautiful repeating patterns on every type of wool.

So much so that she'd realised: this was her job now. This was where she belonged. Her firm in London had originally given her a leave of absence to work with Colton, but that was over and she had to formally resign. Joel had too: he was working for Colton full time. Flora had been putting off going to London, hoping they'd be able to go together to sign off the paperwork, but it didn't seem to be very likely.

So she helped Isla, one of the two young girls who worked with her, open up the Seaside Kitchen for the day. They'd repainted it the same pale pink it had been until it had gone to seed and started to peel. Now it fitted in nicely with the black-and-white Harbour's Rest hotel, the pale blue of the tackle shop and the cream of many tourist shops that lined the front, selling big woollen jumpers, souvenir shells and stone carvings, tartan (of course), small models of Highland coos, tablet and toffee. Many of them were shut for the winter.

The wind was ripping off the sea, throwing handfuls of spray and rain into her face and she grinned and ran down the hill from the farmhouse, the commute that was all she had these days. It might be freezing – although she had a huge Puffa jacket on that basically insulated her from absolutely everything – but she still wouldn't swap it in a second for an overheated, overstuffed tube carriage; a great outpouring of humanity pushing up the stairs; hot, cold, hot, cold, pushing past more and more people; witnessing shouts and squabbles and cars bumping each other and horns going off and cycle couriers screaming at cabbies and tubes roaring past, free sheets being blown by the wind up and down the street with fast-food wrappers and cigarette butts … No, Flora thought, even on mornings like this, you could keep your commute. She didn't miss it.

Annie's Seaside Kitchen was lit up and golden. It was plain, with ten mismatched bric-a-brac tables scattered artfully around the large room. The counter, currently empty, would soon be filled with scones, cakes, quiche, homemade salads and soups as Iona and Isla busied themselves in the back. Mrs Laird, a local baker, dropped off two dozen loaves a day, which went fairly speedily, and the coffee machine didn't stop from dawn till dusk. Flora still couldn't quite believe it existed, and that it was down to her. Somehow, coming back to her old stamping ground and finding her late mother Annie's own recipe book – it had felt like a happy choice, not a desperate one, or a sad one.

It had felt like a great, ridiculous leap at the time. Now in retrospect it felt entirely obvious, as if it was the only thing she should have done. As if this was home, and the same people she remembered from her childhood – older now, but the faces were the same, handed down the generations – were as much a part of her world as they ever were, and the essential things in her life – Joel, the Seaside Kitchen, the weather forecast, the farm, the freshness of the produce – were more important to her somehow than Brexit, than global warming, than the fate of the world. It wasn't as if she was in retreat. She was in renewal.

So Flora was in an unusually good mood as she removed the MacKenzie family butter from the fridge – creamy and salted and frankly capable of rendering all other sorts of spreads redundant – and glanced to see all the locally fired earthenware ready and in a row. There was an English incomer living up past the farms in a tiny little cottage who made it out the back in a kiln. It was thick and plainly fired in earthen colours – sand, and grey and off-white – and they were perfect for keeping your latte warm with a thin, slightly turned-in top and a much thicker base. They'd had to have a polite sign made saying that the mugs were for sale, otherwise people kept nicking them, and the sales had provided a rather handy sideline and a completely unexpected new lease of life for Geoffrey from up off the old Macbeth farm road.

As soon as she turned the CLOSED sign to OPEN, the clouds parted, making it look as if they might get a ray or two of sunshine with their gale-force winds, and that made her smile too. Joel was away, and that was sad. But on the other hand, once she'd got this stupid London trip out of the way she could maybe get Lorna over to watch *TOWIE* on catch-up and split a bottle of Prosecco with her. She didn't make much but they could still go halfers on a bottle of Prosecco, and truly, in the end, what more was there to life than that?

A song she liked came on the radio, and Flora was as full of contentment as anyone can truly feel in the middle of February, when a shadow passed in front of the doorway. Flora opened the door to their first customer of the morning who stepped back slightly from the arctic draught, blinking as they blocked out the light behind them. Then her good mood dissipated slightly. It was Jan.

When Flora had first arrived on Mure, she'd met a nice man – a very nice man – called Charlie, or Teàrlach. He led outdoor activity holidays on Mure, sometimes for businessmen and lawyers and organisations, which paid the bills, and sometimes for deprived children from the mainland, which he did for charity.

Charlie had liked Flora and Flora, resigned to the idea that she was never going to get together with Joel, had flirted with him a bit – well, more than a bit, she thought. She was

11

always embarrassed to look back on it: how quickly she had gone from one to another. But Charlie was a gentleman and had understood. The other thing was, though, he had been on a break from his girlfriend, Jan, who worked with him. Jan had subsequently decided that Flora was a feckless tart and that it was all her fault that she'd led him astray. She had never forgiven Flora, but instead did her down fairly loudly and publicly whenever she got half a chance.

Normally this wouldn't bother Flora terribly much. But on an island the size of Mure, it could be quite tricky to avoid bumping into someone fairly regularly, and if that person didn't like you, it could get a little wearing.

Today, however, Jan – who was tall, with short sensible hair, a determinedly square jaw and a constant conviction that she was saving the world (she worked with Charlie on the adventure holidays) and everyone else was a feckless wastrel – had a smile on her face.

'Morning!' she trilled. Flora looked at Isla and Iona, both of whom were as surprised as she was at Jan's jolly mood. They both shrugged their shoulders.

'Um ... Hi, Jan,' said Flora. Normally Jan ignored her completely and ordered from the girls, proceeding to talk loudly the entire time as if Flora didn't exist. Flora would have barred her, but she wasn't really a barring type of person and had absolutely no idea how she'd have done such a thing. Anyway, barring one person who worked with the adventure programme while simultaneously funnelling food near its sell-by date to the children who came to visit, via Charlie, seemed a little self-defeating in the end.

'Hello!' Jan was swishing her left hand about

12

ostentatiously. Flora thought she was waving at someone across the street. Fortunately, Isla was slightly more up on this sort of thing.

'Jan! Is that an engagement ring?'

Jan flushed and looked as coy as she could, which wasn't very, and shyly displayed her hand.

'You and Charlie tying the knot then?' said Isla. 'That's great!'

'Congratulations!' said Flora, genuinely delighted. She had felt bad about Charlie; the fact that he was happy enough in his life to pop the question to Jan was wonderful news. 'That's just great. I'm so pleased!'

Jan looked slightly discombobulated at that, as if she'd been secretly hoping Flora would throw herself to the ground and start rending her garments in misery.

'So, when are you doing it?' asked Iona.

'Well, it will be at the Rock, of course.'

'If it's ready,' said Flora. She didn't know what Colton was prevaricating about.

Jan raised her eyebrows. 'Oh, I'm sure some people know how to get things done around here ... Do you have any raisin splits this morning?'

And Flora had to admit, annoyed, that they didn't.

'Well, it's wonderful news,' she said again. Then she didn't want to push too hard in case it looked like she was angling for an invite. Which she very much wasn't. More than a few people had seen her and Charlie about town last summer and remembered Jan's meltdown after she'd found them kissing. The last thing she needed was gossip sprouting again, not when things were finally calm and quiet.

So she went back behind the counter. 'Can I get you anything else?'

'Four slices of quiche. So. I know normally your stuff is too full of sugar and you waste a lot ... ?'

Supreme happiness hadn't dented Jan's love of stating the worst possible take on practically everything, Flora noticed.

'Sorry, what was that?'

'Well,' said Jan, a smile playing on her lips. 'We thought you might like to cater the wedding.'

Flora blinked. She was desperate to get into catering; there was no news on the Rock, and she really did want to turn over some more money. She'd be able to pay the girls a little more. She'd rather not have to watch everyone watch her watch Charlie get married. But on the other hand, she didn't really care, did she? And they could really, really do with the money. And she'd be backstage all the time, looking after things in the kitchen. Actually, this might be the best possible solution.

'Of course!' she said. 'We'd be delighted!'

Jan frowned again. It struck Flora that Jan had had some kind of scenario playing out in her head in which she, Flora, would be rendered somehow humiliated by this. She didn't quite understand where the benefit was, but she certainly wouldn't give Jan the satisfaction of thinking that deep down, Flora was anything other than pleased.

Jan leaned closer. 'It would make a lovely wedding present,' she said.

Flora blinked.

A silence fell, broken only by the bell above the door ringing, as their morning regulars started to file in, and Isla

14

and Iona scuttled along the counter to serve them, judging a safe distance between being away from the difficult conversation and still being able to eavesdrop.

'Ah,' said Flora, finally. 'No, I think . . . I think we'd have to charge. I'm sorry.'

Jan nodded as if in sympathy.

'I realise this must be hard for you,' she said finally. Flora could do nothing but look ahead, cheerfully. 'You'd think with that rich boyfriend of yours you'd want to do something good for the island . . . '

Flora bit back from mentioning that that wasn't how it worked, not at all, and she wouldn't have dreamed of taking a penny from Joel, ever; in fact, the idea of ever asking him for anything filled her with terror. They'd never even discussed money. She was conscious as she thought this that they hadn't discussed anything much, but dismissed it.

Joel, who didn't understand this kind of thing particularly well, found it something of a welcome relief from the women he had dated in the past who pouted and always wanted to go shopping. But he also assumed that Flora didn't actually need or want anything, which wasn't true either.

But more than that, it was the idea of Jan and her wealthy, well-fed family tucking into one of the Seaside Kitchen's famous spreads – lobster, and oysters on ice, and the best bread and butter, and local beef, and the best cheese to be found around, glistening pies, and freshly skimmed cream. That they would take that, guffawing among themselves that they hadn't paid anything for it . . .

Flora bagged up the pieces of quiche and rang it up on the till without another word. Jan counted out the money

15

very, very slowly, with a patronising smile on her face, then left, Flora gazing hotly behind her.

Iona watched her go. 'That's a shame,' she said.

'That woman is a monster,' growled Flora, good mood almost entirely dissipated.

'No, I mean, I really wanted to go to the wedding,' said Iona. 'I bet there'll be loads of good-looking boys there.'

'Is that all you think about – meeting boys?' said Flora.

'No,' said Iona. 'All I think about is meeting boys who aren't fishermen.'

'Oi!' said a party of fishermen who were warming their freezing hands around the large earthenware mugs of tea and tearing into fresh warm soda bread.

'No offence,' said Iona. 'But you are always smelling of fish and having not enough thumbs because you got them tangled in a net, isn't it?'

The fishermen looked at each other and nodded and agreed that that was fair enough, fair enough indeed, it was a dangerous business mind you.

'Right!' said Flora, throwing up her hands. 'I have a plane to catch.'

## Chapter Two

Flora drove the battered old Land Rover past her friend Lorna MacLeod's farmhouse on her way to the airport, but missed her by moments. That morning it was very windy, with a breeze off the sea and white tips of the waves beating against the sand, but it was definitely brightening up – the tide was in, and the beach known as the Endless looked like a long, golden path. You still needed a stout jacket, but in the air you could sense it somehow: something stirring in the earth.

On the way down from the farm, Milou bounding joyfully at her side, Lorna, the local primary school head teacher, and in fact teacher (there were two: Lorna took what was commonly known as the 'wee' class which covered the four- to eight-year-olds, and the saintly Mrs Cook covered the others) saw crocuses and snowdrops and daffodils beginning to push through their snaked heads. There was a scent in the air; over the normal sea-spray, which she never even noticed, there was an earthier scent – of growth, of rebirth.

Lorna smiled to herself luxuriantly, thinking of the months ahead, of the longer and longer days until the middle of the summer when it barely got dark at all; when Mure would be full and joyfully thronged with happy holidaymakers; when the three pubs would be full every night and the music would play until the last whisky drinker was happy or asleep or both. She put her hands deep into the pockets of her Puffa jacket, and set off, her eyes on the horizon, where the last rays of pink and gold were just vanishing and some cold but golden rays of early spring sunshine were pushing over.

She was also feeling cheerful as she now awoke when it was light, for starters. The winter had been mild, comparatively speaking – the storms had of course swept down from the Arctic, cutting off the ferries and causing everyone to huddle inside, but she didn't mind that so much. She liked seeing the children charge around in their hats and mittens, pink-cheeked and laughing in the school yard; she enjoyed cosy hot chocolates in town and curling up beside the fire in her father's old house. She'd inherited the house – to share, technically, with her brother. He worked the rigs and had a cool modern apartment in Aberdeen though, and he didn't care really, so she'd sold her little high-street flat to a young couple and set about trying to build a home in the old farmhouse in a fit of spring exuberance. In fact, it was a shame she'd missed Flora, as Flora could have done with a good dose of Lorna positivity, for what came after.

She did, however, see Saif.

Saif spotted her at the same time from the other end of the beach. He lived in the old manse – the smaller, crumbling one, not the one Colton had lavishly updated – up on the hillside, empty since their vicar had moved to the mainland, the ageing population here no longer large enough to justify a full-time padre, on an island which, even though it had strong overtones of religious severity and Knoxism, had never torn itself away entirely from its earlier roots: the many, fierce gods of the Viking invaders; the green earth gods of its primary inhabitants. There was something on the island that was deeply, utterly spiritual, whatever your beliefs. There were standing stones on the headlands – the remains of a community that had worshipped heaven knows what – as well as an ancient, beautiful ruined abbey, and scattered stern plain churches with stubby steeples standing stiff against the northerly winds.

The house was rented to Saif as he did his two years' service to the community in return for which, it was promised, he would receive his permanent right to stay. He was a refugee, and a doctor, and the remote islands desperately needed GPs, although his promised right to stay of course was not guaranteed. Saif had given up reading about British politics. It was a total mystery to him. He was unaware that it was an equal mystery to everyone else around him; he just assumed this was how things had always been.

He had been having the dreams again. He wasn't sure he'd ever be free of them. Always the clamour, the noise. Being in the boat again. Clutching on to his leather bag as though his life depended on it. The look on the face of the little boy he'd had to stitch up without anaesthetic after a fight had broken out. The stoicism. The desperation. The boat.

And every morning, regardless of the weather, he woke up determined not to sink beneath his own waves – his own waves of waiting: waiting to hear about his wife and his two sons, left behind when he went to see if he could forge a passage to a better life for them all in a world that had got suddenly, harshly worse.

He had heard nothing, although he called the Home Office once a week. He was unsure if the distant neighbourhood he had left behind – once friendly, chatty, relaxed – even existed any more. His entire life was gone.

And people kept telling him he was one of the lucky ones.

Every morning, to shake the night horrors from his head, he would go for a long walk down the Endless to try to get himself into an appropriate state of mind to deal with the minor complaints of the local population: their sore hips, and coughing babies, and mild anxiety, and menopauses, and everything that he must not dismiss as absolutely nothing compared with the searing, apocalyptic misery of his homeland. A couple of miles normally did it. Through the winter, he had walked as the sun barely rose, half by instinct, welcoming the handfuls of hail that felt like rocks being thrown into his face, a phenomenon he had never experienced until he had come to Europe and which he had found almost comically inconvenient.

But at least the weather allowed him to feel something other than dread, and he let it scour out his head. When he was chilled to the bone – and exhausted – then, he felt clean. And empty. And ready for another day in this half-life – an eternal waiting room.

And he was thinking this when he saw it, and he threw up his arms in surprise.

Lorna saw this happen from the other end of the beach, and her brow furrowed. It was not like Saif to be enthusiastic. If anything, you had to work pretty hard to draw him out. Life on Mure was chatty – there was no way around it. Everyone knew each other and everyone used gossip as the lifeblood of their community. It wasn't unusual to know the goings-on and whereabouts of three generations of Murians at any one time. Of course, everyone was a millionaire in America or doing fabulously well in London or had the most brilliant and amazing children. You just accepted that as a given. Still, it was nice to hear, regardless.

But Saif never, ever spoke about his family. It was all Lorna knew that he had – or had had – a wife and two sons. She couldn't bear to ask anything more. Saif had landed on Mure stripped of everything – of possessions, of his status. He was a refugee before he was a doctor: he was something pitied – even, in some quarters (until he stitched up their injuries and tended to their parents), despised for no reason. She couldn't bear the risk of upsetting him, of taking away the last bit of dignity he had left, by prying.

So when she saw him waving, the bright empty Mure morning full of whipping clouds and promise, her heart started to beat faster immediately. Milou caught on to her excitement and bounded cheerily up the beach. She ran to keep up with him, arriving panting – the Endless was always much longer than you thought it was; the water played tricks on your concept of distance – and trepidatious.

'Look!' Saif was shouting. 'Look!'

She followed his pointing finger. Was it a boat? What was it? She screwed her eyes up.

21

'Oh. It's gone,' said Saif, and she looked at him, puzzled, but his gaze was still fixed out on the water. She stared too, trying to get her heart to calm down. Just as she was about to ask him what the hell he'd been going on about, she saw it: a ripple at first, not something you could be sure of, then, straight out of the blue, a huge body – vast, vaster than it had any right to be, so big you couldn't believe that it could possibly propel itself. It was like watching a 747 take off – a huge, shining black body leaped straight out over the waves and, with a vibrant twist of its tail, shaking off the droplets of water, plunged back underneath.

Saif turned to her, eyes shining. He said something that sounded like 'hut'.

Lorna squinted. 'What?'

'I don't know the word in English,' he said.

'Oh!' said Lorna. 'Whale! It's a whale. A weird … I've never seen anything like that before.'

'There are many of them here?'

'Some,' said Lorna. She frowned. 'Some normal whales. That one looks weird. And it's not good for them to be so close to shore. One got washed up last year and it was a heck of a palaver, remember?'

Saif didn't understand whether a 'heck of a palaver' was a good thing or a bad thing, and did not remember, so he just kept looking. Sure enough, after a few moments the whale leaped again, and this time the sun caught the droplets dropping from its tail like diamonds, and what looked bizarrely like a horn. They both leaned forward to see it.

'It's beautiful.'

Lorna looked at it. 'It is,' she said.

'You do not sound so happy, Lorenah.'

He had never been very good at pronouncing her name.

'Well,' she said. 'For starters, I'm worried about it. Whales beaching is a terrible thing. Even if you can save them once, sometimes they just do it again. And the other thing . . .'

Saif looked at her quizzically.

'Oh well, you'll think this is stupid.'

He shrugged his shoulders.

'For Murians . . . on the island, I mean. They're seen as unlucky.'

Saif frowned. 'But they're so beautiful.'

'Lots of beautiful things bring bad luck. So we'll welcome them in,' said Lorna, her eyes fixed on the horizon. 'We need Flora. She can handle these things.'

Saif looked doubtful, and Lorna laughed. 'Oh, it's just silly superstition though.'

And the whale leaped again through the breaking waves, so strong and free, and Lorna wondered a little why she didn't feel joyous; why she had, unexpectedly, an ominous feeling in the pit of her stomach, quite at odds with the blowy day.

# Chapter Three

Flora alighted at Liverpool Street from the airport and came up from the warm bowels of the subway, reflecting, briefly, how shocking London is when you've been away and aren't used to it; how there are more people, probably, on the railway concourse than live on her entire island. Then she realised that she'd been standing on the escalator a microsecond too long because somebody barged into her and made a loud tutting sound.

It seemed very strange to her that she'd only been away a few months, as the London commute used to feel as natural to her as breathing. Now she couldn't imagine why anybody would put themselves through this if they didn't absolutely have to.

Now, this morning was something she was not looking forward to. Not at all. It was ridiculous: all she had to do was go in, pick up her stuff, sign some forms for HR to tell them she was leaving and promise not to work for any more high-flying law firms in the next three months, which wouldn't be difficult, seeing as there weren't any high-flying law firms on Mure. There was no high-flying anything. That's what made it so nice.

So she shouldn't be nervous. But she was. The trouble was, Flora couldn't help herself remembering, now she was back in London. She remembered what it was like here, when Joel was constantly dating ridiculously beautiful models; when he used Tinder and hook-ups and all sorts of things Flora had never been particularly good at; when you would never, in your wildest dreams, have put a senior partner – a handsome senior partner too – together with some pale paralegal.

Flora was unusual-looking, she knew, but not traditionally lovely. Her hair was a very pale strawberry blonde, almost fading away to nothing, and her skin was white as milk. Her eyes were the colour of the sea; they changed almost constantly from grey to green to blue. She was the product of generations of island folk and Vikings.

But she wasn't like the gorgeously, beautifully made-up Instagram girls of London, with their amazing clothes – everyone in Mure just wore a fleece every day – and blow-dried hair – there was never any point doing this in Mure, for windy reasons. Here, everyone seemed so self-assured and busy and rushing and glamorous. And she felt herself shrink. Whereas Mure felt like her home, her place to be. It didn't, however, stop London making her feel like a failure.

Focus, Flora told herself. Focus on the good stuff. Their life together. She blinked.

There was no doubt that being with someone as driven, as tough as Joel was, was as her best friend Lorna said, difficult. A pickle. He had grown up in foster care, in and out of other people's homes. Flora wasn't exactly sure he'd ever managed to properly attach to anyone. She worried, genuinely, how much it was her he loved, how much her family – she and her three brothers adored each other, mostly through the medium of slagging each other off – or how much the island itself, with its calm atmosphere, where everyone knew each other. That it gave his anxious heart a berth, which was all very well. But Flora wondered if that was enough; if she, herself, were enough.

Because they had worked together, in this building, for four years, and he'd never noticed her. Not once. Never even known her name. Even though she'd spoken to him several times, when he first called her up to discuss Mure, he'd acted as if they'd never met before. Kai, her best friend in the office, had found it absolutely astounding that they had got together. And Kai was someone who cared for her. What on earth the rest of the office must be thinking she couldn't bear to imagine.

She steeled herself. In, out and it would be over. And she could get on with the next, massive stage of her life, whatever it was going to be.

# Chapter Four

Fintan MacKenzie, the youngest of Flora's three elder brothers, blinked awake to the sight of his boyfriend, Colton Rogers, stretching in the sun.

'What are you doing?' groaned Fintan. They'd been finalising possible whisky suppliers for the Rock the night before – the development was coming on at an extremely leisurely pace – with fairly predictable results, and the early spring sunshine coming through the huge paned windows of the hotel room was messing with his head.

'Sun salutations!' said Colton bouncily. 'C'mon, join me?'

Fintan put his head back under the covers. 'No thanks! Also, you know, that is not your most flattering angle.'

Colton grinned and carried on. 'You won't say that when you see how bendy it makes me. Come on, get up. I've got green juice and green tea on the go downstairs.'

'The only thing green around here,' complained Fintan

as he headed off to the bathroom, 'is me. What have you got planned today?'

'Seeing my lawyer this morning to go over a few things,' said Colton.

'Is that the weird American guy?' shouted Fintan from the bathroom.

'Weird guy would suffice,' said Colton, 'seeing as you are talking to an American. Anyway, you should know. Isn't he marrying your sister?'

Fintan groaned and popped his head out of the bathroom. 'Don't ask me, for God's sake. Flora is a law unto herself. And anyway, marrying? Really?' He made a face.

'What have you got against marriage?' said Colton, stretching himself out again like a cat and bending his back.

'Only that it's for idiots,' said Fintan. 'Look at Innes.'

Innes was the eldest MacKenzie brother, who had married the beautiful Eilidh. It had ended badly, she had raced back to the mainland and now he saw his gorgeous, wilful daughter Agot not nearly as much as he would like.

'Mmm,' said Colton. He changed position and didn't say anything more, and there was a slightly odd silence between them. Then Fintan disappeared into the shower and promptly forgot all about it.

Colton kissed him when he got out.

'That's your "going away for ages" kiss,' grumbled Fintan. 'I don't like it.'

'Neither do I,' said Colton, a smile playing on his lips.

'What?'

'Nothing.'

'What?'

'Well, now I've got that tame lawyer working for me . . . '

'Can we stop talking about him please?'

' . . . I thought I'd go, maybe close down a few things – make it easier for me to spend more time here.'

'Seriously?' said Fintan, his face lighting up. Colton looked at him for a while, just enjoying the effect it had. 'That would be awesome,' said Fintan.

'I know,' said Colton. 'I'm going to . . . well. I have some ideas.'

Fintan embraced him. Then he looked up. 'Can we still go to the Caribbean in February though?'

'Yes.'

## Chapter Five

Adu on reception smiled happily to see Flora and she was grateful to see a friendly face.

'You're back!' he said.

'Oh, no, I'm off,' she said. 'I'll turn in my pass later. I'm leaving.'

Adu looked surprised. 'You're leaving the firm?'

'Uh-huh.'

'Why?'

'To ... um. I'm running a café in Scotland now.'

Adu blinked. 'But this is ... this is the best law firm in London.'

Flora tried to smile. She tried to make herself think of all the punishing hours she'd put in here, the early mornings, the late nights, the endless tedious paper-work she really hated. She'd done everything her mother had wanted her to do – get a degree, get a career – and then, she'd been forced to go home, thinking she didn't want to – and realised she'd loved it all along. It was the strangest feeling.

And somehow, in an awful way that sometimes felt like a betrayal, it also had set her free.

It wasn't Adu who worried her. It was Margo, Joel's high-powered assistant, who had protected him from the outside world and run his life and diary with exceptional ruthlessness. Suddenly Flora wished they hadn't decided that it would have been ridiculous for them to turn up together. She wanted Joel there, his quiet presence calming her, her amazement every time she felt him by her side, as if every hair in her body lifted when he entered a room, like a sunflower gravitating towards him. She knew, deep down, it wasn't right to be so amazed, to be so bowled over.

She had handed him her heart in her hands without truly knowing whether this quiet, enclosed man could be trusted with it. But it had gone; it had flown from her as if it had always been his, regardless of what he wanted to do with it. She sighed. Maybe she wouldn't see Margo. Maybe she wouldn't see anyone.

'SURPRISE!'

Flora blinked. Her old desk, situated in an open-plan space and now occupied by a slightly insultingly young-looking girl called Narinder, was covered in balloons, and standing behind it, looking jolly, was her best work friend, Kai. Never one to let things pass undercelebrated, he had covered her desk with cakes and bottles of fizz, and everyone she knew (and many she didn't: things moved fast at the firm, but who cared when cake was involved?) was standing round, looking pink and cheerful.

'Hooray!' shouted Kai. 'You're making it out of here alive!'

Everyone cheered, and Flora also went pink. 'Och, I'm only . . . I mean, I'm in the middle of nowhere,' she muttered.

Kai said, 'Listen to you, you've gone all Scottish and you've only been away five minutes.' He popped a cork and poured fizz into plastic cups, and more people arrived every minute. Flora had kept her head down and worked incredibly hard for the four years she'd spent there, and she was touched by how many people came up to thank her for what she'd done or to say how much they'd miss her.

'See?' said Kai. 'You think no one ever notices you.'

'Come on, serve free cake and they could be saying bye to a pencil sharpener,' said Flora, but she was pleased nonetheless.

One older woman, one of the senior lawyers, who Flora had always looked up to as almost impossibly suave and glamorous, took her aside. She was on her second glass of fizz.

'Tell me about Mure,' she said. 'Are there jobs there?'

'Well, tourism mostly,' said Flora. 'Catering, always. Farming if you like. It's not easy up there to make a living. Doctors and teachers always welcome.'

The woman nodded. 'It was my dream, you know,' she said. 'To move away. To make money here, then go somewhere beautiful where I could . . . ' She smiled. 'This sounds silly, I know. But where I could set myself free.'

Flora nodded. She knew what she meant.

'You could,' said Flora. 'You could go any time. It's not

32

expensive to buy a house or anything. The people are nice. And there are lots of English people there,' she said, encouragingly. 'I mean, we have shops and everything. Well. Three shops. Okay, forget what I said about the shops.'

The woman smiled sadly. 'Oh, I'm too old to start over now, I think. Everything I know is here, and, well ... But you doing it ... amazing. I think it's amazing. I look at your Facebook.'

'Oh,' said Flora.

'And it's so beautiful and ... well. I'm jealous. That's all.'

And she patted Flora on the arm, rubbed briefly at her eyes and sashayed off on her amazing high heels which cost more than Annie's Seaside Kitchen turned over in a week. Flora watched her go.

'So,' said Kai. 'There's something else people want to know.' He leaned in conspiratorially. '*Spill!*'

Flora blushed. 'What do you mean?'

'Shut up! You know exactly what I mean.'

Flora's skin was so pale that she couldn't possibly hide a blush. She went scarlet.

'Seriously,' said Hebe, an incredibly beautiful girl with polished skin and long braids. She was pretending to be joking but Flora didn't think she was really. 'I mean, why you? I mean, obviously you're awesome and everything ...'

Her voice trailed off.

'Who are you talking about?' said a voice. It was Narinder, her replacement.

'She somehow pulled Joel Binder,' said Hebe in the same tone of voice. 'Basically, she held him hostage on an island until he gave in.'

'That's it exactly,' said Flora, determined not to take the bait.

Narinder shook her head. 'I never met him.'

'You never did?' said Kai. He googled the company's home page and brought up the picture of him. It was an image Flora knew incredibly well – his smart suit, the thick brown curly hair, the horn-rimmed glasses, the strong jaw and slightly disconnected expression. It was all him. She couldn't deny what she felt for him. Couldn't downplay it.

'Look at her!' said Kai. 'She's off in a dream. Are you choosing wedding dresses?'

'No!' said Flora furiously. 'Shut up! I don't want to talk about it.'

'Why, is it over already?' said Hebe. 'Has he definitely resigned too?'

'He's coming in next week,' said Flora defiantly.

'Are you a hundred per cent sure about that?'

Kai sensed the situation was getting a little out of hand. 'Come on,' he said, steering Flora away. 'Early lunch. Bye, everyone. Tell my clients I'm on it.'

'Bring back the real story!' shouted Hebe.

'Actually, I hate her. She can't have any cake,' said Flora as Kai ushered her along, picking up her bagful of belongings – which included a pretty pair of spare shoes in a ballerina style that would be rendered instantly useless by the mud of the farmyard in almost any season Mure had to offer and some expensive Chanel lipstick she'd bought to cheer herself up once following a disastrous Tinder date. It felt like another life.

She was pondering this as they waited for the lift and

then, just when they were nearly out of danger, Margo strode up to her. Flora's heart sank. Which was ridiculous. Margo had been the closest thing to an intimate Joel had ever had at the company. He had lots of acquaintances but hardly any friends as far as she could tell. He'd had a million girls, which she tried not to think about too much, but very few girlfriends who'd lasted longer than a week or so. He had no family, or at least not the type she would recognise. He may carry on talking to Margo. He might even – and Flora felt a momentary panic at the thought – want to continue working with her once they'd sorted out his move.

'Hello.'

Margo looked at her as if she hadn't recognised her first off. Then she smiled. 'Flora MacKenzie,' she said.

There was a long pause. Where the hell was that stupid lift? Kai suddenly was very interested in his phone.

Margo cleared her throat. 'So, how's Joel?'

Flora again went bright pink. 'Um, he's great.'

'And is he ... in *Scotland* right now?'

She said 'Scotland' like someone might say 'Candyland': a ridiculous and temporary concept.

'Um, no,' said Flora. 'He's in New York at the moment, working for Colton.'

At this Margo's face brightened. 'Of course he is,' she said. 'I knew he wouldn't be able to stay in the country for long.'

She sniffed as the lift finally arrived and Flora and Kai went to step inside.

'No, but, he's, but ...'

Kai jostled Flora into the lift as she stumbled over her words.

'Very nice to see you,' said Margo, walking on. 'Good luck with everything!'

'She's just jealous,' said Kai, two cocktails later.

Flora stuck out her bottom lip. 'No, she's just like everyone else! She doesn't think it's possible for people to change!'

There was a delicate pause. Kai had known Joel's self-obsessed, diffident ways for as long as Flora had.

'And he has, right? I mean, of course he has.'

Flora bit her lip. 'Yes,' she said stiffly. 'Of course he has.'

## Chapter Six

Flora got home the next day feeling rather chastened. She was pleased to slip back onto the island, into the farmhouse kitchen where she arrived about five seconds after Fintan, who had travelled in rather more style than she had, and straight into an argument.

When Flora had arrived home months before, the farmhouse she'd grown up in had been a tatty thing, uncared for and unloved since their mother – the centre of their home and thus, really, their lives – had died, in the bed they all had been born in.

Fintan had locked himself away. He was almost unrecognisable these days from the bearded recluse he'd become. Innes, the eldest, and jolliest, had just about run himself into the ground through overwork, trying to hold the farm together. Her father had ploughed on, looking neither to right nor left, and that had nearly ended very badly too. Only big, sweet Hamish, who was generally believed to have been dropped on the head as a baby, was relatively unchanged. Although the first thing he'd bought with the money they got from the farm changing hands was a bright red convertible, so who could say?

Innes and Fintan were arguing about when the Rock was going to open – there was no point in them running the farm ragged for a clientele that hadn't arrived, and the summer season was bearing down on them at full speed. Fintan was saying sulkily that it had to be right; Innes was sarcastically pointing out that if Fintan and his lover boy ever stopped kissing for long enough they might be able to get something done, which was going down about as well as could be expected, especially when Hamish started making kissy noises.

'Hi, everyone!' said Flora, putting her bag down on the old kitchen table. Her father, Eck, awoke with a start.

He'd been taking an afternoon nap. Even stopping some of his work hadn't been quite enough to prevent him waking at 5.30 a.m., up with the milking, and that would never change now. They had been farming in the MacKenzie family for as far back as anybody knew. It was hard, sometimes, to think that this generation might be the last to do it.

Innes's daughter Agot, who'd just celebrated her fourth birthday, was there too, and now she clambered up and down Eck's armchair and all over his legs and shoulders. He looked up with pleasure at seeing Flora; partly, Flora knew, because of the distraction she would bring to the only MacKenzie grandchild. And so it proved.

'ATTI FLOWA!'

Agot had the famous selkie hair, not just colourless like Flora's, but a great rippling mane of silvery white. It looked

38

as if it would glow in the dark. She was, too, a bewitching thing, full of confidence and the absolute belief that whatever she said was very important to everyone. Sometimes Flora caught herself looking at Agot and wondering what happened to girls when they grew up.

Flora gladly lifted her into her arms. 'Hello, my darling.'

'She's being a fiend,' said Innes. 'Can you distract her please?'

'I need to test a new recipe,' said Flora. 'Agot, do you want to help?'

'AGOT DO IT.'

'You can help.'

'ME DO IT. ALPING.'

Flora gave her a wooden spoon and took out the absurd tiny apron Colton had had made for her niece for her birthday. It was the same design as Annie's Seaside Kitchen – yellow on a pale-blue background, like the sun and the pale-blue sky – and it made Agot more certain than ever that she actually worked for the organisation – or, possibly, owned it.

'AGOT SPOON!'

Flora glanced at Innes and wandered across the kitchen. Bramble, the fat retired sheepdog who was snoozing by the fire, got up in case she was doing anything interesting, then went back to his busy day job of sleeping, farting and looking for pastry.

'You know,' Flora said quietly, 'doesn't Agot speak quite a lot like a baby? I mean, she is four . . . '

'*CHAN E ENGLISH A'CHIAD CANAN AGAM GU DEARBH!*' hollered Agot across the kitchen.

'Oh yes, sorry,' apologised Flora. She forgot Agot lived on the mainland, she was on Mure so often: English was her second language.

'Joel still away then?' said Innes, raising an eyebrow. Flora didn't look at him. It was exactly the wrong question. She didn't want to talk about it. Yes, he was away a lot. She realised other people saw their relationship as strange. In London, they couldn't see what he saw in her. On Mure, it was the other way around: people couldn't see what she saw in this tall, unsmiling, taciturn man. To be taciturn on Mure – it really stood out. There were a few hermit types here and there, of course: one or two more distant hill farmers; some confirmed bachelors.

But for most, island living meant sharing. Community. Knowing your neighbours when the snow swept down from the high north and the nights were dark and you'd run out of sugar, or you'd lost some sheep on the high crags, or your tractor was stuck in a bog, or you just needed some simple human contact in this world. A cup of tea and a wee dram and the gentle passing of the seasons could heal most things.

Someone whose head was always in their phone, who zoned in and out, who always seemed in a hurry, was not polite, did not ask after people's children and didn't even try to join in with their community – Flora disliked remembering the quiz night. Well. He was definitely seen as not quite right.

She couldn't explain – how could she? – how different he was in the small hours of the morning when he clung to her like a rock in a wild sea, their sweat and tears intermingling, far, far out to sea beyond the need of words at all. That

40

wasn't a conversation she was about to have with anybody. So maybe they would just have to think that he was odd, that he didn't really care for her. And she would treasure those moments deep in her heart, even though there were precious few of them.

'Yup!' said Flora. 'Gives me a chance to get on with stuff.' Innes nodded and went back to looking at his books. 'Eilidh was always desperate to get back to the mainland too,' he said quietly. Eilidh was his ex, mother of Agot, who had fallen in love with handsome Innes when he was studying at the Scottish Agricultural College in Inverness, when there were parties and gigs and all sorts of things going on. But she hadn't at all acclimatised to a place where the social highlight of the month could be a golden eagle sighting, and they had eventually separated, which had broken both of their hearts. Agot seemed fairly sturdy about the entire thing, but, as Innes had confessed once to Flora after a couple too many whiskies, who knew? He hated being Island Daddy.

'Where is he?'

'New York,' said Flora. 'It's minus-twenty apparently. Makes Mure look like the Bahamas.'

They both listened to the barn door banging in the distance.

'Does it now?' said Innes dryly. 'You should go with him.'

'He won't let me,' said Flora. 'Says it's all work and stuff and wouldn't interest me. Plus I have the Seaside Kitchen.'

'Yes, but it can be pretty quiet round about now, can't it?' said Innes. 'I mean, it's really going to get crazy in the summertime, when the Rock opens up. We'll all be 24/7. I've heard New York is nice in the spring.'

'"I've heard New York is nice in the spring"?' mimicked Flora. 'Oh my God, who are you, Woody Allen? Anyway, I just got back from London. Look at me. I actually smell of London. It's a town; they have pavements and everything. Ooh, and they have staircases that move. You'd find it quite frightening.'

Innes shrugged and looked back at the accounts. 'No need to be so arsey just because your boyfriend keeps leaving the country every time he remembers that you have a nose like a piglet.'

'I do *not* have a nose like a piglet!' said Flora.

'PIGLETS NICE, ATTI FLOWA,' came a small voice. Looking round, Flora saw that Agot was attempting to pull an old blackened saucepan out of the cupboard that was twice the size she was.

'Agot!' she yelled, dashing forward, as the entire pile of pots and pans came clattering down on the flagstone floor. Bramble started up from his nap in front of the fire. Their dad started up too, both man and dog glancing round with remarkably similar whiskery expressions.

'AGOT NOT DO IT!' shrieked the little one, her face red with defiance.

'It's okay,' said Flora, starting to pick them up. 'Help me?'

But Agot had fled to her beloved father and had buried her face in his neck as if she had somehow been gravely insulted.

'You are such a monkey!' said Flora. She glanced over. Agot was slyly peering out of her father's cuddling arms to see if Flora was looking at her. As soon as she saw that she was, she buried her face again. Flora smiled briefly to herself, pleased it wasn't she who would be dealing with Agot's teenage years.

Fintan came in, carrying a vast bunch of fresh flowers. There were huge peonies; white roses; all sorts of things you couldn't possibly find on the Scottish islands in March. Flora stared at them as Fintan hummed around and looked for a vase.

'What are those?' she said crossly.

'Oh,' said Fintan. 'Colton sends them every day while he's away. God, I love that man.' He set about snipping the stems carefully.

'Well, that's not very sustainable,' said Flora, in a mood.

'Oh, I don't know,' said Fintan, arranging them carefully in an old earthenware pot of their mother's. 'I think we are.'

# Chapter Seven

'*Oh yes.*'

'This,' said Flora, 'is one of the many, many reasons we are friends.'

She and Lorna were sitting in Lorna's front room on Saturday night. Flora had brought the food; her experimental leek and cheese twists were absolutely melt-in-the-mouth tremendous, particularly when accompanied by a rich red wine. The weather was throwing handfuls of rain against the windows out of a deep, pure blackness while they sat on a cosy sofa in their PJs and best woolly socks with a roaring fire in front of them and no work tomorrow.

Flora told Lorna about Jan's catering request and Lorna burst out laughing, which made Flora feel better immediately.

'Did she actually say that it would also be a charitable gesture?'

'It would,' said Flora. 'It would be a charity gesture towards the expansion of her gigantic bloody gob.'

Lorna shook her head. 'Some people are never satisfied. Have you spoken to Charlie about everything?'

'No,' said Flora. 'Should I? I mean, that would be dickish, wouldn't it? Like I somehow was implying he'd settled for second best.'

'He didn't,' said Lorna. 'He settled for ninetieth best. On Mure alone.'

'Oh, she's all right really,' said Flora, feeling bad. She picked up her phone. 'OMG.'

'What?'

'There's a message on it from her. Maybe she's standing outside the door listening to us!'

'No more wine for you,' said Lorna.

Flora looked at it. 'Oh no. Now I feel bad. She does want us to cater after all – wants me to give a quote.'

'Who are you competitively tendering with? Inge-Britt making greasy sausage sandwiches?'

'That's probably what I'd like at my wedding,' said Flora.

'She really wants you there to see Charlie and her getting married,' said Lorna.

'Well, that is totally fair enough,' said Flora. 'And it'll be a good test for when the Rock opens. Then we really will be swept off our feet. Hopefully.'

She and Lorna chinked glasses.

'How's Saif?' asked Flora, which was a question she could only really ask after a couple of glasses of wine.

Lorna shrugged. 'He got excited when he saw a whale.'

'Oh God, they're not back?'

Flora frowned. Her grandmother had always said she had a way with them – part of the daft old family lore she ignored about how the female line were all selkies who came from the sea and would go back there. But it was true in part: she felt an affinity for the great creatures, and worried about them when they were in danger.

'Anyway,' sighed Lorna. 'Apart from that, the usual. Sad. Bit foggy.'

'He's foggy?'

'No, it's foggy ... He says it got really cold in Damascus in the winter. But, to quote, "You couldn't see your hand in front of your face at ten o'clock in the morning."'

Flora grinned. 'I quite like it. It's just nature telling you to get indoors and be cosy and have a slice of cake and sleep for a long time.'

'I told him that,' Lorna said. 'He said he was going to start prescribing vitamin D supplements to literally everyone on the island. I still don't think he's used to the NHS.'

'Any news about ... ?'

Lorna shrugged. 'I assumed he'd tell me. But the way he looks out to sea ... I mean ... Surely he'd have heard something by now?'

'It's such a mess over there. Jesus, his poor family. Wouldn't he have heard if ... if they were dead?'

'They had ... have two boys, you know,' said Lorna. 'Two sons. One of them is ten. At that age ... you know, if they're captured by the wrong side. They train them up, you know. Train them to fight. And nothing else.'

Flora shook her head. It was beyond imagination, the torment of their tall, gentle GP. She had thought Joel and Saif might get on, but when they'd met they had little to say to one another. 'God,' she said. 'I can't even think about it.'

She sighed. 'What do you think he does with his Saturday nights?'

In fact, two kilometres up the road, Saif was spending his Saturday night like he spent every Saturday night, even though as a doctor and a clinician this was exactly what he would have told himself not to do. Amena had had – oh, years ago now, so many years – a YouTube account they'd uploaded little films of the boys onto for their grandparents. But in fact neither set of grandparents had ever learned to use the internet, so it had in the end been a pointless exercise and there were only two: Ibrahim's third birthday, and Ash at four days old. Thirty-nine seconds of the first – a confused, serious-looking Ibrahim spitting over some candles, his long eyelashes casting shadows on his cheek. To Saif's utter frustration, Amena was behind the camera. He could hear her voice, encouraging and laughing; he could not see her face.

In the second, the focus was all on Ash, but it was just a baby's face – just a baby, and his own stupid voice. There was a half-millisecond of Amena, as the camera moved up and then what . . . how . . . what had he done? Cut it off, in the full expectation that he would be able to see that face every day for the rest of his life. What had he done . . . ? He watched it. Froze it. Watched it. He glanced briefly at the counter of views. Four thousand nine hundred and fourteen. It was a habit he had to break. He had absolutely no idea how.

'Tell me more about the whale.'

Flora was refilling their glasses and steering the conversation away from boys, as it seemed to be dangerous territory at the moment.

'Not sure what type,' said Lorna.

'Oh, for goodness' sake!' said Flora. 'Call yourself a teacher?'

'We're not all sea creatures in human form,' said Lorna. Flora smiled, but her face was pensive.

'I don't want another beaching,' she said. 'They're so horrid. Sometimes you're lucky, but sometimes ...'

'I know,' said Lorna. 'I think the sea is getting too warm.'

'Are you sure you didn't see what kind it was?'

'Does it matter? It looked like it had a funny horn thing.'

'Really?!'

'Yeah, on its nose. Or maybe it was eating something pointy.'

Flora waited for the internet to slowly download a picture of a narwhal – a large whale with a unicorn-style tusk on its snout. 'Did it look like that?'

Lorna squinted. 'A nar-what? Are those real?'

'What do you mean, are those real? Of course they're real! Where do you think Scotland's unicorn symbol comes from?!'

'Um, I've never thought about it,' said Lorna.

'What do they teach in schools these days?' said Flora, grinning. 'The unicorn. On the union flag. The lion and the unicorn. Three lions on the chest for England. A unicorn for Scotland, described in ancient texts. Of course that's not what they saw.'

'That's the thing I just saw?' said Lorna.

'That's the thing you just saw. Incredibly, incredibly rare.'

'Is it lucky?'

Flora paused. 'The myths say ... well. Opinion is divided. Could be either.'

'I don't believe in luck,' said Lorna.

'I'm not sure if it matters whether you believe in it or not,' said Flora. 'But we'd probably better alert the coastguard and Whale Rescue anyway. A narwhal is a very special thing.'

'Yeah, all right, fish-whisperer.'

And they refilled their glasses, put a film on and finished the leek twists, and felt, for two girls in by themselves on a Saturday night, pretty contented with their lot.

# Chapter Eight

Saif normally welcomed the distraction of work after his empty weekends, but today he was having a particularly trying morning. Old Mrs Kennedy was in with her bunions. The waiting list on the mainland was over eighteen months but she could have got it done privately in a week. She owned a croft and four holiday cottages. He couldn't explain to her that, in terms of her remaining lifespan, eighteen months represented probably quite a large percentage of it, and she really ought to spend the money.

'Aye, och no, I don't want to be a bother,' she'd said.

'But wouldn't you be less bothering if you could walk properly, Mrs Kennedy?'

Lorna had once told him, to his considerable surprise, that his normal timbre of speaking voice could sound aggressive to the locals, particularly the older ones, who'd watched too many American films where anyone who sounded Middle-Eastern was automatically a terrorist. Even though he found this profoundly annoying, he had tried to soften his voice and follow the gentle sing-song pattern characteristic of the island speakers. His English now, in fact, was both strange and very beautiful, a wonderful mix of both accents, with a music all of its own. Lorna loved to listen to it. When he was frustrated, however, it tended to sharpen up again.

'Aye, but you never know when that money might be needed!'

Saif blinked. What Mrs Kennedy did with her own money was, of course, absolutely none of his business. But the difference between being able to walk and not . . .

He shook his head and wrote her out another prescription for painkillers. She was putting weight on too which meant she'd need cholesterol checks and could possibly develop gout . . . Still. Next!

Straight after was Gertie James, an incomer from Surrey who'd given up a high-pressure dual-income lifestyle to come and do weaving and fire her own pottery and grow her own vegetables. Her husband had lasted about fifteen minutes, then given up and decided to rejoin the rat race. Now she was raising three completely assimilated and semi-feral island children, who were happy as clams running around muddy streams all day, knowing every single person on the island, building their own kites, speaking a mix of two tongues and eating tablet. They were no more likely to take to living back in a small Guildford semi with an au pair and after-school Mandarin, lacrosse and Kumon maths lessons than they were to fly to the moon.

'I just feel ... I just feel so ... '

Saif had learned over the last few months that, in the West, going to the doctor and saying you were 'feeling ... ' and just kind of letting the sentence run out was considered a totally acceptable and viable reason for accessing healthcare. This was new to him. Even before Syria had turned into a warzone, going to the doctor cost too much money for you not to be very clear that there was a distinctly pressing reason for you being there.

He didn't deny for a second that mental health issues were real and overt and almost certainly underdiagnosed in his home countries. He had been born in Syria and raised in Beirut; the irony of his moving back to Syria after medical school for a brighter future had never once been lost on him.

But he found trying to guess the subtleties of people's malaise a little tricky still. He was not an unempathetic doctor – not at all. There wasn't a child who arrived scared and anxious who didn't leave with a lollipop, a jolly plaster and the sense of being taken seriously. But in some areas, he was less tested than others, and the 'I've just been feeling a bit ... ' symptoms he did find tricky.

He looked up at Gertie, who, in common with more than a few of the single or divorced women on Mure, found the plight of the tall, handsome, lightly bearded doctor terribly romantic. Alas, despite the lasagnes that regularly turned up on his doorstep (he had, truly, no idea why people did this) and invitations to the town's many social activities, he remained separate – a little distant, entirely focused on the old phone that was never far from his side. This only made him more attractive in many people's minds. Gertie sighed.

'I just . . . I just feel I've lost my sparkle.'

'I do not know if the NHS does sparkle,' said Saif. This was a joke on his part, but like many people Gertie was unclear when he was joking and when he wasn't, and simply looked concerned.

'I mean,' he said, trying to look professional, 'are you sure it isn't just the time of year?'

This was undeniably true. The very end of March was difficult for everyone; the winter had been long and dark, but Christmas had been wonderful. There was something cosy about the depths of winter. Now the evenings were meant to be getting longer; the equinox had been and gone; surely spring should be on its way? But lambs were being born into fierce storms and wet grass, into a world that still felt cruel, when it should start to feel welcoming and new. There were daffodils, yes, and crocuses, and the hardy little snowdrops; and green was beginning to wreathe its way across the land – but when you still had to scrape the ice off your car in the morning, when you still had to run across the road in howling gales and lashing rain, when it felt as if you were holding your breath, waiting for the year to begin, even as days of your life passed you by . . .

Yes. He understood what the half-sentence meant. He did. It was hard.

He looked up at Gertie. 'Spring will come,' he said. 'Things will get better.'

'Do you think?' said Gertie, her voice a little quavery. 'The winter is just so long.'

'The spring makes it worth it. Now, I could put you on the strong drugs, I suppose, but you have children, yes?'

53

Gertie nodded. Everyone knew Gertie's children. Lorna up at the school had wanted to tell Gertie this was actually a functioning modern island, not an Iron Age settlement, but she was slightly worried that Gertie would immediately withdraw them and attempt to home-school which, as well as making for a dangerous outlook for Mure's cats, would lower the school roll yet again. It was a constant balancing act to keep the island's only school open, but without it the island would die, and that was that, so Lorna was going to protect it to her dying breath.

'You want to be present for them, yes? Feel their joys and sadnesses? Because it is not like that for everyone, but for some people ... these drugs, they take away the lows but they can take away the highs too. They can isolate you from the world, you know? Wrap you in cotton wool ... remove you a little. For people whose pain is unendurable, of course. But can you wait, maybe for ... ?'

Gertie looked out of the window. That day, for what felt like the first time in so long, the sun was out again. It felt as if the world was coming alive. 'Do you think?'

'I do think,' said Saif. 'I am old-fashioned doctor. If I could prescribe, I would say get dog. Take walk every day.'

Gertie smiled. 'Do you think that would help?'

'I think that helps most things. But get outside. See the world. See how you are. And if you are still ... no sparkle. Well. Then we have a problem. Please come back then.'

Gertie nodded. 'I'll try it,' she said. 'But I'll blame you if it goes wrong.'

Saif allowed himself a smile. 'But of course.'

He stood up politely as she left.

He wasn't feeling any better though, and he tried to figure out why, as he considered wandering along to the Seaside Kitchen for lunch. Flora had tried her hand at falafel for him. They were terrible, absolutely awful, but she had tried so hard and so sweetly that he had told her they were great. Now she made them all the time and he felt slightly duty-bound to eat them as everyone looked at him expect-antly. Old Mrs Laird, who 'did' for him, would nudge him and say, 'Ooh look, there's Flora's flannels,' which was, to be strictly accurate, more or less what they tasted like. He'd much rather have one of her cheese scones, which were heavenly.

He wasn't in the mood for it today. He would stay here and finish off his paperwork ... He swung round to the computer. And that was when he saw it.

He didn't know why. It must have been to do with how the dates looked so different on his computer – or in his mind, maybe? Because they were in English and not Arabic? Because – and this made him swallow – perhaps because he thought all the time now in English? He even dreamed in English; he dreamed sometimes that his family could not understand him, that he was shouting at them, shouting at them to come, and the only reason they did not was because he could no longer change his voice to the only language they understood. That had been a nightmare from which he had awoken sobbing, on damp sheets – sobbing even harder when he remembered, once again, that the nightmare was true. There was no respite from the nightmare that went on every day: he did not know. He did not know what had happened to his family.

But now, as he glanced down at the phone, he realised. That he had missed it. That he had known on some level that it was today.

The venetian blind on his window, with which Saif was not particularly familiar and usually got tangled horribly, was thankfully already down. He got up and locked the door, even though he knew he was never meant to lock the door from the inside. He glanced around one last time. The morning surgery was finished and the afternoon house calls were not due for an hour.

Then he pulled down a roll of hospital paper, crouched down behind the examination bed, made himself as small and quiet as possible and wept, quiet racking sobs that felt more painful the more he tried to stifle them, conscious that he must be making the oddest of noises. Ash, his youngest, was six years old. Today. Or would have been six. He didn't even know that. Didn't even know.

And he had forgotten the day. And suddenly, once again, everything was too much to bear.

# Chapter Nine

'Mwah. Just one more kiss.'

'Fintan!'

Flora was trying to do the Seaside Kitchen accounts at the table, and listening to Fintan on the phone was too much.

'Homophobe,' said Fintan, not looking remotely sorry.

'I'm a show-off-o-phobe,' said Flora. 'And you are *showing off*.'

'She's on her period,' said Fintan down the phone. 'No, I don't know either. Some girl thing.'

'FINTAN! Hamish, eat the phone.'

Hamish glanced up from the corner, looking quite happy at the prospect, but Fintan flicked them all two-finger Vs.

'That's it, I'm telling Dad,' said Flora. She looked around. 'Where is he?'

He wasn't dozing in the armchair as usual. Bramble was gone too. Flora got nervous when her dad wandered off. She stood up from the accounts – she tried to tell herself she needed a break, but really it was because they were just such bad news – and went off to stretch her legs.

'Colton says bye!' shouted Fintan jovially as she left. She would have slammed the door if it hadn't been warped.

She found her father round the front of the farmyard. He was leaning on the stone wall at the front of the property, over the wide mouth of the road that led down. It was quite the view: low-slung clouds across a wide sky, all the way down to the cobbled streets of Mure below; the beach beyond. He wasn't doing anything. Flora thought he was from the last generation that were content just doing nothing – not fiddling with their phones, but simply standing, waiting, watching. When she was little, he used to smoke roll-ups, but that had stopped a long time ago. His ruddy face was perfectly still, contemplating the only world, really, that he'd ever known.

Bramble's tail thumped on the cobbles.

'Hello dair, dhu,' he said. His voice retained the ancient speech patterns of his homeland.

'Daddy.'

He smiled.

'Fintan getting a bit much for you?' Flora asked.

Eck sighed. 'Ach, Flora. You know.'

Flora looked at him.

'Don't think of me as an ancient dinosaur.'

'I don't,' said Flora. She didn't. She thought of him as a rock, deep set in the soil, immovable; reliable and strong.

'It's just ... it's very new to me, all this.'

'I know,' nodded Flora.

'I mean ... do you think they'd get themselves married, do you?'

This hadn't occurred to Flora. She felt something of a little stab when she realised that Fintan would probably get married before she did. 'I don't know,' she said. 'We haven't really discussed it.'

'I mean, it would have been all right for your maither.' His pale-blue eyes scanned the horizon. 'But, you know. I mean. What would the Thurso boys make of it?'

Flora shrugged. 'I think you might find these days there are more Thurso men with gay people in their families than you'd expect.'

'You think that, so you do, do you?'

'You might be surprised.'

'I might at that.' He shook his head. 'It was simpler when me and your ma were young.'

'For you it was,' said Flora. 'For other people it was impossible.'

'Aye yes, that, right enough.' He sighed again. 'I just want you all to be happy.'

'Well,' pointed out Flora, 'Fintan's the happiest of all of us.'

Eck's eyebrows rose. 'I suppose he is at that.'

They both watched as Innes and Agot came marching up the hill from the ferry port. Agot was jumping up and down noisily at something. With her white hair she looked exactly like the new lambs bouncing in the fields.

'Ach, that girl wants a maither and a faither,' said Eck. We all do, thought Flora, but she kept it to herself, kissed her dad on the cheek and went down to try and get Innes to help her with the accounts, which he did with the highly disappointing outcome that she'd been right all along about how badly she was doing.

## Chapter Ten

Colton was coming home for the evening – one evening! – and not bringing Joel. That was what really did it.

He jetted in on Thursday, looking slim and a little drawn from working too hard, but nonetheless he threw a huge dinner at the Rock for everyone and they all went and had a rip-roaring time. Hamish tried to chat up Catriona Meakin, who was fifty-six if she was a day, a part-time barmaid, full-time sweetheart, comfortably upholstered and very kind and welcoming on the whole; he looked unbelievably delighted when he succeeded.

The Rock had been opened up; from the jetty there was a great red carpet leading up the steps, where braziers were lit to show the way to the old wooden front door. Toasts had been made and plans had been drawn up for when the venue would be open – all very speculative, it seemed.

Flora had finished work and gone back to the farmhouse to find it empty; no one had thought to tell her where they all were. Eventually she'd figured it out and gone stomping down to the jetty, where Bertie Cooper, who helped Colton with transportation, beamed happily to see her (he'd always had a soft spot for her). He took her round the headland to save her walking the length of the Endless. It was a chilly night and Flora dug her hands into the sleeves of her jumper. She'd heard nothing about the lightning visit. But maybe, she thought, just maybe, Joel had come as a surprise ...

Colton was sitting holding court in the warm corner of the bar, next to the crackling fire, Fintan on his lap. Lots of people from the village had spied the lights on and 'popped by' to see what was occurring; there was laughter and merriment and young Iona was singing in a corner, hardly pausing when she saw Flora except to wave cheerfully.

Flora scanned the room slowly. No sign of Joel.

'Hi, Colton,' she said, going over and kissing him, and he hugged her back.

'You didn't bring your lawyer with you?' she said, trying to sound playful and failing mightily.

'He's too busy,' said Colton, 'doing good things for me.' He saw Flora's face. 'Aw, hey, listen. He just wants to get everything done. Sorry. I gave him a lot to do. I decided at the last minute, okay? I haven't even seen him.' At least he had the grace to look ashamed of himself. He ruffled Fintan's hair. 'Sorry, Flora. I've had a lot on my mind.' He kissed Fintan lightly. 'I just ... I just had to get home, even for one night. I dropped everything.'

Flora nodded. 'Sure,' she said.

She wandered back to town. It looked like being a jolly rowdy night, but she had to be up at the crack of dawn. And somehow, she just wasn't in the mood. She picked up the phone to call Joel, then put it back down again. There was no point in starting a fight, even if he picked up at all.

The next time Joel was home they'd talk. They had to talk. She'd said this the last four times he'd come home, then he'd walked through the door and pulled off all her clothes and somehow the moment had gone. She sighed and pulled out her notebook to see if there was anything she didn't have organised for the wedding of the . . .

Speak of the devil, for Charlie himself was walking up the high street pursued, as usual, by a long line of mites – wan, thin children from deprived areas of the big cities of the mainland. Flora waved to him. 'Well met, Teàrlach,' she hailed him cheerily. 'I haven't seen you since I heard the good news. This is great!'

Charlie didn't say that he had been deliberately avoiding her. He had had a very soft spot for Flora the previous summer, and had hoped that they might be able to start something. But as soon as he'd set eyes on the handsome, square-jawed lawyer up from London, he'd realised he didn't have a chance.

And he had known Jan for a long time. They worked together. She had a good heart. They were a good match. All would be fine. It was only for a millisecond, watching Flora's pale hair flutter in the breeze, that he felt a tiny twinge for what might have been. And what was even more difficult, if he was honest with himself, was the sense that she genuinely was very happy for him and Jan – that she was not thinking about what might have been at all.

'Thank you,' he said, going up to her and accepting her kiss on each cheek, although they got it slightly wrong and

Flora remembered about halfway through it was only people from London who did this and it might look a bit weird. It was too late to extricate herself even though both of them separately wished that actually people still just shook hands.

'And where are you all from then?' she said, deflecting attention onto the boys.

'Govan!' said one, and the rest all cheered.

'And how are you liking it here?'

They shrugged. 'There's nae PlayStation,' said one and they all nodded.

'And nae Irn-Bru.'

Flora looked at Charlie mock-crossly. 'I can't believe you're depriving them so badly!'

'Och no, it's all right, it's good, it's all right,' said one of the boys, a tiny mite dwarfed in the orange waterproofs they wore in the hills. He looked terrified, as if Flora had the power to send him home.

'Yeah, it's fine,' chorused the others rapidly.

Flora smiled. 'Well, you can stay then.'

She glanced at Charlie. 'We have some leftover raisin scones tonight – Isla was on Snapchat and let them burn a little bit. We can't sell them, but if you'd like them, they won't kill you.'

Charlie smiled gratefully as the boys jumped up and down in delight. 'Thank you,' he said, and she darted in to get the bag.

He turned to go with the boys. 'I am really pleased for you, you know,' Flora said as he walked away. He glanced back. His blond hair glistened in the evening sun, and his kind face looked a little conflicted.

'I know you are,' he said. 'I know.'

But Flora was already looking back down at her phone. Maybe she should call him after all.

Lorna passed by five minutes later, seeing Flora still trying desperately to get a signal. 'Are you not coming up to the Rock?' she said. 'There's a hoolie on.'

'I know,' said Flora crossly.

'Well, why don't you just go there?' Lorna was saying. 'For the weekend. Can't Colton take you back?'

Flora blinked. 'But there's so much on . . .'

'There's always a lot on,' said Lorna.

'Fly to New York for the weekend?' said Flora. 'Don't be mad. I might as well fly to the moon. Plus, I'd still have to get a flight home. Anyway, Colton wouldn't take me in case I distract Joel.'

'Come on,' said Lorna. 'Just buy yourself a ticket then. Joel is absolutely minted.'

'Well, that's got nothing to do with me,' said Flora stiffly. She didn't like discussing Joel's money; it felt grubby, like it got in the way. She didn't even know how much he made. 'And I've got a wedding to organise.'

'Don't be daft. Four vol-au-vents per head and a few sausage rolls and they'll be delighted. You could do it standing on your head. Haven't you got that farm money?'

Flora looked uncomfortable. Last year the farm had been sold to Colton, who was using it entirely to supply his own enterprises. Her share, obviously, hadn't been as big as her father's or her brothers', who'd worked on it and run it. But she had got a share nonetheless.

'I was saving it,' she said. 'This place ... it doesn't give me a pension or anything, and I didn't save a penny from London, even though I had a big salary.'

Lorna found this astonishing. 'Why not?'

'Because rent is insane and travel is insane and lunch and going out and ... '

'Could you not have gone out less?'

'No,' explained Flora patiently. 'Because all your money goes on renting a horrible place, so you want to be out as much as possible.'

Lorna nodded like this made sense.

'Anyway. I should probably keep it. For a rainy day. I don't think the Kitchen is going to make me rich.'

'But if you're as worried as you say ... ' Lorna let the sentence tail off. 'I mean, are you in a relationship or not?'

'Possibly not if I turn up by surprise.'

'Well, tell him you're coming.'

Flora looked up, and Lorna was amazed suddenly by how unhappy her friend looked. 'What if he says no?' she said simply.

'Is it really that bad?'

'I don't know,' admitted Flora. 'I don't know if he's playing at being here, or what. He emailed me yesterday to say he's going to be away another full month. I mean, for God's sake ... '

'Well then. I don't think you have any choice. Come back to the Rock with me.'

'No,' said Flora. 'But I will think about it.'

## Chapter Eleven

Colleen McNulty, of Liverpool, England, did not talk about her job. It made people act weirdly towards her, either overly empathetic or massively racist – and both were, she didn't really like to admit, quite equally tiresome.

'I'm a civil servant,' she would say coolly, in a way that discouraged further conversation. Her grown daughter (she'd been divorced for a long time) was always interested, but otherwise the line between interest and prurience was hard to navigate sometimes, and she certainly had no interest talking to those who'd never known a day's hardship in their entire lives but thought that desperate people should be allowed to drown in the Mediterranean Sea for want of a little humanity.

She was equally dispassionate in the office, a featureless building on a forgettable industrial estate with only the tiniest of Home Office logos on the signage. She carried out the wishes of the government of the day, that was all. It wasn't her fault or her responsibility; she did it or she didn't. This wasn't cruel: there was simply no other way to deal with it without being overwhelmed – in the same way battlefield doctors kept up a black sense of humour. You had to distance yourself, otherwise it became unbearable. You couldn't get involved in individual people's stories – individual families – because then you couldn't do your job, couldn't function, and that was useful to precisely nobody.

If you had to deal with her, you might have thought her rude, curt and unfeeling. In fact, Colleen McNulty thought being efficient was the very best way to get through her day, and to please the God she fervently believed in.

As she took off her large, practical anorak that morning, hung it on the back of the door where it always went, checked that no one had touched 'her' mug and murmured good morning to her opposite number, Ken Foley, with whom she'd shared an office for six years and had never had a personal conversation, she expected little as she powered up the computer and looked down to see what the day would bring. It would be numbers on a page, that was all, boxes on a spreadsheet: not people but problems to be organised and sorted out and arranged until she left promptly at 5.30 to heat up her M&S pasta sauce carefully at home and watch YouTube videos about crafting.

She glanced at the header of the first email. And for the first time in six years, Ken Foley heard the very upright Mrs McNulty let out a tiny gasp.

'Colleen?' he said, daring to use her first name.

'Excuse me,' said Colleen at once, recovering her composure.

Every Friday, regular as clockwork ... You could set your watch by it, month after month, every week, the English growing more confident – even the accent coming in, the doctor she'd placed miles and miles away, up on that tiny island, asked if she had any news. She didn't get involved, ever, with her clients.

But he had always been so polite. Never ranted or raged like some family members (and indeed, of course, who could blame them?). Never accused her of being unfeeling or being responsible for the government's policies. Never beseeched or begged. Simply asked politely, his gentle voice calm, with only the slightest quiver betraying the desperate angst behind the question. And every week she reassured him that if they had any news, they would contact him immediately, of course, and he would apologise and say that he knew that, of course, but just in case, and she would politely shut him down. But she didn't mind him calling – she never did.

She took a peek at the email again, but she knew the boys' names off by heart. One of them, she noticed, had just had a birthday.

Colleen made it a rule never to look into circumstances – it was prurient, and not her job.

Today she found herself making an exception. Found in a military hospital. Sheltered in a school by what looked like a clutch of rebels and some leftover nuns, of all things. No mother, but the brothers together. Alive.

Colleen McNulty, who never displayed emotion over the exceptionally hard task she did day in, day out – well ... She swallowed hard.

She wanted to enjoy this call – to savour it. She really,

truly did. She glanced over at Ken and did a most uncharacteristic thing.

'I would like to make a private phone call,' she announced pointedly. 'Would you mind?' And she indicated the door.

Ken was delighted to go down to the little kitchen area and announce to all and sundry that the buttoned-up and silent Mrs McNulty was almost certainly in the throes of some tumultuous affair, probably with Lawrence the stock boy.

# Chapter Twelve

The woman in the surgery was crying. Saif handed over the box of tissues he kept for when this happened, which was regularly, although not normally for this reason.

'I was just so sure,' she was saying. It was Mrs Baillie, who had four enormous dogs currently all baying their heads off outside the surgery. Mrs Baillie herself was a tiny woman. If he had had to put money on why Mrs Baillie would have to visit a doctor, he would have suggested that one of the dogs had fallen on her. He hoped she remembered to feed them on time.

'I was just so sure it was a tumour,' she said again.

Saif nodded. 'That is why we tell you not to look up things on the internet,' he said.

She sobbed again, repeating her grateful thanks. 'I can't believe what you've done for me,' she said again. 'I just can't believe it.'

'It was my pleasure,' said Saif, standing up. Lancing boils

wasn't his favourite part of the job, but this level of gratitude was both unusual and pleasant.

'I'll make sure to drop you in a wee cake!' Mrs Baillie smiled up at him through her tears as she got up to go. Saif privately wondered how much dog hair would get into a cake mix in Mrs Baillie's house but smiled politely and stood up as she went to exit. His phone rang, and he frowned. He had at least one more patient before lunch, and he wanted to check back on little Seerie Campbell's whooping cough. He pressed the intercom.

'Jeannie, I'm not done,' he said to his receptionist.

'I know,' she said apologetically. 'Sorry. It's the Home Office.'

Saif sat back down. They rang from time to time to check on his paperwork. It was routine, nothing to get excited about. Although he couldn't help it; he always, always did.

The voice was calm on the phone. 'Dr Hassan?'

He recognised the voice; it wasn't his London caseworker. It was Mrs McNulty at the Complex Casework Directorate.

He found his eyes straying to the blood pressure sleeve on his desk. He wouldn't, he found himself thinking ridiculously, want to try that at the moment. 'Hel- ... hello,' he stuttered.

'This is Mrs McNulty.'

'I know who you are.'

His heart was racing, incredulous.

'I believe I have some good news for you.'

Saif's breath caught in his throat.

'We have managed to locate two children we believe may be your sons.'

71

There was a long pause. Saif could hear his own heartbeat. He felt slightly disconnected, slightly out of body; as if this were happening to someone else.

'Ibrahim?' he said, realising that he had not said the name out loud in so long. Whenever he had spoken to her, he had always said 'my family'.

'Ibrahim Saif Hassan, date of birth twenty-fifth of July 2007?' said Mrs McNulty.

'Yes!' Saif found himself shouting. 'YES!'

Outside, Jeannie glanced up from her notes, but the remaining patient hadn't turned up, so she carried on tidying up morning surgery.

'Ash Mohammed Hassan, date of birth twenty-ninth of March 2012?'

Saif found himself simply saying thank you over and over again. Oddly, he sounded not entirely unlike Mrs Baillie. But he was babbling, and he realised he had to say something.

Mrs McNulty smiled to herself and let it play out.

'I'm going to email you through all the details, Dr Hassan. The nearest centre is in Glasgow. They'll be taken there ... there are various protocols ...'

Saif couldn't hear any of this.

'And ...' he said when he'd managed to wrest back control of his breathing. 'And of my wife?'

'There is no news,' said Colleen. 'Yet.'

'Yet,' said Saif. 'Yes, of course. Yet.'

And they both pretended that it was simply a matter of time.

'Oh my goodness,' said Saif suddenly, astounded anew.

'The boys! The boys are here! My boys! My boys! My boys . . .'

'I am,' said the unemotional Mrs McNulty, 'very, very pleased for you, Dr Hassan.'

And she made herself put the phone down on his over-enthusiastic thanks, as there was a team briefing at 11 a.m. and she had to redo her make-up because she was chairing the estates sub-committee.

'Good luck to you,' she said quietly.

Five hundred miles north-north-east, a tall, slender man with a neatly trimmed beard jumped up and punched the air, shouting so loud a flock of magpies took off into the nearby field, up across the scarecrows and into the clouded sky.

# Chapter Thirteen

Lorna continued on down the harbour, enjoying a bit of sun on her lunch break even as work was piling up back at school, relishing just a tiny break from the sticky clatter of tiny hands, however fond of them she was.

She headed back to the farmhouse to pick up some of the leftover marking she'd forgotten. Unusually, someone was waiting for her there; she heard the shout before she made it up the track.

'LOREN-AH!'

She blinked. She knew immediately it was of course Saif.

'Lorenah . . . !' Saif stopped short when he realised she was right there. He hadn't even known what he was doing. Jeannie was away on her lunch break; he had had to get out, do something before he burst.

The email had come through but the details had swum in front of his eyes. Lorna was the obvious solution. He'd run fleetly through the town to worried looks from passers-by

74

who assumed there was a medical emergency in progress, but he noticed none of it.

The chickens pecked noisily around his feet as he stood there, panting. Lorna lifted her eyebrows. In his agitation, his tie was loose around his neck, his top buttons undone. She looked away quickly from the smooth skin beneath it. He was out of breath, and wild around the eyes, and in his hand he was waving something frantically.

'Where were you?'

'At school, of course! What is it? What's the matter? It's just a whale!'

Saif shook his head. 'Read this! Read this! Um ... Please. Please to read it. Thank you.'

He proffered it. Lorna squinted at him. 'You can read English perfectly,' she said reprovingly.

'I need ... I need to be sure,' panted Saif.

Only the noise of the birds in the trees and the chickens crooning and looking for their breakfast broke the surrounding silence. Lorna looked down.

It was an official email. From the Home Office. Lorna checked the stub of the sender address first. There were so many scams around these days; she got emails from fake iTunes accounts practically every day. But it was legit.

Then she read down slowly, aware of Saif's agonised trembling a metre away from her. Then, to check, she read it again.

'Do you need to sit down?' Lorna said, keeping her voice very calm in order to be understood by someone in a highly strung emotional state, something she was well trained in.

Saif nodded, feeling as if the blood were rushing to his

head, as if he were somehow outside his body just for a second. He staggered over to the wooden bench outside the farmyard door. Lorna went straight inside the house and brought out two glasses of water. Saif hadn't moved. She handed him the water and he took it without thanking her, just staring straight ahead.

'Yes,' said Lorna simply and softly into the clear air. Saif's gaze was still rigid. 'Yes,' she said again. She grew worried about him; his face was completely frozen. Then she realised, a millisecond too late, that he was trying with every fibre of his being not to cry. 'Your boys are here. They're coming home. Um . . . Here . . . They're coming here.'

She jumped up.

'I'll go and make some tea,' she said, and vanished back into the house.

Then she stood over the kitchen sink and, very quietly, sobbed her heart out.

# Chapter Fourteen

After a little while, Lorna emerged from the farmhouse, able to speak again, carrying two fresh cups of tea. She'd boiled the kettle three times over to give them both time to gather themselves.

The sun had burned off nearly all the fog now and it had a fair chance of being a lovely afternoon – for the next half-hour at least, which was as far ahead as anyone could forecast on Mure.

'Ibrahim,' said Saif. 'Ash.'

'Your boys,' said Lorna, warmth in her voice.

He nodded. Then looked down at his hands. 'Amena . . .'

Amena, Lorna knew, was his wife. There was no mention of her in the letter. 'No news. That doesn't mean . . . it doesn't mean there isn't hope,' said Lorna softly.

Saif shook his head. 'She would never have left the boys,' he said fiercely. 'Never.'

'Maybe she had no choice. Maybe they were ... taken,' said Lorna.

It was bad enough tormenting herself with what Saif had endured to reach safety. What had happened to those he had left behind was even worse; what had happened to two children, no older than her own pupils, beyond imagination.

Saif glanced down. 'It doesn't say anything.'

'Well, they'll need to check ... There's an official process. Look, you have to go to Glasgow for a blood test,' she pointed out.

'I don't need a blood test to know my sons,' growled Saif.

'I know,' said Lorna. 'But probably best to go along with it, don't you think?'

'Authorities,' sighed Saif. He took the paper back from her, his hands still trembling, then folded it very carefully and precisely, once, twice, and tucked it into an old battered wallet he carried in his back pocket. Lorna privately predicted, correctly, that he would carry it there for the rest of his life.

Flora was restocking the cheese counter with a rather sensational marbled cheese Fintan had concocted when a sixth sense caused her to look up. Lorna and Saif were approaching. They both looked ... She couldn't tell. She thought, not for the first time, how natural they looked together, like they were meant to be seen side by side. They just fitted somehow. Flora reminded herself that Saif was married and that it was none of her business anyway, and tried to look busy.

Just outside the shop, Saif stopped.

'What?' said Lorna.

Saif shook his head. 'I don't ...' He looked at Lorna. 'Please, don't tell ... Don't tell anyone.'

'I think they're going to find out when two children arrive who look exactly like you,' pointed out Lorna.

'I ... I realise that.'

Saif looked down. For the first time since he'd arrived, nine months before, he'd begun to feel a part of the community; no one, any longer, stared at him when he shopped in the village, or took much notice of him down on the beach in all weathers. No longer did the old ladies insist on waiting an extra hour to see the 'other doctor' rather than deal with someone foreign with an accent. Now he was just Dr Saif (most people had simply given up the Hassan), as much a part of Mure as anyone else.

The idea of voluntarily going back to the whispers behind hands, the stares in the bakery, the speculation, because of his boys ... It would come, of course. But until then, perhaps he could enjoy being normal, just for a little longer.

Also, he did not want to share it. It was treasure: impossible, dusted gold that he wanted to clasp, to hold inside, to deal with the immeasurable astonishment of how this might come to be. It was close to overwhelming.

Lorna blinked. 'Okay.'

'Can you keep it to yourself?'

'Of course.'

And she truly meant it when she said it, and Flora watched as they swerved and, after all, didn't come in. She thought it was peculiar but, caught in dreams of New York, promptly forgot all about it until the day she was due to leave.

# Chapter Fifteen

Flora couldn't sleep with excitement. She was going to see Joel! She was going to see him! And New York too, which she'd never been to before. She knew which hotel he was staying in, and had vague plans of simply going to meet him in the lobby – he would be so surprised! She packed her best new bra set, ordered specially from the mainland, and the best of her old London wardrobe. Her Mure wardrobe mostly consisted of fleeces, big jumpers and a variety of hats, and she wasn't sure it was quite the thing for New York.

Fintan came round in the morning to take her to the airport, smiling all the time and giving her a long list of things he wanted her to bring back from Dean & DeLuca, now he considered himself quite the international globetrotter from being at Colton's side.

'And if you see Colton, give him a big smooch from me,' he added.

'I bloody will not,' said Flora. 'He's the one keeping my boyfriend from me.'

Fintan beamed cheerfully. Flora had no idea how her brother's relationship seemed so uncomplicatedly happy. She wouldn't admit to being jealous. But she was.

They bumped into Lorna at the airport, who was waiting for her brother, back from the rigs.

'I'm doing it!' Flora shouted.

Lorna grinned. 'Woah, I wish I was too.'

'Come!'

'What, and watch you guys make out all over Manhattan? No, thanks!' Lorna smiled. 'It's great you're going to see him on his own turf.'

Flora winced at that. 'Don't forget I saw him on his own turf in London for years. He never noticed me once. Don't all the girls look like fashion models in New York?'

'How would I know?' said Lorna. 'I'm doing Ancient Egyptians with the primary threes . . . '

They called the flight; the half-dozen passengers stood up and shuffled forwards. It wouldn't take long to board.

Flora remembered something. 'Hey, what was with you and Saif the other day?'

Lorna looked up, immediately guilty. 'What do you mean?'

Flora had been merely trying to distract herself from panicking about New York by focusing on something else, but Lorna's furious blush and quick answer piqued her curiosity immediately. 'Ooh . . . ' she said.

'Flight's leaving,' said Lorna. She could see her brother Ian, who'd come on the inbound, crossing the tarmac.

'Something's up! Something's up! I can tell!'

'No, it isn't. Shut up.'

'This is why you want to get me out of the way. Are you planning a night of seduction?'

'No!' said Lorna, going a very dull shade of red.

Flora blinked, concerned. 'What's up?' she said. 'What's the matter? Did you ...? Something happened, didn't it? Did you come on to him or something?'

'No!'

'Well, what then?'

'I can't ... I can't say. I can't tell you.'

Flora looked at her for a few seconds more. There was a last call for the flight.

'Oh God,' she said. 'It's something. Is it about ... is he leaving? No, he can't, can he? Oh my God. Have they ... have they found his family?'

'I can't talk about it!'

'Shit! Oh my God! Really?! Oh my God! Mrs Hassan! I bet she's, like, super-beautiful. Not as beautiful as you though, of course.' She put her hand on Lorna's arm. 'God. I'm sorry. I really am.'

Lorna was choked up. 'It's not that. It's not her they've found.'

Flora blinked. 'Not the boys?'

'Flora MacKenzie!' Sheila MacDuff, who ran the airport, knew her family well. 'Did you no' hear the bing-bongs? Get on that aeroplane before I tell your da'!'

Lorna's face betrayed her.

'Oh my God. Oh my goodness.' Flora was frozen to the spot.

'You can't tell anyone,' said Lorna. 'Please. I promised

I wouldn't. Not until he's got everything sorted out.'

'Well, I shan't,' said Flora. 'Because I am off to New York!'

Lorna smiled weakly.

A thought struck Flora as she hoisted her bag and Sheila hustled her away. 'They'll go to your school.'

'They will,' said Lorna.

'They won't speak any English.'

'I'm sure Saif will teach them pretty quickly.'

'Oh, Lorna,' said Flora. 'It's great. It's wonderful news.'

'It is,' said Lorna. 'It is. It's wonderful.'

And neither of them said what was both true and unutterably awful: that as wonderful as the news was, it was yet another reason added to the great big pile of reasons that already existed as to why Lorna would never – could never – be close to the man she was absolutely, indubitably in love with.

Flora ran back across the concourse to give her friend a huge hug, even as the propellers had started turning.

'You can't,' said Lorna. 'You can't tell a soul.'

But her voice was lost in the noise of the plane.

## Chapter Sixteen

The little hopper plane to Iceland went twice a week, stopping in the Shetlands, the Faroes and on up to Reykjavik. It was more of a bus than an aeroplane, but Flora was too excited – particularly at going north, instead of south – to mind the stopping and starting. She couldn't even read her book. She was going to see Joel! She'd sent him a brief text last night to say goodnight but she hadn't called him in case she betrayed her excitement. She just wanted to be with him. That was all, and she couldn't concentrate on anything else.

The Norwegian flight was nearly full and she settled excitedly into her seat. She'd never travelled like this before, casually hopping on a plane. It felt very grown up. And New York! She wondered if Joel would mind doing some sightseeing. Or whether he'd just want to stay in the hotel room all the time. Either, she thought, would suit her perfectly well. No! She would grab him as he came in from work and he would be amazed and he could take her out, to some fancy glitzy bar like she'd seen in the movies, and they would catch up properly and it would be amazing. Yes. She was happy now she had a plan.

She dozed off slightly just as they were coming in to land, and missed the swirling heights of the skyscrapers; then, slightly confused and more nervous than ever, she bumped through customs and found a taxi to take her into the city.

It was late at home on Mure, but at six o'clock in the evening, the sun was still shining brightly down on the gleaming skyscrapers. The sight of Manhattan after the great expanses of emptiness of her home island felt very strange; it gave her an oddly dissonant feeling, on top of the jet lag. This wasn't just another town; this was another world. Even years of working in London hadn't prepared her for its hyperreal appearance nor, as she got down from the cab, the full sensory overload of the hot dog stands on the corners of the blocks, the steam from the subway, the vast number of people, the honking of the yellow cabs or the height of the great towers.

She stood, for just a second, on the pavement – on the sidewalk, she thought – and took it in. Here she was. In New York. In America. Joel's America.

Her heart beat incredibly fast. She looked around her. It was full of people streaming out of buildings for rush hour, moving quickly, smartly dressed, slim, on the move. She felt intimidated, even though of course once upon a time she'd thought herself just like this: catching the Docklands Light Railway; moving through Liverpool Street. But these people! Their teeth were so white, their clothes so expensive. They wore sunglasses and carried juice and barged past the obvious tourists in a clear two-speed system, and Flora, trundling with her carry-on bag, knew she wouldn't be mistaken for one of 'them' for a moment. And she knew equally that Joel absolutely would, that he would be a part of their slipstream without even thinking about it.

She entered the hotel cautiously. It was extremely grand, with high ceilings and columns and expensive fresh flower arrangements. It was filled with incredibly rich-looking middle-aged people, obviously there from out of town: well-fed, well-dressed types, as well as a smattering of beautiful young things. The reception staff, in chic black uniforms, were beautiful too, with small badges on their chests indicating how many languages they spoke. They all spoke at least three. Flora felt like addressing them in Gaelic to give herself a boost, but didn't dare.

'Hi,' she said. 'Joel Binder's room?'

It was only 6.30. Of course he wasn't back yet. It occurred to Flora suddenly that maybe he wouldn't be back until late after staying at work then going to a dinner or something. Maybe she could call him, find out. But then wouldn't she give it away? Wouldn't it come up as a local call? She wasn't sure at all.

The receptionist looked at her, Flora thought, with doubt. Then she dismissed the doubt as her just being paranoid.

(Actually, it wasn't in the least bit paranoid. The receptionist had been madly in love with Joel since he'd checked in and wandered in and out looking Byronic, distracted and completely lonely – but with lovely manners – ever since.

She'd had her hair recoloured, tried to be on duty whenever he came in, always had a sweet smile and a friendly word for him – he was working too hard, she speculated, and how amazing that he lived in Scotland – and had entertained several private fantasies about simply letting herself into his suite to be waiting there for him, naked, one evening.)

The receptionist was nothing but professional. She didn't know who this bedraggled person with the strange hair was, but she wasn't someone she'd have put with him in a line-up. I mean, if this was the competition . . .

'I'm afraid he's not in, ma'am,' she said in a slightly accusatory fashion. After all, if this person, or stalker, or whoever she was, couldn't even work out his movements, she barely deserved to be here.

Flora meanwhile suddenly felt overwhelmingly tired and desperately jet-lagged and grimy and in need of a shower and thirsty all at the same time.

'Um, could you let me in to wait for him?' she said. 'I'm kind of here as a surprise.'

The receptionist looked at her. 'Well, obviously not, ma'am,' she said. 'I mean, you could call him . . .'

'That kind of does for the surprise . . .' said Flora.

'Yes, ma'am.'

Flora sighed. She looked around. There was a bar in the lobby. 'I think I'll just sit down for a little while,' she said. 'Wait for him.'

The receptionist was curious to see how this would play out. 'Of course,' she said, nodding.

Flora looked at the prices on the menu and tried to do the mental arithmetic to convert them, but found it difficult. She sighed. Whatever it was, it was very, very expensive. She ordered a cup of tea, then realised when it came (and was awful) that actually she didn't want tea, she wanted wine, but she felt too awkward and uncomfortable to call the waiter back. Suddenly, all the great hope and excitement that had propelled her across the Atlantic – and left her, she knew, very, very, very skint – seemed to be draining away.

She went to the bathroom. The flight had left her skin blotchy and dry, her lips chapped and her hair frizzed. She wanted to go out and see if she could find somewhere to buy some new moisturiser – probably not a Tesco Express but there'd be something, surely? – but what if he showed up when she was gone? She'd have to ask that eye-rolling receptionist again, and Flora wasn't a hundred per cent sure she trusted her to tell her the truth.

Flora sighed and did what she could with the body lotion the expensive hotel had sitting by the side of the sink. It smelled of lavender and didn't really do the job properly. As she was doing her best with the feeble contents of the make-up she still had in the plastic freezer bag she'd taken through customs, an enormous girl, like a huge blonde giraffe, came into the bathroom, talking loudly on her phone about, crap, no way was she going to Loopy Doopy you idiot, what are you, twelve?

She didn't even notice Flora was there – she towered about a foot above her, it felt like to Flora – but instead examined herself critically in the mirror next to her. She was utterly gorgeous: flawless skin, a long aquiline nose, clear blue eyes and pulled-back, silky blonde hair. The girl frowned at her perfect features in the mirror, then dabbed at a non-existent blemish on her chin. Then she realised Flora was there and rolled her eyes, as in, aren't we all girls together, what can you do?

'You look great,' said Flora impulsively. It was impossible, really, to say anything else when faced with such fabulousness.

'Oh, so do you,' said the girl unconvincingly, reapplying lip gloss as someone barked down the phone. 'Well, have a nice day . . . No, Sebastian, no, I don't *want* to go to Ann Arbor . . . '

She left a light, expensive scent on the air. That, Flora thought, looking back in the mirror after the goddess had gone, feeling dumpier and more washed out than ever, that was what Joel should be with. That was what New York girls were like: pulled together, groomed, fabulous, confident of where they were going and what they wanted. Everything she had seen Joel with in London, over the years, everything she remembered so well. What was she doing? What was she thinking? Was this all a ridiculous mistake? She looked at herself, sighing. Then she realised she'd better get out there, in case she missed him. And would there be disappointment in his eyes when he did see her? Was it only on Mure where there was only her, and a lot of seabirds and some sheep to look at?

Stop being ridiculous, she told herself. Stop being ridiculous. She came back out and sat down again and tried hard not to worry and to remember back a few months, midwinter, just the two of them, back on Mure, in the pitch black of January when it never really got light and they had stayed in for a whole weekend, spending the entire time wrapped up on the sofa, in blankets, watching old DVDs because they couldn't stream Netflix, eating hot buttered toast, with salted butter from the farm on bread Mrs Laird had made that morning, nutty and golden brown and simply heaven on the old earthenware plates, and the noise of the fire crackling upwards and the scent of the browning bread and the nearness of Joel and his body and . . .

Joel stalked straight past her. He didn't even glance around at the seated or milling tourists who wandered in and out of the hotel lobby at all hours of the day and night: jet-lagged, confused, stressed out or just plain lost.

He moved smoothly over to see if the contracts he was waiting on had been delivered. The same receptionist always seemed to be on duty, he had subconsciously registered, but not actively thought about. She looked at him now with something important to impart on her face. He hoped it wasn't hassle, like a room change. He just wanted a shower, some work, some food and, even though he had blackout curtains, a high-up, soundproofed room and almost silent air conditioning, he was hoping for sleep, although it was doubtful: he was grinding out the days and making his billable hours for Colton up until he could get home.

Home. The word felt so strange and tentative whenever he thought about it. Was it even possible that there was somewhere he thought of as home? Somewhere he could keep, treasured, secret in his heart even as he walked through boardrooms and hotel lobbies a million miles away; somewhere special, just for him, that was waiting for him at the end of this city, and all the other cities exactly like it . . .

The receptionist nodded her head. 'Are you expecting someone, sir?'

'No,' said Joel, his face wrinkling with distaste. He didn't want to deal with any of Colton's clients face to face if he could possibly help it, particularly the way Colton kept pulling out of their marketplaces without warning. Plus they were blowhards that went on about clean eating too much. He sometimes wanted to make them try some of Mure's very best carbs and fats, just to see their faces recoil in horror. The receptionist of course knew fine well he wasn't; she'd just wanted to see the expression on his face. It gave her some satisfaction.

'Well, there's someone here to see you. Maybe it's a surprise?'

When Joel first told Flora about his upbringing she never really realised its import.

He had told her in such a matter-of-fact way and felt no need to expand on the issue. There had been no tears, no histrionics. He had simply told her that his parents couldn't look after him and he had been brought up in the care system. Flora had always, looking at him, found it difficult to imagine that of Joel, who was so sorted, so handsome, so confident, so seemingly impregnable. He didn't seem broken about it, didn't seem even particularly fussed. It was his reality, and that was all it was.

In later years, Flora was to realise how naïve – how dangerously naïve – she had been to think like this. Of course, her upbringing hadn't been perfect – whose was, when you thought about it? Nobody's. But she'd had two parents, who had stayed together, who had loved her and encouraged her to the best of their abilities, sometimes successfully, sometimes less so. That was what family was: everyone muddling along.

She didn't get it. Not really. Not properly. She felt the sadness in the abstract, of course – not having a family, how awful. But she had had Joel on such a pedestal for so long, had seen him always when he was her boss as a great epitome of triumph and success and everything she longed for.

He had told her, but she had not understood, and would not for a long time.

If you have ever known a child in care, the one thing you do not do – you *never* do – is spring surprises. They have known surprises. They have known all the surprises they ever need to know. Surprises like: you won't be seeing your parents again. Or you won't be staying here any more. Or you're moving schools. Or we're so sorry, this placement hasn't worked out quite as we'd hoped.

If you want to show your love to a child of difficult fostering, be entirely predictable. In every way. Tediously and relentlessly. For ever.

Flora didn't realise this even as she started awake, not knowing at all where she was or what time it was. She was surprised, in fact, to find herself in the lobby of a very upmarket New York hotel, still in her Mure overcoat on this hot day, feeling bleary and completely discombobulated, only to find Joel looking down on her with an expression of abject horror on his face – the sum of her worst fears.

# Chapter Seventeen

'Hey,' Flora said weakly.

She rubbed her eyes. He didn't say anything. Behind him, Flora gradually realised the receptionist was watching, hungrily.

'Hey,' said Joel eventually. There was no embrace. He was staring at her like he didn't know what the hell she was doing there. And she didn't either, she realised. She didn't know what the hell she was doing there. Why hadn't she obeyed her first instincts? Suddenly she wanted to cringe, to fold herself up or vanish into the ground.

'I thought I'd surprise you,' she said timidly.

'Consider me surprised,' said Joel shortly. He cursed himself for the look in her eyes: so disappointed in him. What the hell did she expect him to do? He was at work, trying to get through it, so he could come home. He wasn't over here playing up with other women or whatever she seemed to think if she was checking up on him.

'I just thought ... I've never been to New York.' Flora couldn't believe how lame she sounded, like she wanted to be his girlfriend so she could go on a school trip. 'So here I am!'

'And you're staying here?'

Joel said it without thinking. He was very tired, at the end of a long couple of weeks, and as soon as he'd said it he could have kicked himself. He didn't even know what he meant, but even so.

Flora's face went very white and very still. 'I'm sorry I inconvenienced you,' she said, and she went to grab her bag and leave.

After a second, Joel realised that she meant it and headed after her. The receptionist wished she could follow him. This had to be the end; he was absolutely furious with her. Obviously this was nothing serious. She definitely had an in.

'Flora!' he shouted as she headed through the bustling lobby. 'Come back. Sorry. I'm sorry. You just ... you just took me by surprise that's all. I hate surprises.'

Flora's voice was trembling and her eyes were full of tears. 'Well, I hate being an annoying idiot so I guess we're even,' she said.

'Don't ... I'm the idiot,' said Joel. 'I am. I'm sorry. Please. Please. Come upstairs. Let's get a drink. Let's ... I just wasn't expecting to see you here.'

'Really?' said Flora. 'Well, you dealt with it very gracefully. I'm going. I can stay somewhere else and I'm flying back on Sunday.'

'Don't be ... don't be ridiculous. Come on. Please. Come on. Come upstairs.' Joel glanced around. They appeared to be making a scene, which he absolutely could not bear. 'Please,' he whispered urgently under his breath.

><

All the way up in the elevator – the receptionist had huffily made up a spare key for Flora, her displeasure very clear – they were silent. Neither of them wanted to talk about what had just happened. It was as if the first – of how many? – barriers had been held up in front of them. And they had both failed, in ways that weren't clear to either of them. And now they were like strangers.

Flora almost unbent when she saw the suite – not one of her nobler instincts, as she would have been the first to admit. It was large, with a huge sitting room overlooking the whole of Manhattan, glowing pink in the early evening spring light: south to downtown and the new spaceship of the World Trade Center site; east to Brooklyn.

All the furniture was cream and grey: sofas and cushions, floor-to-ceiling windows and, oh my goodness, the terrace . . . Flora was drawn towards it. It was utterly entrancing.

She thought of how it was exactly what she'd dreamed it might be like . . . and how she and Joel would be sitting on that terrace, laughing at how brilliantly secretive she'd been, ordering cocktails . . .

She rubbed stubbornly at her eyes. 'I'm tired,' she said. 'It's 1 a.m. for me. Can I go to bed please? I'll sleep on the sofa.'

Joel didn't like crying women and he didn't like being emotionally manipulated. He'd drawn back; she was here. That was enough, wasn't it? Or was he going to have to feel guilty the entire evening? He was sick of feeling guilty. Feeling guilty was his default. 'Fine,' he said, going over to his desk and setting down his briefcase. 'Are you hungry? You can order something.'

Flora was starving. 'No, I'm fine.'

'Good.' His fingers strayed towards the briefcase.

'Are you ... are you *working*?' said Flora.

'I have a major conference with Colton. There's a lot he needs done. That's why I'm here.' His jaw was set.

Flora looked out at the lights popping on one by one over Manhattan – an amazing, astonishing world of amazing things out there she'd never experienced – and wanted to cry even more in frustration. Everything was out there and she was going to miss it all. Again. Because she wasn't really Joel's girlfriend. She'd wanted to find out and now she knew. She was just his ... what. His bed and breakfast? His country retreat?

Ignoring him, she went to the minibar, and pulled out a vodka and tonic without looking at the prices. She dumped her coat on the back of a chair, pulled off her big jumper – she'd been absolutely stifling – pulled the bobble from her hair, then poured her drink and took it out on the balcony, letting the mild spring breeze blow away the plane and the cobwebs and the jet lag.

Here, even twenty floors up – or perhaps especially – she could feel the city coming at her in waves. The honking of the cabs, impossibly distant below; the setting sun slanting shadows of enormous buildings, one on top of another; the width of the bouncing boulevards and avenues all heading in the same direction, unlike the little winding paths of her home; the hundreds of lighted windows across from her. She eyed up roof gardens and balconies enviously; people out on fire escapes and terraces on such a mild night; parties and friends and lovers and the oddity of a life lived far more closely and intimately with each other than she knew back in Mure, but at the same time distinct and anonymous and different. It was the oddest feeling. And, she thought, with a strange sadness, anyone looking her way right then would just have seen a girl with pale hair standing by herself. She might have been local, might have known New York like the back of her hand, might have been coming here all her life.

Flora found she quite liked this thought and, if this was to be – and here was a thought so frightening she put it to the back of her mind – but if this was to be her first and last trip ever to New York, she vowed to enjoy it. She would go and see everything tomorrow. She had thought Joel might accompany her, or take her to places he liked, but no matter. She would visit the Empire State, and the Guggenheim, and Ellis Island and everywhere she fancied, and she would stop in nice areas and eat at places recommended on the internet and ...

Well. She needed to have a plan. She had made a mistake ... and one, deep down, that she thought on some level she'd been making all along. He was out of her league. She was all right for what the Scots called a 'bidie in' – Flora MacKenzie, sitting at home, weaving and keeping the fires burning while the man went out and did whatever it was he was going to do in the great wide world. The bigger world beyond their quiet beaches and churning tides. Out there. Without her.

She drank her drink and tried to think calmly about it. It wasn't as if she hadn't been warned. By Margo. By her friends. It hadn't been as if she hadn't known.

Music drifted up to her from some bar or concert far below and she listened to it gently swaying on the warm wind, trying to feel, at least, in the moment; trying to salvage something in fact. She was in New York, and the stars were popping out at the purple edge of the skyscrapers and, as the tears rolled down her cheeks, she thought: Isn't that something? Doesn't that count for something? Maybe, one day, she could say: Well, once I listened to music at the very top of New York on a warm spring night, and I was young, or young-ish, and it was beautiful, and very, very sad ... and she wondered who she might even be telling that to.

And she didn't hear the door slide open silently behind her, and she was unaware of anything until she felt on her bare shoulders the softest kiss, the sense of his presence behind her, and she squeezed her eyes tight shut and when she opened them again he was still there, saying nothing, this time putting his arms right around her, sheltering her from the wind, holding her, and he leaned his head against her back, just laid it there. And she thought of an old story of her mother's – of the sea sprites that came in the night, and you couldn't look at them to break the spell, even though they were the most beautiful, the most extraordinary of all the faerie world, but you could not look at them in the day. Not until the sun had gone down could they reveal themselves, and if you could not help yourself, if you took even the faintest peek, then they would vanish for ever into the mist and you would spend the rest of your life on the

98

lonesome road, searching for their traces in all the world up and down but never would you find them or see them again. And that weeping and wailing was the sound the wind made through the rushes at night. So, her mother had said. Do not be afraid of the noises you hear at night. But never, ever look at a faerie if you love them.

So Flora stood, frozen, staring out still, her heart a waterfall, not daring to move, barely daring to breathe as Joel held on to her as if his life depended on it, kissing her softly up her shoulder. She shivered, and, thinking she was cold, he took off his jacket and put it round her, until gradually, reluctantly, as the moon rose behind the buildings, she turned round to face him.

# Chapter Eighteen

Lorna pulled out her pad and paper.

'Okay,' she said. 'Blood test.'

'Check,' said Saif.

They were sitting on the harbour wall, preparing for Saif leaving, which he was doing the following week. His locum was the scattiest person either of them had ever met, so Saif was just privately hoping everyone avoided getting frightfully sick until he got back. And when he got back, well . . .

'Toys?'

'Wait and see what they like.'

'Good call. I will tell you that as of ten past three this afternoon it was Shopkins and Fidget Spinners. Which means it's now something else completely.'

'I don't understand what you just said.'

'Oh, Saif, you are so in for a . . . No, it'll be fine,' said Lorna. 'New clothes.'

'Waiting to see sizes.'

He had shown Lorna two screengrabs from the videos. His original wallet, with photographs, had been lost to the sea a lifetime ago.

'They are very handsome boys,' said Lorna.

Saif had smiled. 'They are.'

'Here.' Lorna handed over a parcel. 'Don't get over-excited. And I think this will just be the start of a deluge of gifts when everyone finds out.'

'Don't tell them,' said Saif urgently. Lorna felt slightly uncomfortable, but didn't say that Flora already knew.

He looked at the parcel.

'It's buckets and spades,' said Lorna, indicating the Endless Beach, where the hardiest toddlers were already marching up and down busily to the waves, making dams and digging holes, despite the chill breeze. 'They never go out of fashion. And you can't live on Mure without them.'

Saif blinked. 'Thank you,' he said. He clutched the parcel. 'They're really coming,' he said. 'They're really coming.'

'And it's wonderful,' said Lorna gently.

'I am as scared as I have ever been,' said Saif.

Innes came by. He was walking freely and Hamish was carrying vast loads of boxes: supplies for the Seaside Kitchen. Lorna was quite impressed by the division of labour.

'Hey!' She waved. 'Hey, Innes, how's Agot?'

He grimaced. 'She's a fiend. Bit her entire nursery class because she doesn't want to go to school on the mainland.'

'Good!' shouted back Lorna. 'We need her for the school roll.'

Innes shook his head. 'I'm not sure wolverines should get enrolled. Have you heard from my gallivanting sister?'

'Nope,' said Lorna cheerfully. 'I'm taking that as a good sign.'

She turned back to Saif as the boys marched on. 'And wellingtons,' she added when they were out of earshot. 'Don't forget wellingtons! Buy all the wellingtons!'

## Chapter Nineteen

Flora turned round to face him.

'No more surprises.'

'Thank you.'

They stood there, frozen.

'I shouldn't have come,' she said after a long pause. 'I thought you'd want to see me.'

'I do,' he said. 'That's why I want to ... to get my head down, to get finished, just to work. So I can get home. That's all I do. That's all I care about. I thought you'd see that.'

Flora blinked. 'But ... '

'But what?'

'But I'm not just for ... for coming back to when you're tired of doing other stuff.'

Joel squinted. He really was very tired. 'What do you mean?'

'I mean, you go to all these amazing places and it's all

right to take me sometimes ... you know, I'm not just a scullery maid.'

'I never thought of you as a scullery maid. Also, what's a scullery maid?'

'You never take me out to nice places like this!'

Joel screwed up his face. 'I'm working fifteen-hour days in a windowless conference room fuelled by American coffee, the world's most disgusting drink. All I think of is getting through it, so I can get home to you. That's all I think about.'

'But I'm here.'

'I know. And I hate it here.'

Flora looked around. 'How can you hate it here?'

She was weak, and put up with too much, and all of those things, probably. But oh my God, here she was, under a purple New York sky with a man, the very smell of whom made her want to turn herself inside out – with so much love she felt she would die from it. It was all she wanted to do ...

Joel shrugged.

'Come on,' she said, shaking herself awake suddenly. 'No, I have a plan. Let's go out.'

She couldn't, she knew, just let him take her to bed. That was what always happened. And it was amazing, but nothing got fixed or moved on at all.

All Joel wanted – he so desperately wanted – was to take her to bed, tear that dress off her, lose himself in the pale beauty of her curves and her skin, then finally, blessedly, find some sleep because she was near him. Just being so close to her again was bewitching, almost made him forget his cases, his workload, the strangeness of being back in America, the pace of it all.

'Can I take you out tomorrow?' he said.

'Aren't you working tomorrow?' she said, teasing.

'I want you so much.' He pulled her very close to him on the terrace, so she could feel it.

'Tough,' said Flora, smiling at him. 'You get me into bed, I'll fall asleep. You need to take me somewhere noisy. With dancing.'

'I don't dance.'

'I don't care.'

~ ~

But Friday night in bustling New York, with a reluctant Joel and a clueless Flora, was a mistake, to say the least. Anywhere that looked nice had a two-hour wait for a table and rude, beautiful girls on the doors, looking doubtful when they hadn't booked, while anywhere else was full of tourists. Avoiding the ridiculously fake Irish bars that Flora absolutely had no wish to go into, they ended up in a dark oak bar full of lawyers – exactly the type of people Joel had absolutely no wish to see – and their gorgeous dates, obviously picked up from Tinder or just around and about the place. And Flora, exhausted and strung out, misjudged completely the strength of the cocktails. She drank two and ordered another at top speed and was, not to put too fine a point on it, drunk in half an hour, while Joel was not. And every time she tried to bring up the subject of the two of them, she realised she was repeating herself and not making any sense at all.

Drunk people horrified Joel – too many memories – and

he tried, gently, to convince Flora to go back to the hotel. She argued against it and told him he was a dreadful guy who didn't really care about her at all and was never any fun, and while Joel disagreed profoundly with the first accusation, he couldn't help seeing that she probably had a point about the second. On the other hand, they had come out to have fun and hadn't had the slightest bit of fun at all, and now Flora was the worse for wear and he was concerned about bundling her into the lift at the hotel in case she started yelling at him inside.

'Need any help, sir?' said the receptionist, smiling perkily at him in what she considered to be an unthreatening way. He tried his best to smile bravely back while Flora muttered unpleasant words in Gaelic under her breath about the receptionist, and kept trying to press the down button and stumble off to the bar as Joel was doing his best to encourage her upstairs. Finally back in the room, Joel went to use the bathroom. He came back prepared for a diatribe about how dreadful he was. Instead, fully dressed, Flora was lying diagonally across the bed, fast asleep.

Sighing, he drew the blackout curtains, gently took off her shoes, put a glass of water and two ibuprofen by her bedside and rolled her carefully under the duvet – then, knowing sleep had no interest in coming anywhere near him that night – put on the desk light in the main room, ordered up some coffee and returned to his files.

Flora woke incredibly early, woozy, with a headache and not a clue where she was in the pitch dark. She rolled over, remembered, then groaned heavily. She had messed things up ridiculously. She remembered being rude to Joel last night, yelling at him. She realised to her horror that of course he'd put her to bed. Oh God. And then . . . what? Where was he? He wasn't in the bed. Had he left in disgust? When she hadn't immediately gone to bed with him . . . then had gone out and rolled around like a loony. Oh God. She thought of him, all buttoned up and restrained and her wanging on like a drunken harpy. She saw the glass and the ibuprofen next to her bed, and dropped her head in her hands. Oh Christ. She had never had a worse idea in her entire life. What on earth had she been thinking? What an utter idiot she was.

Her eyes were getting more used to the dark room and she saw the line of golden light coming from next door. She got up to use the loo and brush her teeth, then glanced through the door. He was sitting, staring at his files, hadn't noticed she was there, and he took off his glasses and put them down for a second, and rubbed his dry eyes. He looked so young and so lost with this little gesture that Flora wanted to go to him, but she was afraid of his judgement, could not face him quite yet, she was feeling so bad, so she went back to bed and lay there in the dark, unable to sleep because of the time difference. Eventually, when he finally came to bed, she still lay there and did not move towards him, nor did he move to her, even though neither of them was sleeping, and it felt like the dawn would never come.

## Chapter Twenty

Joel was up early the following morning to go into the office. Flora apologised and Joel said stiffly not to worry about it, it was nothing. They had still not even made love, and this was terrifying Flora because it was in that space they had together that nothing was ever wrong, and nothing was ever misunderstood; it had always felt like their bodies could talk to each other in a way that their brains could not: directly, with total honesty and utter mutual understanding. Whereas this . . . this was just a mess. And she had absolutely no idea how to fix it.

Still feeling utterly dreadful, she made coffee and sat in front of some strange American television, finding it odd to think that this was normal for everyone who lived there. It was going to be a beautiful day, she realised eventually, after trying to convert Fahrenheit to Celsius. And there was the city at her fingertips . . . once she felt a little better. She had a long shower, which felt like being pummelled by water, in the amazing rainforest bathroom, and that definitely helped. Then she looked through her hastily packed suitcase to see if anything was suitable. Nothing was. She could go and buy some light, pretty dresses, she thought suddenly. But when would she wear them? It wasn't like they got many hot days on Mure, or that they'd be suitable in the Seaside Kitchen.

She felt homesick, suddenly. It would be afternoon there; the trade would be coming in – the walkers, hungry for big sticky slices of millionaire's shortbread and raisin pies and steak bridies and everything they needed to refuel; the wee old ladies down from their grocery shopping who wanted scones and cups of tea; the farmers, in for their weekly look around the bright lights of Mure Town, who would take big sides of fruitcake back home to sit on their dressers all week to be consumed with small glasses of whisky and large hunks of cheese.

Then she told herself to stop being ridiculous; to buck up. They would fix it tonight. Definitely. Wouldn't they?

She looked around the sitting room, which Joel had left incredibly tidy, as was his wont. Then she opened the cupboard, where his row of suits was hanging. She found a jumper, the only thing there not freshly dry-cleaned, that still smelled of him, and buried her face in it, trying not to cry.

Suddenly the phone rang in the suite. Flora blinked. It must be Joel! Maybe he'd be free to meet her for lunch! Maybe he'd got to the office and changed his mind, realised he should take a day off to spend with her! Realised he loved her even if she was a … well, a sloppy drunk with a loud mouth, she reflected, with another stab of agony. Oh God.

Tentatively she picked it up. 'Hello?'

'Hello? Joel?' It was a woman's voice. Flora bit back her inevitable disappointment and tried to ignore her growing fear.

'Um, hi, no,' said Flora stiffly. 'This is Flora. Can I take a message?'

There was a pause. Flora's heart was beating painfully quickly.

'Sorry, who is this?' she said. She couldn't stop thinking of that blonde girl in the bathroom, or even those girls in the bar last night, what she remembered of it, the ones Joel had thought were cookie cutter, but she had thought were beautiful.

'Oh my, sorry ... Are you *Scottish*?' The voice seemed older now to Flora, who was wrong-footed. 'Mark!' The voice on the other end was talking to someone else now. 'Mark! It's the Scottish girl!'

'Excuse me?' said Flora again.

'Oh, I am *so* sorry,' said the woman's voice. She sounded nice: mumsy and friendly. 'We had ... we had absolutely no idea you were in New York.'

'He never tells us anything!' came a voice from a distance behind her.

'I thought we'd just leave a message! Well, my dear. It is *so* nice to speak to you.'

Flora blinked. If she hadn't known ... or thought she knew ... she'd have thought these were his parents.

She suddenly felt how little she really knew about this man and it chilled her.

# Chapter Twenty-one

'Sorry,' said Flora. 'Sorry if this is rude, but ... who are you? Can I take a message?'

'Of course ... I'm Marsha Philippoussis and ... Has he really never mentioned us?'

'No,' said Flora, more and more worried.

'Well, Mark – that's my husband – he ... he used to be Joel's ... Well, I'm not sure if I can say. We're friends.'

'Friends.'

It wasn't that Joel didn't have friends, Flora knew. He had squash buddies and lawyer buddies in most cities in the world and everyone was always pleased to see him. But he didn't have best friends, or intimate friends as far as she could tell. He didn't have a friend like she had in Lorna. But then, maybe most men were like that.

'You can tell her,' shouted the voice.

'Oh, okay. Well, dear. Mark was Joel's psychiatrist. When he was younger. But now we're ... friends.'

'Friends who never call each other when they're in the city!'

Clearly Marsha and Mark were quite the double act.

'Well … yes. We were hoping, since he's in the city, we might have dinner … Would you like to come, dear? Tonight?'

'Um, I don't know what he's got planned.'

Marsha laughed. She remembered what Joel's plans used to be – head for the nearest bar; pick up the most beautiful girl in the room; walk out with her. So she was very keen to meet the girl who had finally – at last – apparently tamed the odd, serious, driven boy she'd known since he was a child. She was hard to imagine; in Marsha's head she looked like a will-o'-the-wisp: a strange, exotic, bewitching creature.

'I'll call his cell,' said Marsha. 'It'll be turned off, but usually if you call four or five times he'll pick up eventually.'

Flora wondered how relaxed she would have to be with Joel to call him four or five times in a row. She didn't know many people who'd dare.

She left the hotel tentatively, relaxing instantly in the warm spring sunshine. Oh, it was glorious after the long dark months on Mure. She checked she had enough sunscreen in her handbag (island skin and hot sunshine did not normally work together too well), then, despite everything, she felt herself unfurl luxuriously as she moved between the long shadows on the busy pavement, getting in people's way but not even caring. The first hit of sun after a long winter made, she decided, everything about a long winter totally worth it. She breathed in the hot scent of New York pavements – hot dogs, pretzels, fuel, perfume, bodegas – and loved it. She let the sun tickle the backs of her arms; felt it soak through her dress and warm her back. She wanted to lift up her hands and twirl in it, to take a bath in sunshine.

It was hard to feel so down. Okay, last night had been . . .

It had been awful, she couldn't deny it. Absolutely the opposite of everything she'd hoped it would be. There had been no delighted sweeping her up in his arms. There had been no impressed head-shaking at her amazing appearance. No happy astonishment and brutal kisses in the shadows of the world's greatest buildings, him showing her round the sights, taking some time off for the weekend so they could behave like . . .

She was honest with herself. Like a proper boyfriend and girlfriend. Not what she sometimes felt they were: shipwrecked sailors thrown together on a desert island, clinging together for sanity and safety amid the wreckage of their own hearts.

That was not what they were, she vowed. They could do better.

She quenched her hangover with an enormous freshly squeezed juice in a huge cup and a pepperoni pretzel – which was utterly delicious, larger than her head and couldn't possibly be good for her, although she did consider appropriating the recipe – then set off to walk to the Empire State Building even though she realised quite early on that walking the huge blocks of the city took rather longer than she'd expected, and that there was rather more of Broadway than any street she'd ever been on before.

It didn't matter though. She was so entranced by looking at everything: the people; the shop windows; the little apartments perched in the sky; the business of everything. Maybe, she thought, she even fitted in. Well, at least until she got to the Empire State Building and had to join the enormous line of other tourists just like everybody else, but even so. She looked thoughtfully at her phone. What if he didn't call her? What if she'd come all this way not to see him? She tried to think of a way to spin this to Lorna, who'd sent her several envious texts already, telling her it was hosing it down and asking for pictures. There wasn't one. She glanced at Fintan's Instagram – yes, Fintan had an Insta now for when he and Colton were flying about places having an amazingly romantic time. She tried her best not to be jealous of her brother's relationship but there seemed to be absolutely no doubt who was having all the fun now, even if he had done nothing but sit in a barn by himself making cheese in the freezing cold for three years after their mother had died.

She sent Joel a message:

Sorry about last night – not used to NYC drinks!!!

She had added too many exclamation marks, then she reckoned they looked a bit desperate and took them away, then decided the message looked too downbeat so she added one and then one more and decided that a) this was definitely it and b) she was going crazy. Then she sent it and held her breath and tried not to check her phone every ten seconds while the queue inched forwards.

'Joel! You didn't tell us you'd brought someone to New York!'

Marsha just launched into the conversation; she didn't

give him a chance to say anything or tell her he was too busy or use any of his usual deflection techniques. She just bulldozered over him. Normally Joel would freeze up or become rude when faced with someone behaving like this. But he didn't mind Marsha doing it. Quite liked it even. It showed how well she knew him, deep down.

'So this is her? This is the girl?'

Joel thought back to Flora ranting at him on the pavement last night outside the hotel and groaned. He really didn't want to see the look on the Philippoussises' faces if something like that happened again. He knew they would want to meet her, but he had absolutely no idea what they were expecting. Someone more model-like, maybe? More chicly dressed? Marsha was always immaculately turned out. But that was just New York women. Would they see that there was more to Flora – that maybe she didn't have perfectly manicured fingernails but underneath it all was a good heart and a spirit and a fire?

And it felt private to them as a couple – something only they shared – and he didn't feel entirely comfortable exposing that to daylight. But, he realised, it was time. He hadn't really had conventional relationships, but this had to be one of them. This is what he would have to do. It was what Flora wanted, of course it was. And Mark and Marsha were … well, they were the closest thing to family he had. It would have to be done. So Marsha was extremely surprised – she had a list prepared of nine reasons as to why he should agree to bring Flora to dinner – when he said laconically, 'Sure. Can I bring her to dinner?'

Marsha was so taken aback she could hardly speak. But

she rallied pretty fast. 'Joel,' she said. 'You are being nice to her?'

And the pause told them both what they needed to know.

'Leave work,' said Marsha. 'It's a Saturday.'

Joel looked down at the papers. Colton had loaded so much on him it wasn't even funny. Something was up and he was being expected to handle all of it.

'And I'll see you later,' said Marsha, hanging up.

Flora was on the top of the Empire State Building, looking out at one of the most iconic views in the world, doing something she had dreamed of her whole life since she'd watched *Sleepless in Seattle* four times in a row one weekend. And all she could do was check her phone.

This wasn't right, she thought to herself. These endless nerves. He was her boyfriend. Okay, he'd never said the word – but on the other hand, he'd moved hundreds of miles to a tiny dot in the middle of the North Sea to be with her. If that wasn't commitment, what was? He could have moved and not lived with her if it was just the island he liked, couldn't he?

She tried to take in the stunning surroundings, the amazing ability of New York to be so strange and yet so overwhelmingly familiar at the same time; she took photos for other, happier couples and tried not to look bitter as she did; she googled where to go for lunch, for which she got thousands and thousands of responses, and glanced down at the list of amazing-sounding restaurants and wished she felt remotely hungry.

She was just turning round to head back when she heard

a ping on her phone. Somehow she knew straightaway that it was him – for good or for bad.

'Hello?'

'How are you feeling?'

Joel's detached, amused tones made Flora shut her eyes with overwhelming relief. She had been sure that he would find an excuse to withdraw even more, upset at her drunken rantings. Instead he sounded just like normal.

'Awful,' she said honestly.

'Good,' he said. 'I should have warned you about American drinks. Although on the other hand, you probably shouldn't have four cocktails in half an hour anywhere.'

'They don't do a lot of cocktails at the Harbour's Rest,' muttered Flora.

'They don't,' said Joel. He took a breath. 'Anyway . . . tonight. Would you like . . . ? There are some people I'd like you to meet.'

Flora straightened up. It must be the lady who rang.

'I'll check my schedule,' she said, and Joel laughed.

Flora then spent most of the afternoon in something of a panic, looking up and down and around Fifth Avenue – completely paralysed by the sheer choice and range of things on offer – to find something appropriate to wear. She got lost in Sak's, wandered through Bloomingdale's far too overwhelmed to even approach anything, got shoe blindness, and realised that in her life she had rarely needed to buy summer apparel and didn't appear to have the knack.

Joel stared at the phone. Stared at the laptop. Thought

117

about what Marsha would say that night, then swore mightily and went to meet Flora.

He worried briefly about what Marsha and Mark would think, but they'd never met any of his girlfriends before; they rarely lasted long enough, and even so he seldom had the slightest bit of interest in sharing his upbringing. He hated – despised – the tilted-head look girls had often given when they heard about his past, as if they immediately saw him as some wounded bird only they could heal, so often he didn't mention it at all. It had been different with Flora; she was so wounded by her own mother dying that it felt they were sharing in something they both understood. Even though she couldn't understand it, not really. Losing a mother you had loved was not at all the same as never having known one.

But Marsha and Mark ... There was no hiding there. Mark had read all his childhood files; Marsha, he surmised, had intuited the rest.

He hoped they'd like Flora. He hoped they'd think he was good enough for her.

He came across her panicking in Zara on Fifth, carting large amounts of clothes into the changing rooms. She looked hot and red-faced – sunny days didn't exactly suit her – and her hair was hanging damply from a ponytail. She had a huge pile of coloured dresses in her arms, none of which, he could tell, would suit her.

'Having fun?' he said mildly.

'Not really,' said Flora crossly. 'American sizes are weird and everything makes me look pale.'

'That's because you're translucent.'

'And nothing suits me and absolutely everyone else looks

118

amazing in these colours and I just look like a peely-wally washout.'

Joel wasn't sure what this was but guessed it wasn't good. He glanced around. There was no doubt about it: Joel was good at clothes, Flora reflected. He wore suits every day, that was what he did, but they were subtly different – better – than other people's suits: the slim lines of them, the positions of the buttons, the crisp shirts. He wasn't a dandy; he just got it effortlessly right. That life he used to have . . . Everyone dressed well. She wouldn't have dared buy him so much as a tie. She sighed. Now he was eyeing her, frowning.

'What?'

'I'm not sure this is the right place for you,' he said. 'Zara is Spanish. It's designed for beautiful tanned señoritas who don't eat till 11 p.m. each night. Come with me.'

She followed him out and he guided her expertly to a very quiet corner of Bergdorf's, up on the fourth floor. She eyed him suspiciously.

'What?' he said. 'I dated a lot of models.'

'Well, *that* makes me feel better,' she said.

'They're very, very boring. Do we need to go through this again?'

Flora looked at the shop assistant, who had skin as pale as her own, but topped with a severe black bob and bright orange lipstick. 'No,' she said.

'Okay.' A smile played on Joel's lips. 'Let me do this.'

And Flora watched in mild amazement as he quickly blew through the racks, picking out some clothes, eyeing her, and putting most of them back. Finally he came up with three.

There was a deconstructed dress in the palest of

119

millennial pinks, with a soft Lycra top and a parachute silk skirt in softest teal that looked far too floaty and strange for anything Flora would ever have picked up. It swirled with her as she walked and made her look, with her pale hair and white shoulders, like a mermaid.

There was a very pale-silver see-through dress with tiny, almost invisible sprigs of flowers embroidered on the outer layer. The inner layer was a heavenly comfortable silk sheath, and the outer layer hung to the floor. From the second Flora put it on she found herself walking differently; it made her willowy and elegant, rather than slightly too tall and Viking-ish – it was a vision of a different type of person than she thought she could be, particularly as Joel came over and untied her hair carefully until it fanned out over her shoulders.

'Now you're a sprite,' he said.

The final dress was of palest green, in grosgrain, off the shoulder, slightly tighter and designed to be worn with heels. It was definitely a sexy dress.

'Oh yes,' said Joel appreciatively. He was sitting in a large armchair leafing through a magazine and glanced up as she left the changing room.

'Really?' said Flora, turning around. She blushed bright pink and Joel got an enormous jolt simply watching it happen. How he loved to raise that colour in her. He looked around to check how private the changing rooms were. The snotty-looking shop assistant immediately looked up as if she could sense what he had in mind.

'Let's go,' said Joel in a hurry, glancing at his watch. 'You've got time to go home and change.'

Flora checked the price tag. It was astronomical. 'Ah,' she said. Joel waved his hand.

'Stop it, please,' he said. 'All of them,' he said over his shoulder to the assistant.

'No, Joel, don't.'

He shook his head. 'I want to.' He pulled her close. 'You are literally the only woman I've ever met who hasn't asked for a thing.'

Flora swallowed. She knew he was complimenting her. But it felt like he was warning her too.

She shook that thought out of her head as she got changed, and the shop assistant bagged everything up for her, all wrapped in tissue, and they ran through the crowds as quickly as they were able. Joel started kissing her before they were even in the lift, and Flora looked around guiltily, then realised of course she didn't know anyone here so who cared, and she kissed him back with abandon and he practically carried her into the lift and they were completely oblivious, even as the receptionist watched them jealously.

>~ ~<

Marsha and Mark lived uptown. Flora and Joel were still rather giggly when they turned up, a little late, Flora with her hair still wet at the ends but glowing in her silver dress. Joel made a mental note to buy her some earrings to go with it.

The Philippoussises lived in a fancy apartment building with a doorman on the Upper East Side, and Flora was intensely impressed by the old oak lift and the beautiful parquet flooring, as well as the views of the park.

Marsha answered the door, and Flora liked her

immediately. She was tiny, with short brown hair and a round figure dressed in something obviously expensive. There were large jars of lilies in the hallway and soft lighting all around. She had dark, beady eyes that took in everything – including the fact that the poor girl, she thought to herself, was obviously wearing a new dress. She wondered if Joel was up to his old tricks again, trying to control every environment he was in.

Joel leaned forward and kissed Marsha lightly, but he didn't get away in time as she stretched her arms up and insisted on giving him a hug.

'I swear you are still growing,' she said.

'Marsha, I'm thirty-five years old.'

'Yes, well, even so.'

Mark came through, holding a wooden spoon with a tea towel over his shoulder. Flora felt Joel relax beside her.

'Hello, sir,' said Joel respectfully.

'Come in, come in,' said Mark, beaming. He had a trimmed grey beard and his eyes twinkled. Flora immediately felt their warmth and intelligence and felt envious of them both. 'You must be Flora, our Scottish friend.'

He did not attempt a shot at the accent, as many Americans did, for which Flora was grateful.

'You look lovely,' said Marsha. Flora wasn't at all what she'd expected. She'd assumed she would be another of Joel's favoured willowy blondes. Although she had always suspected that it wasn't that Joel had a type as such, just that those kinds of girls were considered by the culture to be particularly desirable so he had made his choice in the same way he chose his watch or his apartment or anything else: by what appeared to be the best available to him at the time.

But this girl wasn't like that. She didn't look like anyone else Marsha had ever seen, and she lived in New York where eventually you saw everyone, more or less. Her pale hair; her skin was practically albino; those strange silvery blue-green eyes ... You didn't quite notice her at first glance; she was average ... then you took a closer look and she was extremely striking. Her voice when she spoke wasn't always easy to understand, but it sounded to Marsha like music. Please, she thought to herself. Let her be kind. But not too kind.

'So, how are you finding New York?'

'Amazing,' said Flora. 'It's weird – it feels like I know it already. And also: hot.'

Marsha looked puzzled. 'Oh, I think it's quite a cool spring.'

'It's hot compared to where I'm from.'

'Well, don't come back in July ... Would you like a Martini?'

'A small one, please,' said Flora, as Joel smirked. 'Stop it!' she whispered to him, as they followed through into the large kitchen-diner with its extraordinary city views. 'This is amazing,' said Flora as they moved back out to the terrace. Joel had stopped in the kitchen, where Mark was making a moussaka, and was updating him on his new job. Mark was nodding solemnly.

'So,' said Marsha, drawing her in. Flora remembered what she'd heard about Americans: that they were perfectly upfront in asking direct questions. 'You're the one.'

'Oh, I don't know about that,' said Flora, although she was thrilled by the statement, secretly – especially while sipping her Martini, which was incredibly strong but also rather delicious. She watched the long lines of the lights of cars, up and down the park.

'You're the only person he's ever brought to meet us,' said Marsha. 'And we've known him since he was eleven years old.'

Flora kept staring out. 'What was he like then?'

Marsha thought back. 'Clever. Sad. So tightly closed in on himself, you couldn't have peeled him open any which way. I'm not sure anyone ever has.' She left the unspoken question in the air.

'What happened ... I mean, he told me he was raised in care. Why? What happened? He's never said and it felt a bit strange to ask.'

Marsha shrugged. 'I haven't seen the files, of course. So I don't know. I will tell you this. With other wards, when they turn eighteen, Mark legally asks them if they want to be reunited with their birth family.' She sipped her drink. 'In this case, never.'

'And he never got adopted? Did no family want to keep him?'

Marsha shook her head. 'The system doesn't always work, alas.'

'What about ... do you have children?'

'Yes,' said Marsha. 'Of course, we couldn't have adopted Joel. Professionally, it's unconscionable. And our own children were too young at that time. But we ... we tried to do what we could for him.'

'He is very grateful,' said Flora.

Marsha grimaced. 'I don't want him to be grateful. I'd

really like him to take us totally for granted, fling his washing down and turn up whenever he feels like it. I'd love a world in which we don't have to beg to see him.' She looked up.

'But, Flora,' she said. 'You shouldn't have to be asking me. You know that, don't you?'

Flora nodded.

'That's all love is, you know. To know someone: to be fully known.'

And Flora couldn't speak as they headed back into the kitchen, where Joel and Mark were deep in a discussion of the intricacies of potential impeachment trials which, both the women intuited immediately, was their way of telling each other how much they loved each other. The evening passed pleasantly as Mark and Marsha talked about a disastrous trip to Italy that appeared to include a tour of the country's craziest hotels; about how Mark was refusing to retire, pointing out that half the people he saw were miserable because they had done so and had lost their purpose in life, plus he loved what he did; Marsha talked about her interior design course and the awfulness of the women who went on it; Joel did not talk much, as usual, but he laughed in the right places, and neither of their hosts did the thing Flora had been most excited about while also dreading: asking the couple what their plans were or where they were headed.

At 10.30, Flora let out an involuntary jet-lag yawn and Mark jumped up to get the coats. Joel went to the bathroom and they left, both thinking that it had gone as well as could be expected. Flora fell asleep against Joel in the car, Marsha's words ringing in her ears. As she nodded off, she swore to herself she would do it – she would know him.

# Chapter Twenty-two

Flora tried to act nonchalant but she was fundamentally terrible at it. She sat on the huge bed, still staring out at the sensational view – she wondered if the people who lived here ever got tired of it, even as she wondered whether Paul Macbeth's lambs had been born yet and hoping she didn't miss their first days of bouncing cheerfully about. She was looking forward to going home tomorrow. She wished Joel was coming with her. She watched him untie his tie and he looked so alone, suddenly, standing in the dim light of the bedroom, and she walked up to him and put her arms around him.

'So they knew you as a child,' she said. 'What were you like?'

Joel shrugged. 'I don't know. That's the problem with psychiatrists. They never give you an end-of-year report.'

'Did you like being a child?'

He stiffened. 'Not terribly,' he said. Then he pulled her

round swiftly and hard up against him and looked straight at her, his hands locked on to her back in that way that made her gasp.

'Last night in New York,' he said. 'Let's make it count.'

He was up early on Sunday morning and she sat up and wrapped her arms around her knees, watching him. She told him about Saif's children coming back, and was gratified by his happiness at the news, and concern for how they would be. She lay back, faux casually.

'So was it mostly in New York you were brought up?'

Joel eyed her. 'Why do you ask?'

'I'm interested,' said Flora. 'It's quite a normal thing to want to know, isn't it?'

Joel shrugged. 'Well. Here and there.'

'You said that before.'

Joel looked at her, his dark eyes unblinking. 'I told you about my childhood.'

'You didn't,' said Flora, hating herself for sounding like she was nagging at him. 'You told me you grew up in care. You didn't tell me anything else about it.'

'There's nothing else to tell,' said Joel, glancing at his watch. 'I was fostered. I moved around families. Then I escaped and went to boarding school. Right, I have to shoot.'

'Do you ... do you know what happened to your parents?' said Flora gently. Joel's face closed up tightly.

'I have to go,' he said again.

Flora looked around in dismay. 'You can't have brunch or anything before I go? It's Sunday.'

127

'Colton doesn't recognise Sundays. It's the big meeting today. For which I am not remotely prepared, thanks to being distracted by you. And the faster I'm done, the faster I can leave this place!'

And he kissed her and left, and that was that.

# Chapter Twenty-three

In truth, although he'd tried to shake it off, Flora's visit had bothered Joel far more than he could bring himself to say. That he'd had a message from Marsha saying how much they'd liked her made matters worse. It felt like she was a cop, moving closer and closer to the truth about him. And he couldn't bear that. He wanted the soft-skinned girl who sat in the firelight, whose presence soothed his tortured soul, who acted as a balm to his troubled mind.

Not someone else like all the others – like all the legions of others whose hands he had passed through, who had wanted a full history, who had wanted to hear the whole story again and again and again, and you would think it would lose its power but it didn't. And the one decent thing he had in his life . . .

He had had to leave the hotel room as quickly as he could in the faint hopes that this would not be spoiled too.

He was under no illusions that she hadn't noticed.

Had the meeting with Colton gone well, then he might have been able to smooth it over; deflect it. The meeting did not go well.

The room was closed and private. There was nobody else there. This was very unusual. When Colton did business, he usually had a massive entourage around him, even if they were just there to laugh at his jokes. No Fintan, which was rarely a good sign. Fintan had done Colton Rogers nothing but good. He had toned down his abrasive side and made him laugh.

But here, in this huge conference room on the eighty-sixth floor of a midtown skyscraper mostly owned by Colton, was nothing but a vast table, a pot of coffee and the two men.

Joel took out the paperwork. 'I just . . . I realise it's not for me to question your decisions. But consolidating absolutely everything . . . I mean, what does Ike say?'

Ike was one of Colton's local money men.

Colton waved his hand. 'Doesn't matter,' he said. He pulled out a sheaf of paperwork from his hip backpack. Joel furrowed his brow; this was new.

'Here,' said Colton, hurling it across the table. 'Look at this.'

'You want me to take it away?'

'You can't take it away,' said Colton. 'You read it and redraft it and I get it typed up. Now. Today.'

Joel blinked, then put his head down and started to read. Colton watched him intently. There was absolute silence in the room.

After half an hour, Joel raised his head. 'Colton, you can't do this.'

Colton shrugged. 'I can do what I like.'

Joel looked at it again. 'But ... but, Colton. It's wrong. What it'll do ...' His voice trailed off. 'I mean. Seriously. Are you sure?'

Colton shrugged. 'Well, it's my money.'

'But ...'

There was silence. Colton's face became mutinous. 'Joel, you're my lawyer.'

'Yes, but ...'

'No buts about it. You're hired. You're my lawyer. I don't want anyone else. You do what I ask. Or I can fire your ass and you can leave the island and break that sweet girl's heart and wash up fuck knows where, like I give a shit. Or a reference.'

He stared at Joel, very hard.

'But ...'

'Joel, you're a *lawyer*. You get murderers out of jail.'

There was a long silence.

'You gotta do it. Or I'm just going to find someone else, and you'll just make this whole thing take longer. Oh, and by the way, you breathe a word of this and you'll find yourself in more trouble than you can possibly imagine. I will dedicate the rest of my life to making yours a misery. And don't you forget that.'

There was a very long silence. Then Joel spoke up. 'I can redraft from these notes.'

'Good,' said Colton. 'Do it. And hurry up. I'm getting out of this hellhole.' He gesticulated to the stunning Manhattan views outside his window. 'And getting back to where things really matter.'

## Chapter Twenty-four

'Are you absolutely, totally, one hundred per cent sure he isn't just a dickhead?'

Fintan was doing his best to be encouraging.

Flora thought back to how Joel had been as her boss in London: squiring a selection of models; never even glancing at people he considered his inferiors; his rude manner.

'Well,' she said, as Fintan parked the car. She was jet-lagged and exhausted. 'Well, I can see how people *might* think he was a dickhead.'

She looked up. 'He likes dogs.'

'Mate,' said Fintan. 'Only psychos don't like dogs. I didn't accuse him of being a psycho. Just a dickhead.'

They turned onto the little soil path up the hill to the farm. Bramble and the other family dogs immediately went utterly bananas. Flora almost raised a smile at that.

'Don't upset Dad,' said Fintan.

'Why?' said Flora, instantly stricken. Her father had

been very down after the death of her mother three years ago.

'No reason,' said Fintan. 'Only, he's so happy that you're settled – and Joel's someone Mum would have liked.'

'Unless she thought he was a dickhead,' said Flora mournfully.

'Well, yeah, that's possible too,' said Fintan. 'Anyway.'

Innes and Hamish came wandering in from the fields cheerfully. Since the farm had been bought out, the cushion of a little money, plus a new, guaranteed home for their organic produce, had taken a lot of the strain and worry from their lives. Farmers' lives were never without worry, of course – but even so, you could see a lightness in Innes's happy face as he took off his big boots and waved at them. Agot was inside the farmhouse.

'ATTI FLOWA!' She jumped up.

'You are not still watching *Peppa Pig*,' said Flora, smiling, and she picked the girl up in her arms and whirled her round.

'I'S LOVES PEPPA.'

'Well, I'm glad to hear it.'

Agot looked around mischievously then leaned towards Flora's ear and announced in a loud stage whisper, 'YOU GOT PRESENT FOAH AGOT?'

'Agot!' said Innes. 'Literally that was the exact and precise thing I told you not to say when Flora walked through the door.'

The imp looked utterly unrepentant. 'BUT LIKE PRESENTS,' she said, as if this was a ridiculous demand to have placed on her.

Flora smiled and sat down. 'Well,' she said, and drew out

of her bag a snow globe that had all the New York landmarks underneath it. She shook it for the little one, who gave a great gasp.

'SNOWZING!'

'It is snowzing, yes.'

Agot snatched it from Flora's hands, eyes wide.

'Be careful with it,' said Flora. 'Don't drop it.'

'NOTS DROP SNOWZING,' agreed Agot, nevertheless waving it about in a highly dangerous fashion, her eyes fixed on it.

'What do you say, Agot?' said Innes, watching happily.

'THANK YOU, ATTI FLOWA.' Agot's little face looked up, then creased into a frown. 'WHAT WRONG?'

Flora blinked. 'There's nothing wrong,' she said.

'YOU CRYING? SAD ATTI FLOWA? YOU SAD? YOU SAD? NOT CRY.'

Agot scrambled up into Flora's lap and started using her little hands to wipe away the remnants of tears from Flora's eyes.

'I'm fine!' said Flora, slightly desperately. 'Just a bit tired, that's all.'

'Are you missing Joel?' said Innes.

'Neh, he was being a dickhead,' said Fintan.

'Shut up, Fintan!'

'DOAN BE SAD.' Agot was unswervable on the topic.

'I'm not sad,' said Flora. 'I am very happy. Why don't you play with your snow globe?'

Agot looked at it. Bramble was trying to eat it.

'SNOWZER WAN WATCH PEPPA,' she said, snatching it back.

'Well, good,' said Flora. 'I think that's an excellent idea.'

'WAZ A DICKHEAD, ATTI FLOWA?'

The boys had already started squabbling about who was making dinner, and suddenly Flora felt overwhelmingly tired.

'Actually, I think I'm a bit jet-lagged,' she said. 'I think I'll just go to bed.'

# Chapter Twenty-five

Dear Colton,

I regret to . . .

Joel stared at the blinking cursor in frustration.

He couldn't think straight. He could barely think at all. He had messed everything up so thoroughly . . . Maybe he should resign. Resign and leave Mure and stay here in New York or Singapore or anywhere else . . . He would always be in demand.

The thought of leaving all of it behind: the only place that stilled his restless damaged heart; the only place he could breathe, away from the wretched air conditioning and the constant traffic noise and the beep-beep-beeping of everybody's phones and the endless lines of people and issues and problems all jangling up against him and crackling across the air . . .

Christ. He deleted the email.

Dear Flora,

He flashed back suddenly to that weekend they'd spent together in the depths of winter: Flora pretending to be reading even though she kept falling asleep; he was working. Every time he looked up, her head would be drooping, then she'd see him looking at her and smile and say, 'It's actually very interesting,' and he'd smile back as the flames crackled in the wood-burner. The room had felt cosy, and Bramble, who had appeared to become a permanent feature ever since Flora had returned and disliked leaving her side, had turned over with a groaning noise that sounded exactly like a seventy-year-old man – which is what he was in dog years. Joel had suddenly found that he had completely lost interest in the work he was doing. He had pushed aside the folders and got up and put her book down. He had pulled her up towards him in the firelight and kissed her ferociously and she had leaned into him with such hunger, instantly and completely awake, those pale eyes of hers taking on a characteristically misty distant look he had learned to recognise very well. Then they had fumbled as she tried to take off the four layers of ridiculous clothes she was wearing and they had laughed – which was strange for Joel, as he rarely laughed – and they had locked Bramble in the bathroom and the flakes of snow had swirled around outside and settled on the harbourside so prettily as the heat of their bodies was magnified by the licking of the flames that threw their shadows against the wall. And he thought he had never been so happy – no, that he had never been happy at all.

And what had he done afterwards? He had slept. He had slept for nine hours.

Joel never slept anywhere. He had learned not to early in life: in foster homes, with children of the family who might make their displeasure at your appearance obvious in different ways, at unpredictable times of day; at boarding school, where one was never entirely safe from a master looking for miscreants, or older boys looking for trouble. His entire life was lived on guard.

Except for Mure. There, he was ... there he was safe.

New York wasn't safe. It was confusing and busy and made him anxious. It made him have to keep a tight lid on himself, and what had he done? He had looked at her and seen in her eyes not the clear gaze of trust she gave him when they sat on the harbour wall; not the calm, focused look she had when she was working in Annie's Seaside Kitchen, perfectly following recipes handed down from her mother; not that clouded, melting look whenever he placed a hand on her, cheeks reddened, every time, her hands trembling in a way he found utterly irresistible ...

No. She had looked at him in pain and confusion and disappointment, and in all the kinds of terrible ways Joel couldn't bear to be looked at – that triggered the panic, so deeply buried, of a little boy who, if he wasn't pleasing people, couldn't be certain of a roof over his head and food to eat, never mind someone to love him. And to make matters worse, now Colton was working to destroy it all.

There was no connection in Joel's life that you could screw up and still be loved. None. It simply had never happened to him. That was why he had fought so hard to be the best: to be the most successful, to turn in the most billable hours, to always beat the other guy, to seduce the most beautiful women, to always succeed.

To fail in Flora's eyes felt like the worst failure of all and he wasn't sure if he could bear it. And he didn't know what to do about it.

He deleted the email, cursing. He was no good for anyone or anything, it seemed.

Joel paced the suite, trying to distract himself. Something occurred to him – something that, even if he had screwed everything up, even if he had to move, he could do. One useful thing.

The country may be different, the context might be strange, but there was one thing that nobody knew more about than Joel: child services.

He reopened the laptop.

Dear Saif,

I just wanted you to know I have heard your wonderful news, and would be delighted to represent you, pro bono, for anything that may lie ahead.

# Chapter Twenty-six

Sometimes a good night's sleep can solve everything. Sometimes you get two seconds before you realise that, no, everything is still pretty rubbish. Flora blinked at the ceiling and sighed. She hadn't called Joel. She didn't know how. She didn't know how she felt or where she was going to go, or where they were. She stared at the ceiling. Oh yes. And she had a wedding to prep for that she'd completely ignored while dashing off to the other side of the world.

The wind was coming in off the sea but it was salty and fresh and helped get the jet-lag cobwebs out of her brain as she opened up the kitchen door and let the dogs out, their huge tails wagging cheerfully in the morning light. She headed into the kitchen. 'Ta-da!' said Fintan. He held up some freshly made sausages in a paper packet. 'Haggis and herb.'

'That sounds gross.'

'And that is where you are wrong,' he said, turning up the Aga. 'Just you wait. These will cure all ills.'

Flora smiled sadly. 'How's Colton this morning?'

Fintan's face lit up. 'He's great! He's in LA shouting at share-holders. If it wasn't for this stupid wedding I'd be there too.'

Flora smiled. 'Ah, good.'

Fintan leaned over. 'If he's not making you happy . . .'

'Don't start,' said Flora. 'I can't think about it just now.'

'That means you'll just stay in the same place for ever, if he thinks doing this kind of thing is okay.'

'I know,' said Flora. 'I do know that. It's just . . . I met his psychiatrist.'

'He took you to meet his *psychiatrist*?'

'It's an unusual situation.'

'Does he have literally no friends? Did he have to pay him?'

'It's not like that,' said Flora, going pink. She had never mentioned Joel's past to anyone, which was difficult, as it made it harder to excuse him. 'He's had a rough time of it.'

Fintan paused and turned the sausages, which were spattering in the pan. 'He's a rich, handsome lawyer who can travel the world.'

'Rich, handsome lawyers have problems too.'

Fintan looked at his sister. 'I think . . .' he said slowly. 'I just think . . . he should be treating you like a princess.'

Flora smiled. 'Cinder-bloody-ella, you mean. The jobs list for tomorrow is insane.'

'I know,' said Fintan. 'Isn't it brilliant?'

><   <

Charlie and Jan's wedding was booked in the ancient chapel that overlooked the headland, the lines of ancient graves standing sentinel against the waves. It was old – *old* old. By the time the missionaries had arrived, there had already been people living on Mure for thousands of years. Conversion had been swift – too swift, some said. The people had accepted the new religion, but had never quite forgotten the old, layered stories of sea gods, of seals and of Viking gods and princes in ice towers that were brought over the cold sea and told down the generations round the fire and out of earshot of the minister.

The reception was to be in the Harbour's Rest, slightly to Flora's surprise – she had expected a marquee in Jan's rich parents' garden, rather than the old, slightly slovenly hotel on the edge of town. Still, it would be handy that you could just leave when you'd had enough rather than waiting for the entire town to go, and the Rock of course still wasn't open. There was a guest list, obviously, but it was accepted that locals – and particularly the town's elderly residents – might well just turn up anyway at the church, weddings being rare on Mure in their small community (although outsiders came to get married there all the time for the picturesque backdrop and as a bit of one-upmanship, wedding-style, in terms of how complex they could make getting there for their guests). These extra guests would probably tag along to the reception too, so Jan had requested a buffet rather than a sit-down, and a reasonable limit on the cash bar.

But for the food, she wanted everything. Flora cursed her, under her breath, and tried to think of the money as she rolled out hundreds of individual sausage rolls; miniature scones, all light fluffy and perfect, to be served with local cream and bramble jam; tiny immaculate simnel cakes; pies of every description; jellies and possets, even though Flora had had to dig deep into her mother's recipe book even to find out what they were. But not the wedding cake, of course, Jan had said smugly. That would be sent over from the mainland, the implication being that of course they wouldn't entrust Flora with the really important stuff ... Flora had just smiled and bitten her tongue and said that was fine.

There was – she could not fail to admit – a tiny bit of her thinking: what if?

Could it have been her waking up this bright and breezy spring morning, not with a sense of dread, but with a secure sense of happiness? Knowing that she was going to marry a handsome, kind, upstanding man with whom she could build a life, straightforwardly and happily? With whom she could raise children who would speak Gaelic and English and who would go to Lorna's school? Seeing each other every day; working reasonable hours ... ?

A very simple kind of happiness ... That had been offered. But Charlie had seen the doubt in her eyes, the way her head turned whenever that damned impossible American had entered the room; he had seen it and known it and left her alone. She was doomed – never to have a simple, happy life like everyone else.

Flora felt incredibly sorry for herself – even as she fired up soda bread to be served with plenty of butter and island whisky, smoked salmon and local roe, and iced ginger buns that popped in the mouth with crème pâtissière squirting out, and endless eclairs, as Isla and Iona cut cucumber sandwiches in the back kitchen with the radio turned up loud and talked about what boys they hoped were going to show up and how short they could wear the black skirts Jan had requested.

By eleven o'clock, however, when the ceremony was going on – she didn't know if Jan thought she might have tried to crash it – she surveyed the room in pleasure. The carpet was faded (and a little dusty around the edges) and the ceiling was still tobacco-stained after all these years, but the long tables were absolutely stuffed and groaning with food around the centrepiece of a cake (which was very plain and unadorned and nothing Flora couldn't have knocked up in the Seaside Kitchen). There were heavy jugs of cream, two sides of locally smoked salmon and little hot bowls of Cullen skink, and it really was quite beautiful.

Flora allowed herself a little smile. So . . . A bride she was not. But she was definitely edging closer to being able to call herself a cook. Fintan stuck his head round the door, and gave her two thumbs-up.

They heard the wedding party before they saw it; it was a lovely bright and windy shining day and there were no wedding cars on Mure, unless you wanted to put flowers on a Land Rover (and some people did), so the entire party simply walked down the main street, to shouts and congratulations from holidaymakers and passers-by, delighted to find themselves in the middle of a wedding procession, as the bells rang out from the church. Flora steeled herself a little. This was Jan's day, and there weren't many people who didn't know that she and Charlie had had something of a flirtation the previous summer. She wished just for once that Joel could be by her side for something that mattered to her. Fintan, as if he could sense this, moved closer to her and squeezed her arm. He also dusted off some of the flour that had fallen on her apron and in her hair.

'Don't worry,' said Fintan. 'You have nothing to feel bad about.'

Flora didn't think that was true for a moment. But she stuck a smile on her face and did her best.

To be fair, Jan looked nice. Okay, she hadn't dyed her hair, so it was short and rigidly quite grey, or removed her glasses. But it was the first time Flora had ever seen her out of a fleece, and for sure, she had the most tremendous legs. She wore a chic, straight knee-length dress that showed them off nicely and a slightly 1980s-style but somehow appropriate white jacket. No veil, but she looked like herself. Charlie of course was in his kilt, as were the other men, with a black tie for once and a Bonnie Prince Charlie short black jacket with a black waistcoat underneath it.

Flora ducked out of sight as he came into view, back in the kitchen like Cinderella, while the plates with the hot canapés on them were rolled out – scallops, and neatly cut venison, and little haggis bonbons, piping hot with a horseradish cream. Inge-Britt, the manager of the Harbour's Rest (and one-time amour of Joel's, which Flora tried uncomfortably to forget and Inge-Britt, who had a fairly healthy Icelandic attitude towards this kind of thing, already had genuinely forgotten), was laying out glasses of ordered-in Prosecco, some of which had been poured too early and was already going flat – although Flora didn't like to mention that.

Flora squinted at the crowd coming through. There really

did seem to be an awful lot of people ... Jan had been insistent that there was catering for a hundred people, which was plenty, obviously, but there were far more than Flora had been expecting showing up.

Not only that, but there were lots of children. Jan had definitely not mentioned children ... Many of them, Flora assumed, were part of Jan and Charlie's outreach groups that they ran together, taking children from the mainland in difficult situations out on adventure holidays. While this was an entirely laudable aim and a wonderful thing to do, Flora sometimes wished that Jan didn't show off her moral virtue quite so regularly.

But the problem with these children was they couldn't wait for a buffet. They didn't know they were meant to hold off until everyone had a drink and was settled and organised so the speeches could begin and everyone could behave reasonably. They went straight to the heaving buffet table and immediately began stuffing their faces with whatever they could find.

'No!' said Flora, horrified, as her lovely display was being ruined before the guests had even got in to see it.

She came out of the kitchen, not even caring that she hadn't cleaned up or put some lipstick on. The boys, startled, looked up at her guiltily and a hush fell on the room. Jan turned round with an expectant look on her face. Flora immediately felt herself blush bright pink.

'Um. I mean, hello. Would you like to wait until everyone is here and everyone can start the buffet together?'

She put on her most ingratiating face and was aware how fake her voice sounded. In fact, she sounded like she'd been chasing away hungry children from food. This was not really the look she'd been after.

Jan bustled over, a pitying smile on her face. 'Not to worry, Flora ... Everyone here is our guest.'

Flora tried to pull her aside. 'But ... but we've only got food for a hundred guests! You said a hundred!'

The room was now absolutely packed, and the boys had gone straight back to stuffing their faces.

Jan tinkled a little laugh Flora hadn't heard before. 'Oh, it's hardly difficult, what you're doing, is it? It's lovely to welcome *all* our friends to celebrate our marriage ... '

Charlie came up behind Jan, grinning nervously and looking rather sweaty.

'Oh ... yes ... Congratulations,' said Flora. 'I'm very ... I'm really pleased for you.'

Jan tightened her grip on Charlie's hand proprietorially. 'Well, of course you would have to say that,' she said. She looked around. 'I see the American appears to have left.'

Flora blinked. There were even more people slipping in through the door, including a few disreputable Harbour's Rest drinkers that she was reasonably certain wouldn't have received an invitation in a million years. 'So, anyway ... Do you know how many you're expecting?'

'Flora,' said Jan. 'This celebration is important in our community. It's important to all of us. Obviously you moved away from the islands.'

And then I moved back, thought Flora mutinously.

'But for those of us who've always stayed here, who believe in the island as our home ... this is an important day for all of us.'

147

'So ... how many?'

'Everyone is welcome,' said Jan. She glanced over at the rapidly diminishing buffet table. The boys were throwing vol-au-vents at each other and crumbs were getting underfoot. 'Oh dear, it's looking a little thin.'

And she glided across the floor as if the situation were nothing to do with her.

Flora turned, grabbed Isla and Iona into the kitchen and hooked Fintan, who'd been heading over for a gin and tonic.

'Everything,' she hissed. 'We get everything we've got in stock.'

Fintan frowned. 'Well, she's not having the ageing range.'

Fintan had started to lay cheese down, like wine, in preparation for the Rock reopening. It was extraordinary stuff, really beautiful, and Flora sometimes wished they could sell it on the open market. It would make a fortune.

'Anything,' she repeated. 'Anything that's in the freezer, anything lying about, and everyone start baking. The quickest thing – Iona, you do sandwiches. Run down to the Spar.'

She was sad; up until now they'd used the best of everything.

'Buy up whatever ham they have. All the cucumbers.'

She thought about the local shop's cucumbers. They could be a little tired, to say the least. Cucumbers had to travel a long way to reach the Northern Isles.

'Put loads of butter on everything. Oh Christ,' she moaned. 'We won't have time to make any more bread. See what Mrs Laird has.'

The girls, to their credit, worked at lightning speed with what they had. They found every piece of fruitcake – Flora stockpiled them for the kitchen, did them in huge batches. They also found a vast pile of frozen gingerbread Flora had forgotten she had, and ended up microwaving it into a pudding and adding custard. They scraped every crumb out of Annie's Seaside Kitchen and served it up to an increasingly drunken and demanding crowd, even stooping, eventually, to ransacking Inge-Britt's stock of crisps simply to give Jan's guests something to eat.

Finally, after what seemed to Flora about twenty hours of rowdy people and dancers and bar bores and singers, and after the speeches were made, the cake was cut and the free bar was shut, there was not a crumb to be found, and people, sensing the main affair was over, started to drift off.

In the kitchen, the girls were working like Trojans washing up, and Fintan had pitched in like a good one. Flora was flat out, her hair pulled back in a ponytail, sweat on her brow. She looked around. There wasn't a scrap left; they'd even used the sausages Inge-Britt served in the morning, and the eggs, to make a last-minute frittata they'd cut into slices. There wasn't a single thing left untouched. The mess, though, was everywhere.

Flora wanted to weep. She barely knew what people had eaten. All the lovely, delicately handmade little cakes and hors d'oeuvres she'd had ready at the start had been shovelled carelessly into the mouths of boys who couldn't have cared less what they were eating. People had been looking around with hungry looks on their faces until they got drunk enough not to care or were happy enough with a bag of crisps. The idea of anyone wanting to book her after this was unthinkable. Plus they'd spent all their petty cash in the local shop and probably owed Inge-Britt money for the crisps.

As the straggling members of the wedding party headed outside to watch Charlie and Jan go to pick up the night ferry to the mainland – they were going to Italy, Flora had heard Jan say a million times – Flora laid her exhausted head against a doorframe and let a tear run down her cheek. Then she told herself not to be so silly, there were still hours of clearing up to do. And she didn't even want to think about the envelope that had been pushed into the kitchen by Jan's taciturn father.

It would contain, she knew, a cheque for the precise amount that they had agreed in advance – to feed a hundred people. It would be nowhere near enough to cover the extra food and extra hours or the use of Inge-Britt's kitchen. The wedding was meant to make them money – launch them. Instead, all that people would remember were the empty plates; the messy sandwiches.

Oh, there was no point, she told herself. No point in worrying about this or dwelling on it too long. Perhaps she had been getting complacent; the Seaside Kitchen had been running so well she had taken a weekend off. She had taken her eyes off the prize and forgotten what it was actually like to run a catering situation, day after day. Well. Now she knew. She rolled up her sleeves and filled the sink, and tried to chalk it up to experience. But her teeth were definitely gritted.

There was a quiet knock at the swing doors of the kitchen. Flora glanced up wearily. There wasn't, truly, a single soul she was terribly desperate to see at that precise moment, and that in itself made her sad. The woman standing there was a stranger, although Flora had glimpsed her in the wedding party. She was wearing a flowery dress and white sandals; she had thick glasses and long black hair and an apologetic look.

'Um, hello?'

'I don't work here,' said Flora. 'You need Inge-Britt. Hang on.'

'No, no,' said the woman. She had a Glasgow accent. 'I just wanted to say ... I'm so sorry ... I'm the youth worker. With the boys. I'm so sorry – I realised when I came in what they'd done to the buffet ... I was caught behind them at the church.'

'That's okay,' said Flora. 'They did quite a lot of stamping, though.'

'They were over all week doing Outward Bound and they just had such a wonderful time, and I was meant to be escorting them back when they found out about the wedding and just pestered and pestered to be allowed to stay.'

She looked down.

'You know ... they get so few happy events like this, some of them. A lot of them, they barely go out at all. And there certainly aren't a lot of weddings in their backgrounds. Some of them.'

At this, Flora felt absolutely stricken with guilt. All she'd thought about was the boys making a mess of her lovely spread. She had forgotten completely about who they were, and where they'd come from. She tried to think about what they would be like teasing Charlie, who, despite his size, was the softest lump ever to walk the earth, and the hope in their little faces and how on earth you could turn that down.

'I meant to come out and control them, obviously.' The woman twisted her fingers nervously. 'But I got caught up in the pews, and one of them had to go to the loo and by the time I'd showed him the rest had kind of pelted down the street and ... I'm really sorry.'

'That's okay,' said Flora. Weirdly, just saying that, and getting the apology, did somehow make it feel a bit better.

The woman glanced around. 'Do you want me to send them over to help clear up?'

'Oh gracious, no,' said Flora. 'No. I want them to enjoy their holiday.'

The lady smiled. 'They're on the same ferry over as Jan and Charlie, so I don't know how much of a wedding night they're going to have.'

Flora grinned. 'I'm glad they managed to come.'

'So are they,' said the woman. 'Thanks for being so understanding. I thought you'd be writing furious letters to the council demanding my head on a platter!'

'I would not be doing that,' said Flora. 'Although I might have served it if I'd thought of it earlier. Do you want a cup of tea? Or, sod it, there's some leftover Prosecco here ...'

Kind Inge-Britt had secreted away a bottle for her.

The woman looked guilty. 'Oh, I shouldn't. I've got to see the boys back ... okay. Half a glass. Don't tell anyone.'

'I shan't. Where are they?'

'They're all early for the ferry. Charlie's arranged a kick-about match for them on the green.'

Flora shook her head. 'On his wedding day?'

'He's a good man.'

'He is,' said Flora, musing. 'He really is.'

They sat together in the kitchen.

'Can I ask you something?' said Flora.

'Sure.'

'These kids ... They're in care, aren't they?'

'Some of them ... Some of them are sometimes with a parent. Often the best situation is when you can get them with a grandparent.'

'What makes care places fail?'

'Aggression usually. If there are other children in the family, and the child can't handle sharing the attention ... sometimes they kick off if that's all they know.'

Flora frowned. This didn't sound like Joel at all. He could be distant, but she couldn't imagine him being violent or having uncontrollable rage. If anything, he was far too controlled.

'Any other reasons?'

The youth worker took another sip from her glass. 'Well,' she said. 'Sometimes kids just don't fit. It's not their fault. Trauma at home knocks them off-kilter, but they're a little unusual to begin with. Asperger's syndrome can be difficult to place. Or, weirdly, sometimes the opposite. A lot of our foster families come from lower to middle incomes. We had a child once who was a genius, more or less: unbelievably clever, really unusually good at maths, a bit of a prodigy. We couldn't settle him in foster care at all. Either his foster family thought he was too snotty or showing off or they just didn't know how to deal with him.'

'How is he now?' said Flora, breathless. This was more like it.

'He was lucky. We found him a scholarship, parachuted him out of the care system. To boarding school.'

'Wouldn't he be lonely there?'

The woman looked sad. 'That's the deal with my job,' she said gently. 'They're all lonely, dear. So lonely. Something a child should never know how to be.'

She got up to go and poured the last of her glass down the sink.

'One more question!' said Flora. 'I have a friend. A friend who . . .'

And she explained the situation with Saif and his boys.

'It will probably be fine,' said the youth worker. She handed over her card. Her name was Indira, Flora saw. 'But, any problems, you call me, okay? I won't forget you feeding the five thousand today. I owe you one.'

## Chapter Twenty-seven

Saif didn't mean to yell. He had never been the yelling type. But Lorna was so damned enthusiastic, as if this was a school project, not his life.

Lorna hadn't been able to think of much else, was desperately full of ideas of what they would be like and how it would be, and what she could do to welcome them, and how troubled they would be – would they be violent? Brainwashed? So traumatised they upset the other children? She would have to work out a strategy for dealing with the other children – she would possibly need help from refugee resettlement groups which meant people coming from the mainland – and, gosh, it was exciting, of course it was, but so complicated too.

So she was spilling over with plans and thoughts when she went to meet Saif that morning for an early walk. It was a windy day and fun to feel blown down to the Endless Beach, the breeze waking her up, making the waves dance – although going back would be harder – only to find him there, staring out to sea, his face absolutely set in stone.

He had turned round slowly, and it was only then that she realised his eyes were full of rage.

'Are you all right?'

'I trusted you!' he shouted furiously. He was brandishing something; he'd obviously expected to see her. 'I trusted you with the biggest . . . I trusted you with my entire life. My life and my family's life in your hands. And . . . '

Lorna felt her heart drop to her stomach, that awful way when you begin to suspect that you have made a terrible, terrible mistake.

'What?' she said, trying to sound breezy but hearing the tremor in her voice.

'You tell everyone! You tell everyone on this island now and they know!'

'I didn't!' said Lorna, panicking. She'd told Flora, but she'd sworn her to secrecy, hadn't she? 'I didn't!'

'Joel! He knows!' He showed her the email. Lorna read it in silence.

'Flora guessed!' said Lorna. 'I didn't tell her.'

'And now she tells everyone!'

'It will only be Joel.'

Surely, thought Lorna to herself. Please. But she could understand the impulse completely – the joy of spreading good news, for once, was powerfully strong. Of course Flora wanted to make people happy and rejoice in something good happening – for Saif, for the island, for the world – out of the desperately awful situation.

'There is no such thing as "only" here,' said Saif, who

156

found the tight-knit community very like the world he had left behind in Damascus with its extraordinary combination of it being both delightful and infuriating that everyone knew about every step of your life before you'd even taken it half the time. 'It will be in the papers and in the grocer shop and whispered round my surgery and you will turn my children into zoo animals before they even arrive and you will give me no chance to prepare and we will be overrun ...'

'Overrun by people who mean well – who care,' said Lorna, stung. 'Who want to do the best for you and your family. Why is that a problem? Joel is offering you free legal advice! I want to make the school ready and appropriate for the boys. Everyone will want to help!'

Saif shook his head. 'No,' he said. 'Everyone wants to gossip and be nosy and find out what it was like and poke at the little brown boys. And take pictures and talk about them.'

He turned his face to the sand.

'What if they are injured, Lorenah? What if one of them has lost a hand, an arm ... You still want everyone looking, asking? Huh?'

Lorna didn't say anything for a long time.

'I'm sorry,' she said eventually. 'I'm sure Flora hasn't told anyone else.'

Saif shook the paper furiously. 'Are you?' he said. 'I ... I am not sure.'

And he turned round and stalked off down the beach and Lorna watched him go in absolute dismay, wanting to be cross with Flora but knowing full well deep down that the fault was entirely her own.

It was odd. Saif was to remember every second of the next two weeks in the same way as he remembered the very first night of his eldest son Ibrahim's life: in the house, every second weighing upon him with the enormity of how his world had changed for ever as he gazed down at this tiny, tiny being, while Amena slept in the back room, torn and utterly wearied.

That first night had been quiet. He remembered every sound the cicadas made in the courtyard; the distant rumble of Damascus traffic that didn't permeate into their pleasant suburb; the little bundle, with bright red cheeks, tiny fists, a wobble of black hair. It wasn't crying exactly, just snuffling and twisting slightly crossly. Saif had been a doctor for long enough to know that he should of course leave him to settle and on absolutely no account lift him up. He lifted him up.

In that tiny yet huge new world and new dawn, he had walked Ibrahim up and down, out into the blessed cool of the courtyard, where the heavy scent of the hibiscus petals opening up in the night lay upon the gathering dew and mingled with the dusty smell of the city streets and the last remnants of the delicate scent of evening meals passing on the breeze. They had paced up and down, Saif and his baby, as Saif pointed out the moon and the stars above and told him how he'd love him to there and beyond, and the little thing had snuffled and nuzzled into him and fallen asleep on his shoulder and Saif had promised to protect him with his life.

He had not done that. He had failed. The world Ibrahim

had been born into – and Ash too – had slowly, then to their mounting disbelief very suddenly, crumbled around their ears. And worse: it had crumbled as the rest of the world had stood by, wrung its hands, prevaricated, wobbled.

But that first night. The heavy scents, the quiet rumbling; the tiny, snuffling, incessantly alive creature in his arms; where it had all begun. And now, did he have the chance to begin again?

'I'm sure he'll be fine,' said Flora. 'I am so, so sorry.'

Flora had closed the shop on the Monday. Partly because she was just so exhausted after the wedding and partly because they had literally nothing to sell and she was going to have to wait for supplies to be replenished – flour, and milk for more butter to be churned. There was a real problem when you promised to make everything locally. You couldn't just nip to the cash and carry and stick everything back in the cupboard.

'Oh, don't worry about it,' said Lorna. 'I shouldn't have told you.'

'You didn't tell me! I guessed!'

Flora had gone to fetch Lorna from school, where she had nervously covered over a book she was reading in her office.

'What's that?' Flora had said suspiciously, but Lorna had shaken her head and refused to answer. 'If it's *How to Leave Teaching*, I will kill you,' said Flora.

Lorna shook her head. 'God, no,' she said, waving at the collection of pupils who liked to stay behind in the playground for some fairly competitive inter-form football

159

matches. It was easy to have inter-form matches in a school with only two classes, and sometimes the bigger ones would make up the numbers in the littler class.

The little school sat at the top of the hill overlooking Mure Town. Made of red sandstone, it still had the original carved letters over the doors for 'Boys' and 'Girls'. It was a windy spot in the wintertime, but in the summer the high vista with water on two sides of the hilltop, the town down in the sheltered harbour below, the boats steaming off to far-distant lands and the oil rigs on the horizon was a beautiful sight. Of course, the view was entirely unappreciated by the children who ran freely back and forth there, blithely unaware of their unfettered childhood – unconstrained by helicopter parents. Everyone knew all the other parents and the children roamed at will – the few cars on the island rarely travelled at more than twenty miles an hour anyway – up and down the lanes and in and out of each other's houses.

There was danger on Mure – in unattended burns; in climbing the fell in bad weather; or jumping in the sea on a day when the rip tide wanted to pull you out, and regardless of how warm the summer's day might be, the water was never going to be warm. But the normal dangers – of heavy traffic, of abduction and strangers and muggings – were not present. Children were free to play. In the long winter months, they had to hunker down, like everyone else, with books or video games. But as soon as the light returned, desperate to be free, they were outside as late and as long as possible. It was not unusual, in the height of the summer when the sun never set, to see children playing in broad daylight at ten o'clock in the evening.

'No,' said Lorna again. 'Actually, I want to do more of it. I just need more people to have some damn children.'

'Probably starting with us,' said Flora gloomily as they headed down to the Harbour's Rest. There was a pretty beer garden there, as long as you were wearing a fleece, and they sat outside, smiling happily at other friends coming past.

'Hahaha,' said Lorna. 'God, there's more chance of Mure getting the Olympics.'

'Tell me about it,' said Flora. 'Oh God, can you imagine? All those *rowers*?'

'You're going to fix it, aren't you, Flores?'

'I don't know,' said Flora soberly. 'I seriously don't know where his head is. He'll be back soon. And meanwhile, I don't dare look at the accounts.'

'Just send Jan another invoice.'

'I would,' said Flora, 'except I know exactly what will happen: "Ooh, Flora, I know you're so jealous of our amazing happiness but I would have thought you could have spared a thought for penniless orphans, blah, blah, blah . . . "'

'Can't you talk to Charlie on his own?'

'Oh God, no, he's terrified of me now, like I'm suddenly about to cast my womanly wiles and try to ensnare him, like I *totally* didn't do last time. Gah.'

'Maybe it's Mure,' said Lorna. 'Maybe it's being on this island makes our love lives totally suck.'

'Has to be,' said Flora. 'Can we go drinking on a school night more? I mean, if you can pay . . . '

'Seriously?'

'Yes,' said Flora. 'Yes. It really is that bad.'

# Chapter Twenty-eight

Saif had had a flurry of checks. A woman had come to check the house, and as he looked at it through the eyes of a stranger – the first person apart from Mrs Laird who had stepped over the threshold since he'd moved in the previous year – he realised how unsuitable it was for children: still full of the last occupant's heavy dusty furniture; an ancient creaky fridge; no television.

He tried to cheer up the bedrooms upstairs by ordering some stencils from the mainland – boats and rocket ships, who knew what boys liked? But they made the old sofas with their antimacassars and the damp, sagging beds somehow look rather worse. The woman, however, simply checked a bunch of boxes on a form and said nothing either positive or negative. Evidently he had passed as he soon got an email requesting that he present himself at an address in Glasgow on a certain date – and to expect to book lodgings for a fortnight. His young, rather ditzy-seeming locum had arrived from the mainland, and tried to slip away without anyone noticing. He also tried to sleep at night, a million questions swirling around his head. It was not, he thought morosely, the best of times to fall out with his only friend, who also worked with small children every day. But his pride stopped him from calling her – he never called her anyway; their relationship was much more casual. To call her felt like it would be crossing a line. And his thoughts were so overwhelming he couldn't bring himself to do it.

At last the day came.

He tried to slip into Annie's Seaside Kitchen without attracting attention – which is actually quite difficult when you are a six-foot-one Middle-Eastern man on a small Scottish island where you are one of only two doctors.

'Hello, Dr Saif!' chorused Iona and Isla as he walked through the door. He looked nervously around for Flora – he was reasonably sure Lorna would have told her everything – but she wasn't out front yet. She was still finishing off some chive and herb focaccia out the back with the expectation that in today's mild but windy weather something that could be eaten by the harbourside but wouldn't blow away might be just the ticket, and trying to balance the accounts, which was an upsetting job at the best of times.

'Um . . . can I have some kibbeh?' he said. He had absolutely no idea that Flora had finally got wise to the falafel catastrophe and put the hot spiced lamb sandwich on the menu purely for him. It had never even occurred to him. Now they had become instantly wildly popular in the village and were beginning to be seen as quite the speciality, excellent lamb being something Mure had no shortage of.

'Of course!'

The bell tinged, and old Mrs Kennedy and Mrs Blair came in together, quite flustered.

'That whale is back! Look! It's not safe!'

'It'll block the ferry.'

'Flora, you need to do something!'

'No, I don't,' said Flora immediately.

Iona immediately grabbed her phone.

'I'm going to stick it on my Insta.'

'It always just looks like a blob,' said Isla.

'Well, I'll zoom in then. Whale selfie.'

'It's not a whale,' said Mrs Kennedy seriously.

'Okay, well why did you just say, "The whale is back"?' said Iona petulantly, shuffling with the camera on her phone.

'It's a narwhal,' she said. 'It's very wise, very rare, very beautiful, and absolutely is going to overwhelm this entire island before they sort it out.'

'What do you mean?' Saif couldn't help himself asking.

'Oh hi, Saif. Now, I really am having a terrible bit of trouble with my . . . '

Saif was used to this kind of thing and brushed it off.

'Make an appointment with Jeannie . . . I mean, why will we be overwhelmed?'

'Tourists,' tutted Mrs Kennedy, as if tourism wasn't the lifeblood of absolutely everything they did. 'Everyone wants to see one. Then the authorities will want to tow it away. Then the Greenpeace campaigners will turn up.'

'What do they want with it?'

'They don't know either. I think they just like their

pictures being taken next to it. Flora, just go talk to it.'

'It's not like that!' said Flora. 'I'm not a seal! And you're being . . . seal-ist!'

'All the women in your family can talk to whales.'

'Is this true?' said Saif.

'Yes, Man of Science, it is,' said Flora, rolling her eyes. 'Do you want coffee?'

'Yes please.'

Flora passed him his customary four sugars. 'I need to catch the ferry,' said Saif. Flora blinked. She wanted to ask why but didn't dare.

'The ferry won't go if it's in its way,' said Mrs Blair.

'I am trapped,' said Saif, trying to sound casual but actually panicking. His meeting in Glasgow was at 4.30. He had to make this ferry – he had to – and it had to be on time. He hadn't slept a wink. He had spoken constantly out loud to Amena as if she were there, but he'd felt stupider than ever. He was terrified. He wished Lorna and he were still friends, that she could come with him; he knew what she was like with children. But of course she didn't speak Arabic and the children would be even more confused, and, no, that was a terrible idea too. Oh God, why couldn't they have found his wife?

But no. This was his to do alone. But on what should be the happiest, most amazing day of his life – the day he had dreamed and dreamed would come when his babies would be returned to him – he was filled with terror and foreboding. If he said the wrong thing, would they refuse to let him take them? Would they think they'd been radicalised? Surely not – they were only little.

As a rule, he tried to avoid the sensationalist headlines – most people on Mure read the local news and little else. The passing crazes of Edinburgh and Westminster and Washington meant little to people whose lives were measured by the changes in the weather and the length of the days, not Twitter and politics and shouting on television debates.

But still, he knew it was out there: ugly, ill feeling that infected people whether they wanted it to or not; every terrible tragedy; every spitting, postulating right-wing and left-wing and all sorts of crazy given air time. He just kept his head down, tried to do his job as well as he was able. And of course, as people got to know him they knew what was more or less intrinsic to human beings: everyone was pretty much all right, just bumbling along trying to make the best of it like everybody else, although he disliked it when people felt the urge to point out to him that he was all right, you know? Because he knew it meant 'for one of them', however kindly said.

He accepted his coffee and bade everyone a good morning.

'Why are you going to the mainland?' said Mrs Blair suspiciously. She hadn't been to the mainland since her daughter had married an Aviemore snowboarder, and, well, look how *that* had all turned out. It had confirmed to her absolutely that going off the island was pretty much a bad idea, and why would anybody have to, seeing as everything anyone could ever possibly want was here, in her opinion?

Saif hadn't thought about people asking him this, although he had a brief moment of relief that she didn't know already.

'Um, bit of shopping?' he tried vainly. It was a reason he'd heard from people before, which was specific enough to give a reason and vague enough to discourage speculation, so hopefully it would do. It would be all round the village by nightfall that he was some kind of crazed shopaholic, but there wasn't very much he could do about that. Flora didn't catch his eye.

Mrs Blair nodded. 'Well, be careful on that mainland,' she said. 'It's not all it's cracked up to be.'

'Thank you,' said Saif.

By the time he reached the harbour and nodded to the other passengers – there were more than usual as the flight had been cancelled – the narwhal had, he assumed, moved on. There was no hold-up and soon the mate was unwinding the thick rope from the harbourside, and the pastel-coloured houses of Mure, jolly and sparkling in the windy sunlight, started to recede from view. The water grew choppier and the puttering noise of the boat tilted them up and down in a way that reminded Saif unpleasantly of another journey across the sea – memories of which faded into dimmer images in the daytime but were never terribly far from him in dreams that were filled with the weeping women and, somehow worse, the silent children who had learned how to stay very quiet and still as their world was torn apart around them. He remembered the rough shouting of the smugglers, who would send a swift kick to those they didn't think were moving fast enough, and the freezing cold of the waves – he had never known such cold as they broke over the side – and

167

the strong smell of cheap diesel infiltrating everything, even over the unwashed bodies and fear of the people crammed together inside. It had been a glimpse of hell.

Saif shut his eyes briefly and tried to dispel the memories and focus on the task ahead. His heart was glad, but still so fearful. He wished ... Oh, how he wished Amena was there. He imagined – let himself imagine briefly as he stood with his hands gripping the railing far too hard – walking into a small windowless room, like the many he had passed through as he'd been singled out and processed into the new world of the British Isles. He imagined himself walking through the door, and Amena there, her long hair shining, smiling at him, as beautiful as she'd been on their wedding day, her face lighting up, the boys as beautiful and loving as ever, saying, 'It's okay! It's okay! I took care of them! They're fine! And now we shall all be happy!'

His eyes shot open. This was a ridiculous fantasy and it would not help him in the slightest to deal with the real world: to deal with things as they were. Spray splashed up against the side of the boat. And then ... He squinted. Surely not. Surely ... Was he still dreaming? Was that ... ?

He stood alone, most of the other passengers having decided the wind was just a little too bracing so they had taken happy refuge in the cafeteria or the bar below. He stared straight ahead, but his brain couldn't make sense of what he was seeing. It was a whale – the whale he had seen, he was sure of it, the same deep belly, the white tinge to the skin, the same beautiful twist of curves, as if a child had drawn parabolas on the sky.

But there really was something different he could clearly

168

make out now. This whale had ... There was no denying it ... It had a horn, like a unicorn's. It was huge, twisted like barley sugar, and it protruded from the animal's mouth. It was the single strangest thing that Saif had ever seen: stranger than the phosphorescence on the Greek shore, or the scarab beetle his brother had once kept in a matchbox, marvelling over its jewel-like brilliance.

But this ... This must have beamed in from space, or from some other magical realm. It really was quite the most amazing thing Saif had ever seen, and it frolicked in the wake of the big ferry as the water churned up behind it. Saif was worried it would get sucked underneath the great propellers, but it seemed perfectly happy, swimming under and over the bouncing wake, curling itself up and down.

Was this a symbol? A message, even, from Amena? Saif was not the holiest of men: he was a scientist and had been trained to be rational. But surely it would take a harder heart than his not to think it possible, as the great, impossible beast tossed in the sunlight glinting off the waves ... If wonderful, amazing things could happen ... Well ...

Meanwhile, five hundred miles south, in Liverpool, Colleen McNulty looked sadly at her packed lunch and wondered if there was any way to find out what was going on today. But she only sent out the letters after all. She was only a clerk. As soon as Ken was out of the room, disappearing for an overlong toilet break as he did every day at around 10 a.m. (it was, she sometimes mused, all the unpleasant bits of marriage without any of the nice parts), she reached down into her bag and double-checked the two little parcels – a stuffed bear and a fluffy dog she'd been unable to resist. She knew the boys were older, possibly too old for stuffed toys, but she couldn't think of anything else children might like. They were simply addressed to the doctor's office in Mure – no signature, just a little note saying, 'From a well-wisher'. She'd be in big trouble in the office if she was suspected of interacting with any of the unit's clientele in any way. She would slip out at lunchtime and go to the post office and hope that, in some tiny way, it might help, just a little.

# Chapter Twenty-nine

The interview room was exactly as Saif had predicted. Two women were there waiting for him.

'Now,' said the obviously senior caseworker. She was slightly taller and thinner and better-dressed than other people, though not in a way you could necessarily put your finger on straightaway. She had high cheekbones and her hair was a short flat top, and Saif was impressed and a little intimidated all at once. 'I'm Neda Okonjo. Would you like to speak in English or Arabic?'

'English is fine,' said Saif. He had got so used to living his life in English, it felt like speaking Arabic again would be a challenge. Arabic was his old life; English was his new. Here, in this anonymous bunker somewhere on the outskirts of the huge grey city of Glasgow ... Here they were about to collide. 'Can I see them please?'

'I'm sorry,' said Neda. 'You understand we have to ...'

She introduced the other woman, who was a doctor, and

who took the swab. He obediently opened his mouth as she scraped around. He had sent a blood sample already; this was just to check that he was the same person the sample had come from.

'You realise it's just a formality.'

'Of course. And then I can see them . . .'

The two women exchanged a glance.

'We need to fully debrief you.'

'Of course . . . Are they . . . are they all right?'

'Be right back,' said the doctor, and Saif and Neda sat in pained silence, Saif staring into space, Neda tapping on her phone. Presently the doctor returned, and nodded gently at Neda.

'Good,' said Neda, leaning forward.

'Can I see them?'

Neda pushed the full notes across the table. Saif read them incredibly quickly, his heart racing. It was hard reading.

'You should know. When we found them . . .'

'My wife . . . ?'

'I am so sorry. We simply don't know.'

'She would never have abandoned them.'

'I realise that. The area they were found in . . . It was basically shredded. A bombsite. Anyone who could have fled had fled.'

'She would never have left them!' He scanned all the papers again. She wasn't mentioned at all.

'Please, Dr Hassan. Sir. Please keep calm. I'm not insinuating that for a second.' She frowned. 'You didn't have anyone you wanted to bring with you?'

Saif shook his head, terrified suddenly that if he showed displeasure or anger she would somehow prevent him from reuniting with his boys. 'I apologise.'

Neda nodded and went on. 'They were living with a group of other children ... effectively feral ... Some deserting soldiers helped them with food, found them things to eat, but there wasn't much.'

Saif shut his eyes.

'Ash ... Ash, we believe, broke his foot at some point and it wasn't reset properly. We'll be looking into doing the procedure here before you leave.'

Tears immediately sprang to Saif's eyes at the idea of his baby hurt, limping, getting around on his wounded leg with no mum and no dad.

'I realise this is upsetting,' went on Neda. 'And Ibrahim. We have reason to believe he spent a lot of time with the soldiers. There's psychological help available – not as much as I'd like, I'm afraid. Austerity. But we will be here for you, as much as we can.'

Saif nodded, but he wasn't really listening. He needed to have his arms around them immediately. 'Can I ... can I see them now, please?' he asked as calmly as he could.

Neda and the doctor looked at one another. They passed over several pieces of paper, all of which he signed.

'Follow me,' said Neda.

The second room, down a long corridor, had windows in it, and, Saif noticed through the window in the door, toys of all kinds. His heart felt like it would stop. He wanted to go to the bathroom, was slightly afraid he was going to be sick. Kindly, the doctor put her hand on his arm.

'It will be fine,' she said softly. 'It might take a while, but it will be all right.'

But Saif, blinded by the tears in his eyes, could hardly hear her as he blundered through the door, then stood there, trembling, blinking in the natural light, in the middle of the low-ceilinged room. Two thin boys, barely taller than the last time he had seen them nearly two years before, turned round, their huge eyes wide in pinched faces, both in terrible need of a haircut, and Ibrahim shouted loudly, and Ash whispered, tentatively and wonderingly . . .

'*Abba?*'

# Chapter Thirty

Saif held his breath. Ibrahim had, after the first time saying his father's name, been silent. He had retreated to the corner table of toys, where he had been banging pegs into a wooden board with a toy hammer – a game far too tiny for a boy of ten, although he looked younger.

Ash, however, who was six now, wouldn't let his father go. He had shrieked and raced towards him and clambered onto his lap and refused to budge. The last time Saif had seen him, he had been a round-faced babyish angel of a boy, only just four, still with the folds of the baby he had been on his knees and elbows.

Now he was so thin it was heartbreaking; his eyes were huge in his face, his cheekbones hollow and his legs and arms like sticks. When Saif picked him up, he weighed about as much as the well-fed Mure four-year-olds he treated in his surgery. He frowned and looked at Neda, who glanced at her notes.

'They're both on high-calorie meal drinks as well as food,' she said. She read down further and smiled. 'Apparently neither of them like them.'

Saif buried his head in Ash's shoulder, so he couldn't see him cry. 'I'm so sorry,' he whispered in English so Ash wouldn't understand him. The child replied, 'Abba's back!' in Arabic, as if he'd been away for a day.

Ibrahim's head shot up at his father speaking this strange language, and his brow furrowed in a way that reminded Saif painfully of his mother. He indicated for him to come closer, and said, 'Come here, my darling boy,' in Arabic. But Ibrahim still regarded him warily.

'Don't worry,' said Neda quietly. 'This is all totally normal.'

'Stop talking the way they talk,' Ibrahim hissed quickly at Saif.

'My darling,' said Saif. He walked over and knelt down beside his boy. He put his arm around him. Ibrahim flinched at his touch, and he backed away.

'That is how we are going to speak from now on. It is not so difficult. You're very clever. You learned some already at school, remember?'

Ibrahim blinked. Of course, thought Saif. He hadn't been in school for so long. He thought of the report again. Hiding out with resistance soldiers. What he had seen ... He couldn't bear it.

'Have the people who speak English not been kind to you?' he asked. Ibrahim shrugged.

'They brought you home to me,' said Saif.

'This isn't home.'

'No,' said Saif. 'But you'll like where we're going.'

'Going home to Mama,' muttered Ash, his face still buried in his father's neck, even though Saif's beard tickled him. Saif closed his eyes.

'I keep telling him,' said Ibrahim, his face still cross. 'Mama is gone. Everyone is gone. Everything is gone.'

He hit the block in the children's game very hard with the hammer. Silence fell in the room.

Neda stepped forward. 'There are new homes,' she said. 'You will have a new home now. Tell them what it's like.'

'Well,' started Saif. 'It is very windy. It's fresh and blowy and sometimes you get blown right across the street.'

He could see Ash looking up at him, interested.

'And it is very old, and there are lots of green hills and . . . boats . . . and sheep and . . . Oh, you will like it, I'm sure. Lots of dogs!'

Both the boys stiffened. Saif immediately realised what a mistake he'd made. They knew about the border crossings, when the soldiers would appear, their snarling beasts sniffing vans and lorries, looking for stowaways: looking for problems. He realised suddenly how much he'd changed and even relaxed. The island felt so safe, so much a haven for him, that dogs no longer scared him, and he couldn't even remember how this had come about. He thought of Lorna's daft dog, Milou, who rushed up to him every morning when they were on the shore at the same time. He had definitely helped. Then he remembered that Lorna wasn't his friend any more and that God knew what was round the island by now. Then he thought, bitterly, none of this mattered. All that mattered now was in this room.

Mrs Cook peered in to where Lorna was, once again, working late.

'Don't stay too late!' she said. Lorna looked up. She'd just received an official confirmation from the refugee resettlement council. It wasn't a secret any more: the boys were on the school roll. She showed it without comment to Mrs Cook, who'd have Ibrahim in her class.

Sadie Cook read it slowly, then took off her glasses. 'You knew about this?'

At least someone knew she could keep a secret, Lorna thought. She nodded.

'Good God. I mean, this is going to be huge . . . Can they speak English?'

'Those Galbraith children can't speak English!' pointed out Lorna.

'Good God, yes,' said Sadie. 'They'd have to go some to be worse than that lot of ferals.'

'Well,' said Lorna. 'Quite.'

Sadie looked at the paper. 'And the mother?'

Lorna shook her head. 'No news.'

'Christ. It's awful. Just awful.' Even so, a slightly mischievous twitch played around her mouth. 'Oh my goodness, that poor man isn't going to know what hit him.'

# Chapter Thirty-one

Over the next several days in Glasgow, there were numerous psychological evaluations, the beginnings of some English lessons and many, many forms to fill in and go over.

Neda was patient and useful throughout, and the doctor, whose name Saif never learned, was on hand to make sure the boys had their vaccinations and to build up red books for them – the British medical history they would need throughout their lives – as well as testing them for everything possible. They were malnourished, obviously: small for their size and underweight. They had internal parasites from eating God knows what, and lice, and Ash had his foot reset under a local anaesthetic. While he clung onto his father the entire time, he was so heartbreakingly quiet and brave Saif couldn't bear to think of what else he'd had to endure.

But apart from that, they were fine; there was no lasting damage, on the surface at least. Saif's graver nightmares, of lost limbs and head injuries, were not coming true.

Psychologically, things were quite different. Ash had not left Saif alone. Neda had counselled that it might not be a good idea to let him sleep in the same bed, but he had howled so piteously – and in the hotel room too – that Saif had given in, and the hot restless figure had tossed and turned next to him all night. It was like carrying about a small koala bear. Ibrahim, on the other hand, was distant and cold; not overtly aggressive, but sullen and wary. He point-blank refused to look at the English storybooks or repeat basic words. He would not touch his father, and he endured the vaccinations and endless blood tests with a stoic look on his face and a refusal to be comforted. Ash started to go the other way. It was as if he'd learned, belatedly, that if he cried he'd be rewarded with some attention or a sweet, which Saif was also very unsure about. But it must have been so long since he'd had any attention at all.

At the end of the first week, Neda somehow sourced a DVD of *Freej*, let one of the other charity workers babysit and took Saif out for coffee in a little Lebanese restaurant she knew in Glasgow.

'How are you doing?' she asked.

Saif shook his head and answered honestly. 'I haven't slept. I'm ... It's ... I mean ... I thought it would be like getting my boys back. These ... They've changed so much.'

Neda nodded. 'Don't worry,' she said gently. 'It will just take time. But it *will* take time. It won't happen fast. But kids ... they have a lot of resilience. They've been through a lot. Routine, good food, fresh air ... Plenty of that, and they'll start to heal. They need to be out of this centre, stop being poked and prodded by grown-ups. They need to be around other kids.'

'But Ibrahim ...'

'It's very common.' She smiled. 'If it helps, I've got a twelve-year-old, and he's like that all the time.'

Saif smiled. 'It does actually.' He played with the sugar bowl. 'I wish Amena were here.'

'You've heard nothing your end?'

Saif shook his head. 'Ibrahim must have been the last to see her ... I mean, I haven't heard from my cousins, or anyone ...'

Neda looked at him, so full of pain. 'You have no family left at all?'

Saif shrugged. Yes, he did, but they were fighters, and he never mentioned this to the authorities. 'Not really,' he said quietly.

Neda changed the subject. 'So you're going to be a single dad?'

He smiled. 'Yes, I suppose ... There's a lady who helps out who said she'll babysit while I'm at the surgery, and they'll be at school and ... It is a lot to take in.'

Neda glanced at her watch. 'Well,' she said. 'Don't forget to enjoy it.'

And Saif hadn't the faintest idea what she meant.

# Chapter Thirty-two

Tentatively Saif took the boys out, shops on Mure that didn't sell bagpipes or whisky being rather thin on the ground. He kitted them out with big fleeces and waterproofs, which were comically large, and treated them to a burger, which turned out to be a terrible idea. Ibrahim remembered drinking cola with a group of soldiers and turned terrified, and Ash wouldn't let Saif put him down even to pick up the order, and everyone looked at them and someone tutted, and Ash started screaming and in the end Saif just left everything behind and scurried back to the refugee centre, his heart beating wildly, convinced that he wasn't up to it, that he couldn't possibly deal with the two traumatised little lads.

But Neda was perfectly stark about it: either he took responsibility for his boys or they would have to go into care, or, even worse, back. (This wasn't remotely true, but she was cross with Saif for being so scared of taking up his responsibilities and was trying to scare him straight.)

'I'll be up to visit very soon. Any questions, night or day, you ring me. Except for night, if you love me at all.'

And she smiled to show she forgave him for the disastrous outing.

'Look,' she said finally. 'You'll be fine. All over the world, mothers do this every day. Fathers do it every day. You'll be fine.'

And Saif, with a finally sleeping Ash clinging onto his arms, hoped she was right.

Meanwhile, he'd called Jeannie, the receptionist at the surgery. And, realising it was ridiculous not admitting what he was coming back with, and how it would be, he explained the situation and confessed everything.

Jeannie's shocked silence made him realise, with a start, that the news wasn't around the entire village at all. He'd just assumed Lorna and Flora would have told the world between them. Realising they had not, humbled him.

'Ah,' he said. Then added, 'Can you explain to everyone?'

'Of course!' said Jeannie, who would, Saif knew, be delighted to be the bearer of gossip, knowing, as she did, more about the health and medical history of every single person on Mure than anyone else and unable to breathe a word of it. 'Don't worry. I'll tell them not to bother you. Hang on, does the school know?'

'Of course,' said Saif. 'They're enrolled, ready to go.'

'And what about childcare?'

'Well, I'm their father.'

'Yes, but you'll be working . . . You know school finishes before surgery, don't you? And you'll be on call still.'

Saif blinked. Why hadn't he thought of all this before?

He knew why. Because until he'd held them in his arms, he couldn't let himself believe that they were real.

'Could you . . . ?'

He could hear the smile in Jeannie's voice.

'Let me ask around. Mrs Laird will have some hours for you. She's very fond of you, you know. There'll be plenty of help. Oh, Saif, this is wonderful. Such wonderful news. Lorna must be delighted.'

'Why?' said Saif instantly.

'Well, you know . . . to fill up the school, of course!'

'Oh yes, of course.'

'How are things?' said Jeannie, changing the subject. 'I can't imagine. You must . . . Oh, you must be so happy.'

Saif glanced around their little room at the cheap hotel. Ibrahim was in the corner, furiously playing a war game on the iPad Saif had thought at the time would be a good thing to buy him and was already deeply regretting. Ash was sitting staring at nothing, his arm tight around Saif's ankles, twisting a lock of his hair around his finger over and over again.

'Oh, it's, ahem, fine,' he said.

'Must be hard for them.'

Saif couldn't say it was hard for all of them. So he simply thanked her profoundly and hung up the phone. Ibrahim was still refusing to speak English and said he didn't have to go to school – school was for losers, for people who didn't trust in God to see them through – and Saif had absolutely no idea

184

how he was going to win this one. Ibrahim had always been a sensitive child: curious and questioning. How he used to make them laugh with his complex questions about how the world worked, and his desire to get things figured out.

Now as he sat, obsessed with the game on his lap, Saif wondered what answers he'd found out there on his own, tossed on the seas of a war.

➤ ⟵

He had thought the overnight ferry might be a fun treat for them. Once again, of course, he had thought wrong.

They had said goodbye to Neda, Ash clinging to her and sobbing like his heart would break, which made nobody feel at ease, and Ibrahim shrugging as if he didn't care, which was equally bad. They both balked at the boat, even though they'd been flown to Britain originally. They were fearful of the way it bucked and rolled; a swell had risen up and the crossing was difficult. Ash was sick sporadically and Saif ended up spending half the night with him bent over the toilet; Ibrahim refused to glance up from his iPad, which Saif made a promise to himself to get rid of as soon as was humanly and psychologically possible, and by the time they finally got in sight of Mure, Saif was incredibly anxious about the days and weeks and months ahead.

Would they be accepted? How on earth would they learn English? How would he peel Ash off him every day? How would he manage to work too? – and there was absolutely no way he couldn't work; that was the condition of his visa. How could he mother two motherless boys?

Saif had felt powerless before: in the war; on his long

journey. But he had never felt quite so low as this, and the weather mimicked his mood, black clouds glowering down over the top of Mure. There was a crack of thunder and Ash screamed and hid his face up his father's jumper. Even Ibrahim notably tightened his grip on the video game.

'It's just thunder,' said Saif. 'Come on, let's go up on deck and take a look at your new home.'

Up on deck it was freezing, incredible for April, with winds blowing straight down from the Arctic, screaming across the sea. Bouncing raindrops mixed with the high spray from the huge arching waves; vast seagulls screeched round the port. Ash immediately burst into tears. Ibrahim stared at his feet, sulkily refusing to look at the view.

'So, this is going to be your new home,' said Saif, trying to put on a cheerful face although he hadn't slept properly now for weeks. 'See the jolly houses on the front? All different colours? And round the harbour there's a beach that goes on for so long people call it the Endless Beach! And in the summer there's a festival down on the beach! And all the children come and celebrate the Vikings and . . .'

But neither were listening. As the CalMac made monstrous noises going into reverse, Ash was sobbing his heart out and Ibrahim simply turned round and re-entered the body of the ship, and Saif had to run and get him back before he got lost, even though the boy shook him off as soon as he got there.

The amount of luggage that both the lads had was pitiful, even with the new clothes he'd bought in Glasgow. They were two lost souls, washed up here, and Saif was as scared as he'd ever been in his life as the little, terrified, broken family disembarked the large boat into the freezing grey morning of Mure.

Saif was busy trying to carry all the bags and Ash at the same time, and he didn't look up until they'd fought the wind to the end of the jetty, past the terminal building and towards the car park. Then he did look up and saw them.

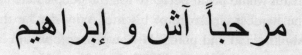

Lined up, frozen and wriggling, along with a large number of townspeople – particularly the older ones, who always liked to see anything that was going on – was Lorna, wearing a huge anorak, with a group of her schoolchildren. As soon as they saw them, the little ones waved wildly and she ordered them to lift up the sign she'd had made, painstakingly and probably, she thought, only being able to get what she could from the internet, entirely wrong.

## WELCOME, ASH AND IBRAHIM.

# مرحباً آش و إبراهيم

Saif prodded the boys to look. Ash blinked, and Saif remembered that although he was six, he hadn't yet been to school or learned to read. It was perfect that there were only two classes in the school here: he could be in with the little ones, starting from the very beginning, even though he would be eighteen months older than many of them. He was, though, about the same height.

Ibrahim, on the other hand, looked up, and Saif saw the first glint of hope in his eyes since he'd arrived.

'They speak Arabic?' he asked, his expression desperate. Saif winced.

'No,' he said. 'We speak English now.' He repeated it, as gently as he was able, in English, just as Lorna raised her arms, and the children started to sing the Arabic alphabet song, quite dreadfully.

At this, Ash lifted his head from his father's jacket and turned to watch in amazement as they sang a song even he knew.

Saif tried to smile. He knew – and could see from Lorna's anxious face – that they were trying the best they possibly could. And when they came to an end, he and the other adults who'd gathered round to watch clapped as hard as they could.

Lorna looked up at him with a hopeful expression on her face, and Saif immediately forgot their row, or any disagreement they had had. How on earth could he not have realised that it would be far better to tell the people here about this, the hardest challenge of his life? Why did he think they would stand and point? His own people would have welcomed him and helped look after him and his family when things had gone badly wrong. What made him think the people here would be any different?

'Thank you,' he said.

'بالحب و السعادة,' said Lorna.

Saif looked up, surprised. 'You speak Arabic now?'

'قليلاً,' she replied. 'I'm trying to learn.'

Then she blushed, and did not want to betray how she had done little with her evenings since she'd heard the boys were coming other than swotting up and being addicted to Babbel, which was better than being addicted to watching Netflix, although it still, she did not like to reflect, left her sitting alone in her late father's house night after night as her youth slipped away.

Flora came running down to the jetty as the friendly policeman, Clark, came up and seriously shook Ibrahim's hand (Ash wouldn't turn round) and beamed kindly in the absence of having anything to say. Flora had a large care box of food, including as much baklava as she'd been able to put together. And Saif took it and wondered, standing there in the howling gale, overwhelmingly grateful, whether this could possibly, possibly be enough.

# Chapter Thirty-three

The storm had passed in a flash, as weather so often did in the high islands, and a glorious afternoon had arrived from nowhere. Fintan was rushing to the airport. He knew Colton didn't need picking up – one of his staff could drive him – but he didn't care.

He hadn't seen the same thing at Charlie and Jan's wedding as Flora had at all. He'd seen happiness and the amazing sight of the entire community there, celebrating together. Since his mother had died, he'd felt so frustrated living on the island, doing the same thing day in and day out. Meeting Colton had changed all that so much; he saw things now through Colton's eyes. He appreciated more and more the beauty of the landscape, the peace and tranquillity they found there, the privacy and peace and quiet of mind. He saw what Colton saw. And he loved his clever, mercurial boyfriend more than ever.

Colton beamed as he got down from the plane. He

looked thin and a bit overtanned. The US always did that to him. 'Oh *God*, I wanna kiss the ground,' he said. 'You know, if you ever don't come and meet me, like one tiny time, I'm going to reckon we're in real trouble.'

Fintan kissed him. 'Then it'll never happen,' he promised. 'How was New York?'

Colton frowned. 'I think I have a very depressed lawyer. On the other hand, that makes him a highly overworked and busy lawyer, so in that sense it's not going so badly.'

'Ugh,' said Fintan. 'Flora is doing nothing but mope around too.'

'Honestly,' said Colton, with the happy confidence of someone who thinks other people's emotional problems will never happen to them, 'I don't know why they just don't figure it out.'

Fintan smiled happily.

'Seriously. My sister is a pain in the arse, but she's not that bad really.'

Colton sighed. He knew he was partly the cause of Joel's unhappiness, and that he was about to make a lot of other people unhappy too with what he was proposing. But he wasn't going to think about that right now. When it came to Joel and Flora . . . well. He had dated a lot of different people down the years, and had come to some conclusions: one, that there was no single person for everyone; and two, if you found someone you were crazy about, who liked you in return, you were the luckiest goddam son of a bitch in the world. He'd spent plenty of time in love with people who only saw him as a friend, or were in denial about their own sexuality and feelings, or were simply wrong place wrong time.

Now he was in his mid-forties, he knew: waiting for what you wanted, waiting for something perfect, was a disaster. It would never work. You had to jump. If you jumped and it went wrong, well, that was that. You could fix it. But if you wouldn't commit, wouldn't settle, kept waiting for the next thing, the thing that would take absolutely no effort, that would be incredibly easy. Well. That was not going to happen.

Fintan had made a meal, but Colton shook his head. 'Neh,' he said. 'I'm not hungry. I think I want to stretch my legs, shake off my jet lag, rebalance my melatonin, you know?'

Fintan did not know, as he rarely went anywhere, but he nodded regardless. 'Sure,' he said.

'Let's walk one of those stray dogs you always have,' said Colton.

'They're not strays!' said Fintan. 'They're loyal working dogs! Who happen to have a lot of freedom.'

This was true. Bramble was in the habit of ambling down the high street to go and visit the Seaside Kitchen from time to time. Residents and visitors had got used to him marching down the street, and Hamish had trained him to pick up the paper and bring it back to the farmhouse, so everyone was happy with the arrangement – except for Bramble, who smelled all sorts of awesome things around Flora, but was never given any of them. All the cuddles he got en route kind of made up for it, but not entirely. However, he was a wise dog, and lived permanently in hope.

'Whatever,' said Colton. He was just so happy, so pleased

to be back on the island again, and it made Fintan happy just to look at him.

'So, apart from your miserable lawyer, how was New York?'

'Shithole,' said Colton. 'Too hot and sticky and I hated it. Can't breathe there. LA was even worse.'

'I brought you something.'

'Is it cheese?'

'Colton!' said Fintan. 'Shut up!'

'I love your cheese,' said Colton. 'I'm just saying.'

There was a silence as they headed automatically through the town to park up at the Endless.

'So,' said Colton.

'It's not cheese!'

'Okay, so what is it?'

'I forgot it,' said Fintan sullenly.

Colton sniffed in the car.

'Stop it.'

'It's just … it smells a bit like …'

'This car always smells like cheese.'

'Well, that's true. You could still surprise me. Soft cheese? Blue? Hard?'

'Shut up!'

'Because I got something quite hard for you …'

They got out of the car, grinning, and sure enough, there was Bramble, trotting up the high street, the newspaper between his teeth.

'Good timing,' said Fintan, patting him and retrieving it.

'He maybe smelled the new cheese,' said Colton.

'Shut up about cheese!'

They set out. It was evening, but the sky still looked like a studio set: a blue that faded to white, or rather, to a colour you couldn't quite put your finger on, a little like Flora's hair, something that faded into itself, that was hard to look at.

Near the harbourside, the beach was busy with brave toddlers paddling in the shallow freezing water, little crab-catchers with their nets and fishermen on the jetty. (There weren't so many fish close in to shore; it was more of an excuse to get out of the house on a fine evening, and chat to their companions and share a nip or two in friendly silence than a genuine activity.)

But as they walked on, the weather changed: the sun swept out again and they both took off their shoes, letting their feet sink into the soft, warming sand, the crowds enjoying the beauty of the evening fall behind them and, sheltered from the wind by the rock behind, they felt the sun on their necks and the soothing noise of the waves and little more.

After a few hundred metres, Colton stopped, a serious look on his face.

'*Okay*,' said Fintan. 'Okay, it was cheese. Sorry.'

Colton shook his head. 'I don't need any gifts from you,' he said, rubbing his greying goatee.

'I know,' said Fintan stubbornly. 'That's why I wanted to give you something anyway. Nobody ever does. They just assume you have everything.'

Colton blinked, surprised. It was true. In his life, Fintan was practically the only person who as much as bought him a drink. He was just so used to paying all the bills it hadn't even occurred to him. He smiled to himself. If he'd had a moment's doubt, it had just been assuaged.

He glanced around. Some sea peeries were circling, far out over the waves, and a heron was lifting off from the rocks. Apart from that, they were completely unobserved, at the far end of the Endless Beach. It was a perfect evening. Colton held his breath and it felt for a second that everything except the waves was still – everything in the entire world. Time was not moving on, the world was standing in place and nothing had changed or ever would, which meant that either you could think that nothing was particularly important – or everything was.

Colton dropped down on one knee.

Fintan's mouth dropped open.

'What . . . what are you doing?' he said, glancing round in case anyone was behind them. Colton suddenly felt a bolt of fear. Had he completely misjudged the situation? Fintan had spoken about men in the past, but nothing remotely serious; he hadn't even come out until last year. Was it possible that he was just practice for the younger man? Before he moved on? He started to panic. Colton was not traditionally one of life's panickers.

Fintan was still staring at him. Then, thank God, to the mournful calling of the peerie above, he bit his lip, and tried to stop a smile of pure delight spreading across his face.

'Fintan MacKenzie,' Colton said slowly. 'I have never done this before, and seriously I never want to do it again as I am getting old and my knees can't really take it, and the sand is actually quite wet when you get down here.'

Fintan's hand had flown to his mouth.

'But I can't imagine being happier with anyone, anywhere on earth, than I am with you. And your . . .'

Bramble thought they were playing a game. He came and sat down next to Colton on the sand and was now pawing him, thinking he was going to throw something for him. Colton giggled. 'Stop it, Bramble!'

Bramble threw his paws over his arms.

'Aw, for goodness' sake, Bramble. I don't want to marry *you*.'

Fintan gasped audibly.

'Shit, what did you think I was doing down here?' said Colton.

There was a pause.

'Is that it?' said Fintan finally.

'What do you mean?'

'My proposal. Is that it? You proposing to a dog instead of me?'

Bramble was now jumping up and down, licking Colton's face delightedly.

'Stop it!' said Colton. 'That's it, I'm getting up. Hang on, I can't get up until you give me an answer . . .'

'I haven't had a question!'

'This is much more uncomfortable than it looks when people do it in the movies.'

'Right, fine. Come on, Bramble,' said Fintan.

'No! Wait. Right. Okay. My darling. Baby. I . . . I adore you. Have done since the first time I met you, all sulky and a bit drunk.'

'That's very much me at my best,' said Fintan.

'And . . . and the rest of my life is going to be here. It is. I've decided. I've been, hell, everywhere. And nowhere is better than this. Fact. I want to be here, I want to be with you, and time . . . time. Well . . . ' He winced. 'It's always later than you think.'

Fintan smiled down at him. Bramble let his tongue loll out and panted from his exertions. Colton wobbled.

'FINTAN! FOR FUCK'S SAKE!'

'Okay, okay, okay. Yes! YES!'

# Chapter Thirty-four

No sleep. Endless work. Nothing from Flora. Nothing from Colton except more work, of the worst kind.

The hotel was bearing down on him oppressively, and he no longer felt he could call Mark ever since both he and Marsha had made such a massive point about how much they adored Flora, of course, and how much they felt this girl was the one for him and how he should settle down and so on and so forth. So he cut himself off from that.

He exercised relentlessly, which normally worked to quell his restlessness, but pounding the city sidewalks for hours didn't help; didn't tire him out enough to sleep; didn't switch off the endless, clouded panic circling in his brain. He tried more work, but the more he did, the more Colton fed him. He tried drink and realised that in the past he would have gone to a bar and found an incredibly attractive woman and tried to screw it out of himself ... but he didn't ... He didn't want to do that any more. There was only one thing he wanted, only one person, and he couldn't seem to get through to her at all – couldn't seem to get it right. He was worried that she would want more and more and more, and all sorts of things that weren't in him to give.

And now that place – the place he thought he'd found, where the endless, self-doubting torment, the desperate running and fleeing wasn't necessary – now was that still there for him? Colton was about to change it irrevocably. Was he even still welcome there? He had no idea, truly, what was going on in Flora's head; he felt merely that he had been locked out of paradise, that Flora's careful, non-committal chats echoed precisely the language he had been used to all his life, when a well-meaning but nonetheless determined social worker had explained, yet again, why he wasn't welcome at this place, that they would try and find somewhere else for him.

He went to the balcony. The heat and noise of the city rose up to meet him. Christ, he hated it here. He hated it. He wanted to be cool, and quiet, and walking a long beach, and smelling the freshest of sea wind, just letting the air blow out every cobweb in his head. No. They weren't cobwebs. They were more like twisted snakes, coiled around the inside of his brain, squeezing tighter and tighter, and if Flora knew ... If she only knew, if she got close enough, if she suspected what was beneath the carapace of him; what it contained ... It was a writhing, choking mass of slithering monsters that tightened every synapse, the great coiling insides of him that he could conceal with a smart suit; with a charming manner; with a fit body; with spending money; with everything like that. For as long as that worked.

He couldn't risk letting her get closer. But if he didn't, he would lose everything. And Colton was taking a sledge-hammer to it all.

His head hurt, as if the monsters in there were trying to burst out, trying to escape. He couldn't ... If he ever let them out, if he ever did, he worried that he would start to scream and never, ever be able to stop.

He staggered along the balcony, peered over the top and stared down to the ground. The suite wasn't on the street side; it simply led down to the roof of another building.

Why was it so fucking hot? Hot everywhere. He'd turned on the air conditioning, but then he'd started to shiver uncontrollably. He didn't know how long he'd been in this room, in this hotel. His brain was cloudy. None of his clothes fitted; he didn't know what the hell was wrong with everyone. He couldn't remember the last time he'd eaten. He blinked; sweat was dripping down his forehead. He staggered forward again.

⌒ ⌒

Flora was closing the Seaside Kitchen and had dismissed the girls and was making Lorna a cappuccino. 'This we can afford,' she said. 'Well done today.'

'Thanks,' said Lorna, blushing. 'Was he pleased? He was hard to read. I think he was pleased.'

'I can't believe you studied Arabic for a month.'

Lorna blushed more. 'It's a beautiful language.'

'You're a dark horse.'

'You're not. God, but those boys are tiny.' Lorna sighed. 'He's going to need a lot of help.'

Flora gave her a look. '*Sexy* help?'

'Oh Christ, of course not,' Lorna said. 'Trust me, I've given up in that department. Can you imagine? Not in a million years.'

'Things that shouldn't happen in a million years do actually happen, you know,' said Flora, licking the foam off the cappuccinos she'd made them. 'I mean, look at this place.'

They looked around at the lovely painted homely café.

Lorna smiled. 'True. But I think he has quite enough on his plate, and I'm hardly going to impinge upon his image of his missing and perfect wife, am I? Anyway, it's inappropriate. I'm going to be looking after his boys. Christ. That's a job ahead. Poor wee mites, they looked miserable. It would be disgusting weather this morning.'

'I know. Want me to send up some buns tomorrow?'

'Nothing in the budget,' said Lorna gloomily.

'Nothing in the charity fund,' said Flora equally gloomily. 'Jan takes it all.'

'Any news from Joel?'

'Um, I'm playing it cool.'

'*You?*'

Flora went pink. 'I know, I know. Shut up.'

'You literally pursued him for four years ... '

Flora ran her finger round the rim of her cup. 'Seriously, I'm desperate enough to try anything.'

Lorna nodded.

'And, by the way, you're *learning Arabic* ... '

'To help the children,' said Lorna piously. 'So, you're giving him the cold shoulder ... '

'Nothing ... ' Flora shook her head. 'Not a thing. I haven't heard from him at all.'

Lorna grimaced. That didn't sound good. 'I mean,' she said. 'You know what those friends of his told you in New York.'

'Yes,' said Flora, 'but they didn't say, "Keep on making a fool out of yourself. For ages and ages and ages."'

Lorna looked sympathetic but glanced at her watch. 'Sorry,' she said. 'I have to go. I have nine miles of marking.'

'I know,' said Flora. 'I've got accounts.'

'Isn't it great, being awesome women completely in control of our lives and destinies?' said Lorna, getting up and giving Flora a hug. 'Look,' she said. 'You love him. Put your cards on the table. If you want him, I don't think waiting is going to do it.'

'Me either,' said Flora. 'But what if he brushes me off and says he's too busy?'

Then she sat, staring at the telephone, pondering and weighing up what to do, without the faintest idea, not the slightest, about the tumult that was taking places thousands of miles away. She had a romantic notion, or had done in the past, that if you were with the person you truly loved, you would pick up on how they were feeling, 'tune in' to their vibes; even if they were far away, you could pick out a star or sense from a passing cloud how they were or when they were thinking of you.

There was every possibility, she now realised, that this was total and utter crap.

On the other hand, as she stared at it, her phone started to ring . . .

Flora grabbed the phone and picked it up.

'Hello?' she said, registering with some disappointment as she did so that it was Fintan, not Joel.

'YAYYYYYY!' came a noisy roaring sound down the phone. It sounded battered and windy.

'Fintan? Where are you? Are you drunk?'

'No!' came the ecstatic voice. 'Actually, now you mention it, that sounds like a totally fabulous, fantastic idea. Let's go and get drunk!'

'Yes, doing my accounts always goes better when I'm drunk,' said Flora. 'What's up?'

'Tell her,' came Colton's unmistakably growly voice behind him.

'*What?*' said Flora.

'We're getting married!' screamed Fintan joyously down the phone.

Flora paused, only for the very briefest of milliseconds, before she screamed 'Yay!' down the phone too.

It wasn't fair, it really wasn't at all fair to be jealous of her brother for getting married first. She was fine about it. Great, in fact. She loved Fintan; she loved Colton; this was all brilliant. Brilliant. And she would be happy, she told herself. Plus, it really *was* a good excuse for not doing the accounts.

'That's wonderful!' she said. 'Who proposed?'

'The one with the grey hair,' said Colton. The phone was now obviously on speaker. 'Obviously. Come join us up at the Rock for some fizz.'

'What did Dad say?'

'He's the next call,' said Fintan. Flora bit her lip. He'd

called her first. Without Mum, he'd called her first. That meant so much.

'He'll be . . . ' She thought for a moment. 'Well. He'll handle it.'

'Do you think he'll walk me down the aisle?'

They both burst into fits of hysterical laughter.

'Oh, Fint,' said Flora suddenly. 'Oh, Mum would have loved it.'

The boys fell silent on the other end of the phone.

'Aye,' said Fintan. 'Reckon.'

'Oh my God,' said Flora. 'Who's going to break it to Agot? She'd better be flower girl.'

'Oh yes,' said Fintan. 'Come on, come on. I'll pick up some food from home. We'll get the fires lit up at the Rock. Come on.'

And that is how Flora didn't get around to phoning Joel until much, much later.

><

Joel hadn't realised he'd emptied the minibar: it just suddenly was empty, and he was staring at it, slightly dumbfounded. Everything seemed very off. He tried to remember when he'd last eaten, then realised he couldn't. He eyed a wobbly Toblerone but decided he couldn't face it. He looked at his phone. Nothing. Nobody to call, nobody to . . . He looked at his computer. The words swam in front of his eyes. Christ, he was tired. He was just so damn tired. Of holding it together. Of doing well. Of needing nothing, and nobody.

And he didn't. He didn't need anybody. He got up, staggered to the terrace again, fell down. Perhaps he should go out. Perhaps he should see if they had any whisky down-stairs. They had to have whisky, didn't they? In Mure they served the best whisky in the world ... What was it called again? Something weird and Gaelic and unpronounceable and you sat round the fire and got cosy and mixed it with a tiny bit of water and the first time Flora had bought some for him he'd mentioned ice and she'd looked utterly horrified and ...

The next thing Joel knew, he was back on the balcony. Perhaps he'd blacked out for a second. He didn't know where he was. He didn't know what was happening. Only that everything was too much.

The champagne cork popped and everyone cheered, their faces bright in the evening light after the sun had made its late appearance. A huge fire still crackled in the grate – you could always do with a bit of insurance on Mure. Everyone was laughing and Fintan was sitting on Colton's knee, occasionally glancing up at him as if in wonder that all of this had come to pass.

'Have you got a ring?'

Fintan nodded and leaned over. Flora gasped. It was exquisite: two bands of silver, between which was a carved metal design of little cogs slotted together. 'Like a butter churn,' said Fintan.

Flora shook her head. It was utterly beautiful, unique and absolutely them. 'It's lovely.'

'What did Joel say?' asked Colton lazily, who was not really listening to the MacKenzies' chatter. When they all were yapping en masse, he found the accent got thicker and became difficult to follow, but he rather liked this. He simply leaned back and let it all wash over him like birdsong – sipping whisky rather than champagne, the man he loved on his lap, the fire flickering in the fireplace, still light past nine o'clock – and felt that a happy life had nothing much more to offer.

Flora froze. You would have to have known her rather less well than her brothers not to notice. 'Um, I haven't . . . '

Innes frowned. 'Are you two . . . ?'

'Sssh,' said Fintan quickly.

'No,' said Flora. This was ridiculous. Of course she would phone him. They were normal people. If he was out in a bar or too busy to talk to her or . . .

Suddenly her heart started to race. This. This was a reckoning. She would call him. She would tell him the loveliest, happiest news that had happened to the MacKenzies in a long time. And if he was truly her boyfriend – a part of her family, her community – he would be delighted, thrilled, interested.

And if he was too busy, if he passed over it . . . Well. Then she would know.

She felt cold inside. But after the disastrous trip . . . There had to be limits. There did. She didn't need a perfectly designed engagement ring that cost a fortune. She didn't need a big wedding or a fancy declaration. But she needed to know where she stood. She needed to know she meant something.

She stood up, excused herself from the table, knowing full well the boys would watch her go then gossip about them. She couldn't think about that just now.

Outside it was colder than it looked. The sun was making a full high arc of the sky, the wide light the palest yellow, almost leached of all colour; the sea, unusually, as still as a millpond as far as the eye could see, a perfect flat calm. It was an utterly ravishing evening, and up here at the Rock, with its manicured gardens and walled terraces – with its red carpet leading down to the jetty where guests would arrive by boat – the fiery torches were lit, a merry path although it was not dark at all.

The air was heavy with the scent of the last of the spring bluebells, neatly serried in rows by the Rock's army of gardeners, the very last of the daffodils fading away.

Flora looked around, took in the beauty of the evening, terrified that everything was about to change so much and spoil and leave her. She thought of Joel, his beauty, his set face, his unexpected flashes of humour which, she now suspected, he had used all along to keep her from getting close. The sex.

Maybe. Maybe she could live like this. Maybe she could handle it. Being ignored. Undervalued. Left on her own for months on end. Waiting around for some crumbs from her lover's table. Or maybe she couldn't.

Joel was sitting down on the terrace when the phone rang, although he wasn't quite sure how. He'd been standing up, hadn't he? Trying to get cool? Or had he? Everything was quite jumbled in his brain.

At first, he didn't realise what was making the sound; his head was full of noises and everything sounded like

207

the scream of a phone, but it persisted and persisted then it stopped – did it? Or did he pass out? – and then it started again and then it stopped.

>⸱ ⸱<

Flora stared out at the sea, furious. She wouldn't leave a message. This was too important. He would see it was her on the caller display, even if he was out. He was never more than two feet from his phone, not even at night when he used it as an alarm clock. He walked about with his life in the palm of his hand, wrapped in plastic. The phone was important to him. Whether she was was a different matter.

She hung up and phoned again, hung up and phoned again, realising this was bordering on craziness but so wound up and anxious and angry she no longer cared how she seemed or came across. If he thought she was some kind of disposable, cool, non-interested girl, well . . . she wasn't, and that was how it was.

She glanced back at the beautiful building of the Rock, tranquil in the evening light: the grey stone so comforting; the glories of the garden just beginning to come to fruition; the small group inside laughing convivially in the soft light. It looked so happy. She felt so on the outside looking in.

She dialled again. Dialled again. Last time, she promised herself. She would dial one last time.

>⸱ ⸱<

Joel half-opened an eye. He felt like a shipwrecked man, clinging to a world that turned round and round and tipped him up and down again until he no longer knew which way was up. And still that persistent sound in his ears. He had to make it stop. He *had* to make it stop.

He grabbed the phone, which had skittered nearly to the very edge of the balcony. There was a gap between the glass protective wall and the floor. He was tempted to kick the phone over. See how it fell, first. See how it soared and twirled through the air; see if it was the right ...

He squinted at it, realising he was seeing double, that he couldn't make sense any more of the words that were there. F ... l ...

'What?'

'Joel!'

'What is it?'

Flora was taken aback. 'Um. Does there have to be a reason?'

'No, of course not. Tell me ... Is it nice there? Not too hot? Christ, it's fucking hot here ...'

'Joel ... I just wanted to call you with the news. Colton and Fintan got engaged! They're getting married.'

Flora waited anxiously for his reaction. There was a long pause, over thousands of miles. Then she heard a massive exhalation of breath.

'Of course they fucking are,' said Joel. And he hung up.

🐦 🐦

Flora slowly put down the phone. Enough. She stared out over the sea. Enough was enough now. She turned to go. She wouldn't say goodbye to the boys; their evident happiness was a little much for her right at the moment. She knew they'd be all right. In fact, better, she'd pop in on her dad in the morning and try and do some good. He hadn't wanted to come out that evening – he slept in the farmer's way, always had: 8 p.m. to bed, 4 a.m. rising. Not that she'd get much sleep tonight.

Bertie, who ran a boat around when they were at the Rock, was waiting at the jetty. He jumped up.

'Hello, Flores!' he said, going bright pink as always.

'Can you take me home, Bertie?'

'Aye, of course! Love to! Boat or car? Come on, take the boat. It's a lovely night!'

'Why not?' thought Flora. It was hardly like it mattered and the fresh air might help her get some sleep at least. So she nodded and followed him to the jetty.

# Chapter Thirty-five

Joel realised he was in a mess. But he didn't know how to get out of it. Everything had come to a head suddenly, and he didn't know how to cope. He couldn't control his breathing.

Gulping, he felt a sudden skip in his heartbeat – a massive electrical jolt. He grabbed the phone like a lifeline. Before he knew what he'd done, he'd pressed the callback button, although in his confused, twirling state he wasn't sure why, or even whom he was calling. His breath came in great shuddering gasps.

There was no signal out at sea, and Flora found a queer sort of quiet and contentment staring out over the wide ocean, feeling alone and facing the world by herself. Whatever happened, she knew, she wasn't the same girl she'd been a year ago: timid, scared, upset to the point of paralysis by the death of her mother; angry at having to come back to the island.

Now, this was home, and despite its many inconveniences she loved it. She had a little business – well, okay, they were pretty much running on empty at the moment, but it was her business and she could manage. She was doing all right. She'd never be rich, but then she'd spent some time with rich people. She wasn't sure it made them remotely happy. And there wasn't that much point in having fancy dresses on Mure.

The worst feeling, she thought, was that she'd failed. She'd known Joel, she thought, as closely as anyone could know him. As close as anyone could get. And still she couldn't crack it. She couldn't get through; she couldn't fix him. Everyone had been right. He wasn't tameable, simply because he didn't know what it was to be tame. But she had tried her hardest. She had.

It wasn't until she got closer to shore, back into the range of Mure's single lone mobile phone mast, that she realised her phone was ringing. She'd taken the voicemail off when she'd left London, not wanting to be a slave to her phone any more.

If anyone had ever checked the records, they would see that it had rung 138 times.

Flora stared at it as Bertie looked at her, a hopeful expression in his eyes that turned to disappointment as she answered it. 'Joel?'

There was a short pause. Then just two words.

'Help me.'

## Chapter Thirty-six

Flora burst through the door of the Harbour's Rest.

'I need to use the hotel phone and the computer,' she said. 'Sorry, the signal is just too shitty. It's an emergency.'

'It is,' said Inge-Britt as Flora scrolled desperately through the internet until she found a listing for the psychiatrist Mark Philippoussis in Manhattan and explained the situation to his receptionist, who patched her through. She remembered the room number and Mark got down there in record time, Marsha following on, plus a police officer in case they couldn't get into the room. Flora had also called the hotel management and caught the receptionist who was in love with Joel and who had, too, been increasingly concerned by his weight loss, his late nights, his odd hours and habits and the glazed look in his eye whenever she tried to flirt or say hello. She could not have been kinder or more helpful to Flora then, and Flora was half glad and half absolutely distraught that she wasn't there when they finally got through the door and found him, sitting on the balcony, looking over the edge, as if he wasn't sure where he was, even with the huge pinkening city spread beneath his feet.

## Chapter Thirty-seven

'Well, fuck that, man.'

Flora couldn't help but be impressed. Having not really contemplated, beyond the buying of holidays and possibly a little flat one day, what money could do, it was quite incredible to watch Colton in action.

He was talking to Mark Philippoussis, or rather shouting at him.

'Let me talk to him!'

Mark was entirely calm about the whole thing. 'One of your staff appears to be suffering from nervous exhaustion,' he said politely, 'while also being tremendously drunk. I think the last thing I'm going to do is let you talk to him.'

'He's my employee and I have a duty of care and if I have to fly him back, I will.'

Flora went up. 'Please can I speak to them? Please?' She grabbed the phone and moved to another part of the hotel. 'Mark?'

'Flora? Is that you?'

'Yes . . . What's happened?'

'Did you know he was working so hard?'

Flora gulped. 'He always does that.'

'I know. It looks like . . . He's dropped a lot of weight, Flora. I think he's just exhausted. Did anything stressful happen to him at work?'

'He never talks to me about work.' Flora shot a look at Colton, who turned away.

'What about you two personally?'

Flora paused long enough for Mark to pick up on it.

'Listen, Flora. Why don't you let me and Marsha take him to our place? Let him sleep it off?'

'Then will you send him home, Mark?' said Flora anxiously.

'Do you think that would be the best thing for him?'

Flora wished she knew. 'Yes,' she said. 'Can I speak to him?'

'He's passed out, Flora.'

'Jesus,' said Flora. 'What is it? What's wrong with him?'

'I'll need to talk to him, but I would say panic attacks and overwork. I don't know what's made him so anxious; he's normally so controlled. As soon as he wakes up, I'll call you.'

'Are you taking him to hospital?'

'Not tonight.'

'Good,' said Flora, relieved. He'd sounded so . . . so very desolate.

Colton snatched back the phone to make it very clear to Mark that he would pay for anything required and could

216

have a jet on standby, but Mark was short with him and the call ended.

Flora sat by the window as, after ten, the evening finally began to darken, the moon at last to rise.

'Did you know something was wrong?' said Fintan gently, twisting the brand-new ring on his finger.

'I ... I just thought he was like that ...' She looked around, stricken. 'He got further and further away. But ... you know ... Men do that.'

Fintan nodded. 'I know.'

He placed a reassuring hand on Colton's knee, even as Colton stared outside as they sat and waited the night through for news.

# Chapter Thirty-eight

Saif's boys hated his house, their new home. It was freezing cold and draughty. A flat handsome grey house made of expensive stone, it had beautiful outlooks, slightly out of the town.

But the previous owner had had little spare money for its upkeep, and the window frames were peeling and cracked, draughts blew in everywhere and the thick curtains Saif used to keep the light out during the long summer evenings were heavy with dust. It was cold and spooky, and as Saif looked around he wondered anew how this had never occurred to him before.

This house had only ever been a place to eat and sleep. He left at the crack of dawn, usually to walk the beach, and to hope and wait for his family; then he was busy at the surgery all day and on call most nights. Mrs Laird came in a couple of times a week to do for him, and she would leave him a casserole or a lasagne – he'd got used to her bland cuisine eventually; the children ate quickly and without comment – and then he'd just make some soup or eat at the Seaside Kitchen and have a sandwich in the evening. He barely thought about food at all.

Now, looking around, he realised how bleak the house really was, even with the pathetic stencils he'd bought to try and cheer things up. It had never been a family home, had never felt like one.

He felt even more the idiot. If he hadn't got so irrationally cross and silly with Lorna, she'd have helped him before to make up nice rooms for the boys – there was plenty of space in the house. All he needed to have done was to buy bright covers and curtains – or whatever it was boys liked. He felt sorry and ashamed.

'I'm scared, *Abba*.'

Ash was still clinging to him. He'd had his foot X-rayed and reset in Glasgow, but he was really meant to be walking on it to strengthen it. Instead, he still refused to be put down at all, not even for a moment.

'That's okay.'

'I sleep in your beb?'

Saif really wasn't in the mood for another night of being kicked in the head by a small boy in a plaster cast. On the other hand, what were his options? He well remembered the first night he'd spent here, freezing, alien, sobbing.

'Of course,' he said, putting on the lamps. 'Bed. It's pronounced "bed".'

'Bib?'

He looked at Ibrahim. 'Do you want to sleep with us too?' Ibrahim shrugged. 'I don't care.'

Saif nodded. He knew this meant yes. 'Okay. Well, let's stay together tonight, okay? I'm sure the storm will have moved on tomorrow.'

He was not remotely sure about this at all.

His phone rang, and he cursed. All out-of-hours calls were still directed to the locum service, surely? Who could want him this late? He glanced down and saw it was Flora MacKenzie. That was strange.

'Hello?'

'Saif? It's Flora . . . I'm so sorry to bother you.'

'That's all right, but . . . Sorry. Is this medical?'

'Yes.'

'You know, I'm on . . . It's the on-call doctor . . . '

'I know, I know. I'm so sorry, Saif. But . . . ' She explained the situation.

Saif nodded. 'That sounds like . . . It sounds like a nervous breakdown, Flora.'

He could hear her swallow. 'He shouldn't stay there?'

'I don't know.' Saif thought about it carefully, even as Ash kept trying to pick his fingers from the phone. 'I think . . . ' he said eventually. 'I think this kind of thing is best treated with care. And peace and quiet.'

'But can you treat it?'

'Yes. I can.'

There was a pause.

# Chapter Thirty-nine

Joel was always very hazy on what happened next. He dimly remembered Mark asking him lots of questions, but wasn't too sure exactly how he'd answered them. Colton had organised a plane to bring him home, and Mark sobered him up with a large amount of coffee and a drip – the hotel was not unused to such scenarios.

'What do you want, Joel?'

And he had found that oddly funny, and then he was so exhausted and Mark's voice was so kind and soft and he just said, 'Can I go home?'

And he got on the plane, and that was the last thing he remembered.

Flora didn't sleep at all. She paced the Endless through the night when it didn't really get dark, just a kind of twilight at midnight, the sun immediately rising again. Colton and

Fintan dozed off together in armchairs, but Flora refused to rest all through the five hours the flight was in the air. It was a light and bright 4 a.m. when the tiny dot appeared in the wide white sky, slowly circling downwards, the only manmade object for miles, above the tin shed that housed the tiny airport. Sheila MacDuff emerged. She would normally be furious to be woken at this time, but was feeling rather pleased this morning because the reason was so big and gossip-worthy. Her husband, Patrick, who worked as air traffic controller and gift shop operator, waved from the little control tower as the plane made a perfect landing in the glimmering dawn.

Colton and Fintan woke up and came out with Flora to greet the flight. Flora leaned her head on Fintan's shoulder as the door opened on the tarmac and a thin, stooped figure, with Mark by his side, limped down the steps. Everyone watched Flora to see what she was going to do, but she just stepped forward, carefully, worried – as if he were fragile.

Mark's cheerful New York tones as he scanned the gravel and the windswept fields around the airfield broke the ice.

'Where the hell is this place? The moon?'

Joel was woozy and quiet in the Land Rover. Flora took his hand and he looked at her. 'I'm sorry about the fuss.'

She shook her head. 'Don't be ridiculous. This is Colton's fault for working you too hard.'

Colton, in front, was uncharacteristically subdued.

'Yeah,' he said, turning round. 'Yeah. I'm sorry. You can sue me if you like.' And he smiled weakly.

Joel didn't take the olive branch. Instead he stared at

222

Colton, his eyes burning. Flora noticed the look, but didn't understand it. It was like Joel hated him.

'You need sleep, man.'

They parked up at Joel's cottage at the Rock. Mark had a room down the hallway. Joel had never been so pleased to see anything in his life.

He walked in by himself. 'I'm not sick,' he said and turned around at the door. Colton was looking at him. 'Thanks,' Joel muttered. 'Thanks for getting me home.'

'You're welcome, man,' said Colton, and once again something passed between them. Joel had hardly looked at Flora at all.

She followed him into the bedroom. He looked up at her, and she was deeply troubled by how thin and haunted he appeared. How had she not noticed when she'd seen him? Why hadn't she questioned the evasiveness, the way he had stopped coming home?

They looked at each other. Then Flora moved into the beautiful bathroom, with its old claw-footed tub, and started running a very hot bath. Joel screwed up his face.

'Come on,' she said quietly, unbuttoning his shirt. 'Get in.'

And carefully, gently, she put him in the bath and climbed in behind him, and tenderly washed him and held him and kissed him gently and every time he started to woozily say something she would hush him and say tell me tomorrow, and he let her. Then he climbed into bed and was instantly asleep. She stood there, gazing at him, wondering what the hell she could do now, until, after five o'clock, she too became overwhelmed with exhaustion, and lay down beside him and drifted off to sleep.

# Chapter Forty

Once again, Annie's Seaside Kitchen did not open on Monday morning. Mrs Cairns waddled down looking for her first cheese scone of the day (Saif had warned her about her weight many times, and she had looked at him and said, quite clearly, 'Doctor, I am seventy-four years old, my husband is dead, my children live in New Zealand and you are seriously telling me I can't have a cheese scone?' Saif had said uncomfortably, 'Madam, I think you can have one cheese scone but you cannot have four cheese scones,' and Mrs Cairns, who had, after huge initial reservations about whether the brown doctor was there to blow up the island, rather overestimating the island's political interest to ISIS as a target, had grown to like him and the way he gravely called her madam, and actually he was rather handsome when you came to think about it, a bit like Omar Sharif . . .) and she sighed heavily when she found it shut. The gaggle of her friends and relations, many of whom she had hated for murky reasons for almost half a century, joined her slowly as they pondered where they could go to discuss their latest ailments and who may or may not have died.

Charlie's face fell as he cheerily led his latest bunch of troubled youngsters off the boat for their early morning sausage roll. It had been a difficult crossing: the ones who weren't throwing up were, frankly, going bananas on the boat, charging about here and there, and the stewards, who knew him pretty well and were usually very tolerant, were raising eyebrows left, right and centre. He'd promised them all the best sausage rolls in the country if they'd behave, and now he was stuffed.

Isla and Iona had been absolutely delighted by the news of an unexpected day off, having not yet caught up with the gossip, and had decided to go sunbathing, even though it was fourteen degrees with a wind that felt like somebody was spinning a fan over some ice, but Isla had waited a very long time for her new bikini to arrive from the mainland and was absolutely not going to miss the opportunity to wear it.

Hillwalkers and holidaymakers, excited by the amazing TripAdvisor reviews (except for 'Very disappointing lack of Chinese food – one star' and 'Couldnt understand wot they was saying, theys shood speek English up here – one star') and in the mood for something delicious to set them off for ten hours' hard walking in goodness knows what weather, realised they were going to have to make do with whatever the supermarket felt like offering them, or the beer-smelling Harbour's Rest. They tried, and failed, to put a brave face on it, particularly the dragged-along hikers, there to make up the numbers but who were now clearly going to do nothing but moan all day. It was not working out very well for anyone.

If Flora could only have seen it, it would have cheered her up immeasurably to see how, in such a short time, the Seaside Kitchen had become such a mainstay of their little community.

But she couldn't.

The confusion in Joel's head as he awoke around ten-ish was hard to deal with. First, he had the mother of all hangovers. He also had absolutely no idea where the hell he was. He glanced around, his eyes scratchy and sore, his brain still furled up in cotton wool, muggy. What? What the hell had just happened? Argh, oh God, oh God, his head . . .

He tore to the bathroom and threw up. He looked at himself in the mirror; he barely recognised himself. Where the hell was he? What was this?

Finally, gradually, he pulled himself up, found a huge fluffy white towel and pulled it around himself. He was so light-headed he staggered against the doorframe. When was the last time he had eaten? He couldn't remember. Oh God, he felt awful.

It was only then, clutching the door, trying to work out what the hell had happened, that he caught sight of the room beyond, and his brain exploded.

Wasn't he in New York? His heart skipped in panic. The panorama in front of him . . .

His first thought was he had died. He had jumped – suddenly it scissored back into his brain: the balcony, the heat, the height. He clutched again at the doorframe, his head trying to focus on what he was seeing.

Instead of the bright reds and oranges of the New York sunset, ahead of him was a palette of washed-out pale greys: a huge glass window looking out onto a dawn that precisely reflected the room they were in, huge grey vistas, clouds and sea, soft white sands, pale flattened grass, deep blues. He blinked. And there, on the bed, stretched out, pale, her hair around her like sea grass . . .

And then he remembered. And he was so grateful he nearly burst into tears. Okay, his career might be in ruins . . .

But she was still here. The worst had not happened. He sat on the bed for a little while, making his breaths go in and out with hers. She shifted slightly in her sleep and he leaned over and kissed her on the forehead and headed out to blow the cobwebs away – to breathe the fresh air he had missed for so long.

## Chapter Forty-one

Lorna turned up at school early and nervous. The news hadn't reached her about Joel yet; she was worried about their two new arrivals. The children wanted to sing their alphabet song again – they had, to be fair, spent an awful lot of time practising it – and it was a fine day, so Lorna decided to let them. Neda Okonjo had sent over the briefing notes on both the children, which she had to keep locked in a filing cabinet. Both gave her cause for concern. She'd had children from difficult circumstances before, of course – there were divorces on Mure like anywhere else, and Kelvin McLinton's father had fallen under the wheels of his tractor one awful stormy day.

But this was something she was worried she wasn't fully equipped to cope with. She'd read as much as she could online about dealing with post-trauma in children and infants. Much of it was reassuring – as she kept telling herself, as long as babies were loved and looked after, they possessed so much resilience. She reminded herself that her grandparents' generation had lived through evacuation and war. But this was a challenge she was desperate not to get wrong, for Saif, and for the boys themselves.

'Just do your best.' Neda had been cool, clear and reassuring on the phone. 'Nobody's going to expect perfection. Just keep to what they can do, and don't worry too much about their English – basically to get that they need to do the opposite of what we recommend for most children, and watch about six hours of TV a day. Just try and make sure the other children are as nice as possible, and let them draw lots of pictures. Did you know children's drawing is universal?'

Lorna did.

'Well. Appreciate that. Every neurotypical child has a way of building up the world through their hands. Let them do it and they'll slot right in with the rest of the class. And keep your Google Translate on.'

Lorna stood. She'd chosen a long skirt, hoping in some odd sense that she might look more like women they were used to seeing, although she didn't really know much about that at all, and she plastered another big smile on as she saw Saif arrive.

He greeted her, trying his best to smile in return. He looked exhausted. Lorna thought it suited him.

'I am so sorry,' he said. 'I had an emergency last night. They haven't had much sleep.'

Indeed, Ash was sleeping on his shoulder, having not quite woken up in the car. Ibrahim was trailing sullenly behind, the sleeves of his blazer hanging down past his fists, kicking the fronts of his new black shoes against the gravel.

'Hope it was okay,' said Lorna, and Saif figured he would leave her to find out for herself; he was on his way to the Rock now anyway.

He shook Ash awake, who instantly started to cry, then held both the boys close.

'It's just school,' he said firmly. 'Ash, you'll like it. They have lots of toys to play with and things to draw. Ibrahim, there'll be other boys to play with.'

Ibrahim shrugged.

'And I'll be back at lunchtime.'

They were starting with some half-days. If they had to come back to the surgery with him, they just would.

Ash set up his shrill, one-note yell again, and Saif tried not to let his irritation show too much.

'أهلاً بالمعلمة,' said Lorna. 'Come in and welcome.'

Saif looked at her. 'One year here and there was a fluent Arabic speaker all along,' he said with a half-smile.

She flushed. 'I'm terrible!'

'Your effort,' he said, 'is the biggest compliment and kindness anyone could do me … I am sorry I ever …'

She shook her head. No apology was needed between them. He nodded.

Then he indicated Ash, whom he had to peel off himself again.

'No, I really am sorry,' he said.

'Happens all the time,' said Lorna with a smile, and looking in Lorna's pretty freckled face, the warmth of her reassuring, slightly nervous smile, Saif felt his world stop spinning, just a little. He was not alone.

'لعب. Toys,' she said to Ash, who stopped screaming for

a second, then shook his head and started again. 'Well, we have toys.'

And, holding him to her as if he were a much younger child, and in direct contravention of about forty health and safety regulations, she took him inside, Ibrahim glancing sullenly at Saif before reluctantly trailing after her. Saif stood and stared in amazement that it had been, in the end, easier than he'd been expecting.

Flora awoke to an empty bed and a knock on the door. She blinked as it all came rushing back, and sat up. Jesus. What time was it? Where was he?

Where was he?

There was another knock on the door, and she jumped, startled. As she looked around, Joel appeared at the French windows that led to the garden, thin as a wraith, frightening her even more. He passed through the room without looking at her and opened the door to Saif.

'Excuse me!' said Flora, pulling up the covers.

She was horrified. Saif looked equally disconcerted. 'Ah,' he said. Flora rolled her eyes.

'Sorry,' said Joel.

'Shall I come back?'

'No, it's . . . ' started Joel.

'Actually, could you give us five minutes?' said Flora. 'You can get a coffee at the lodge?'

Saif nodded and beat a hasty retreat. Flora felt her heart in her mouth as Joel turned round.

'Um.' She cleared her throat. 'Hello.'

'Hey,' he said.

'How are you feeling this morning?'

'A hell of a lot better than I felt last night.'

She yawned and got out of bed and went towards him. 'What happened?'

Joel shrugged. 'I spoke to Mark. He says stress and panic attacks. Brought on from overwork.'

'Is that all?' She looked up at him.

'He doesn't think so.'

'And what do you think?'

'I think you look absolutely ravishing and we should tell Saif to stay away for a bit . . . '

Flora shook her head. 'That doesn't solve things.'

'It solves some . . . '

'JOEL!' shouted Flora. 'This is not the way! You were blind drunk and falling apart. Why? Okay,' she said. 'I think I'm going to have to hand this over to Saif and Mark. I'm here for you, Joel. But I'm not helping you. I'm not making you better. I'm making you exactly the same. I hoped . . . I hoped I'd be able to help, to do something for you. To be with you. But I can't.'

Joel stared, gutted, helpless, unable to move.

'I am here for you. But I am not doing you any good, Joel. And you are not doing me any good either. All I think about is you, and it's torpedoing my business and torpedoing my life and I can't . . . I can't do this to myself either . . . '

She found herself choking up.

'I'll be at the farmhouse. But I am here for you whenever you want me. Not for sex. Not just for sex. I am here when you are ready to be here with me. If you want me. Not Mure, not a home, not an island, not some dream of a sea creature. Me. Just me.'

'Flora, this is ridiculous. It's fine. Everything's fine.'

'One doctor is standing outside this door with heavy medication and another doctor is waiting for you in the lodge,' said Flora. 'That is nobody's definition of fine. If it wasn't for Colton, you could have woken up this morning in a damn hospital.'

'If it wasn't for Colton, I wouldn't be in this mess in the first place.'

'He didn't make you work with a gun to your head.'

'He might as well have done.'

Flora walked up to him and gently stroked his face. 'I love you,' she said, quietly. She had never said this before, not to him, and she wasn't sure if she'd ever get a chance to say it again. She needed to know that she'd done it. Even if nothing happened from now on. Even if this really was it.

There it was. It hung in the air. The very last card she had to play.

He looked at her, stricken, unable to answer, his head desperately trying to make sense of the situation. She couldn't love him just because she felt sorry for him; he couldn't bear it. 'It's … This is just a misunderstanding,' he said.

There was a very long silence after that.

'It is,' said Flora. 'It is, Joel. And the person who has misunderstood it is you.'

And she kissed him and turned to go. She picked her top up off the pillows where she'd left it the night before.

The pillow under her hand was soaking wet. Someone had been crying into it. She turned around and walked away, a pale ghost down the paths of the beautiful gardens of the Rock.

# Chapter Forty-two

Saif came back in again, having taken the opportunity to call the school and check on the boys, but Lorna had had her hands full and hadn't answered, so he was full of trepidation.

He blinked again at Joel being up and about. It wasn't at all what he'd been expecting. He hadn't had much experience in mental health issues, and not as much time as he'd have liked that morning to catch up on the reading, but he wasn't expecting someone greeting him courteously and asking if he'd like more coffee. He focused on Joel's right hand. It was trembling, even as he put his other hand on it to try and make it stop.

'Do you know where you are?' said Saif gently.

'Does anyone?' said Joel, then shook his head. 'I'm fine. Sorry. I got very overstressed and ... combusted. It was good of Colton to fly me home.'

'Now there are several options suggested in this case ...

I think we should start you off on benzodiazepine and see how you react to that ... '

Joel held up his hands. 'Wait ... wait. I mean, there's nothing wrong with me. I had a bad night, that's all. Overworked.'

'That's right,' said Saif. 'You were also dehydrated and you're underweight. This doesn't seem to be a new issue for you.'

'I'm fine.'

Saif blinked. Usually he was trying to keep people off antidepressants. This wasn't one of those cases.

'Joel, there is no shame in asking for help if you need it. It's just an illness.'

'It's not,' said Joel. 'It's a natural response to an intolerable situation. Dammit.' He looked around the room. 'What else would you recommend if you weren't prescribing?'

Saif shrugged. 'Rest. A good diet. Peace and quiet. Gentle exercise.'

'Well, I'll get peace and quiet,' said Joel. 'Nobody's speaking to me.'

Saif nodded.

'And the food here is pretty good. If I can get my hands on some.'

'And you need to keep talking,' said Saif. 'Find someone to talk to.'

'Oh God,' said Joel.

There was another knock at the door. It was Mark.

'Jesus Christ, man, this place is stone-cold awesome,' he said. 'Have you even drunk the water? It doesn't taste like any water you've ever tasted. I don't think it is water. It's like drinking cold light. And that air! It's like you get a detox just by walking about! Right. Let's get you sorted out.'

He shook Saif's hand. 'Did you get him to take anything?'

Saif shook his head.

'Me neither.' Mark rolled his eyes. 'Ornery bastard. Thanks for trying, Doc. And you and I,' he went on, pointing to Joel, 'we have work to do. Like, a *lot*.'

'Good luck,' said Saif, and slipped out. He hadn't even started morning surgery yet, and he had the boys to pick up later. This was turning into a very challenging day.

Saif was late up the hill to the little school at lunchtime, which wasn't strictly speaking Mrs MacCreed's fault. In the normal scheme of things, he didn't mind at all when she went on about her bunions. She came as often as their appointment system would allow, told him cheery stories about her grandchildren and how well they were doing, brought him a pie and beamed at him as he gave her foot a cursory examination. Then he reissued her prescription. He'd told her it could be done automatically either at reception, or, even more simply, delivered straight to the pharmacy, but she had got a very hurt look on her face and he realised that he was simply part of Mrs MacCreed's social rounds. Her children were on the mainland and her husband was long in the ground – the men worked themselves to death; the women, small and wide and wiry, somehow carried on, bent into the wind, for an incredible length of time – and she was lonely, and he hadn't mentioned it again. Today the pie was venison. There was meant to be an official cull on the deer but it was best not to ask where it had come from. Saif had been astounded deer were on the island at all, until he was informed the Vikings had imported them a thousand years ago. He felt sometimes like he was walking through a world of long ago. This pleased him.

But there really was no hurrying Mrs MacCreed.

His long legs stretched out as he sprinted the last few yards up the hill. It didn't occur to him to drive; he very rarely drove on the island, only to night calls, and it wasn't until he was halfway up that he thought he should probably have brought the car so he wouldn't be carrying Ash down the hill, but it was too late.

Lorna watched him, standing with a silent, trembling Ash by her side and a sullen Ibrahim, fists balled, a little further away. They were going to have to talk, but first she had to squeeze out of her head the sight of his strong powerful body in motion. For many, many nights she had lain, pondering on whether his chest was smooth or hairy; wanting to trace the dark hairs on the back of his hand up through his cuffs; wondering about his golden skin and how it would contrast so strongly with her pale . . .

She shook herself. This was completely pointless and entirely inappropriate, particularly so considering she was holding one of his offspring by the hand. She flushed bright red. Saif, looking up, thought she was angry.

'I'm so sorry,' he said. 'I'm genuinely so sorry. I got held . . .'

She shook her head, feeling obscurely that she should be apologising to him for the disgusting pictures of him she'd plastered all over the inside of her head while standing next

238

to his children. They didn't warn you about this in teacher training college.

'No, no, it doesn't matter. It's only lunchtime. We're not late.'

Saif bent down and opened his arms. Ash flew to him, dragging his bad foot behind him. Ibrahim stayed exactly where he was.

'So, uh, how did it go?' Saif asked desperately. It was a parental look Lorna recognised very well, although here it was slightly more important than usual. She bit her lip.

'Don't forget, it's just the start,' she said. 'Nobody expects this to be smooth straightaway.' She didn't know how to put it so she started with the positive. 'Ash mostly stayed very close to me.'

He hadn't unpeeled his fingers from her all morning. There were eleven children in the class; she still had to attempt to work with all of them. She had called in Seonaid MacPherson from the other class, who was eleven and big for her age, and she had managed to get Ash sat on her knee. Seonaid had very kindly gone through a baby book Lorna had dug up, pointing out 'cat', 'dog', 'ball' and so on and trying to get Ash to repeat the words. He hadn't repeated any of the words, but it was a start.

Ibrahim, on the other hand . . . She'd encouraged him to go play shinty with the other boys at playtime, and to her delight he had joined in, the boys making room for him willingly.

That had been until one of them, little Sandy Fairbairn, had tackled him, fairly gently, to take the ball, whereupon Ibrahim had leaped on top of him and started punching him hard in the face while screeching at him.

She had separated them immediately – shamefully, given her lack of Arabic, only able to yell, 'Stop, stop!' at Ibrahim – and comforted Sandy, who was more shocked than seriously hurt. She was dreading confronting his mother at home time. There was understanding and then there were cuts and bruises. And she wasn't enjoying this either.

Ibrahim was staring at the ground, refusing to meet his father's eyes.

'There was ... an incident,' she began, glancing at him. He looked up. He might not understand the words, but he knew she was dobbing him in, that much was clear, and his eyes burned with hatred.

Saif's face fell. Ibrahim looked frightened. Saif and Lorna shared a thought neither could voice. When they had been looked after by soldiers, how had that worked, exactly? What had the boys seen? Ibrahim had been two years in a world of war and violence and still didn't want to open up. Saif flashed back to Joel earlier that morning, all buttoned up. The boy became the man.

'I'll talk to the other child's mother,' said Lorna. 'But I'm afraid you'll have to make it clear ... '

She was worried she was sounding too teacher-like.

'Please,' she said. 'Please make it clear. They are both very welcome here. So welcome. But there are some things that could make it difficult, and violence is one of those things.'

Saif nodded. 'I understand. What they have been through ... '

'I know,' said Lorna. 'I realise that. Everyone does, I promise. But they can't hurt other children.'

Saif nodded again. 'I know. I know. I am sorry.'

Saif ended up taking the afternoon off – much to Jeannie's smirking lack of surprise, as she'd raised four kids and knew exactly what was going to happen – and he tried to bring lunch out into the garden, but the boys refused to eat the food and complained that it was too cold, even though the sun was shining. The boys were shivering and Saif realised in amazement how he'd got used to the weather. He ended up admitting defeat and opening the packs of fig rolls he'd stockpiled, which they ate silently. There had been three casseroles left on the doorstep, but he couldn't imagine them eating any of them. There was also a mystery package of teddy bears that was postmarked somewhere in England. Not a clue as to the sender, Saif had been entirely puzzled and considered throwing them away in case they were from racists or someone who wished them harm. However, Ash had caught sight of the parcel and had grabbed the small bear and was refusing to let it go, so he just had to apply Occam's razor and assume nobody had actually stuffed a bear with anthrax and sent it to a refugee child.

They sat back down inside.

'So,' he said tentatively. 'What do you think of school?'

'I stay with you, *Abba*,' said Ash decisively, from his place on Saif's knee. He was licking out the figs and discarding the biscuit. Saif wasn't sure this was as successful a weight-putting-on strategy as it might be.

'But you're a big boy now who goes to school!'

Ash shook his head.

'No. Me stay with *Abba*.'

It was as if he'd been frozen on the day his family disappeared: crystallised as a toddler. He held his son closer. He wanted to say, Of course. I will turn you back into a baby and we shall start over.

But he couldn't start over. The days had ticked relentlessly past – the months, the years – and they would never ever get those days back again. And there was no point wishing things could have been different. Everyone wished things could have been different.

He held the boy tight. 'You are my big boy,' he said and kissed him hard. 'And I will never ever leave you again except for school, I promise.'

The boy's little body relaxed a little.

'When Mama coming?' he said, sleepily.

## Chapter Forty-three

'No!' Mark said, shooting out a hand. 'I mean, this place! It's awesome! It's just ... I mean ... I thought living in the middle of nowhere ... It sounded like Alcatraz or something. I could never get my head round it. But *this* place ...'

Joel half-smiled. The Rock was perched at the very northern tip of the Endless Beach, and they were walking down it, slowly. He still felt a little fragile.

'It's not always like this,' he said, as two tiny puffs of cloud chased each other across the sky, and the water lapped far up the beach. It was high tide, and it was as if someone had filled up a bath between Mure and the mainland.

'I mean it's just ... it's just so ... clean. So pure. Look at the water!'

Joel nodded. 'Yes.'

'I can see ... I can see why ... Shoot, is that a heron?'

Joel let him walk on some more.

'Joel. Forget me being your friend. I'm not your friend right now, you have to understand that?'

Joel looked up and sighed. 'I just need sleep.'

'You need a lot of things.' Mark glanced around. 'This is better than any yoga class I've ever been to,' he said, mostly to himself. 'I have to bring Marsha out here. She thinks she'll evaporate if she ever leaves the island of Manhattan, but I think this would surprise her.'

'So, what's going to happen?' said Joel.

Mark sighed, and took his glasses off for a moment. His eyes were light brown: clever and penetrating. He looked much more direct and sharp without the spectacles, which gave him a distracted professorial air. Joel wondered briefly how much he really needed them, or how much they let him set up a barrier of professional affability.

'Well,' said Mark. 'That's really up to you, isn't it?'

'Saif thinks I had a nervous breakdown.'

'I agree with him.'

Joel blinked. 'That's . . . Professionally I had some bad news.'

'Well, that will happen,' said Mark. 'Most people develop some resilience to that kind of thing.'

Joel nodded. 'You also made a series of major life changes.'

'I move about a lot.'

'And this move was meant to be the opposite of that.' Mark looked at him carefully. 'This isn't a placement, Joel. You're not being judged on whether you can stay.'

Joel halted. 'Of course I fucking am,' he said. 'By every single last person here. Who don't think I'm good enough for their local princess.'

244

'Can you be?'

'You want me to be better.'

'I want you to get better,' said Mark. 'That's not the same thing at all.'

They walked on again.

'Is this what you want, Joel?' said Mark. 'Because until you're sure and until you're sorted, I don't think you should be breaking that nice girl's heart if you're going to flee again.'

Joel sighed. Everything he had wanted Mure to be felt like it was falling down around his ears. 'You think I should leave her alone ...'

'I just think you need a break from all distractions.'

'Flora's not a distraction.'

Mark didn't answer that. 'I think you just need some time to heal yourself first.'

Joel hated the neediness in his own voice as he said, 'Will you stay?'

'Everyone needs a holiday,' said Mark, beaming as the harbour came into view. 'Now, is there anywhere good to eat around here?'

'Oh God,' said Joel.

# Chapter Forty-four

Almost imperceptibly, a routine developed. Joel was forced to stay in bed until late, even though he protested he was a poor sleeper. He'd be made to eat a huge breakfast, then he and Mark would play Scrabble or read quietly in the empty hotel, before taking huge long walks covering the length and breadth of the island via its many hidden byways and long quiet roads. Mark had bought a sturdy stick and a large straw hat and looked ridiculous but incredibly happy, and both men grew brown under the sun. He kept trying to persuade Marsha to come out, but she refused, pretending she didn't want to leave Manhattan. In fact, Manhattan in summer was sticky and unpleasant, but she intuited that what the two men were doing together was incredibly important, and she wanted to give them every chance to get on with it by themselves.

Mark kept in touch with Flora – and spent plenty of money in the Seaside Kitchen – but kept her and Joel apart.

Joel was either going to come round and face up to things, he figured, or he wasn't, and he wanted to spare Flora as much pain as possible.

In fact, Flora was already in pain. She threw herself into where she knew she was needed: work. Annie's Seaside Kitchen was in very real danger of going under, and Flora was trying to solve its money problems by working harder and longer hours. She wasn't going to add to anyone else's worries by discussing it, but it was constantly on her mind. The holiday crowd was in full swing now, and she spent all day feeding people freshly baked cakes and scones; pies and pasties; endless coffees and thank goodness it got hot enough for them to sell a lot of cold drinks, a major source of their mark-up. She also decided she needed something else to do; Lorna was incredibly busy with the school end of term, and everything had been so tough for everyone.

Then Fintan wanted an engagement party, and how could she deny them that?

'Family rates,' Fintan had said. 'You'll give most of the food for free. I don't want it to look to Colton like we'd take advantage.'

Flora hadn't answered that. She desperately needed to take advantage of Colton Rogers, but she saw Fintan's point.

'Everyone tries to rip him off,' explained Fintan. 'I want him to see ... to realise ... that's not why.' He blushed.

'I know,' said Flora, wincing slightly. But of course they could do it. Of course she could, couldn't she?

'To be honest,' said Fintan, 'I've hardly seen him since we got engaged. And he looks really worried all the time. Do you think he thinks he's doing the wrong thing?'

'I think all American men are completely and utterly fucking useless,' said Flora, scattering flour to roll out dough. 'Next question?'

Colton in fact had finally agreed to meet up with Joel, who was feeling awkward about the fact that he was still living at the Rock.

Colton was looking thin and drawn as Joel knocked and let himself in.

'How are you?' Colton said.

Joel shrugged. He was aware he was the topic of conversation on the island, but he felt insulated from it, somehow. And putting down his laptop and his phone (Mark had threatened to flush it) was also doing him the world of good.

'How are you?' he asked in return. He still couldn't quite believe what Colton was planning.

Colton shrugged. 'Who cares?' he said. 'It might amaze you to know that you managed to finish all the paperwork before you had your ... little turn. I didn't realise I'd hired such a sensitive flower.'

Joel blinked. He didn't want to give Colton the satisfaction of showing him how awful he'd felt.

Colton shuffled his papers. 'So, let's cut the crap, Joel. This is happening whether you want it to or not. You've been with me this far. It's practically finished. There's no more work to be done ... for now.'

Joel nodded.

'But ...' Colton's face suddenly looked uncharacteristically vulnerable. 'I'd still like you to be my lawyer.'

There was a pause.

'Come on, Joel. Someone has to do it. I'd rather it was someone I trusted. Completely.'

Joel looked up at that.

'Please.'

Joel heaved a sigh. 'I can't . . . I can't work much.'

'That's okay. Do a little bit as and when. Stay in the Rock. Eat a lot of cream. You know I don't care about the expense.'

'Thank you.'

'No problem,' said Colton. 'All you have to do is back me.'

Joel closed his eyes. That was, indeed, a problem.

## Chapter Forty-five

The days continued to lengthen – and every single one of them, Saif dreaded once again going to school pick-up. Ibrahim was refusing to play at all with the other boys, who had done what children do naturally in such situations and withdrawn from him, even for shinty.

Ash was still showing no signs of becoming less clingy, although he had begun to say a few English words – 'dog' had come up, and 'sweeties' (Saif suspected major bribery on Mrs Laird's part, which would be correct). Saif was still so worried though. He was up all night doing paperwork he didn't get round to in the day and he barely thanked the old ladies who brought casseroles, even though he couldn't do without them. He also couldn't do without Mrs Laird, who, between looking after his boys and making her incredibly popular bread for the Seaside Kitchen, was working more hours than her arthritic knees could strictly handle. But he still couldn't get a smile out of either of the boys.

Ibrahim was only happy on the iPad, which was a terrible dependence Saif didn't have the first idea how to break. He'd taken them for their counselling classes on the mainland but they had just sat there, completely mute, Ash with his head once more in Saif's armpit. The psychologist had nodded and suggested that they meet by Skype from now on, which wasn't particularly making anything better.

Neda was coming in a week to check up on them. Saif was terrified she'd see what a pig's ear he was making of everything and take the little ones away. And his early morning walks of course had ceased, and he missed them. Now Lorna was his children's headmistress, it felt even harder to have her as a friend, and he was privately amazed by how much he missed her.

There had been one saving grace. The locum covered his on-calls several nights a week when he couldn't get babysitting. One wet and windy night, when she was meant to be on duty, she'd called him, having just half-severed one of her fingers in a bolognese incident.

The boys were both asleep; he didn't know what to do. Mrs Laird was visiting her sister in the Faroes. He tried Lorna first, then Flora, only to discover that apparently they'd gone to the pub together.

'I'll come down if you like,' said the friendly voice from the farmhouse, and Saif hadn't even known which brother it was until Innes turned up five minutes later, apologetically with Agot who'd caught wind that something was up and insisted on coming with him, whereupon both the boys had instantly got up too.

'Thanks so much for this,' said Saif, throwing on his coat and grabbing his bag.

'Aye, no worries,' said Innes.

Ash had been fascinated by the little girl instantly, and put out his hand to touch her white-blonde hair. Agot in her turn tried to grab his incredibly long eyelashes, which made him cry. Agot immediately started rubbing his back suspiciously hard, saying, 'THEAH, THEAH, DOAN CRY, DOAN CRY,' until eventually, to Saif's surprise, Ash repeated 'DOAN CRAH' and Innes and Saif swapped a thumbs-up.

'I'll stick on some cartoons,' said Innes.

Saif looked at him, genuinely touched. 'Thank you,' he said.

'Agot will watch anything as long as it flashes enough to give you a seizure.'

'I'm worried Ash will get a little . . . '

Indeed, seeing that Saif had put his coat on had made Ash very anxious, and he ran over to his father and put his arms around his knees.

'I'll be back very soon,' said Saif, trying to peel him off gently.

'NOT GO.'

'I'm coming back. I have to do my job.'

'ABBAAA!'

Saif looked at Innes apologetically.

'Ach, he'll be fine,' said Innes. 'We have plenty of lambs who are exactly the same.'

'Whom you then kill,' said Saif, then stopped when he saw Innes's face.

'I am joking,' he explained.

'Oh,' said Innes, who genuinely hadn't been sure.

'I have to stop joking in English,' said Saif.

'No, you should joke. It's good,' said Innes, smiling even as Ash started to yell and panic-breathe.

'There, there, young man, don't worry.'

'DOAN CRY!' Agot was back. 'DOAN CRY, BOY!'

There was a moment when Saif was minded to tell the locum to stitch up her own hand or basically just go anywhere where he didn't have to leave his family.

Innes nodded. 'They'll be okay,' he said roughly. 'You have to go sometime.'

'They need a dad.'

'The island needs a doctor. You're going to have to be both.'

Saif did the fastest stitching job of his life and handed over some painkillers to his wildly embarrassed locum, then drove at eighty miles an hour along the deserted country roads to get back to the house, his heart beating. How would Ash have coped? Would Innes have managed the screaming? What would they have done without him? Would they feel abandoned all over again? How much would this set him back? And the horrible, clawing thing at the back of his mind: could childhood trauma turn a grown man into . . .

Well, there was no point focusing on that now. None. He just hoped things weren't too . . .

As he entered the gloomy, foreboding house, a strange noise met his ears. Was it screaming? His heart rate surged and he ran forwards into the sitting room … There was nobody there. He turned round, in full flight or fight mode. Where was he? Where were they?

He followed the noise to the top bedroom, the spare room he'd earmarked for the boys, and entered.

There they were, bouncing furiously on the beds: Ash, on his injured foot, and Ibrahim, throwing himself about in an ungainly way, and Agot, who was screaming, amid fits of laughter from all three of them, 'BOUNCE, BOUNCE, BOUNCE!' and the boys were shouting 'BOUNZ! BOUNZ!' and then Ibrahim fell off and they all collapsed laughing.

Saif looked around for Innes, who was sitting in the corner, half asleep even through the racket.

'Hey,' he said, as the three noticed him.

'*ABBA!*' Ash was back in his arms immediately – but panting, out of breath. Ibrahim looked up, then his face shut down as he saw his father. Agot carried on bouncing.

'Well, I am guessing you are all fine,' said Saif, half cross, half delighted.

'MIDNIGHT FEAST?' suggested the little pagan Agot, but Innes carried her, complaining madly, down the hill, and Saif tucked the boys back into bed, and he lay sleepless until morning time contemplating the school uniforms he'd bought them that hung over the chair, which were made for ten- and six-year-old Scottish children, and made them look as if they were wearing sleeping bags.

Flora and Lorna had missed all this, propping up the bar in the Harbour's Rest.

'Crap,' said Flora, necking a gin and tonic. 'And now I'm apparently throwing a huge party I can't afford for Fintan and Colton to celebrate their perfect love.'

'He's still here though,' pointed out Lorna. Flora nodded. 'He is. Mark doesn't think it's a good idea we have a relationship till he's ... well. Till he's recovered.'

'Do you recover though?'

'Dunno,' said Flora. 'I think I shall also eat some peanuts. You know, Lorna, you can't miss what you never really had.'

'I do,' said Lorna crossly, accepting a handful of peanuts. They sat closer on their chairs.

'How are the boys doing?'

'Also awful. I am failing in every conceivable way.'

'You're fabulous!'

'I am getting older and older every single second, waiting for something to happen. And nothing's going to happen. I have to snap out of it.'

'More gin ...' Inge-Britt sorted it. 'Ooh!' said Flora.

'What?'

'You know who else is brilliant and single at the moment who isn't Saif?'

'This better not be one of your brothers.'

'It's ... Oh.'

'Seriously?'

'Come on. Innes is handsome. Apparently.'

'*Innes?* Seriously, Flora. I've known him since I was four.'

'So, you know he's a decent guy.'

'It's icky. Like Joey and Rachel in *Friends*.'

255

'Or maybe Ross and Rachel in *Friends* . . .'

'Which is also icky.'

'Oh yeah. Come on, let me marry off my brothers.'

Lorna thought about it. 'Flora. I've lived on this island thirty-two years. Innes has lived here thirty-five.'

'Ooh, you know how old he is! You must like him!'

'No, I've just been at every single birthday party he's ever had.'

Flora blinked.

'My point is: don't you think if we fancied each other, we'd have done something about it by now? There's nobody else here!'

'Well, maybe that's it. When you've been through everyone in the world and there's nobody left . . .'

'Seriously?' said Lorna.

'He's been single for ages! Agot and the business take up all his time.'

'What if we got together and broke up and you had to take sides?'

'I'd take yours,' said Flora. 'I've got loads of other brothers.' Lorna smiled. 'Oh, come on, are you telling me you find him disgusting?'

'I've just never thought of him that way,' said Lorna. Innes had been the heart-throb at school but she'd always spent so much time with Flora he'd just been the guy who'd teased her and called her Freckles and touched her plaits. She hadn't liked it one bit. But there was no doubt he was pretty much the pick of what was on offer.

'Plus it'd be weird,' she said. 'Agot will be coming up soon.'

Flora shook her head. 'She'll go on the mainland with her mother.'

'Are you sure? She's here a *lot*.'

'I know,' said Flora fondly. 'I will miss the little wildebeest.' She glanced at Lorna. 'Of course, if you snared her father . . .'

'Stop it, you big weirdo!'

'I just want someone to be happy! Except for Fintan and Colton: they're *too* happy.'

'So you want people to be happy but only to a certain Flora-acceptable extent?'

'This is why I will never run for parliament. Inge-Britt! Tell me what you do for men!'

'Are you stupid?' said Inge-Britt. 'What about the nuclear submarine out in the loch?'

'The what?' Lorna and Flora both said at the same time.

'Whoops!' said Inge-Britt serenely. 'I forget it's top secret.' She picked up the empty glasses. 'Those Russian sailors,' she whispered. 'Wowza.'

And she sashayed off, leaving Flora and Lorna looking after her in confusion and not a little envy.

## Chapter Forty-six

Joel squinted through his glasses as he and Mark took their constitutional. After the first day, they never spoke about Joel's health again. They spoke about books they'd read or baseball. Not a single thing that touched on what was happening or the future, what Joel would do or where he would go. Mark felt he had to decompress the boy within the man, and give him enough breathing space to figure out what to do after that. He was well aware this was a rich man's cure. He was equally well aware that he and Marsha both blamed themselves for not taking the boy in when he was young and raising him as their own. They should have done. If he wasn't having such a nice time, this would have felt like penance.

Up on one side of the fell on a bright breezy day, they came across a group setting up tents. Joel remembered the name in time. Charlie: Flora's ex, the one he'd met before. He was with a grumpy-looking woman with short hair and a large collection of young boys. He looked at them curiously. They were unkempt, many of them, with razor-short hair done cheaply and quickly; bitten fingernails and missing teeth and surly expressions.

Joel recognised them with a start. The hand-me-down T-shirts from goodwill stores. The slightly aggressive stance in children who had been just as likely to receive a blow as a kiss. A belligerent look on their faces that said that they didn't care what you were going to say to them; they'd heard worse. He looked at Mark, and Mark understood wordlessly and nodded at him to go forward.

Joel had heard Flora mention Charlie's work of course, and something about a wedding, but he had been in full work mode then and not paid attention. No. He was trying to be more honest with himself: he had heard perfectly well, but hadn't wanted to listen. Other lost boys were not his concern, and he'd suffered just as badly at the hands of other foster children as he had in other homes; they jeered at him for his bookish ways. There was always that ongoing sense of competition between them: who would get adopted? Who was getting too old to be charming?

Now it was as if he was seeing them for the first time, as he stood, alone in the world, scowling at it, just as the boys did.

Charlie smiled, his wide-open, uncomplicated face simply friendly and welcoming, and Joel suddenly wished savagely that Flora had married him after all so at least one of them could be happy. If she'd married him, he wouldn't have to worry about her any more, could be sad by himself.

'Morning!' said Charlie. 'Say hello to Mr Binder, everyone.'

'He-lloww, Misterr Binder,' chorused the boys sullenly.

Charlie came close. 'I heard ... I heard you'd been having a tough time of it.'

Joel shrugged. 'Honestly, it's nothing. I'm fine. Bit of overreacting.'

'Um, right,' said Charlie, rubbing the back of his head awkwardly. 'I must have got the wrong end of the stick.'

Joel could feel Mark looking at him, and took a deep breath.

'No,' he said. 'In fact, you didn't. I have been finding things pretty rough. Thanks for asking.' Mark beamed approvingly. 'This is my friend, Dr Philippoussis.'

The fierce-looking woman marched up. 'Who's this?' she barked.

'Um, this is Joel and Dr ...' Charlie was not used to Greek names and rather let it peter out. 'And this is my ... uh, my wife, Jan.'

Jan looked him up and down.

'You're Flora's American,' she announced. 'I thought you'd have had a bit more meat on your bones. Like my Charlie,' she said smugly. Joel remembered now that Flora didn't like her, which was puzzling, as Flora generally liked everyone, like a Labrador. But he was beginning to see her point.

'Are you off?' she said. 'You're on mental health leave, aren't you?' She could not have picked a worse term. Joel's face tightened. 'Excellent! We can use you round here. Get your DBS check, and come and join us. Here, I'll drop the forms in.'

'Excuse me, what?'

'We need volunteers! We always need volunteers! Come and help us with the boys.'

'Oh, no, I ... I don't think so.'

Mark coughed meaningfully.

'Everyone else on this island has two jobs. You have none. Seems about right, don't you think? Don't worry; we won't make you do anything mentally taxing or stressful. Just put up some tents and cook some sausages.'

'I don't think it would be appropriate.'

'Or maybe it's your moral imperative,' said Jan in that direct way of hers that brooked no argument.

'This is Joel, who's going to come and help out,' she announced to the boys, all of whom cheered.

'Oh, I really don't ... I really don't ... '

'I'll drop the forms in to the Rock. Bye!'

Jan marched on. Charlie looked at Joel apologetically.

'Is she always like this?' Joel couldn't help asking.

'She gets stuff done,' said Charlie.

'I like her,' said Mark, rubbing his beard.

## Chapter Forty-seven

'Do you know who fancies you madly?'

Flora was in one of those moods when she got home, and she'd had another gin and tonic. She was meant to be cooking for all the family but it wasn't working too well. Hamish was off again in his ridiculous sports car, it being a Friday night, and her father had decided that if she was to come up to the house smelling of gin in a way that would make her mother's eyes roll in her head (it would not have done this), then he was going to have a whisky.

Innes had just arrived, Agot marching ahead. It was true, Flora thought, a little fuzzily. Agot was here a lot more now. She realised Eilidh was busy with her full-time job on the mainland and Innes being his own boss made it easier for him to have her around – plus she'd been raised on the farm, and Mure was the kind of place where everyone kept an eye on everyone else's children. Even so.

'I BORED,' announced Agot. 'I WAN SISTER.'

'You've got me,' said Flora ingratiatingly. Agot looked her up and down.

'YOU ATTI,' she said crossly. 'AND YOU OLD ALSO.'

'Also' was Agot's new word. Flora wasn't sure she approved.

'Agot,' said Innes. 'Behave.'

'AGOT NOT BEHAVE ALSO.'

Flora deftly cut her a piece of the new bread and spread it thickly with butter. 'I think *Robot Wars* is on,' she said optimistically. *Robot Wars* was Agot's new favourite show as she now felt *Peppa Pig* was for unsophisticated babies.

'KILLBOT LIVES!' shouted Agot, marching into the underused front room to turn on the old television set. Innes watched her go.

'So anyway, back to this person who fancies you madly,' said Flora, chopping onions for curry, which her father disapproved of. She thought about adding extra chillies, then thought of an evening of Agot complaining and decided against it.

'Who?' said Innes, with a puzzled look. It was true: in his youth he'd been through half the island. 'I mean, someone I don't "know"?'

Flora smiled annoyingly.

'Stop being annoying.'

'Flora being annoying?' said Fintan, coming through the door wearing a new, incredibly expensive-looking man bag, which he placed reverently down on one of the ancient threadbare armchairs. 'That doesn't sound like her, except for every day.'

'Shut up, Fintan,' said Flora, kissing him on the cheek.

263

'Oh God, hark at the metropolitans,' said Innes, rolling his eyes.

'Someone fancies Innes, and he's so old now he's forgotten what it's like,' said Flora, embracing Colton who'd come in just behind. He was looking tired, but was clutching a bottle of wine a client had given him as a parting gift that they would drink that evening without checking the label – and none of them would ever find out that it was an incredibly rare vintage worth approximately £8,000.

'Well, I'm not surprised,' said Colton.

'HEY!' shouted Fintan, batting him on the lapels.

'What? I'm being gentlemanly. You don't want me to say, Christ, your family look like raccoons.'

'I want you to say everyone in the world looks like a raccoon next to me,' said Fintan, mock-crossly, then they kissed and everyone rolled their eyes.

'Stop it!' said Flora. 'Or I'm cancelling your party.'

'A lady fancying Innes,' said Fintan. 'How strange and unusual.'

He came over, tasted Flora's curry sauce and stuck a heap of extra chilli in it. She hit him on the hand with a wooden spoon.

'Who is it? Mrs Kennedy? Apparently she can take out her false teeth.'

'Shut up, Fintan,' said Innes.

'Well, you are getting on a bit. Mrs McCreedie? If you like a sheepskin bootee, she's the one for you.'

'Actually,' said Flora. 'It's someone you know very well.'

Innes grimaced. 'It's not one of your crazy friends from the mainland again, is it?' he said. 'They're all completely weird and they talk total shit and have stupid hair.'

'I think what you mean there is they're contemporary and fashionable,' said Flora.

Innes snorted. 'Aye, that'll be right.'

'Fine,' said Flora. 'Don't find out.'

'Just invite her to the barbecue,' said Fintan. 'And we can spot her then.'

# Chapter Forty-eight

'Are you sure you're really going to throw an actual barbecue for the party? I don't know anyone who even has one.'

There was a superstition on Mure and indeed many of the islands that to buy anything deliberately intended for outdoor use was simply tempting fate: storms, power cuts and torrential rain. If you wanted to barbecue something, you could use bricks and an old grill like everybody else; you were mad to try something different. It was arrogance that would simply invoke the wrath of the gods.

'Colton's bringing one over. Apparently he has a top-of-the-range, blah, blah ...'

'Colton is bringing a barbecue to your house?' Lorna frowned. 'Why don't you just go to Colton's? *And* he's got flunkies and things.'

Flora shrugged and Lorna remembered that Joel was up there, and changed the subject. 'It will hose it down.'

'It might not.'

'You're planning something for two days away. You're a crazy person.'

'I know,' said Flora. 'But on the other hand ... Come to the barbecue. Toast the happy couple. Have a couple of beers. Stand close to Innes. Eat a sausage in a suggestive manner.'

'Flora!'

Lorna couldn't deny it though. She was so lonely. The idea of dressing up nicely to go and do something glamorous ... Well, not glamorous, but something ...

'What were you going to be doing?' asked Flora annoyingly.

'Bundle up in my raincoat, watching the rain pound against the windows,' said Lorna. 'That is exactly what I'm going to be doing.'

'See you there,' said Flora. 'Wear something sexy.'

'My pink fleece or my brown fleece?'

'Just make sure you've unzipped the top bit as far down as you can.'

'To reveal my other fleece underneath?'

'Something like that.'

'Don't let me stop you going,' said Joel.

'You're not going? I know I said you should be careful of Flora, but this is a big event.'

'I said I'd help out with the boys today.'

Joel couldn't face seeing Colton and Fintan so happy. He just couldn't.

Mark frowned. 'And what might Flora say to that?'

267

Joel shrugged.

'Don't you think you should tell her?' Mark's tone was gentle, but firm. 'I think you've had enough time apart now. Don't make her wait for you, Joel, if you can't be there.'

Joel knew he wasn't just talking about the barbecue.

Saif was just so damned tired. All the time. It was just one thing after another. He hadn't really thought about how much Amena and his mother had done for the children at home; hadn't really appreciated how much they'd tended to their needs while he'd at first gone to work, then later worked hard constantly on figuring out how to get them away and to safety. He thought of those long days in the market square; the low voices and misinformation; the selling of everything they had to sell. The planning and the fear.

But it was the day-to-day stuff he couldn't figure out now. He'd thought he was prepared for the mental anguish, the pain and the difficulty. He wasn't at all prepared for Ash sitting on the corner of his bed, refusing to get up and instead pulling the Velcro on his tiny trainers to and fro, every noise like a wire brush on Saif's brain, no matter how often he told him to stop, or threatened to take the trainers away. Which he couldn't, of course: Ash's huge eyes would fill with tears, and the idea of depriving him of anything, or making him unhappy in any way at all suddenly seemed utterly unbearable.

So they would start over. And he also faced an internal battle about tearing Ibrahim away from his iPad, when it was the only thing he wanted to do … He had succeeded, though, in switching it to English, which was something, he supposed. But every day he approached the school hoping for better news, and every day Lorna was too kind to tell him that he would have to stop carrying Ash everywhere, for everyone's sake, and that the boys still weren't accepting Ibrahim, who lashed out when anyone went anywhere near him, and how she wished she knew what to do, she really did, and it must only be time, mustn't it?

The Thursday before the barbecue was a glorious evening and Saif decided to walk the boys down to the harbour front and buy them some chips and Irn-Bru. He couldn't personally stomach Irn-Bru, even without knowing what was in it, but he understood that it was part of Scottish religion, and respected that. Hot vinegary chips, though, reminded him of the spiced fried potatoes they used to get at home, and he had developed a fondness for them and wanted to introduce the boys. Ibrahim mooched down the hill, looking as if going for a treat on a beautiful day was the single worst thing that could possibly happen to him.

Outside in the queue – for plenty of Murians had had the same idea on such a glorious evening – was Innes, holding Agot by the hand.

'Hey,' said Saif, wondering how Innes, who looked to be a single father to all intents and purposes, managed everything – his job and his daughter – while still looking so at ease in his own skin. Perhaps it just came naturally to some people. Perhaps he had just been a fool for thinking it would come easily to him. 'Thanks again for the other night.'

'ASSSHHHH!' yelled Agot.

And then, in the queue, Ash did the most unexpected thing. He clambered out of Saif's arms of his own volition.

He limped over to where Agot was jumping up and down.

'CHIPS, CHIPS, CHIPS!' Agot was yelling in excitement.

Ash grinned. He'd lost one of his front teeth, which made him look very comical. Then, all of a sudden, 'CHIPS, CHIPS, CHIPS!' he shouted, in a perfect imitation of her broad islands accent.

'KETCHUP ALSO!' hollered Agot.

'KETCHUP ALSO!' echoed Ash.

'Goodness,' said Saif, completely taken aback. Innes smiled distractedly. Agot bossing around other children she'd met was hardly a new experience for him.

'Oh, it's nice they're getting on ... Things going better then?'

Saif was overwhelmed with the desire to say, 'Awful, unbearable, how does anyone cope?' Then he glanced at the two children, Agot a little hopping imp, Ash desperately trying to imitate her.

'Well, you know,' he said weakly.

'We were just heading to the harbour wall,' said Innes in his easy way. 'Want to join?'

Innes never knew how much that simple invitation meant to Saif. A simple outstretched hand of friendship, meant without expectation, neither intrusively nosey, nor desperately worried about saying the right thing. It was just one chap to another, with no agenda. Saif had lived with nothing but other people's agendas for so long: the sheer banality of the invitation made him want to weep.

'Sure,' he said.

So they bought chips and Irn-Bru, except Agot wanted something called Red Kola, so of course Ash wanted it too, and got it, and Saif offered some to Ibrahim too, who shrugged and said he didn't care, which Saif realised meant he desperately wanted some, and they all took the steaming paper-wrapped parcels and crossed the cobbled street to the sea wall. They sat, watching the children on the little harbour beach, shouting at Agot every time she tried to feed the seagulls who swooped around the children and looked entirely huge and alarming enough to carry them away.

'I'S WANTS SEAGULL CARRY ME!' shouted Agot, holding up her arms, whereupon Ash did so too, the chips fell to the ground and there was quite the kerfuffle getting everything sorted out again and drying tears and replacing the chips. But it was, Saif realised, a normal sort of fuss – the kind of thing that would happen to any family, any parent, out with children – and he was deeply and profoundly grateful.

'We're having a barbecue on Sunday,' said Innes casually. 'To celebrate my brother getting engaged. Bring them if you like.'

Something struck him.

'Oh, but also he's getting engaged to a big hairy American bloke so I don't know if ...'

Saif smiled tightly. He knew people meant well, but he didn't like the implication that because he wasn't from there he was automatically a bigot. Innes registered this immediately.

'Sorry, I mean, some of the old buggers around here have been very weird about it.'

Saif nodded. 'How is your father?'

'Oddly cheerful,' said Innes, eating a chip. 'I think he just wants us to get out of the sodding house.'

'YOU COME MY HOUSE?' said Agot to Ash. Ash nodded.

'Yes,' he said.

'Did you understand that?' said Saif in Arabic, crouching down. 'Did you?'

'He's not stupid,' said Ibrahim.

'Did you?' said Saif.

'YES!' shouted Ash in English.

Saif blinked in amazement. This was ... this was amazing.

'Well, uh, well, I'll be off,' said Innes.

'Oh, yes, sorry,' said Saif, immediately reverting to English. 'Thank you.'

And he meant it more than he could convey.

# Chapter Forty-nine

Annie's Seaside Kitchen was quiet, the girls gone, everything cleaned and polished and put back, ready for another day tomorrow. Flora was sitting alone at a rickety table in the corner of the room with a calculator and a mounting sense of panic. She put down her tea and glanced up as there was a knock on the door. Sometimes a hopeful wet tourist would swing past after closing time, and sometimes, if she was in a better mood than this, she'd whip them up a quick coffee and piece of flan and send them on their way happy.

But not tonight. She shook her head, then the visitor knocked again. It wasn't until she looked up that she realised it was Joel.

'Hey,' she said, swallowing hard as she turned the old Yale key. Her heart was beating. Was he here to declare himself? To tell her how much he missed her, how he just wanted to devote himself to her, how he'd made a mistake?

He was looking better, she realised, with something of a

pang. There was some colour back in his cheeks. Fresh air was obviously doing him good. She wanted more than anything to run her fingers through his curly hair. He leaned in to kiss her and she did too, but they both aimed badly, and he ended up half on her cheek and half in her ear and she went bright red immediately and jumped back.

'Uh, hi,' he said.

Flora stood aside to let him come in.

'What are you up to?'

Flora shrugged. 'Just looking at ... accounts and things.'

She wished she had some make-up on. She hadn't had a second all day, that was the problem. She never stopped.

Joel looked at the dusting of flour she had across her forehead and wanted more than anything to gently wipe it off, take her head in his hands ... but no. As Mark said, he had to get himself well.

'How ... how are the accounts?'

Flora suddenly wanted to burst into tears. She was so tired getting everything ready for Sunday, and the one person she wanted was standing in front of her like an accountant giving her an audit.

'Awful, if you must know.'

Joel blinked. 'But you're always so busy!'

'You can talk ... Sorry,' Flora added quickly.

'It's okay ...' He glanced at the computer. 'Can I take a look?'

Flora's eyes widened. He'd never shown much interest in the business before. 'Um, sure,' she said.

'How old is this laptop? Do I have to wind it up at the back?'

'Joel ...'

'It's heavier than you.'

'Glad something is.'

Joel smiled, and it shot through Flora like a dart. Then he wiped his glasses on a clean white napkin, and bent his head.

Flora went through the back to the kitchen, finishing the last of the day's chores and the first of the new day's prep. She made them a coffee, not because she wanted one but because she couldn't think of anything else to do. Then she went back into the main room. It was gently lit. The evening was light but grey, and the round old-fashioned lamp posts on the harbour were glowing softly from beyond the window panes. She briefly leaned her head against the window frame and looked at him. He was as engrossed as ever – as far away, she thought, as ever.

'Here.'

Joel looked up and smiled. 'Thank you. But I'm off coffee.'

'Oh. Really?'

'Coffee, wine, processed food ... Basically Mark's got me eating grass and animal fats and that's about it.'

'Okay ...'

She fetched him a glass of water, just as he took his glasses off and sighed.

'Flora ...'

Her heart leaped. 'What?'

'Flora ... this can't go on. It isn't ... It can't work.'

Flora steadied herself against the counter. Everything was coming tumbling down. Everything was over. Just as she had known it would, just as she'd suspected all along.

'Look,' he was saying. 'Look at your inventory. Look at

your stock control. You can't . . . I mean your portion control is a disaster. Look at this.'

He beckoned her over, but she couldn't trust her limbs to move. 'I thought you were a lawyer,' she said.

'Yeah, good luck to corporate lawyers who can't read a profit and loss account,' said Joel. He looked up at her. 'I mean, you could get cash in, but it would be like putting water in a leaky bucket.'

Flora nodded, biting her lip.

'I mean, you make far more pastries than you sell every week. Why aren't you just making fewer?'

Flora stared hard at the ground. She didn't want to tell him: because she needed something to give Teàrlach's boys.

'And why are you even paying near market value for produce from your family farm?'

'Because your bloody boss hasn't opened the hotel yet, which would allow us all to make a living,' said Flora, her face hot. Joel blinked but didn't comment.

'I mean, you're just charging far, far too little. For everything. Do you really need three different types of sausages?'

Well, she did, Flora thought crossly, because not everyone on Mure ate pork any more, and he should know that.

'But . . . but people are spending their pensions in here,' she said. 'There are young mums . . . and you know what farming is going through.'

'Yes, but you're packed out with rich holidaymakers. Presumably they could spend a bit more.'

'We can't do that,' said Flora. 'We can't have one price for local people and one for tourists.'

Joel arched an eyebrow. 'I don't see why not.'

'Because it's illegal, Mr Lawyer-person.'

'Well, there are ways around that ...'

'I just want to run a good business!'

'I want you to do that too, Flora. I just ... You know I want good things for you.'

And? thought Flora desperately. And? And what else?

'Listen, I'll ... Can I send you an email with some thoughts?'

'I don't need rescuing.'

He stopped short at that, and half-smiled. 'I can't even rescue myself,' he said. 'But there are things you could do. Lots. Positive things. Think about it. Please?'

Flora nodded mutely as he stood up to go.

'Oh,' she said at the door, yearning to take his hand and bury her head in his chest, even though Mark had made it delicately clear that they both needed space. 'Why ... why did you come by?'

Joel put his coat back on. 'I ... I can't come to the party on Sunday,' he said. 'Sorry.'

Her face fell. She had hoped ... just a little ... that he would turn up, see how brilliantly everything was going and what a happy time everybody was having and he'd want to join in and ... Joel joining in. That was a stupid thought, for starters.

'Okay,' she said. 'Thanks for the tips.'

'You're welcome,' he said, and ducked out into the pale-grey foggy evening, and she lost sight of him before his footsteps faded from earshot.

# Chapter Fifty

Saif was still anxious, but not quite as terrified as he had been, when Neda showed up later that week.

His optimism, as they went down to the harbour to collect Neda from the ferry, faded fast. She emerged, tall and glamorous-looking, by the quayside next to the bearded walkers and excited Americans clutching their bumbags. She stood and looked around.

It was a glorious morning, cold and breathtakingly fresh, like a glass of iced water. The chilly waves danced in the light. She blinked, pulled on a large pair of sunglasses and walked up the jetty towards them, her heels clacking loudly on the cobblestones.

Instantly Ash was trembling in Saif's arms, and Ibrahim turned away, back to his iPad.

'It's Neda!' said Saif encouragingly. 'She's nice!'

Ash was still shaking.

'What is it?'

The little boy muttered something that Saif strained to hear, even as Neda leaned over. She shook her head.

'No,' she said. 'Listen to me, Ash. I'm not here to take you back.'

Saif gasped that he would think that. Ash was still flinching, and the tears were running down his face as Neda straightened up again.

'I'm just visiting! I have presents for you!'

But Saif couldn't hear her. He had turned his face away. It felt ridiculous now he was even thinking about it, but nonetheless it was true. There was a tiny part of him that had also worried that maybe they would want to go back. That anywhere would be preferable to living with him. He suddenly felt overwhelmed and grabbed Ash close. Neda glanced at him shrewdly, then smiled.

'Look at this amazing place!' she said. 'Now, is there anywhere you can get a cup of coffee? We need to sit down to unwrap presents!'

Ibrahim lagged behind as Saif showed her up the harbour walkway towards Annie's Seaside Kitchen, where many of the grateful disembarkees – the ones who were home and the ones who'd been warned of poor food on their journey – simply couldn't believe their luck. She turned to Saif and smiled broadly and spoke in English.

'Did you seriously think they'd rather come back with me?'

Saif blinked twice. 'Only for a second.'

She shook her head. 'Honestly. Did you really think they'd be here for five minutes and everything would be rainbows and fairy tales?'

Saif's shoulders sagged. 'But it's so, so hard.'

'Welcome to parenting,' said Neda.

Saif smiled weakly. 'But I can't put Ash down, or get Ibrahim off his iPad.'

Indeed, the boy was walking, staring at the screen, oblivious to everything around him.

'What do you mean, you can't?'

Saif looked at her.

'Just put Ash down.' They had crossed the quiet road and were walking up the pavement towards the Seaside Kitchen, in its little pink building. Neda looked at him. 'Do it!'

'Um, I don't think he wants to go down.'

'He doesn't want to eat his vegetables either, am I right?'

Saif winced. 'One thing at a time.'

Neda shook her head. 'Doesn't work that way I'm afraid, my friend. You can't fight every battle. Just fight one.'

'Which one?'

'The "do as I say" one.'

Saif laughed. 'I don't think so.'

They headed up the road, Saif aware everyone was looking at them.

'Well, you're a doctor. What would you recommend?'

'I would recommend people do not come and visit me for child-rearing advice.'

Neda tutted. 'Come on. What would you say?' Saif shrugged. Neda lowered her voice. 'What would Amena say?'

It was a low blow, and Saif winced a little. 'There is no news?' he said quickly.

Neda shook her head. 'I'm sorry, Saif. But if she were here . . . '

280

'She would say, "Ash, you are a big boy, you have to walk."'

'Mm . . . ' said Neda.

They took another couple of steps. Then Saif whispered in Ash's ear. 'Darling. I'm going to put you down, so you can walk and make your leg all nice and strong.'

Ash's little jaw jutted out and he immediately got a steely look in his eye. 'No, *Abba*.'

'I'm afraid so,' said Neda. 'We're going to the coffee shop to get treats and presents. Want to come?'

She indicated to Saif, who put Ash on the ground. Ash immediately started to scramble back up his trouser leg. For an underfed six-year-old with a damaged foot, he was surprisingly strong. Neda watched Saif to see what he would do, and Saif found himself red and conscious that this was a test – not for Ash, but for him.

Saif uncurled the little fingers, even though it felt unbearably cruel. Ash screamed all the louder. This was great, thought Saif, growing red, Ash having the mother of all crazed screaming tantrums in the middle of the high street, on the thronged harbour, on an early Friday morning. The number of people on the island who wouldn't have heard about the doctor's deranged child by lunchtime was practically negligible.

'Right, let's go,' said Neda. She smiled cheerily at Ash. 'We'll see you in there. I hope they have buns. I love buns, don't you?'

Ash continued howling, his face bright red, his good leg hitting the pavement. Neda kept smiling.

'Am I just supposed to walk away? When he's upset?'

Neda shrugged. 'It's up to you, Saif.' She lowered her

voice. 'It might make things trickier, you know, in the long run, if you can't treat him like a normal kid.'

'He isn't a normal kid.'

But Neda was already marching on. Saif felt torn, looking at the little boy having a paddy on the pavement and the tall, confident woman striding ahead of him.

Saif took a pace towards Neda. There was a pause and suddenly, just for a moment, the screaming let up, as Ash glanced up to take in the new situation. Then he resumed, louder. Saif looked pained.

Neda pushed open the door of Annie's Seaside Kitchen, which dinged loudly.

'MMM,' said Neda loudly in English. 'LOOK AT ALL THESE CAKES.'

This time, the pause in the screeching was much longer. Ibrahim blindly followed Neda. Saif allowed himself another step.

'What kind of muffin are you going to have, Ibrahim?'

Well, this was too much for any six-year-old to bear. The idea of Ibrahim being allowed to choose a big cake all to himself while he was left out on the pavement was an injustice too far. Ash picked himself up and ran, tearfully, to the door.

Flora was regarding them with a slightly puzzled expression on her face, particularly as Neda was holding the door and blocking the way out for three backpackers and their gigantic backpacks, which were now getting in the way of Mrs Blair's new shampoo and set which she'd come down to show off, so that was pleasing absolutely nobody.

Then Flora looked through the window and saw the

boys – she'd seen them in passing of course, but hadn't met them officially. She broke into a grin and beckoned them in. And even with Joel's dire warnings echoing in her ears, she couldn't help but bring out a couple of lollipops she had secreted away.

'Welcome,' she said. 'Welcome, all of you.'

Ash's sobs had slowed to the occasional whimper by the time they were all sitting down, and Mrs Blair's shampoo and set had been patted back into position, but, to Saif's astonishment, Neda didn't let up at all.

'I know how you feel,' she said, as Isla brought over two flat whites. 'Wow,' she added. 'Thanks!'

Flora was always faintly insulted by the patronising way people reacted to the fact that she sold good coffee – she resented the assumption that everyone who lived in the islands was some kind of hunkering rube who thought instant was a treat.

Neda continued, 'And I don't want to lecture, but for the moment, at least, you have to be mother and father to those boys.'

'You mean tell them off.'

Neda shrugged. 'Again, it's up to you.'

'You say "it's up to you" when you mean "do as I say",' said Saif, smiling.

'Do I?' said Neda, biting into an iced finger. 'Oh my goodness, this is terrific.' She turned to Ibrahim, who was slouching in his seat and, as usual, staring at the iPad in front of him, then looked back at Saif.

Saif sighed and leaned over. 'Ibrahim. I need to take your iPad.'

Ibrahim went wide-eyed. 'You can't,' he said. 'It's mine.'

'While we're in the café.'

'Until she goes?'

'She is Neda, please.'

'Until Neda goes?'

'Just give it to me now.'

Everyone sat looking tense at the table, except for Ash, who had a bun in one hand and the lollipop in the other and had quite forgotten his bad mood.

'What lovely boys you are,' said Neda cheerfully. 'Now, are you going to show me your school?'

Flora smiled as she watched the boys leave. Saif made them turn and lisp awkward thank yous to her. Ibrahim was his double, she saw. He had the exact same furrowed brow and grave expression on his face. Ash was a beautiful child, with long eyelashes. But both the boys were too thin. She would fix that, she vowed. A few more cheese scones. Ugh, no, she had to make the scones smaller ... Oh, why was it so hard?

🦅 🦅

Ash managed to make it halfway up the hill before collapsing in dramatic fashion and declaring himself utterly exhausted. Neda asked him to say it in English, which to Saif's amazement he absolutely could. She laughed at his face and said, not to worry, she knew plenty of full-time fathers who also found this kind of thing incredibly tricky, which made Saif relax a little and find his own smile at Ash's dramatic over-acting, which is why the first time Lorna saw them approaching from the staffroom window, the two boys walking, Ibrahim without his iPad, and the beautiful, tall woman walking next to Saif, her heart dropped right into her boots.

She certainly never made him smile like that, or laugh so his white teeth showed. They were a good-looking couple too, she thought. Who was she? It couldn't be ... It wasn't as if Saif couldn't have found a girlfriend, was it? After all, he'd meet someone one day, right? But she had comforted herself so much by thinking that he was just too loyal, too respectful to his wife, to ever ...

'Hello!' said Saif. He was definitely in a better mood than he had been the last few weeks when he'd been exhausted and strung out, picking up his furious, uncommunicative children, watching with a parental heartbreak Lorna recognised very well as his children were left out of playground games, unpicked, alone in the corner of the school.

Today his face was sunnier, more open, and Ash – was that child walking? Lorna had never seen him on the ground before. She waited for him to try and cling to her as he usually did, but instead – and this stung frightfully – he held the tall woman's hand.

'Lorenah. Miss MacLeod,' said Saif, smiling. 'This is Neda Okonjo. She's the social worker who's helping us ... She looked after the boys in Glasgow.'

'Hello,' said Lorna, more stiffly than she meant. She hadn't realised social workers were quite so glamorous these days. Saif wondered why she was being weird.

'Hello,' said Neda. 'Hey, I think you're doing a great job with the boys.'

Lorna blinked. She, personally, had not been thinking that at all. She'd been worried she was failing them desperately. She couldn't get them to say a word of English, or join in, or respond to anything.

'They understand everything we're saying already!' said Neda. 'Great job.'

Lorna frowned. 'Do they?'

'Look at Ibrahim,' said Neda, grinning. The boy immediately flushed and stared at the ground.

'He's pretending he doesn't understand. But he does. He's a very handsome boy.'

Ibrahim blushed even more. Saif couldn't believe it.

'And he's much better at football than he thinks he is.'

'You're a miracle-worker,' said Lorna.

'No. You are,' said Neda. 'Trust the process. Both of you. Trust how clever the boys are and how much they're taking in, even when they don't realise it. Treat them like the other boys. Please. No more carrying.'

Lorna nodded.

'No letting Ibrahim on computers. If he can manage not to hit anyone – eh, Ibrahim? No hitting?'

Ibrahim shrugged.

'Let's make a deal. I bet if you stop it, you'll be playing football with everyone in a week.'

'Don't care.'

'In English.'

And he did. 'I don't care,' he said, pink to the ears.

'You don't have to care,' said Neda softly. 'You just need to play.'

And the bell rang, and for once the children disappeared

inside the school building on their own, getting caught up in the little stream of boys and girls, getting lost in it – just like normal children going about their day. And Saif and Lorna stared at each other in disbelief.

'Right,' said Neda, turning round. 'Let's have a look at the home set-up. Don't worry, I'm just ticking boxes. You're obviously going to be fine.'

'You're amazing,' said Lorna, glancing back towards her classroom.

'Well, it was nice to meet you too,' said Neda and she turned round and marched off down the hill, Saif turning to follow her, in awe, and Lorna reflected that she'd fallen in love with Neda in ten seconds flat, and she didn't blame Saif in the slightest if he'd just done exactly the same thing.

# Chapter Fifty-one

Joel woke up early, feeling trepidatious, like it was his first day at school. Of course it was already light outside. He realised it was at least a month since they'd had to put any lights on at all. Such a strange sensation.

He clambered into the 'rugged' clothes his secretary Margo had bought him last year. They didn't feel right at all – he preferred a well-cut suit, as armour, something that allowed him to vanish subtly into the background of any room he was in. The moleskin trousers and the rough-hewn pale checked shirt with a waterproof lining felt odd. Also, putting them on, he became conscious of how much weight he'd lost and grimaced. Then he set out into a misty morning, the grey haar obliterating all distinction between land and sea; the kind of morning, in fact, that often burned off into a glorious afternoon, but it made heavy weather of the first part of the day. He took the piece of paper which had arrived the day before.

Grabbing a coffee, he set out up the hill. That he was working with Flora's ex-boyfriend, and her arch-enemy, hadn't escaped him. He was aware he hadn't mentioned it in the café. She had looked so disappointed that he wasn't going to the party, he didn't want to make matters even worse.

Not knowing the way, as it turned out, was no problem: the bright orange tents and screams and yells of the boys were visible and audible from miles away, as was the scent of sizzling sausages on the fire.

Charlie was there, on his own third cup of coffee, typically weary as he always was. Every group of troubled youngsters had a bedwetter and some tiny fiends who liked to tell horror stories, although many of them had already lived through their own horror stories. He nodded to Joel, taking in – in a way that surprised Joel mightily – the expensiveness of his outdoor clothing.

'Morning.'

'Hey.'

Joel felt awkward. He held out his envelope. 'I brought this.'

Charlie just tipped his head. 'Give it to Jan. She handles all the paperwork.'

'Who are you, mister?'

A small boy of about eight or nine was standing in front of him. His head, which might have been blond, was shaved down to the wood, his body was skinny and none too clean-looking and there were dark hollows under his eyes. His posture was defensive; he had the look about him of a kid that was always waiting for a telling-off.

'I'm Joel,' he said mildly. They looked at each other. Joel wasn't about to say anything else. Adults asking questions was probably more than this kid ever needed.

'Are you American?' said the boy, eyes widening. 'You sound weird.'

'Yes, I'm from America originally.'

'What are you doing in this shithole then?'

'Caleb,' said Charlie, but in a relaxed way. 'What did we say about swearing?'

'Shit isn't swearing,' said the lad. 'Fuck is swearing.'

'No, shit definitely counts.'

'Oh. Sorry.' He readdressed his question. 'Why are you in a poo-hole like this?'

'I happen to like it,' said Joel.

'Like it more than America? With like sunshine and guns and cars with no tops on and California and skyscrapers and stuff?' The kid's eyes widened further.

'It's not all like that.'

'It's naaat allll laaak that.' The child tried out a dreadful imitation of Joel's drawl, then called the others. 'Aye! Ye gadgies! Yon mon here's a Yank!'

Other shaved heads emerged. Joel knew on one level that small boys having short hair simply made practical sense. But his hair was always shorn when he was a boy because nobody loved him enough to comb it. He'd worn his dark curls longer than was usual for a lawyer, long enough to flop over his high forehead, ever since. Flora adored it, and would have loved it even more if she'd known the reason why.

The boys gathered around Joel as an object of

curiosity, and Joel wished he'd brought some sweets to hand out. They all wanted to know about gangs and guns and the streets and all sorts of notions and appeared to have picked up most of their American assumptions from playing *Grand Theft Auto*, but he helped as much as he could. He noticed Charlie watching him, not in a disapproving fashion.

Jan arrived, looking scrubbed down as usual.

'Hand over that,' she said, gesturing at the envelope in his hands, and he did so. 'Right,' she said, studying it carefully. 'You can take down the tents and wash up while we start our forest walk. Has everyone got their squirrel charts?'

'Can he no' come with?' said Caleb, the boy who'd first spoken.

'Not this time,' said Jan. 'You can stay and wash up if you like.'

There was a pause.

'Aye, all right,' said the young lad.

'You'll have fun on your walk,' said Charlie.

'Neh, he wants to stay behind and get felt up by yon teacher,' said a huge overgrown lad, bulky of shoulder, his voice already breaking, to an outbreak of laughter from the others. Joel went puce.

'You want to go home, Fingal Connarty?' shot Jan, sharp as you like. 'I don't want to send you home, son. I want you to stay. Can you stay?'

The huge boy shrugged.

'Then you keep a civil tongue in this place.'

Caleb, however, heard none of this. He had turned bright

red, and went charging up towards Fingal, fists outstretched, and despite being several inches shorter than the other lad, still managed to get a reasonable uppercut into Fingal's pudgy nose.

'Oi, you little fucker!'

Fingal rugby-tackled Caleb, bringing him down to the ground, and was about to start pounding on him when Charlie and Joel managed to pull them both apart.

Jan then did a surprising thing. She went to both of the boys and put her arms around them.

'It's OKAY,' she said. 'It's okay. Can you apologise?'

'He called me names!'

'So what?' said Jan.

'I've got a bleeding nose! I'm going to kill you!'

It was decided, fairly speedily, that Caleb would in fact stay behind with Joel and help with taking down the camp. Joel was starting to worry he'd made a terrible decision.

Charlie gave him a walkie-talkie, as phones didn't work up the hill, and told him they'd be back in two hours, if he wouldn't mind organising their main breakfast.

'How many are you?' said Joel.

'Thirty,' said Charlie. 'See you later!'

Caleb said that the night before they'd taken the dishes to a nearby stream, so they decided to do so again. As Joel had thought, the haar began to burn off, and from up here the sheep on the farm were tiny fluffy dots, and the sailing boats and great steaming tankers were toys on the horizon.

It was quiet away from the sea, only the birds calling and chirruping to one another.

Joel answered Caleb's questions about America as entertainingly as he could, even into the second half-hour about *Avengers Assemble*.

But oddly, he didn't mind. It was the first time in a long time that he'd spoken to anyone who wasn't telling him terrible news; or trying to ferret information out of him. Caleb was the first person he'd met since he couldn't remember when who didn't want anything from him, who didn't care who he was.

'I want to go to America,' said the boy eventually.

'Well, there's no reason why you shouldn't,' said Joel. 'Just work hard at school and get a job.'

Caleb laughed. 'Ha. What's the point?'

'Well, I wanted to travel.'

'Yeah,' said Caleb, kicking the dirt. 'You're not from where I'm from.'

Joel looked at him. 'I grew up in a children's home.'

The boy blinked. 'Aye?' he said cautiously. They were scrubbing the frying pan, neither of them particularly well.

'Aye,' said Joel, rather clumsily.

'And you went to college and that?'

'Yes.'

'And you still came *here*?'

Joel laughed and splashed him with bubbles. 'Watch it,' he said.

But Caleb still stared at him curiously.

Joel set about making breakfast without too much

clattering. It was odd how he found that the simple chopping up of mushrooms and tomatoes was exactly what he needed: calming and meditative. He could see straightaway what Flora got from it. It was pleasant to be out here, in the breezy early morning air, rather than stuck inside an office staring at a screen. He glanced up and found himself being regarded by a large hare, who flattened its ears then bounded off across a field of wildflowers. Joel found himself doing something uncharacteristic: he was smiling.

He turned round then at a sound. At first, he thought it was just one of the birds, but as he listened he realised it sounded more like a stifled sob.

He walked over to behind a copse and found little Caleb, his face absolutely filthy, desperately trying to stifle sobs. As soon as he saw Joel, he turned his face away fiercely, wiping his nose on his grubby sleeve.

'Hey,' said Joel, as casually as he could. 'Are you hiding to get away from helping with breakfast duties?'

Caleb shrugged. Joel wanted to go and sit beside him but didn't feel that would be the right approach. It was like dealing with a terrified animal.

'I'm sorry,' said Joel, realising. 'I didn't mean to splash you with bubbles. I was trying to mess about, that was all. It's my first day.'

'It's no' you, mister,' came the small voice.

'Are the other boys being assholes?'

Caleb shrugged.

Joel sat down, pretended to be very busy looking at his cup of coffee and didn't say anything for a moment. In the distance, two cormorants circled the cliff at the end of the beach.

'They're stupid,' said Caleb. 'Anyway, their mas are rubbish. Hoors the lot of them.'

'Don't say that,' said Joel gently.

Caleb rubbed his face again.

'Were they talking about mothers?'

Caleb shrugged. 'I don't care.'

Most of the boys had mums, whom they lived with on and off; many were with their grandparents; nearly all had some kind of family contact. Only Caleb was truly alone, it transpired: in a residential home, for as long as he could remember; never adopted. He wasn't cute, with his scrawny rattish features and embittered expression. Oh, Joel knew it all so well.

'Everyone wants girls, don't they?'

He didn't even know why he said it.

Caleb nodded fiercely. 'They want the cute ones. Blah, blah, blah, ooh, kissy cuddle face.'

He scowled again.

'In my day, they wanted boys to work the land,' said Joel. 'I didn't look like I could do that either.'

Caleb looked up. 'Did they make you?'

'They tried,' winced Joel, remembering one particularly long summer on a cotton farm in Virginia. There had been a lot of shouting. He had been so tired he had fallen asleep every night at the dinner table. Theo the farm hand had thought he was useless and bullied him endlessly. The smell of the fields had haunted him for years. Mind you, he'd had no problem with insomnia then, he found himself thinking.

Caleb sat up and they both threw rocks into the stream

for a bit, not speaking even as they could hear the other boys, returning to the camp, shouting things.

'It sucks,' said Caleb.

'It does,' said Joel, throwing a stone with exceptional force. 'It sucks ass.'

Caleb shot him a sideways glance. 'Does it get better?'

And Joel thought about it. 'Yes,' he said, 'it does. Now wash your face and we'll get to breakfast.'

## Chapter Fifty-two

Saif was definitely on a post-Neda high when he decided that a Saturday afternoon walk in the blowy mountains might be quite the thing – it would help Ib forget about his iPad for one.

It had also occurred to him, as Neda had told him, that he would have to talk about their mother at some point. And possibly being high up in the hills might provide … well … a safer space. A space for all of them that wasn't just tiptoeing about the house, with the constant sound of computer games and Ash whimpering in his sleep. He didn't want to carry Ash up the hill – one good thing since they'd got here was that he was filling out and putting on some weight. There weren't quite the hollows under his eyes that there had been before, and he was getting heavier to carry everywhere. Though his hollows had transferred themselves directly to his father.

Nonetheless Saif tried to be jolly as he got them, grumbling, into waterproofs and wellingtons. It was cool and breezy outside, and the grass bent in the wind. Ibrahim moaned and complained the entire way. Ash was bouncier, particularly when he saw a hawk that Saif pointed out to him.

Annie's Seaside Kitchen was busy as he popped in for some rolls to take with them, and Flora was looking slightly distracted.

'How's Joel?' said Saif casually. Joel hadn't come to see him to ask for drugs, and Saif was unsure as to whether this was a good or a bad thing.

Flora stiffened. 'You'd have to ask him,' she said, and Saif regretted mentioning it immediately. Ash was pointing at the big jam and cream scones at the front of the display and Saif made a promise he could have one if he climbed to the top of the hill, which Ash immediately did, whereupon Saif bought it for him and Ash immediately dissolved into tears and demanded it now and Saif eventually gave in and gave him a little bit, which brought on more tears and a full door-slamming stomp-out from Ib and the same sinking feeling in Saif's stomach that nobody – nobody – could be doing a worse job with the boys than he was, and he was their father. He was conscious not just of the loss of Amena, who would surely know what to do in that beautiful smiling way of hers, but his own mother, long dead, and the way she could soothe him when he was upset and the way she seemed to move . . .

He shut it down and pasted on a smile, trying to channel Neda.

'Come on! Let's go! Last up is a loser!'

The boys stomped grumpily behind, Ash moaning that he had a stomach ache, Ib pointing out every five minutes that he was bored. Saif thought for a second what would have happened if he had ever spoken to his own father like that, but again, it wasn't worth bothering about right now.

And the view from high up really was worth it, as they finally reached it and threw themselves down, complaining even though they could see all the little boats in the bay and the grey slate of the roofs of all the houses of the town.

Saif pulled out sandwiches and cans of juice and the boys picked at them listlessly. It had heated up a little bit up here, and he stretched out on the grass and let it tickle his nose. When you got close, you could see the beetles scuttle here and there, a busy world beneath the world they lived in. Were they as concerned? Did such awful things happen? How many bugs had he trodden on just to get here, and did they even notice when children, wives, parents got lost – vanished off the face of the earth?

Even so, it was pleasant up in the hills. Even Ib had lost his characteristically guarded look. Saif stared at him.

'Do you guys . . . ?'

He tried to start casually. It had been the last thing Neda had said to him before they left. They had to discuss Amena. Don't make a big deal out of it, she'd said. Just talk about her. Just let it flow naturally so they didn't feel that anything was their fault, or not up for discussion. It would be hard at first, but the more they talked, the better it would get. He had nodded when she'd said that, thinking how reasonable she sounded.

'Do you think about Mama a lot?'

Ash shot up immediately. 'Mama is coming? She's here? Mama's back?'

Ib read Saif's expression better. 'Of course she isn't,

you idiot. She's probably dead. And even if she wasn't, why would she want to come here?'

The crushed look on Ash's face made Saif more furious with Ibrahim than he'd ever been with anyone in his life. He did his best to swallow it down. He was so upset he could have … No. No. It was a child he was dealing with. A sad, wounded child without a mother.

He did his level best to keep his voice calm.

'We don't know where Mama is,' he said softly. 'But lots of people are looking for her. I just want you to tell me a bit about how you think about her and how you feel.'

Catastrophe unfolded. Ash collapsed into hysterical tears, like those of a two-year-old: endless, sobbing until he was hyperventilating. He cried until he threw up the sandwiches and scones all over the grass, whereupon Ibrahim called him a disgusting baby, which made him cry more and Ib stormed off in disgust.

Saif tried to hold on to Ash and move him away, even as a large column of ants came to investigate the spew, and grabbed his phone to call Neda, cursing when he remembered, yet again, that there wasn't a bloody mobile signal in the middle of one of the most peaceful, technologically advanced countries in the world – and he swore again.

'I just want Mama back,' Ash was howling and Saif rocked him like a baby, while shouting for Ibrahim, at first crossly, and then more and more worriedly. The fell was trickier than it looked; there were plenty of gullies and precipices one could easily get lost down.

'Come on,' he said to Ash. 'We need to go find Ibrahim, right?'

Ash just howled harder. 'Now Ib has gone too!'

'He hasn't gone. We just need to find him.'

Saif's head was instantly filled with horror stories of children drowning in gullies and tripping and falling over rocks.

'IB!' he roared, but the wind carried his voice away. He swore massively and rapidly in English, which he didn't think counted as proper offensive swearing, even though Ash looked up at him as if he totally understood what he was saying.

'Where's Ibrahim? Where's my brother?'

Ash's hysteria seemed to be taking on an even higher pitch. To make matters worse, the black clouds that could appear out of nowhere on even the sunniest days, like a speeded-up film, were gathering overhead. That's all they needed, a quick drenching.

He stood up and gazed around. Nothing stirred, except for the wind through the straw and the lambs hopping through the lower fields. Oh goodness.

Joel was following behind the boys as they walked in a crocodile, finding an odd sense of recognition – even though the dialect they spoke was different – of the memories; of boys together. They bawled and hollered and laughed out loud and Jan and Charlie let them – as long as they were roughhousing and not being cruel – shake the kinks and the wiggles out, bay at the moon, tire themselves out, expend their energy without feeling that they were being troublesome; without having to conform to an institutional-ised Victorian style of behaviour that so many boys simply weren't designed for. There was some singing of songs, including one that got abruptly halted for reasons Joel didn't understand, as it couldn't possibly be worse than the filthily rude rugby song they'd been on a moment or so before. Jan made a face and said 'sectarian' which left him no wiser than before.

The clouds were coming in, but Joel had learned fairly early on that weather was simply a condition of clothing – nothing to revel in or complain about, but merely to be got through with a song and a lot of shouting. The boys had bird-spotting manuals, which Joel had thought they would ignore, but they were actually very officious about spotting the various breeds, and laughing at one another when they made mistakes. They were just about to stop at the top of the river, where there were gentle rapids that Charlie let them kayak down, when he caught a flash of a waterproof out of the corner of his eye.

At first Joel thought it was one of their boys, but when he looked closer he caught sight of a thin, darker-skinned lad ploughing blindly through the trees, tripping and stumbling up the hill. Charlie caught his eye and nodded and Joel peeled off and headed towards him.

He hadn't met Saif's children, but he guessed pretty quickly that this was who this must be. There was something almost transfixing in the boy's misery and rage, and he wished he spoke a few words of Arabic.

As he drew closer, the threatening rain began to fall, and the boy, who still hadn't seen him, grabbed for a tree root, didn't make it and stumbled down the hill, tumbling over the too-large and unfamiliar wellingtons he was wearing.

Joel leaped down the copse and grabbed him by the shoulder just in time to stop him tripping back even further. The boy lashed out.

'It's okay,' said Joel. 'It's okay, it's okay. I can help you.'

'NO ONE HELP ME!' shrieked the boy, and Joel didn't know whether he meant no one ever had or that he didn't want anyone to, and realised of course that it could easily be both.

'NO ONE HELP ME!' the child cried out again piteously. 'NO ONE HELP ME!' and Joel looked at him, and he saw himself, and he saw little Caleb, and he saw a gulf he didn't know how to cross.

He saw all of those things before the boy, to Joel's utter surprise, collapsed into his arms, and Joel stiffly put his arms around him and said, 'There, there,' although he didn't know why people said that, or whether it helped, or maybe it did, and then he said, because he knew this much was true: 'People want to help you. They do.'

Saif was soaked and bedraggled by the time he'd carted Ash halfway across the damn mountain and found Joel and Charlie and a bunch of other people with his boy, warm and dry in a vast tent, a fire crackling outside. Ib wasn't saying much, but the other boys didn't seem to care about that. They'd met plenty of quiet ones in their time too. Caleb was sitting right next to him.

'Oh, thank goodness,' said Saif. He wanted to be cross, to ask the boy what the hell he thought he was doing, but he was just too relieved. Actually what he wanted to do was cry.

'Do you want to stay and have some sausages?' said Charlie jovially. 'They're veggie.'

'Are they?' said one of the lads. 'Chuff's sake.'

'You'll have to pay for them,' interjected Jan. 'We're a charity.'

'Um. Yes. Yes, I think we would,' said Saif.

➤  ➤

'You know,' Neda said on the phone when he finally got a signal again, with a smile in her voice that made Saif think that perhaps everything hadn't been quite as dreadful as he'd expected. 'This is a good start. Tears, anger, shouting, pain . . . These are all feelings. Letting them out. It's a good starting point.'

'Are you serious?' said Saif. 'I nearly lost one of them.'

'Yes, but you didn't,' said Neda.

Saif glanced over to where the two boys were snuggled up to one another back in the house, drinking hot chocolate and watching television – in English, hallelujah, even though it appeared to be some strange adult drama full of people confronting each other in public houses; however, in his state of mind he'd take it. And of course Neda was right: nobody had ever said this would be easy.

Then he took a deep breath and went and turned the television off.

'Let's talk about Mama,' he said, and he brought out the pictures he had stored on his phone, and they looked at every single one of them.

There was no need to talk about the last thing the boys remembered, that Neda had shown him on the transcripts, that he couldn't allow himself to dwell on, not yet, possibly not ever: that one morning, after a night of heavy shelling around Damascus, Amena had gone to fetch bread, leaving the boys at home for safety, and had never been seen again.

Instead, they talked about the food she had cooked and the songs she used to sing until both the boys had inched closer, and Ash curled across his lap, which he'd expected, but Ibrahim fitted himself under his arm, which he had not, and they talked into the night, gradually quieting, until all three of them fell fast asleep on the sofa, tangled up like puppies.

# Chapter Fifty-three

In a funny way, seeing Neda had fired Lorna up too. She had to stop with this ridiculous pining: Flora for once was right. She was going to go to this barbecue on Sunday and she was going to dress up and have fun and stop feeling like a dowdy spinster schoolmarm.

And Flora was right about another thing: come Sunday, the weather was once again kind. The rest of the UK had been battered by the storms, but they had passed through and now the country was bathed in a funnel of high pressure, and the sky was a deep and cloudless blue. Already, the teenagers swigging cider by the harbourside were turning a deep shade of pink for skin unused to the bright rays of a sun that never set.

Lorna took a bottle of Prosecco from the fridge. She wore a pretty flowered dress she'd bought for a wedding down south three years ago – if she breathed in and stood up really straight, she could still get into it – and she curled her red hair round her shoulders and put on lashings of mascara and some light lipstick. As she looked in the mirror, she reminded herself: she was a young woman. She should enjoy it. Especially on a beautiful day like today.

It seemed that the MacKenzies had invited pretty much everyone to the engagement barbecue. To be fair, when you got weather like this, which was quite rare, you just wanted to follow the smell. There were the Morgenssens, all the dairy boys, who got precious few days off and were going to make the most of this one, so they were already quite far into the local ale. The boys had pulled hay bales out so everyone could sit around the farm courtyard, and had set up not just the underused barbecue, but they had dug a pit too and covered it in woodchips Fintan had set smoking the night before. Innes had sniffed and told him he was just showing off, but Fintan was adamant. If they were throwing a party, they were going to do it right. And just as well, as everyone brought engagement gifts, properly gift-wrapped and everything.

Fintan tried not to show how touched he was. In public, he was defiant that this would be the first gay wedding Mure had ever seen. Deep down, he was as keen to be accepted as anyone ever was. It was all right for Colton, who didn't give a toss what anyone thought about him, and hadn't grown up here. But being welcomed meant a lot to Fintan, who, more than almost any of the MacKenzies, desperately missed their mother's comforting ear. She would have had a good time today, he thought, looking around: the musicians tuning up;

the beer cold in the bins full of ice; dogs and children already starting to lark through; Flora's spectacular chocolate mousse chilling in the fridge.

Innes came over. 'Mum would have liked this,' he observed, and Fintan started.

'Yeah,' he said. Innes passed him an already open bottle of beer, and they toasted.

Saif wasn't sure what time to show up and what to bring. He didn't really get invited to many social events on Mure – partly because he kept himself to himself and didn't join the golf club or the pub quiz team; partly because he was foreign; but mostly because he'd seen absolutely everyone's private parts, and nobody likes that. So he was excited to go, and dressed the boys in clean white shirts.

When he'd woken up – very cricked and cold and uncomfortable on the sofa with a dead arm and broad daylight outside, even though it was 4 a.m. – he'd had a sense that things were changing. Not quickly, but changing they were, and for the better. And now, he had the inclination to believe Neda. He'd see her again in a month; he wanted to show her how much they'd improved. He thought, for the first time, that it might be possible. Then he looked back into the bedroom and sighed.

'I DON'T WANT TO GO!' Ibrahim was shouting. He'd returned to his bedroom and was lying full-length on the bed.

'There'll be other kids there.'

'I hate them!'

'Agot will be there,' said Ash happily.

'Exactly.'

'She's a baby.'

'She's not a baby! Just play nicely.'

Ibrahim sighed in a very teenage way. 'Can't I just play on the iPad today? When there's no school?'

'No,' said Saif. Saying no did not come easily, but he was trying it out for size. 'If you're polite and speak English, then I will let you play on it tonight.'

Ibrahim weighed this up and declared it officially acceptable.

'But not with that baby Agot.'

'Deal,' said Saif.

They walked through the farm gates – late, obviously: he'd got it wrong again. A group of people were in the corner playing a piano they'd trundled out of the house, and there was a fiddle, and various already quite drunk people were standing up to do a song. Huge numbers of children were tearing round and round the house playing with the dogs. The smell of grilled meat went all the way down the drive and was driving the dogs potty. He felt suddenly nervous as they walked through the gateway, feeling that awful party feeling when you think you won't know anyone or that everyone is looking at you, and he realised that bringing a bunch of flowers when the field in front of the farmhouse, which was lying fallow this year, was absolutely teeming with poppies and wild daisies, was perhaps a little unnecessary. Agot came tearing up to them, her almost-white hair glinting in the sun. She was wearing a medieval princess dress of velvet with a long train, goodness knows how or why. But, oddly, it rather suited her.

'MY FRENS!' she yelled.

From Agot's point of view, she had been feeling most out of it, as all the other children went to the local school and had been ignoring her, and she had been on at her father to let her attend simply by calling it 'MY SCHOO!' whenever they drove past it. Eilidh's parents were elderly, and on the mainland. When she was with her mother, Agot got farmed out to a succession of babysitters and, it seemed to Innes, anyone who could take her. It wasn't that Eilidh was a bad mother – she was a wonderful mother. But trying to keep together the fabric of family and home and work when her ex lived a body of water away was so tough on both of them. It gladdened his heart to see so much of his daughter; he knew many divorced fathers didn't or couldn't. But he had no idea what to do with Agot's apparently implacable will to move.

Ash lit up. 'AGOT! PLAY!' he demanded. His small vocabulary of English words tended towards the imperative.

'YES!' said Agot, equally happy to respond in shouts, and the six-year-old and the four-year-old took themselves off. Saif looked for Ibrahim, who was staring rather longingly at a rowdy football game that was going on at the end of the low field, consisting of several boys, a couple of girls, some drunk dads and some dogs.

'You could go and play,' said Saif.

Ibrahim shrugged. 'They won't want me.'

'This is a party. It's different from school. You're good at football.'

'I'm not,' said Ibrahim.

'Well, you can't be worse than that dog there.'

The ball came soaring towards them. Saif nudged him. 'Go on.'

'*ABBA!*'

'Just return it. Then you can come back to me.'

'You are *so* embarrassing.'

Saif found himself grinning. That was all he wanted to be. An embarrassing dad.

He straightened up as Ibrahim slouched off, handed back the ball and was ushered in by one of the fathers. He smiled once more to himself and moved forward.

Two things struck him, almost simultaneously. The first was Lorna. He would barely have recognised her. Gone was the fleece she wore for cold walks in the early morning, hair pulled back. Instead, she was wearing the prettiest summer frock – Saif didn't know a lot about women's clothes, but he could see the tumbling flowers and the way the long skirt swayed in the light breeze, and it looked pretty to him. Her hair was loose and glorious – that shimmering red that looked so exotic and foreign – and tumbled down her back. She was wearing a little make-up, and her eyelashes were long, and she was laughing in the sunshine, and Saif felt a jolt of something he hadn't felt for a long time, and he remembered suddenly last year, when they had nearly, just for a moment, kissed at the town ceilidh. Suddenly he found his throat was dry, and his cheeks were pink, and as the sun glinted off her hair he felt a way he hadn't felt for a long time. It was several seconds before his reflex guilt kicked in, before he told himself, I am married, I am, I am, in the eyes of God and the world, to a woman I love, even though every day brought less and less news; even though even the boys now only asked at night.

Then Lorna turned and saw him and her heart leaped, and every idea she'd had of playing it cool or not reacting or ignoring him in favour of Innes . . .

She stopped, frozen, caught in mid-smile, unable to disguise her delight at seeing him, her heart lurching. Oh, he was exactly the only person she wanted to see and they gazed at one another . . .

'Hey, beer?' Saif blinked, and tried to focus on the person handing him a drink. It took him a moment to realise it was Colton, and he was about to make his excuses and move towards Lorna when he stopped and looked twice, and suddenly everything changed.

# Chapter Fifty-four

Colton wasn't Saif's patient – Saif presumed he had a private doctor elsewhere – so Saif hadn't seen him for a long time.

Probably it wasn't as noticeable if you saw him day to day.

But Saif knew. In his country, where medicine could be expensive, many people put off going to the doctor until as late as they could. Often far too late. And when they came into his surgery, they had a look about them. It was experience that taught you, and Saif knew it very well.

Saif stared at Colton, who was looking at him cheerfully, beer still outstretched.

Gradually, Colton took in the look. Saif glanced around to make sure nobody was standing too close to them. He didn't see Lorna's face fall rapidly into deep disappointment, as he had seen her and then immediately snubbed her to talk to Colton.

He did not see her tip the rest of the glass of wine down her neck in double-quick time, grab a huge refill, then march off, face hot, to look for someone – anyone – else to talk to, and to stop herself bursting into tears.

'What is wrong with you?' Saif said quietly and urgently. He never realised how direct and rude his English could sound sometimes. The English language not having a formal tense meant he just assumed nobody minded how you spoke to them.

'What are you talking about?' said Colton. 'Have a beer, enjoy the lovely day. You drink beer, right?'

Saif rolled his eyes and didn't answer, taking the beer. 'You have not been to see me.' His voice was barely louder than a whisper.

Neither was Colton's. 'Why would I have to do that?' he said uncomfortably.

'You have lost a lot of weight.'

'I'm getting married. That's what people do.'

Saif shook his head. 'I do not want to alarm you. But I would like very much for you to come in and see me. In fact, I would like to send you for some tests. I do not want to scare you or spoil your party. But I would highly recommend that . . .'

Colton grabbed Saif by the arm and marched him over to the quiet side of the barn, where there was no one else around. 'Shut up,' he hissed. 'I don't want to hear it. And I don't want you shooting your mouth off either.'

'What would I be shooting my mouth off about?'

Colton spat on the ground. Saif looked into his clouded eyes and heaved a sigh. 'Doesn't he know?'

There was a long pause. Colton stared at the ground.

'You're getting married! You should tell him! Where is it?'

There were so many options now. Treatment in the West was astonishing to Saif. For all the complaints about the NHS, he found it passionate and compassionate and mind-bogglingly successful.

'Pancreas. Well. It started there.'

Saif never swore, as he was never sure which taboo words in his new language were mild and which were unfathomably insulting. But now he did. There was barely a worse prognosis.

'Fuck,' he said.

'You sound funny when you say that,' said Colton.

'Stage?'

Colton held up four fingers. 'You're a doctor, right? You can't tell anyone.'

'You should perhaps tell your husband.'

'After the wedding,' hissed Colton.

They glanced round. The scene under the wispy clouds in the sky was idyllic. The football match; the dancing; the laughter in the air; the children running; the fiddle music; and the green hills stretching down, dabbed with lambs and wildflowers and bright waving poppies all the way to a deep blue sea that went on for ever.

'There is nothing they can do . . . ?'

'You think I can't afford the best doctors, Doc? No offence. You think I haven't checked this shit out? That that hasn't been my full-time job for months? I have my own morphine supply, my own whisky distillery . . . Hell, I'm just happy it isn't dementia.'

Colton's bravado was touching, but he wasn't even fifty.

'Doc.' Colton leaned over. His voice was slightly slurred. It seemed impossible Fintan hadn't noticed.

'I have one. Last. Summer. I want to spend it here, on this place I love. I want to get married to the boy I love, without everyone giving me fucking puppy dog face. I want to be happy, and then I want to drift away. Chemo will give me an extra six months of throwing up in a fucking bucket. It doesn't matter anyway, because this shit is spreading to my brain and you know what that means.'

Saif did. Delirium. Hallucinations. Mental incapacity. The full checklist of horrors.

'I'm not having it,' said Colton. 'I control my life. I control what I do. I always have. And I am telling you. I'm not having it.'

'Don't say any more,' said Saif. This was perilously dangerous, legally speaking. 'Please don't say any more.'

Colton swigged from a paper cup of whisky. 'I find I worry less these days,' he said. 'About how much alcohol is good for me.'

He pointed at Saif.

'Vow of silence, right? Hippocratic oath.'

'Who knows already?'

'That piss-ant lawyer of mine,' said Colton, sighing. 'I sure wish I'd never told him. He fell apart. That is the one thing I feel bad about.'

Agot suddenly appeared, her little witchy face sly.

'UNCO COLTON! UNCO COLTON, IS AGOT YOUR BRIDESMAID?'

'Yes, of course you are, Agot. Always.'

'WE NEED HORSIE! ME AND ASH NEED HORSIE!'

Ash was jumping up and down, pretending he knew what was going on.

'AND YOU, ASH DADDY ALSO,' said Agot indignantly.

Which was how, after receiving the devastating news, Saif and Colton, after another slug of his whisky, ended up on all fours in the long, sweet-smelling green grass, riddled with tall daisies and dandelions, each with a child on their backs, roaming the garden and making appropriate noises.

And Lorna gave up, and drank another too-large glass of wine, and decided to go and see what Innes was up to.

Flora was going crazy in the kitchen, bustling about, taking cling film from the tops of salads and things people had brought, sending Hamish out with bottles to top people up. Anything, in fact, to save her having to smile and answer questions about Joel. She sighed heavily just as Mark walked in, carrying the most expensive bottle of wine the little supermarket sold (which was not very expensive), and with a huge pile of hog roast on a roll. He looked as happy as a clam, but his face fell when he saw her.

'Ach, my Flora,' he said, putting his arm around her. 'I know. I know.'

'I haven't even seen him,' said Flora. 'I haven't seen him at all.'

'You need to let him recover. Let him get there on his own.'

'What if he doesn't?!'

Mark patted her on the shoulder. 'Life is difficult,' he said. 'Your food, on the other hand ... it is amazing. And it is a wonderful afternoon, and the sun is shining and there is wine ... Life could be worse.'

'Yes, it could. But, Mark. Why can't . . . why can't he just let me in?'

Mark sighed sadly. There was so much he could say. But he couldn't say any of it.

'It's very difficult for him,' he said.

'It's difficult for everyone,' said Flora. 'Can I ask you one question?'

'Um, I don't know.'

'If you were me, would you wait?'

Mark rubbed his neck. 'Come on, Flora. There's only one person who can answer that.'

'No, there are at least three, and two of them won't talk to me. By which I mean you and Joel, by the way, in case it wasn't obvious.'

'It was quite obvious, thank you,' said Mark amiably. 'But that only leaves one person to answer the question.'

# Chapter Fifty-five

Saif finally managed to persuade Agot and Ash there was ice cream in the kitchen if they went and asked Flora nicely. He looked closely at Colton, pulling himself up. His face was grey, and he was sweating and breathing heavily. Saif didn't say anything.

'There you are!' Fintan came up to Colton and slung an arm casually around him. 'You look hot. Are you too hot?'

'I'm fine!' said Colton. 'And a man in need of a beer.'

Fintan kissed him. 'Your wish is my command,' he said. Then he added, 'Don't expect it to be like this after we're married,' and headed off to the kitchen.

'I won't,' said Colton, watching him go. Away from the noise of the musicians, the afternoon suddenly felt quiet: the sun not so warm; the sky not so bright; the music slow and getting slower as the two men stood there in silence.

Saif badly wanted to go home, but he couldn't. Agot was showing Ash *Frozen* in the back parlour, and to Saif's total surprise when he'd wandered in to check, Ash knew all the songs in Arabic. When he asked him how, Ash, not wanting to tear his eyes from the screen, had muttered something about the soldiers having it, leaving Saif wondering precisely what had happened then, and whether Ash would ever really remember. He would have asked Ibrahim but the boy had finally – *finally* – got himself insinuated into the football game and there was absolutely no way Saif was going to mess with that. So he watched with the little boy and girl for a bit – Agot having decided she wanted to sing the same words as Ash – rubbing his beard, then reluctantly went back outside.

Lorna had definitely found her courage from somewhere, somewhere being a chilled glass of rosé on a warm summer's day. Innes was standing watching the football, talking hay prices with some of the farmers who'd driven their tractors here from over the hill. She walked over to him, feeling the sun warm on her back, her dress fluttering around her legs.

'Hey,' she said, handing him the beer she'd picked up for him on the way.

Innes blinked at her, took in the dress, the pretty hair . . . Oh my God! This was Flora's mystery woman! Of course it was: those two were thick as thieves! He'd rather assumed Fintan and Flora had just been teasing him, but now here she was . . . He'd never given Lorna a second thought; she was his annoying little sister's best friend after all, always closing the door and giggling and smelling the place out with what he had learned was nail polish (with the occasional undercurrent of cider and black in their teenage years).

'I'm here to persuade you to enrol Agot,' she said, grinning.

He looked at her. Her face was smiling.

'I think you could persuade anyone to do anything,' he said frankly. His blues eyes crinkled in his suntanned face, and Lorna felt her insides suddenly turn a little watery. She felt defiant too. Why shouldn't she have some fun? Why shouldn't she stop moping after some ridiculous, completely out-of-reach man she was never going to be with? Was she going to sit on a shelf for ever?

'Well, that's fortunate,' she said, moving closer. 'But we don't have to talk about school.'

Lorna wasn't very experienced at flirting, and not particularly good at it. But suddenly, there was something in the evening that made them both not care.

'We don't need to talk about anything,' said Innes, taking a grateful swig of the beer. The fiddlers had started up a fast jig. 'Dance?'

Lorna held out her hand.

$\rightarrow\quad\smallfrown$

Joel glanced at his watch. The streets of Mure were empty. Every single person on the entire island was up at the barbecue. And he should go, he really should, even if it was the last thing he could handle right now.

Joel took the hill road, expecting to see the boys – it was their last day today; they'd catch the morning ferry back, but Jan had said they didn't need him. He had watched, genuinely surprised as the boys had complained less, laughed more, seemed to stand up straighter by the end of their stay. They had gone brown as nuts in the sun, laughing and splashing about in the stream. He was going to have to have a word with Colton, make sure they didn't lose their funding, as Jan kept threatening they were about to . . . No, he wasn't going to think about Colton.

He wandered up and the boys crowded around him.

'Well,' he said. 'Nice to meet you all.'

They cheerfully chorused a goodbye and Joel had the pleasant sensation of doing something positive, something that wasn't just for him.

Before he'd got too far, Caleb had caught up with him. 'Oi! Mister! Joel! Mister!'

Joel turned round. He glanced up, expecting to meet Jan's disapproving face, but she just smiled.

'He wants to come into town with you!' she yelled.

As usual, Jan didn't ask whether this would be all right or not. She said what was happening and you had to deal with it.

'Okay then,' said Joel.

They walked in reasonably companionable silence. Joel stopped at the grocer's and asked the boy if he wanted anything, expecting an order for sweets, but Caleb shook his head. 'That's all I get,' he said quietly. 'Can I have proper food?'

And Joel's heart sank and he wanted to take him to the Seaside Kitchen to buy him something wholesome, but of course it was shut for the party, so then naturally Caleb wanted to know where everyone was and when he found out they were at a party his eyes got very wide and he rushed back and told everyone. Almost before Joel knew it, they all appeared to be marching up the hill road to the MacKenzie farm, where the boys could smell the most delicious barbecue. Caleb gleefully slipped his hand into Joel's, as the other boys congratulated him on his magnificent scheme. Joel looked down at him and grinned.

Caleb gazed at him wonderingly. 'Can I see your watch? I won't steal it.'

Joel unstrapped the heavy Jaeger-LeCoultre he always wore, which had been knocking the boy's slim wrist. He had bought it when he got his first bonus, solely because Mark had one and it seemed a nice, heavy, centring thing to have. Caleb looked at it in awe.

'How much is this worth?'

Joel smiled. 'It really doesn't matter.'

'Can I have it then?'

For a moment, Joel was tempted to give it to him, before he realised the horrendous amount of trouble they would all get into if he let this happen.

He looked at Caleb. 'When you finish school,' he said. 'If you get all the way through and pass your exams – because you're obviously smart – then you come and find me. And I'll help you in any way I can. And then you can have the watch.'

'Whoa! That's going to be my watch!'

'If you get your head down,' said Joel. 'And ignore all the crap. And just get on. And try your best. Caleb . . . '

The boy was staring at him as if he held the meaning of life.

'There is a way out. I promise there is. You just have to work harder than the next person. Which doesn't seem fair and it doesn't seem nice and you'll think nobody will care, and you might be right. They might not. But then it doesn't matter, because you'll be old enough and out of there and you can make the world care about you. It just takes time.'

Caleb nodded. 'Well, I'll have time,' he said cheekily. 'Because I'll have your watch.'

'You'll have my watch,' agreed Joel, feeling very nervous as they approached the farm gates, and very unsure of the welcome awaiting him.

## Chapter Fifty-six

Flora walked out into the courtyard, glass in hand. She noticed to the side that Innes now had his arm around Lorna's waist and, across the room, that Saif was trying very hard not to look at it. She saw her father, happily oblivious to all of this, beaming at everybody there, obviously quite surprising himself with the speed with which it had become completely normal to him that his son was marrying another man – a foreigner at that. Amazing. Almost as amazing as Hamish, who was sequestered in a corner with a girl Flora had never seen in her life before – busty, and incredibly overdressed for a Sunday barbecue, in a low-cut top and a very short skirt. Hamish wasn't saying much, but he looked utterly delighted.

Flora cleared her throat.

Colton and Fintan were holding each other closely, looking expectantly at her as the crowd quietened. God, Colton had lost a lot of weight. She thought only brides did that.

Joel was nowhere to be seen.

'Um,' she said, her voice growing quieter.

'I just wanted to say ... thanks for coming. To celebrate the engagement of Colton and Fintan, even though obviously that's very annoying as two people shouldn't get married whose names sound exactly the same ...'

There was some appreciative laughter.

'But we are so happy that they are and that they're going to be staying here on Mure ...'

A cheer went up.

'... and Colton will be getting the drinks in. Hopefully.'

Colton raised a glass with a half-smile.

'So. Eat, drink, be merry, everyone ... and here ...'

There had been a collection box in the Seaside Kitchen for weeks, hastily hidden if either of the happy couple came in. Flora didn't think anyone hadn't contributed. She lifted the cloth she'd had underneath the trestle. There it was. A swing.

She didn't know when it had occurred to her that a swing would make a nice gift. It was for the tree just outside the Rock before you got to the walled garden where the vegetables grew. It just seemed the perfect spot for it. It was a large swing, built for two by the endlessly talented Geoffrey, and inscribed carefully by old Ramsay at the forge: 'Colton & Fintan, September 2018' in immaculate letters.

The men knew immediately where it was for. Fintan jumped up, grinning and pink. Colton didn't move for a little bit, and when she glanced back up at him – this guy who had received honours and prizes his entire life, who had done little but win acclaim and awards wherever he'd been – she saw tears in his eyes, and suddenly, for the first time, he looked his age.

Fintan held it up.

'This is beautiful,' he said wonderingly. 'Geoffrey, was this you?'

The old man, who rarely said more than was strictly necessary at any given moment, nodded shyly.

'We'll treasure it,' said Fintan. 'Outside the Rock, don't you think? On all those freezing evenings! We can swing on it to keep warm.'

Colton did his best to smile, but still didn't seem quite able to trust his voice.

Fintan embraced Flora. 'Thanks, sis,' he said and she hugged him back.

'I'm so glad you came home,' he added under his breath, and Flora grinned.

'That's not what you said at the time.'

'I'm an older, wiser man now,' he grinned back.

'No, you *have* an older, wiser man,' corrected Flora, and watched as Fintan put the swing down – very, very carefully – and went back to embrace Colton, who still hadn't moved. He seemed very overcome by emotion, she thought.

Everyone else was clapping and turning back to their drinks and the fiddles were starting up again, and as she stood there she realised that everyone had turned away. And she was still there, alone, her brothers engulfed.

'That was a nice idea, lass,' came a voice, and she realised her father was by her elbow, surrounded, of course, by the omnipresent dogs. 'Very nice.'

He clasped her arm. She could never quite get used to being taller than him.

'That chap of yours?'

Flora winced. How could she say it? Joel had let her down. Or she hadn't been enough. Either way . . . There was to be no excusing it. No understanding it, even. If even her father had noticed . . .

She just shrugged.

'He's over there,' her dad said.

# Chapter Fifty-seven

Joel stood, looking awkward, holding a small boy by the hand.

'Uh, hi,' he said.

'You came!' said Flora, unable to conceal her delight. He looked so much better: much, much healthier than he had a few weeks ago, stumbling off the plane. Then her eyes travelled to the little mite next to him.

'Hello,' she said kindly. 'Who are you?'

But then the entire party traipsed up behind them, and she clocked the entire band of boys, with a smug-looking Jan and an oblivious-looking Charlie bringing up the rear.

'HELLO, FLORA,' shouted Jan loudly. 'So lovely to have your ex working for us now! He's just wonderful; I can't believe you let him go.'

Flora blinked twice and turned round and headed straight into the house.

This was her home – the place she had lived most of her life, in happy times and sad. But there was nothing here for her tonight. Her hands scraped the corridor wall, covered in old pictures of her and the boys: riding ponies; blowing out candles. Her parents, getting married in black and white, nervously beaming at each other, looking like children dressed up in wedding clothes. Rosettes from long-forgotten dancing shows; small trophies here and there. The detritus of a long family life in an old family home.

She picked over the various people having loud, slightly pissed-up but very intent conversations in the kitchen, and glanced again out of the window at happy couples dancing in the golden early evening light, including Innes and Lorna.

Even if you took away the fact that Innes was her stupid big brother, you couldn't deny they made a good-looking pair: his hair blond in the sun, hers a shimmering red-gold glinting in the light; both laughing; dancing with practised ease, Innes from many nights seducing girls on and off the island and Lorna because she had to teach all the little ones for the Christmas party. They were lovely together, and Flora felt a mixture of happiness and sadness all at once. She caught a glimpse of Saif suddenly, sitting to the side sipping a beer while getting his ear bent by Mrs Kennedy, who thought that her medical woes were of interest to everyone, and probably took this even further with the doctor. But his eyes were watching the dancers too, and his face was sad.

Flora slipped out of the side door and walked down the hill, not even turning to say goodbye to her father, who was now happily ensconced in an old chair they'd pulled outside, chatting to his cronies. She wouldn't be missed, and even if she was, she certainly didn't want to draw attention to herself leaving, or spoil anyone else's fun.

The harbour was uncharacteristically quiet. The campers had obviously retired, finding that Sunday trading laws were still very strict on Mure, and that there really was nothing open, particularly in the afternoon. They'd all be on the Endless Beach, Flora assumed, making the most of the glorious day. Or, if local, it seemed that everyone on the entire island was up at her house.

She stared out to sea, desperately looking for the narwhal dancing – anything to lift her spirits. She wondered briefly why Colton had been so emotional. It was sweet really; he'd never seemed like a terribly emotional man.

But seeing Joel again. That's what had really set her off. When he hadn't even come to see her.

The realisation was like a wave breaking over her head. He was getting better – it was obvious. And still he didn't want her. And she couldn't keep kneeling at the edge of the table for crumbs. She couldn't survive off closed minds and turned backs and things – so many things – left unsaid. It was like trying to love a rock. No, she thought bitterly to herself. At least rocks were solid and stayed put. Joel was a law unto himself. She felt horrible deep down in her stomach.

The tide was high, lapping against the harbour wall. The Endless Beach had disappeared almost completely; it must be a lea tide, that rare mystical confluence of moon and water that made the world feel entirely enslaved to the gentle deep blue.

She knew now. The Seaside Kitchen was leaking, but summer was coming on strong. She could do it. They were going to make it up, she knew they were. She could keep it together. She could make it on her own, after all these years of yearning so much for Joel. She was still here. And the tide would still come in and go out, and the sun would still rise – well, until the clocks went back, at any rate – and she would persevere. And sustain. She could.

'Flora!'

She squeezed her eyes tight. She didn't want to talk to anyone and she certainly didn't want to talk to him, not here, not now.

'FLORA!'

Joel couldn't get her to turn round. She was walking away from him. How many other people had he seen walking away? He couldn't bear it. He ran ahead of her across the walkway to the harbour, as she kept walking, head down, not looking at him.

'Go away, Joel,' she hissed. He dived up in front of her on the wall, and she blindly put her arms out to move him out of the way. He stumbled, surprised for a moment, as Flora looked up, also surprised, and without warning he found himself off balance and slowly, and entirely without cere-mony, he fell sideways off the harbour wall into the water.

'JOEL!'

Flora's face was a picture as she peered over. The water was shallow but utterly freezing, about knee deep, and he immediately tripped in the rip. He had managed to hurl himself into a forward roll as he fell – and landed rather beautifully, Flora was unsurprised to note – but he was choking and coughing and utterly drenched, and completely shocked by the sheer temperature. He stood up, his brown hair dripping and curling more now it was wet, falling over his glasses.

Flora couldn't help it. She burst out laughing.

'Why do we live in the Arctic?!' shouted Joel, and Flora couldn't help noticing the 'we'. But she was too helpless to respond. His trousers were utterly ruined.

'Thank you for your sympathy and kind help,' said Joel. 'Oh my God, I'm going to die of hypothermia.'

'It's only up to your knees,' pointed out Flora. 'Also . . . '

She pointed to the far end of the Endless, where the sand backed into the dunes and the tide never took over completely. You could just see a family playing there, the children in swimming costumes splashing in the water.

'Oh, for Christ's sake,' said Joel. 'Okay, I get it; you're all Nanook of the North.'

He waded towards the wall and tried to scale it, but without success. Flora watched him but didn't follow him, as he waded round to the slip. Her heart was beating incredibly fast.

'Please,' he said, hands out as he approached, dripping all the way. 'Can we talk?'

'I don't know,' said Flora. 'Can you?'

# Chapter Fifty-eight

Feeling distinctly hazy, Lorna clocked somewhere that Saif had left – without saying goodbye; without speaking to her at all. Fine. If that was what he wanted, Innes was looking handsomer and handsomer in the bright early evening; the noise was growing louder and everyone was having an absolute ball; Colton and Fintan were dancing together, completely wrapped up in one another; a few midges were circling, but lazily, as if even they didn't want to ruin the perfection of the day.

Innes checked that Agot was busy – she was, climbing up Hamish, who happily pretended not to notice she was using him as a climbing frame. Or, possibly, he hadn't actually noticed ...

'Come for a walk?' he said to Lorna. Lorna, giggling and none too steady in her heels, agreed and Innes pinched a bottle of fizz from the big bin full of ice and two plastic glasses, and they set off.

Saif had not gone; he had been rounding up the children, amazed that they appeared to have had a good time. He just caught sight of Lorna, still laughing, her gauzy dress floating behind her, following that handsome brother of Flora's. He shouldn't feel anything, he knew.

He felt a lot. He refused to admit it to himself, pressed it down. This was ridiculous. He was a married man. He was.

Innes and Lorna headed off, by mutual consent, not down towards the town and the Endless, where partygoers were staggering up and down, but behind the farm, climbing up the stony hill. Lorna abandoned her shoes, which they both decided was quite hilarious, and they clambered up over the grass and the moss, as the view expanded in front of them.

Finally, they came to a rock with an outlook over the top of the farm, tiny below them now, sheep dotted about like cotton buds. You could see for miles, right across, Lorna felt, the top of the world. Innes passed her the bottle and she drank, and they laughed nervously, and then Lorna giggled some more and then Innes laughed too, both of them conscious that they had known each other since childhood. He moved over and tentatively put a hand around her shoulders and she flushed.

'So,' said Innes, who, Lorna knew already, was incredibly practised at this kind of thing. She, on the other hand, was definitely a bit rusty.

Innes moved closer.

'You look pretty in that dress,' he said.

Lorna realised that he was about to come in for a kiss. And simultaneously she realised that she was sitting here,

335

feeling the pleasant weight of a man's arm around her and pretending – desperately fantasising, even, as they sat out on a hillside overlooking the most beautiful bay in the world – that he was somebody else. Oh, to hear those words – but from Saif. Innes was great, but . . .

He moved closer again. She told herself, just go for it. For goodness' sake, she was a living, breathing woman, wasn't she? She liked sex, didn't she? It was a beautiful summer night and there was a handsome man sitting right next to her and she had absolutely no other prospects on the horizon of anyone quite so nice, and she should enjoy it. She should . . .

Then she turned, and realised again it was Flora's brother – *Flora's* brother, of all people – and she realised she was laughing again and it wasn't polite and Innes was actually looking a bit wounded.

'What's wrong?' he said.

'Oh God. Sorry. Innes, I'm sorry. I'm just remembering that time you came home from Cub camp and you'd got into a fight defending Hamish because he'd eaten all the sausages . . .'

Innes smiled at that too.

'Well, he did eat all the sausages. But the other kids weren't very understanding about it.'

'You had this bloodied nose and you were so furious!'

Innes smiled. 'Maybe I'm the patron saint of lost causes.'

He passed over the bottle.

Lorna smiled back and took it. 'You were cute.'

'Cute.' Innes's brow furrowed. 'Not a word any man ever wants to hear, if I can be totally honest with you.'

Lorna leaned her head on his shoulder.

'I know. But now we're here … I mean, it's ridiculous. I remember you eating that slug.'

'Hamish ate one first!'

'Yeah, and he liked it.'

They both smiled.

'I remember when you got all those spots on the end of your nose and locked yourself in Flora's room for the evening,' said Innes.

'Yes, and none of you were remotely helpful,' said Lorna, screwing up her face in mortification.

'Oh, come on, you were my wee sister's annoying friend! Of course we weren't.'

'But did you have to make up a song about me?' She smiled at the recollection. 'Except for Fintan. He lent me his tea tree oil. Where did he even get tea tree oil?'

'How did we never suspect?' said Innes, shaking his head.

'I think what I'm saying is …'

'We're family,' said Innes. He nodded his head. Then he looked at her.

'You do look good in that dress though. Compared to, you know. Spotty Muldoon face.'

'Thank you.'

Innes frowned. 'Flora totally told me you had the hots for me.'

'She told me the same thing!'

'Oh my God! Let's kill her!'

'She was trying to promote incest!'

'No,' said Innes. 'Let's pretend we had a massive outdoor session.'

'Abso-bloody-lutely not!' said Lorna. 'There are parents down there!'

'Come on, I have to tell them something. Tops?'

'Tell them we really appreciated Colton's champagne. Or don't tell them anything!'

'I'm sure everyone's too pished to notice we've even left.'

'That,' said Lorna, watching the remains of the barbecue waltzing crazily around the farmyard far below, 'is absolutely right.'

And they toasted each other with the little plastic glasses and smiled – at an accident averted and a friendship renewed – and everyone went to bed alone, although some felt more alone than others.

Back at the Manse, Fintan was still shaking his head.

'Quite a gift, eh? And you thought the pitchfork-wielding locals would set us on fire.'

Colton scratched his neck.

'I don't remember putting it quite like that.'

'Remember when you arrived . . . ? Ooh, I'm in Mure to keep private . . . I can't speak to any locals or hire them . . .'

Colton smiled. 'Well, that's before I got to know you.'

'You sound so dodgy. Come here.'

Colton smiled sadly as Fintan widened his arms, and came in for a reluctant hug. Fintan started kissing him.

'Ah, babe, I'm exhausted.'

Fintan blinked. 'Are you sure? I thought it was after the wedding you were meant to start going off me.'

'It's not that,' said Colton. His painkillers were in the

338

locked cupboard behind the bathroom door. He needed to get to them and quickly. How many weeks to the wedding? he calculated. Could he hang on until everything was signed and done?

Well. He had to.

'I'm just exhausted. It's been a great day. I love you.'

'Are you sure?' said Fintan suspiciously. He started to kiss up Colton's neck.

'No, baby, honestly.'

'Fine,' said Fintan, slightly insulted, but too good-natured to take it personally. 'Hey, did you taste that new cheese?'

'I did,' said Colton, relieved to be back on safe ground. 'You've done a terrible thing to cheese.'

'It's Mrs Laird who pickled the onions. All I did was put them into cheese.'

'A terrible, terrible thing.'

Colton's hand shook as he opened the cabinet. He couldn't bear, couldn't deal with the idea of the fuss and upset that would be unleashed if what Saif had unearthed – and Joel already knew – got out. It would be horrendous.

All that pity, and people thinking Fintan was only marrying him because he felt sorry for him, or worse, because he wanted his money, and all those hospitals, and tests, and being forced into shit he didn't want.

If he could just make it through the wedding then Fintan would be his next of kin – without being suspected of being in cahoots with him – and they could make the right choices. Together. That was all he had to do. In Colton's life, he'd always done what he needed to do. Normally by just working harder than other people. By gritting his teeth and getting

339

on with it. He was going to grit his teeth and get on with it for as long as he was able.

'Are you still taking all those vitamins? You're going to rattle, you big Californian freakbag,' came Fintan's voice from the other room.

Colton washed them down, wincing.

'Yeah,' he shouted back. 'On the other hand, they might also make me more in the mood ...'

'Yeah, baby!'

## Chapter Fifty-nine

Back at the Rock and somewhat drier, Joel wanted to drag Flora to bed immediately. He felt, for the first time in so long, good and positive and suddenly – as soon as he'd seen her face – so much more sure. About everything.

Flora was having none of it.

'You have to talk to me.'

'About what?'

'About you. About your life. About what makes you be like this.'

'Like what? Come on, Flora . . .'

'No,' said Flora. 'Otherwise we'll start up again and it will be just the same and you won't let me in, and it'll end. Badly. And you'll go off and work for my evil arch-nemesis so she can sneer at me.'

'What?' said Joel, bamboozled.

'I'm not kidding,' said Flora. 'I want to know. All of it.'

'There's nothing to know,' said Joel. 'I told you. I was brought up in care. Get over it.'

'You can't get over it!'

'I'm fine!'

'You're not fine!'

'This isn't your business.'

'It is!'

'It isn't! Goddammit, Flora! I just wanted ... I just wanted to have something pure. Something that isn't part of that life. My selkie girl.'

He couldn't have picked a worse thing to say.

'That's not me, Joel! That's not me, some easy-going water bloody sprite that comes and goes and asks for nothing. For *nothing*. Because I'm not a real girl; I'm some stupid fantasy you have of an island and a life that just does nothing but sit around and wait for you and takes care of all your needs but doesn't get anything in return. Because I get *nothing* from you!'

He was suddenly furious. 'You have *all* of me. You have everything I have ever had to give.'

'IT'S NOT ENOUGH!' screamed Flora.

Suddenly, in his fury Joel threw the chair on the floor. Flora stared at it, then up at him.

And then he was right in front of her, breathing hard, and she was staring back up at him, her heart pounding furiously, and, even as she cursed herself for her utter stupidity, she couldn't help herself: she grabbed his face and before she knew it he was kissing her, furiously hard, almost painfully, and she was tearing at him, half from frustration and rage and everything she felt overspilling as if she didn't know how

342

else to express herself. Every word she had spoken had been pointless. Everything had been a waste. What did she have left, after all? And she grabbed him and pulled him tight towards her and they fumbled their way to the door, both of them aware that Mark might be back at any moment. They opened the door. A cleaner was at the bottom end of the corridor wielding a duster and pushing a trolley full of towels.

Both still breathing heavily, Joel tucked his shirt back into his trousers, Flora's hand went to her burning face and they tried to half-walk, half-run as normally as possible down the corridor.

Joel fumbled with the electronic key in the door of the guest cottage, and looked incredibly close to kicking it in before the green light finally showed, and they collapsed through it, without words, letting it slam loudly behind them. Joel immediately turned to Flora and pushed her hard against the wall, as she found herself absolutely frantic: ripping the expensive shirt buttons when she couldn't unfasten them; tearing at them to get through to the smooth chest; pulling off her own top so he could bury his face in her breasts. All the sadness, all the anger and grief and frustration needed to be swept away, the only way they knew how. He stopped briefly, looked at her with furious lust in his eyes and dragged her over, throwing her on the high bed. As she pulled back the crisp white sheets, he was already on her, pushing down her jeans, and she responded with equal fervour, grabbing him as if she wanted her body to swallow him up, to rip through her skin, to become a part of her and she didn't want him to stop. She didn't recognise the noises they were making; she was screaming at him and he was responding, furiously, tumultuously, as it burned through them like a purifying fire. Flora wasn't sure if it was love or rage or both, and they shouted, both of them, as he collapsed finally on top of her, a maelstrom of sweat, breathless, with items of clothing they hadn't managed to remove from the bed all round them. Joel swore, uncharacteristically, and rolled off and lay facing the wall. Flora tried to get her breath back and felt her heart rate slow, very gradually, and stared at the ceiling, trying to come back down to earth – trying not to think, What now . . . ?

Eventually, Flora had to get up and go to the bathroom. Joel still hadn't moved. She hadn't touched him or spoken to him; his broad back was motionless beside her on the bed. She moved, slowly, her muscles aching. As she got out of bed, he flinched beside her. She turned her head.

'Come back to bed.'

His voice was low, almost imperceptible. The mood had changed completely, like all the fight had gone out of him. Flora blinked. He was still lying facing the wall.

There was a pause. Outside, somewhere, a lost lamb baaed loudly, repeatedly, looking for its mother.

Joel still wouldn't turn around.

'Well,' he said. She stared at the back of his head.

He heaved a great sigh. When he spoke, his voice was very low and calm.

'When I was four years old. My father,' he said finally. 'When I was four years old, my father killed my mother. In front of me. He would have killed me too, but my mother . . .

My mother screamed and ran to the doorframe and there was a lot of blood and noise everywhere and he tried to run away.'

Flora was utterly winded.

She found herself kneeling on the bed, but didn't want to go any closer.

'I remember everything. I remember being there very clearly. My father killed my mother. The police took him away. He died in jail. I never saw him again. I didn't speak at all for two years. The government tried to foster me out but none of the placements ever worked out for me. I did well at school, got a scholarship and the government paid for me to live there until I got a full scholarship to college. Dr Philippoussis was the guidance counsellor connected to the school.'

'He is,' said Joel very slowly, 'the only person who knows.'

Inside, the snakes were writhing, coiling themselves more tightly around his brain. Sex had stopped them, shut them up for long enough, allowed him to break through and speak out. But now, he could feel them moving again.

'Did you love your mum?' Flora's soft voice was like balm.

'I don't know,' said Joel, his voice faltering. He had to, he knew. He had to push on through, defeat the things in his head. 'I don't remember. I found out later she and my father ... They took a lot of drugs. They got in a lot of trouble. She was a dropout.'

'Their families?'

'I didn't ever know my father's family. I don't know if he even did. He was just feral, through and through.

345

My mother ... she was from a wealthy family. Gave up everything for him. They cut her off completely.'

'But what about you? What about when you were left all alone?'

'They didn't want to know. Didn't care. I was some mistake by the daughter who'd gone bad. She had a lot of siblings, I know. Maybe they were worried about their own kids' inheritance, that kind of thing. Who knows? I don't, and I don't care.'

'But ... your grandmother?'

'That's right,' said Joel. 'I come from a long line of absolute bastards on both sides.'

The snakes in his head tightened their grip, as Flora shook her head in disbelief, but he was too far in to stop now.

'That's ... '

'It happens all the time,' said Joel. 'Four times a week in your country, did you know? A man kills his partner. Leaving God knows what chaos behind.'

Flora blinked. 'Jesus ... '

'So,' said Joel. 'Now you know.'

'Now I know,' said Flora. 'And I don't care a bit.'

And then she pulled up the bedsheets and she dived right underneath them and crawled over and found him in the dark and held him – pinned herself to him from behind – held him fiercely tightly and neither of them wanted to talk any more, not then, and so Joel turned around and once more took her fiercely on the large bed. They turned off their phones, and made love, and slept, and held each other, and ordered room service and said as little as possible, to let the detonation and the dust settle – to see if they could deal with

346

the new reality now that it was out there, now it was a part of their existence, now Joel had brought the wolf through the door, the violence unleashed; the boy become man, and the damage it had wrought.

# Chapter Sixty

'No more secrets,' Flora had whispered lying next to him on the bed, and she had never been so happy in her entire life.

'You say that while I can't see your selkie tail.'

'Stop talking like that,' she said, kissing him in a warning fashion. Then she got up, groaning. 'Argh, wedding planning day.'

'Did you give any thought to the finances?'

Flora didn't want to confess that she had found his email almost incomprehensible and grimaced. 'One nightmare at a time.'

'Quite,' said Joel, who was dreading the wedding more than Flora could possibly have imagined.

Flora sat in the Rock with Colton, looking at her ring binder. Fintan and Colton were going big. Really, really big. She wasn't a hundred per cent sure she was up to it, not after the

Jan controversy, but she was doing her best – the barbecue had been a success after all, although a lot of that had had to do with the farmers' cask of ale and their incredible luck with the weather.

Colton was flying in champagne from a small vine-yard, which would be completely wasted on the local residents but presumably not on the investors and rich Americans she assumed must be coming. But she'd assumed wrong, it turned out. Apart from a handful of friends – both his parents were dead – from college there was almost nobody coming for Colton at all. He'd shrugged it off cheerfully.

'Billionaires don't have friends,' he said. 'Or else they have to buy them. And my family are a bunch of tightass Republican birther homophobic bastards.'

'All of them?' said Flora.

'Every single last one. I just want people I love. Actual people I really love.'

'And all the drunks from the Harbour's Rest who'll want to come,' pointed out Flora.

'Collateral damage,' said Colton.

Flora looked at him critically. 'Stop losing weight for the wedding. You're not trying to get into a Kate Middleton dress. Are you? *Are you?*'

Colton shook his head. 'Neh. It's just being fed properly by your brother.'

'Well, that's odd,' said Flora. 'Because every time I eat Fintan's latest batch of cheese, I put on half a stone.'

Colton smiled weakly and changed the subject. 'Okay, so, anyway, the cloudbusters.'

'The what?'

Colton shrugged. 'I know, I know. Sometimes it's beautiful. But sometimes it isn't.'

He gestured outside, where it didn't look remotely summery. A sideways sweep of rain had appeared from nowhere and the Seaside Kitchen was pleasantly full of steamed-up tourists in cagoules sitting out the storm and finishing all the cheese scones and moving on to the potato scones.

'Yes, and?'

'Well, I want to have the wedding outside. I want it to be perfect.'

'You can't control the weather though.'

'Ah,' said Colton. He pushed over a brochure to Flora, who took it in amazement.

'"Cloudbusting Services",' Flora read in puzzlement. She looked up. 'You're joking, right?'

Colton shook his head. 'Nope. They seed the clouds with silver and it clears them away.'

'Where do they go?'

'I don't know. Science,' said Colton.

Flora leafed through. 'So they guarantee you a clear day on your wedding?'

'Yup.'

'That's *insane*!'

Colton looked serious. 'You know, Flora, I'm only planning on doing this once.'

'You'll have to,' said Flora. 'I don't care how rich you are: how much is this costing?'

'Never you mind,' said Colton. 'Just remember that I give a lot to charity.'

'I can google it, you know.'

'I give a lot to charity. Right, I have to go. Do you think you know what you're doing?'

'Making the most amazing meal anyone's ever had ever?'

'Great! Thanks.'

'I'm googling cloudbusting, you weirdo.'

'Can't wait to welcome you as a sister.'

'And please,' Flora genuinely was begging. 'Please, when are you opening this place up for business?'

Colton looked shifty. 'Ah, don't you like having it just for us?'

'Yes,' said Flora. 'But I like paying my staff even more.'

'Okay, here's a thought,' Flora said, testing out yet another wedding cake recipe on everyone as they sat at the kitchen table in the farmhouse. Joel looked up, desperate to get out of unsuccessfully attempting to have a conversation with her father about farming.

'What if I change everything that needs butter to margarine?'

Joel winced.

'Not likely,' said Fintan.

'Yuck!' said Hamish.

'Come on, you guys, you're not helping. Hamish, come work for me for free.'

'Look,' said Innes. 'Running a business is hard. Maybe you're just not cut out for it.'

'Shut up, Innes! You're the one who nearly lost the farm.'

'Hey, don't have a go at Innes,' said Fintan. 'I was the

one who nearly lost the farm. There must be other things you could try.'

Flora looked at him. 'I could marry a billionaire. Where is he, anyway?'

Fintan shrugged. 'He's up to something secret on the mainland. I hope it's buying me a really large present.'

Flora caught Joel looking dismayed at that remark, but thought little of it.

'Do you need more investment?' said Innes.

'No,' said Flora. 'It's just pouring money down a black hole. Oh God. The only thing I can do is whack the prices up.'

'You should do that,' said Joel. 'It's absurdly cheap.'

'But I don't want to gouge everybody in the neighbourhood!'

'Can't you gouge the tourists then?' said Innes, who was cross because someone in a hire car had beeped his tractor as he'd been driving up the hill. 'They're bloody annoying buggers.'

Flora thought about it. 'I suppose ... What if I had a discount card?'

'What do you mean?' Joel took off his spectacles.

'Well ... We talked about this ... I can't charge my locals more.'

'You could ...'

'I shan't!'

Joel smiled to himself.

'*But*,' said Flora, 'what if I bumped up all the prices then gave every single local person a discount card that brought it back down to what it was and only took extra money off the tourists? And Jan ...'

The boys stopped what they were doing.

'Hang on,' said Innes. 'Did our Flora just have quite a good idea?'

Fintan shook his head. 'Flora, are you sick?'

'And every time you're rude to me,' said Flora, 'I'm adding another hundred quid on to your wedding bill.'

'Shut it!'

'Two hundred!' She smiled gleefully. 'That could work, couldn't it?'

'You'd have to explain it four times to Mrs Blair,' said Innes thoughtfully. 'And get the cards printed.'

'I can do that. Agot, draw me a card.'

'I DO THAT ALSO.'

Joel put his glasses on and grinned at her wolfishly. 'You might just have cracked it,' he said, glancing at his watch. 'C'mon, let's go home.'

'WOOOO!' said Fintan.

'Three hundred!' said Flora as they walked out of the door – Flora blushing, Joel practically pulling her along.

'And,' she said as they walked down the cobbled road to town, even though he kept trying to smother her with kisses on the way, 'your boys owe me one by the way. Well, not those exact boys. But even so. Do you think they'd fancy helping me out as wedding staff?'

'I'm not sure child slavery is as good an idea as your other one about the cards.'

'Work experience?'

'I'll ask Jan.'

'Ask Charlie.'

# Chapter Sixty-one

Saif was surprised to see him there in the waiting room. He was running desperately behind: the children had had to get dressed up for Viking day and Ash had run up and down the stairs brandishing a sword and refusing to answer to any other name than Storm Cutter.

But he welcomed him in politely.

Colton sat down and took a deep breath. 'I need my medication increased.'

Saif stared. 'I haven't got your medical notes. I can't just do these things willy-nilly.'

Colton made a quick phone call, and the notes appeared on Saif's computer ten seconds later as if by magic. He sat in silence while Saif read them. The prognosis was very grim indeed. Pancreatic cancer was not one of the sexy high-profile ones that got celebrity campaigns. And Colton was very far along. It was so clear when you looked at him, but what was obviously jaundice had been covered up with

Colton's heavy Californian tan. He'd had his teeth whitened, wore sunglasses permanently and absented himself on business. Even so.

'How are you keeping this from Fintan?'

'A lot of effort and lying.'

'I haven't read much but . . . I mean, there are experimental treatments . . . '

'None of them worth a dime, Doc. The one thing I do know a bit about is where to put my money. And none of them are worth a nut.'

Saif frowned.

'And it says here you've turned down chemo?'

'Chemo is fucking barbaric, man,' said Colton, shaking his head. 'I throw up and fall apart and feel like crap so I get an extra three months.'

'Three to six . . . '

'Yeah, but that's the winter anyway . . . '

Saif blinked at Colton's dark humour and decided to risk responding to it. 'Won't that feel longer?'

Colton's laugh turned into a coughing fit. 'Thanks, Doc. It's nice to talk to someone who gets it. That lawyer of mine completely fell apart.' He leaned forward. 'Morphine and whisky,' he said. 'That's how I'm doing this.'

'I can't prescribe whisky,' said Saif.

'That's all right: I bought a distillery.'

Saif raised his eyebrows, unsure if Colton was joking. (He wasn't.)

'I'll get my prescriptions filled on the mainland. Don't need any busybodies around. But you make sure it's generous.'

'There are guidelines,' said Saif.

'Fuck 'em,' said Colton.

Saif stood up. 'Mr Rogers,' he said. 'If you are looking for me to do something I should not do . . . You know where they would send me back to.'

Colton blinked. He hadn't thought about it. 'Gee,' he said. 'Sorry.' For sure he'd find a pharmacist he could bribe somewhere. Things weren't that hard when you were rich. He stuck out his hand. 'I shouldn't have asked.'

'It's your right to ask,' Saif said. 'Believe me, I am sorry to refuse.'

'Just give me as much as you can.'

Saif had given him as much as was possible without an alarm being raised. 'Done.'

'And . . . you'll be here for me, right?'

Saif nodded. 'Any time,' he said. 'But please, please get the support of your family. I can't do a thing without them, you know that.'

He couldn't understand the need for secrecy when more than anything, surely, you needed love and support around you. Pretending everything was fine wasn't going to make this go away.

Colton grimaced. 'Soon,' he said. 'Let me just get through my wedding day.'

## Chapter Sixty-two

The wedding day dawned pale and clear. Flora never found out if Colton had used the cloudbuster or not, but it couldn't have been more perfect. The ceremony was being held in the back garden of the Rock, its green lawn trimmed within an inch of its life. There was a marquee, but it looked like people were going to be able to spend the entire day outside. An orchestra was playing.

Flora was wearing the green dress Joel had bought her in New York and almost all of the work had been done: Isla and Iona were busying themselves and, to her amazement, Jan and Charlie's group of boys were making themselves incredibly useful fetching and carrying.

As well as the Mure spread, there were lobsters in tanks and a special sushi chef flown in from LA, an edible flower salad and a green juice cocktail bar Colton had insisted on and presumably everybody else was simply going to ignore. There was a cascade of macaroons and an ice sculpture – but

357

nothing, Flora thought, looked quite as lovely as the long board of Fintan's magnificent cheeses, laid out with fresh green grapes, Flora's best oatcakes, Mrs Laird's bread, local apples and imported white peaches amid chilled pitchers of rosé. It looked like a painting.

Innes and Hamish were both the best men for Fintan. Innes was in charge of the stag night, which had ended with fourteen young farmers jumping off the end of the dock at midnight, thirteen young farmers landing in the water and one young farmer landing on a fishing sloop and breaking his wrist. Saif, who had been invited but was trying to save up his babysitting, tried not to be too disapproving when woken by loud singing outside his window at four o'clock in the morning and instructed to get his plastering kit out.

Innes was also in charge of the transport, the rings, the bridesmaid, the speeches and making sure everyone had the right tartan on. Hamish was just to stand there and look handsome in the photographs, Flora said, patting him on the hand. Colton didn't want a best man; he said he already had the best one. Flora had mentioned to Joel how odd she found this, but he had been completely uninterested; he didn't seem to care to hear about the wedding at all. Flora wondered if he was secretly prejudiced, although she hadn't noticed anything like that about him at all, but in the business of the day had put it to the back of her mind.

The MacKenzies were of course getting dressed at the farm-house and Flora went up to fetch them.

She stopped at the farmhouse door, looking in at the scene. Innes was straightening their father's bow tie. Hamish was trying to smooth down the bit of hair that wouldn't ever smooth down, and already looking hot and uncomfortable in his tight collar. Fintan was putting on just the tiniest bit of mascara. Agot was standing in a great heap of tulle and flowers and bounced up.

'ATTI FLOWA!'

Flora smiled and the boys turned to her, and with the sunlight behind her, suddenly she looked so like the one person missing from the room, and they all knew it. And she stepped forward and they all gathered in a group hug.

Hamish wanted to drive his sports car down, but of course they wouldn't all fit. Instead, on such a glorious day, Flora swapped out her shoes, and they decided to walk, arm in arm – Agot and Flora in the middle, Fintan and her father at their sides, Innes and Hamish making up the ends – and everyone who saw them marching straight through the centre of Mure, the four kilts swishing, waved and honked and sent good wishes and followed them as they walked the full length of the Endless, up to the Rock. The church bells pealed them on their way, and Fintan was nervous and giggly and they told old stories and made old jokes that only siblings could ever understand. They talked about their mum, and it wasn't until they drew near the Rock, which already was full of cars and people milling about, that Fintan's nerves really kicked in.

Flora took him aside, as she had to just check on the food one last time.

'Amazing,' she said. 'You look gorgeous.'

Fintan shook his head. 'You know,' he said, his voice cracking slightly. 'When Mum was sick … it felt like I'd never be happy again.'

'I know,' said Flora. 'Now, give me a hug before you ruin your mascara.'

Innes, hand in hand with Agot, saw Eilidh, Agot's mother, waiting by the gate. She smiled nervously. Agot pulled Innes over and took her mother's hand in her free one, joining them.

She looked good, thought Innes. Really good, in fact. He smiled, and she smiled back, and he asked her if she would like to sit together and she said she would. Lorna, passing by, also smiled when she saw them and resolved to corner Eilidh and drone on about how wonderful her school was. Just in case.

Hamish darted after one of the new seasonal barmaids he'd had his eye on to ask if she liked sports cars.

And old Eck, ramrod straight, walked out into the sunny garden behind Agot, who was making a very careful and serious job of throwing rose petals out along the red carpet, and in front of all his friends and neighbours, walked his youngest son down the aisle.

# Chapter Sixty-three

Flora looked closely at Colton standing at the altar. He didn't look terribly well; he must have real wedding nerves. Which was strange. Since he'd met Fintan, he hadn't seemed remotely in any doubt about it. Well, she'd never got married and probably never would. She glanced at Joel standing beside her. Oddly, he looked furious, his hands gripping the chair in front of him tightly. She squeezed his hand, but he didn't respond, so she concentrated on watching the service and lustily joining in the 'Hebridean Wedding Song' as Joel squinted at the incomprehensible words on the hymn sheet.

Finally, the vicar joined Fintan and Colton's hands together and produced the long white cords for purity; pink for love; blue for faith for the handfast.

'Will you love and honour and respect one another?' she asked.

'We will,' Colton and Fintan replied.

'And so the binding is made,' she said, tying the first cord.

'Will you protect and comfort one another?'

'We will.'

'And so the binding is made.'

'Will you share each other's pain and seek to ease it?'

'We will.'

'And so the binding is made.'

'And will you share each other's joy and laughter, every day of your lives?'

'We will.'

'And so the binding is made.'

And they kissed, and the congregation erupted, and a full pipe band (Colton had insisted, much to Fintan's eye-rolling) suddenly appeared from the depths of the grounds and led the grooms, followed by everyone in the wedding party, back down the aisle to a rousing march, and Mure's first ever gay marriage ('that you've heard about,' Fintan had sniffed whenever it came up) was ready to be properly celebrated.

Flora was in the kitchen when it happened. She had decided to make up a separate buffet for the boys so they could gorge themselves on sausage rolls and cheese sandwiches and crisps in the back of the catering tent. However, plenty of Murian residents had decided they actually preferred this to the sumptuous spread on offer outside and kept sneaking in, muttering about 'fancy food' and helping themselves to cheese and pineapple on sticks – and Flora had to keep chasing them out again.

At first, only catching a glimpse out of the corner of her eye, she thought it was one of the old geezers that haunted the Harbour's End, grey and wheezing. She could certainly spare a few sausage rolls, she was thinking, when she turned around and realised to her absolute horror that it was Colton.

It was as if he was hiding behind the door, leaning against the wall. His bow tie was looking rather wilted and he had a crumpled-up piece of paper in his hand. He was sweating and looked green and in pain.

'Colton?' She ran over. 'Oh my God! Are you okay? Aren't you meant to be having your picture taken? Do you need to sit down? Is it the heat?'

Anything above fifteen degrees counted to Murians as dangerously extreme temperatures.

He turned to her, momentarily confused, swallowing hard. 'Can I get a glass of water?'

'Sit down.' Flora studied him. He looked awful. She suddenly hoped it wasn't anything she'd served. Was the seafood all right in the heat? 'Are you okay?'

'Just ... just ... '

Colton was suddenly so desperate to tell her he could have cried.

'Just the heat.'

'Well, that's your fault!'

Flora whisked round suddenly at the voice to find Joel there behind her, his face grave. Next to him was Saif. They'd both noticed him slipping into the kitchen, and, for the first time, shared a glance of their common knowledge, then run to him.

'Excuse me,' she said, still thinking little of the situation. 'This is a working kitchen, *actually*.'

They both ignored her. Saif knelt down and took Colton's blood pressure.

'You should be in hospital,' he said quietly. 'Now. It's done. Come on. Enough.'

'I'm still doing this,' said Colton. 'It's my day.'

'You're nuts,' said Joel. 'You've signed the paper. Let us take care of it.'

'What the hell's going on?'

Joel glanced at Flora, who turned pink. 'Can you give us a minute?' he said.

'This is my kitchen and this is my brother-in-law, so no, *actually*, Joel. What's going on?' said Flora.

'Please,' said Saif, turning his liquid eyes on her, and after that, Flora could do little but retreat. Joel grabbed her wrist as she left.

'Everything's fine,' he said quickly. 'But could you waylay Fintan for a moment?'

'How is everything fine?'

Flora's heart was beating fast. Something was obviously terribly wrong. And Joel had that face on again. That closed-up face.

'Please, Flora, don't ask me.'

🕊 🕊

Flora, terrified, peeked out of the door of the marquee.

Fintan was there, looking gently buzzed on champagne in the glorious, ridiculous afternoon sunlight. He was handsome in his kilt, a smile and a word for everyone, as well as happily receiving compliments on the food and the sheer beauty of the day. He was surrounded by the locals, people who'd known him as man and boy, who had seen how troubled he'd been during their mother's illness and subsequent death and how Colton had brought him back to life. He stood in a pool of golden light. Very close by him, Agot was twirling round and round to make her ridiculous dress ride out, and next to her Flora noticed Ash was doing exactly the same with his little baby kilt someone must have unearthed for him; and they were both hysterical with laughter.

She stood, watching Fintan for a moment. He was so happy. He glowed with it, in the perfect sunlight, in Colton's perfect garden.

She glanced back at Colton – he looked sick, so sick. Why was Joel in there? What did he know? Saif made more sense but it was as if they knew something . . .

Her heart beat faster still, even as Fintan threw back his head laughing at something Innes was saying. She backed away. Speeches next, then lunch . . . Everything had a schedule, had been planned perfectly. She glanced round. Joel was heading back towards her, a concerned look on his face.

'What's the situation?'

'He's just overexcited . . . hot,' said Joel.

'He needed his lawyer to tell him that?'

'He'll be fine. He's coming out to cut the cake. Too much fizz on a hot day.'

'Well, that's his fault,' said Flora.

Joel blinked. 'Sure.' He looked at Fintan.

'He looks so happy,' said Flora. She turned round. 'You'd tell me if something was . . . '

Joel had already vanished back inside the marquee

though, and Flora signalled to Iona and Isla to start circulating with more canapés.

Back inside the tent, Saif was all but ordering Colton to get to the hospital, and Colton was absolutely refusing. This was his day and he was getting through it, goddammit. He drank another glass of water and asked Saif if he had anything he could give him. Saif had anticipated this moment, and he did. Ten minutes later, Colton was on his feet again, but Saif wasn't remotely happy about it.

'It's my wedding day,' said Colton hoarsely. 'Now I'm going out there before the bastards notice I'm not actually there.'

Saif and Joel both gave him an arm, helped him up and walked him to the flap of the marquee, where he shook them off and walked over to Fintan, putting on a wide and unconvincing smile.

All eyes turned to Colton as he tinked his glass for attention. Amid the exquisite gardens, the green of the lawn and the blue backwash of the sea, he looked almost translucent, and as he stood there he shook. Flora glanced at Fintan, who looked confused, suddenly, as if this was just dawning on him too. Then, with a sudden horrible cold feeling in her heart, she went and linked arms with Innes, as Joel was nowhere to be seen.

'What's up with . . . ?' Innes began, but Flora shook her head and shushed him. The speech was beginning.

'I just wanted to say . . . thank you to all of you, those of you who have come a long way and those of you who just wandered round the corner . . . to all of you in this place who have done so much to make me feel welcome, make me feel at home . . . '

'That's because you bought us all champagne!' shouted a wag in the crowd and there was a welcome ripple of laughter.

'I have never . . . I have never been so hap—'

Colton's eyes were brimming with tears and he grabbed hold of Fintan, whose eyes were also moistening. Flora frowned. He wasn't cuddling Fintan. He was leaning against him.

Fintan realised something was wrong and turned round, just as Colton mouthed ' . . . happy' once more and collapsed onto the ground.

# Chapter Sixty-four

Immediately there was pandemonium. Fintan leaped down straightaway, calling Colton's name. Saif and Joel ran from the marquee straight past Flora, who stood watching them open-mouthed. Saif cleared a way and put Colton in the recovery position, gently persuading him to come round. More water was brought. Joel pulled his phone out and the helicopter, which was there ready to take the boys off to start their honeymoon, was pressed into rather more urgent service to take Colton to the hospital. And all around, people fanned themselves and said, after all, he hadn't looked well, and hadn't he got thin, and they tutted and tried to shelter themselves from the ridiculous heat and worried together.

Flora went straight to find Joel and wanted to throw a tray at his head. 'He's sick!' she shouted at him.

'Flora, you know I can't talk about it. It's privileged. I can't say a thing.'

'So he's really sick! And you let him marry my brother!'

'Why? Would your brother have dumped him flat if he thought there was something wrong with him?'

'No! But don't you think he has a right to know?'

Joel was furious. 'Of course I do! It's not my decision to make! If it was me . . . '

'If it was you, you wouldn't tell anyone either,' snarled Flora. 'You'd keep it all locked up from everyone, just as usual. I thought we'd *finished* doing this.'

Joel stared at her, wounded. 'But. I. Can't. Say,' he said through gritted teeth. 'You know that, Flora.'

'But it is something they can cure?' said Flora in anguish. 'Can't they? Oh God. Just *tell me*! JUST TELL ME!'

'I. CAN'T. SAY.'

'You would screw up my entire family so you didn't lose a job?!' said Flora. 'You would literally risk the lives of people I love so that you could keep on making lots of money?'

'That's not how it works!'

'You let this happen,' said Flora. She was so white-hot with rage she couldn't see straight.

'Actually, I think I'm going to find out how a sick man is doing,' said Joel furiously, pulling out his phone and heading out of the marquee.

'Don't forget to NOT TELL ME, ONCE YOU KNOW!' screamed Flora after him in front of half of the guests. She turned round to also leave, but of course she then had to walk past everybody she knew in the gardens, all of them looking to her as if she knew. Innes and Hamish were approaching, and her father – oh Christ, her dad – was looking utterly confused standing next to the vicar. What a mess.

Joel reached the other end of the marquee. The

369

helicopter was still circling overhead, but oddly not landing on the clearly marked 'H' over to the side of the orchard. Colton was sitting on a chair, his head nodding a little, an obviously deranged Fintan sitting beside him, pleading with him, but Colton was, of all things, on his phone.

Joel moved forward, glancing at Saif who was shaking his head in disbelief. Before figuring out what would be best, Joel turned to the watching crowd.

'Would you mind . . . ?' he said awkwardly. Most people had never heard him talk and turned round. 'I'm sorry. Would you mind . . . leaving, or going back to the marquee please?' He looked at the disgruntled and concerned faces and had an idea. 'Actually, no, hang on – Inge-Britt – can we continue the party at the Harbour's Rest? Send Colton the bill? And we'll keep everyone updated. I'm sure it's nothing, just overexcitement.'

There were a few disappointed faces, but Joel looked smoothly authoritative and they had no choice but to turn away and head back up towards the house. Joel instructed the minibus driver, and let people tell Colton to get well soon, and hopefully they'd be back in time for the famous but terrible 1970s rock band he was rumoured to have flown in for the occasion.

By the time he got back to Colton, they were no further on. The helicopter was still circling without landing. Fintan was still shouting in a way that couldn't be heard over the din.

Joel moved quietly over to Colton's other side. 'What are you doing? You need to get on the helicopter.'

'I'm not getting on any fricking helicopter, dicks, and I don't know how to make myself any more clear,' hollered

Colton. He was sweating and looked dreadful and spoke into the phone again.

'Back off, Jim. I won't tell you again. Get back to the mainland before you run out of fuel.'

'Please,' said Saif. 'Please.'

'SOMEBODY, JUST TELL ME WHAT'S GOING ON?!' Fintan yelled in pure frustration.

'JOEL KNOWS!' shouted Colton suddenly. The helicopter at that moment chose to peel off to the side, its blades whirring against the blue, taking off over the sea. The men watched it go for an instant. Then they switched their attention to Joel.

'What?'

'Joel knows,' said Colton again, wild-eyed.

Joel froze. Fintan was looking at him, eyes wide with incomprehension and fear.

'Knows what, Colt? What do you know?' he asked, his voice bitter and low.

Flora came out from the marquee to see how the boys were; she'd seen everyone else head back to town, but she was damned if she was going. She folded her arms, ready for the fight. Her hair had escaped the bun she kept it in for catering, and it was flapping in the wind behind her back, the pale dress Joel had bought her, what felt like a million years ago in New York, blowing out in the breeze. Joel, glancing up, almost lost his breath. She looked like a fury: a beautiful, alluring avenger.

'Tell them.' Colton sounded husky. Saif folded his arms too, absolutely furious even as Flora stepped forwards and Joel found himself surrounded by accusing eyes. All the

MacKenzies: Innes, who'd sent Agot back with Eilidh and Saif's boys; big Hamish, who wasn't quite sure what was going on but was standing with his family anyway; Eck, trembling a little and quite confused. Everyone was staring at him, except for Colton who was resolutely looking away and out to sea, ignoring Fintan's hand on his shoulder.

'What?!' said Fintan, looking petrified.

'For God's sake, Colton,' Joel swore under his breath. He closed his eyes. For a moment, nothing could be heard except the rasp of Colton's laboured breathing.

All of this stuff. All of this stuff he had been carrying about for so long. All of this pain. His head tightened and twisted. He felt the snakes again, writhing, squeezing in his head.

As he stood there, Colton stretched out a gnarled hand, the skin tight over the knuckles, took Joel's long fingers and squeezed them. His watery eyes stared into Joel's.

And Joel nodded in resignation.

'Uh,' he said, standing up straighter. 'I have legally signed papers in my possession indicating the wishes and living will of Colton Spencer Rogers . . . '

'The *what*?' said Fintan. And before Joel could get any further he burst into tears and flung himself on Colton.

Flora watched Joel in disbelief. The entire day had cracked like an egg. She saw his hands trembling, even as Colton held on to him with one hand and tried to cover Fintan's sobbing head with the other.

'It is his recorded wish that he remain on the island at all times, regardless of his health situation.'

Joel's voice sounded robotic. Flora looked at Saif. He looked sad, but not at all surprised, and she realised with a jolt that of course he must have known all along too. Her fury rose even further.

'And you were going to tell me when?' shouted Fintan in disbelief. 'We're married! We just got married!'

Colton looked up at Fintan with terrible sadness in his eyes.

'Oh my God. You're sick. You're sick. You didn't tell me. You bastard. You absolute bastard. How sick are you?'

Colton sniffed. 'About a hundred per cent, as it happens.'

'And you weren't going to tell me?'

'No,' said Colton.

'Why? So you could trick him into being your carer?' shouted Innes suddenly, unable to contain himself. Everyone looked at him. Fintan looked up at Colton, tears falling down his cheeks.

'Did you not think I'd look after you? Did you think I'd walk away if I knew? Did you think I'd ever walk away from you?'

There was silence.

'Of course not,' said Colton eventually. He stared at Joel again, who cleared his throat.

'Mr Rogers ... ' he said carefully. 'Mr Rogers has made it very clear in all of his paperwork that there was absolutely no evidence of coercion or weakened resolve when you agreed to marry and indeed when you did marry.'

'What? Why?' said Fintan.

'So that there wouldn't be potential complications ... later ... '

373

'Nobody,' croaked Colton. 'Nobody could say you married me for money, knowing what you know now.'

'But I don't know anything now!'

'Saif?'

Saif stepped forward, very unhappy to be singled out. 'The prognosis with this type of cancer . . . '

Fintan let out a howl of animal misery and buried his head in Colton's lap. Colton stroked his brown hair.

'Sssh, it's all right. Listen to the man. Don't make him say it twice.'

But Fintan was muttering, 'I can't do this again, I can't do this again,' and did not respond.

Saif had done harder things than this. ' . . . is . . . We don't like to talk in terms of time, but months. Depending on what types of treatment are used.'

'Months for some and years for others?' said Innes.

'Some or more months.'

'But where is the cancer?'

'It is widespread.'

Fintan raised his head. 'You said you had the flu!'

'I had that too.'

'And when you were always away . . . and you didn't open the Rock?'

Colton nodded. 'I had to . . . finalise a few things.'

Fintan looked at him. 'How can you be so calm? This is the worst day of my life.'

Colton cradled his head to him closely once more. 'It can't be,' he said quietly. 'Because it's the happiest of mine. And from now on, every day has to count.'

# Chapter Sixty-five

Joel had backed away, but Flora followed him.

'What have you done?' she said, her voice icy. 'What have you done to us?'

'I was following his wishes. Someone would have had to have done it.'

'So what exactly is the stupid fucking plan? What?'

'Well, he didn't want anyone to know.'

'For fuck's sake! He's going to die? But there must be treatments ... new experimental stuff they let you have if you're very rich?'

'Apparently nothing that'll work longer than a couple of months. And he said he doesn't want that. He doesn't want to go to hospital. He wants to manage it at home, fly anyone in he needs to. Sit by the beach, watch the tide go out. Here. Home.'

'Oh God,' said Flora, her voice cracking. 'Poor, poor Fintan.'

'Poor everyone,' said Joel, staring at the floor.

Flora looked at his exhausted face, the stress the last few months had put on him, carrying all of this around, and could have wept for him. 'You've carried this around all this time? You made me think it was all my fault!'

Joel was bamboozled. 'How could it have been your fault?'

She turned and walked away. She glanced around at the remains of the feast, of the washing-up the boys had done so diligently, but still there remained half-eaten crumbling pieces of cake, birds on the grass looking for crumbs, everything falling and decaying away.

Outside it was growing dark. Finally, the light summer nights were beginning to come to an end, reminding her that the long dark winter was coming, when the sun never rose at all, and everything was collapsing around her – and would get worse and worse.

She walked slowly back towards Fintan and Colton, still entwined in one another down by the water's edge, even as the sun was setting and the stars were starting to appear behind their heads. As she did, a little figure moved towards her.

'UNCO FINTAN SAD?'

Flora turned round. Oh my goodness, why was Agot still here? Everyone was meant to be at the Harbour's Rest; Agot must have run back on her own. She was such a minx.

'I'S HELPING!'

And she ran towards the two figures, her white hair streaming out behind her, and clambered up onto them, pushing her way in, surprisingly strong for such a tiny girl, until she was sitting between them.

Both of them immediately closed their arms around her too, making a trio, and as she saw that, Flora started to run, and knelt down next to them and added her own arms, and Innes and Hamish did too, and Flora got up and grabbed her father, who was still confused, and they all stuck together like glue. Joel saw them there, and he turned around and began to walk away. Flora's head went up and she saw him, once more out on his own – once more alone of his own choosing, even in the very depths.

# Chapter Sixty-six

Joel walked through the darkening night, down the path from the Rock towards the Endless. It grew cold, but he didn't care. Somehow, blundering around in the dark summed things up better than he could have predicted. Creatures scattered at his approach, as if he were some kind of incoming monster, and he pushed his way on through, completely and utterly unable to work out how his life had become such a mess.

He looked down the long stretch of pale sand, glinting now under the full moon rising.

Then suddenly at the end of the beach he saw something sparkling. And, simultaneously, out at sea, he heard a great thudding noise and saw a huge head tilt out of the water; it was unimaginably vast, a truly extraordinary-looking thing, with – Joel squinted – was that a horn? Did it have a horn on its nose? Like a unicorn?

Almost convinced he was dreaming, Joel moved forward

to where most of the town was standing, watching the beast as it moved irrevocably closer to the shore.

'It's going to beach itself!' someone yelled from further down the beach, closer to the Harbour's Rest. Joel looked at the poor creature, thrashing desperately about in the sea.

'No!' he said. He took out his phone and falteringly googled what to do about a beaching whale. For once the internet held, and he read, blinking, that you could lure a whale off a beach with fire. He glanced around to Inge-Britt, who had come up to see what was going on.

'Have you got anything we could set on fire?' he shouted. Then instantly he realised and turned around, running.

'Come with me!' he shouted to the group of Charlie's boys who were also clustered by the waves, watching intently. They ran towards him instantly, and they all rounded the head of the beach in a tearing hurry.

'The torches!'

Of course, all the torches were set up at the Rock, lining the steps between the jetty and the building.

'CAREFUL!'

They grabbed as many as they were able, and Joel shouted for them to be handed over to the grown-ups (although a couple of the older boys demurred and followed him anyway), and, without thinking, he ran headlong into the sea, waving madly.

The creature was coming closer and closer as more and more of the islanders ran into the sea. It felt like the entire town was there now. One of the boys, who had done some fairly excellent cat burglary back in the city, had found the gardener's hut where the torches were stored and had broken more of them out.

This alerted everyone at the Rock. There was a good view from there, up high.

Colton and Fintan were still sitting there with Agot between them. Now she wriggled out from underneath them and began dancing excitedly on the grass, shouting, 'ALLO, WHALE! ALLO! DOAN GO, WHALE!'

The entire town now waded in deep, under the starry sky, frantically waving their flaming torches in the air, moving closer, shouting furiously at the huge beast who tossed and turned this way and that.

Flora moved down towards the waves, worried someone might get hurt. And then, and only then, did she see the person who was furthest out and deepest in, waving his torch so desperately in the air.

A quietness stole over her. It was a sense she had always had when close to the creatures of her island: the island of her ancestors, deep back into Viking lore and further even, back to the myths and dreams of selkies, and the people who came from the sea. It was a sense that this was something she understood.

She kicked off her shoes and walked slowly down to the water's edge. The people with torches – she didn't take one – parted to let her through. Fintan sat up to watch, wiping his eyes. The water was freezing but she didn't notice or mind; the waves parted for her as she left the land behind; the noise of everyone screaming and shouting was drifting away and still she walked deeper and deeper into the water, feeling the cares of the island fade behind her, feeling the fear and panic of the huge animal even closer as she moved through the waves, her thin dress streaming behind her, her hair wet.

Finally, she was shoulder to shoulder with Joel, who looked at her, incredulous, but didn't say anything, just held his torch as high as he could.

'Don't say anything,' she said.

'My beautiful selkie girl.'

'I only wanted to be your girl, Joel.'

Her attention was caught by the huge beast, and suddenly a change came over her as she stepped further into the water. *'Much-mhara adharcach,'* she called out softly. Joel couldn't make out a word she was saying, but she wasn't talking to him. She seemed, although it was absolutely crazy, to be talking to the huge creature. Certainly it looked as if it were looking straight at her – at them – but that couldn't be right, could it?

The thrashing tail seemed to quieten somewhat and Flora moved forwards, even though the water was up to her neck, and he wanted to grab her and hold her and keep her safe. He glanced back towards the beach. The flames – scores of them – roared high above the waves, the noise reaching them, but Flora was still talking quietly to the creature and, as he watched her, she put her hand out and touched the beast on its grey-blue flank, just once, and as she did so, quick as anything, the creature's tail shot up and hit Flora on the side. It knocked her clear out of the water and through the air, and there was a bounding and a massive churn of the waves, and a huge splash and noise, and Joel felt himself almost slip under the water as he yelled and pushed forwards. He tripped and his head went under, and everything was churning beneath him. When he pulled it up again, he couldn't see anything at all; his glasses had gone and he'd lost sight of the whale and lost sight of Flora and he could see nothing and hear nothing except the roar of the ocean and the cries of the lost.

# Chapter Sixty-seven

Joel washed up on the shore.

By the time he had recovered his footing – if not his glasses – and started to fumble around, looking for Flora, calling her name, realising how freezing the water was, he saw that the sky was already lightening in this ridiculous place at the top of the world. A dawn was somehow coming. He looked around. The narwhal ... The narwhal was gone. The great creature had somehow managed to turn itself around and get away from the island it had haunted all summer.

'FLO-RAAAA!'

Nothing. The sea ahead was just starting to glow with the first rays of light of the morning.

'FLOOO-RAA!'

He could hear nothing above the waves; his teeth were chattering. Then there was a noise behind him. He turned around, incredibly slowly.

All along the beach of the Endless stood a line of islanders, still brandishing their torches. And they were cheering and applauding.

In the middle of all the people was a pale figure with long hair the colour of the sea, and a green dress that clung to her like a mermaid's flesh, and she stepped forward, looking as if she didn't feel the cold in the slightest, and she opened up her arms. And he pulled himself back and away from the waves, looking out into the open sea one last time, thinking he could just – could he? – make out the shape of a fin in the very far distance.

He waded in to shore, utterly soaked, utterly freezing, straight into the arms of Flora, who wrapped them around his neck, equally soaked, and kissed him in front of the entire town.

## Chapter Sixty-eight

'Oh God,' said Lorna, who had been waving a torch next to Saif, who'd wisely decided to stay on shore and try and persuade the more elderly and drunken residents not to get in the sea. 'Oh God.'

Lorna was a little over-emotional and had been up all night.

Saif shook his head. 'I know.' He glanced up. 'Would you mind coming and helping me with Colton?'

'Of course not,' said Lorna. Wild rumours had already been running riot around the Harbour's Rest, unfortunately most of them correct. Together, with Fintan stumbling along behind him like a child, they managed to load him up onto one of the Rock's golf carts to take him back to the Manse.

'Is he going to be all right?' whispered Lorna. Saif shook his head in a warning that she shouldn't ask him about it.

'Oh goodness,' said Lorna and she helped him get the

sleepy Colton down and undressed and into his pyjamas. Saif gave him a shot that should make him feel better and told the maid what to do.

It was fully light by the time they took the cart back across the island, but it didn't seem like anyone was going to bed any time soon.

'Well, that's not how I usually expect weddings to turn out,' said Lorna, making conversation.

Saif was tired and not concentrating and blurted out the first thing that was on his mind. 'I thought you'd be with Innes anyway.'

Lorna turned to him in shock. 'Of course I'm not with Innes! Why would you think that?'

Saif shrugged. 'He's very popular. Why wouldn't you be?'

He wished he could keep the infernal tone of jealousy out of his voice. He couldn't be jealous: it was ridiculous. Absolutely ridiculous.

'Why wouldn't I be?' said Lorna. 'Why wouldn't I be?'

She clambered down and stood on the beach, the early rays of the sun hitting her bright hair. Saif got down onto the beach beside her.

'Well, one, he's practically my brother, and two . . . '

He stared at her. 'Two? What is two?'

Lorna reached out her hands and said, as if he were a complete idiot, 'Saif . . . two . . . is you.'

'*ABBA! ABBA!*'

And then Ibrahim and Ash found their father and over-whelmed them both. They were overexcited, both of them babbling in a mixture of Arabic and English, had he SEEN it, had he SEEN the huge *hawt*, had he seen it, *Abba*? It was huge, it was amazing and it was night-time and only dark for a little bit, and the water was so cold, and there was a BIG MAGIC WHALE ...

Lorna melted into the shadows, wishing the ground could swallow her up, but somehow, deep inside, glad. At least she'd said it. At least she didn't have to go through the rest of her life turning down opportunities – Innes might not be the right thing for her, but it was definitely a start – or wishing for what might have been. Because she knew, she knew one hundred per cent, that it absolutely never could have been and never could be, and there was – even as she watched her friend walk up the beach in a daze, hand in hand with Joel – a satisfaction in that, if nothing else.

# Chapter Sixty-nine

'You saved her,' said Flora.

'How do you know it was a girl?' said Joel later, as they were warming up in the huge bath at the Rock.

'I just do,' said Flora, but wouldn't be drawn any more on what had happened.

'You did it,' said Joel. 'With your magic powers. That are totally made up and I totally don't believe in them ...'

'Good,' said Flora. 'Oh Christ. I should call Fintan. Maybe I'll just go up there.'

Joel put his hand out. 'You should probably give them a bit of time.'

Flora shook her head. 'I can't ... I just can't ...'

'There'll be plenty of time to be with Fintan. In the weeks and the months ...'

They had got into the bath together. Somehow it was the most vulnerable position imaginable: the two of them, back to chest.

'The last time,' said Flora, staring down at the water. 'The last time ... He looked after our mum. When I was ... well. When I was working for you. But when I was too scared.'

She swallowed.

'This time, I can be there for him. At least.'

He soaped her shoulders gently, marvelling once more at their pale shapely perfection, kissing her tenderly, wondering how close he'd come to nearly losing her.

'Very close,' said Flora suddenly.

'What?' said Joel, startled that she'd read his mind.

'I like it,' said Flora. 'When we're very close.'

She in turn couldn't believe how different it was from the last time he'd been in this bath, at the very lowest ebb.

'I need ...' She took his hand and placed it over her heart. 'I need you to feel for me. And let me feel for you. I need to know you, and I need you to know me. And that is all I have to say.' She took a breath. 'Tell me everything about Colton.'

He half-smiled. 'I can't,' he said one last time.

Then, slowly but deliberately, he turned her round. She stared into his eyes fearfully.

'But if you like,' he said, 'I can tell you everything about me.'

She held his gaze for a long moment.

'I would like that,' she said.

# Chapter Seventy

Fintan was standing, silent and brooding, by the window, the dawn light shining in.

Colton stirred.

'Please,' said Colton. 'Please come and lie down with me.'

Fintan took off his kilt, put on that morning with such joy and expectation. He pulled off his shirt, sighing deeply, shaking his head.

'How could you?' he whispered. 'How could you keep it from me for so long?'

'Because ...' growled Colton. 'Because every time you mention your mother you tear up. Because every time I think about what you've been through – what I'm about to put you through – I feel like the biggest son of a bitch on earth. Because I love to see your smile and I love to hear your laugh and, right now, the biggest fear I have is that I'm never going to see those things again, and I knew it would start right the moment you found out. Because ...'

He let out a great sigh.

'Because as soon as I got the diagnosis I should have broken up with you. I'm a heel. An absolute heel not to do that for you. I should have treated you so badly you hated me and were absolutely delighted when I walked out the door.'

Fintan shook his head. 'You couldn't have done that.'

'Well, if I'd been a half-decent man, I'd have given it a shot.' Colton covered his face. 'Man, I am so, so sorry.'

Fintan crawled up on the huge, luxurious bed. It was to have been their marriage bed. No: it was.

'Is there nothing left to try?' he said. His voice was a rasp.

'Let me tell you,' said Colton. 'There is nothing you or anyone else could do about this disease. You could hate me or love me or divorce me or whatever you like. Stage four pancreatic cancer gives no shits about what you do at this point, what I do, what anyone does. You got that?' He put one arm around Fintan. 'Please?'

Fintan looked up at him. 'This isn't fair!'

'I know, baby, I know.'

Fintan crept under his arm. 'Other people get everything they want.'

'I did,' said Colton.

Fintan blinked.

'Now, listen. You're protected,' said Colton. 'I'm not leaving you much. It's all going to Cancer Research. Obviously. But if anyone tries to dispute the will, it's all on paper and it's all known: you didn't coerce me to marry you; you had no idea I was sick; you had no idea what was going on. A hundred witnesses there today. That's why I did it, you understand? You have no idea what hard-asses my family are.'

'Well, they produced you,' said Fintan.

'Yeah.'

Fintan blinked again.

'And you will have the Rock, and the Seaside Kitchen, and the Manse. That's for you. And some years' running costs – not loads. Not enough so you can lie on that gorgeous little ass of yours. And nobody will ever, ever dispute it or try and take it from you. You got the best lawyer in the world protecting that. And you are well within your rights to storm out, or to break up with me, or hell, I don't even care what you do.'

'What will you do?'

'I'm going to stay here. On my beach. In the most beautiful place on God's earth. Eating good food. Drinking good whisky. And if you would keep me company I would be very, very happy. But if you can't, I understand.'

Fintan didn't say anything.

'But right now, whatever Saif brought me is making me want to sleep like a baby. God bless that man.'

Colton looked at Fintan. 'Will you be here when I wake up?' he said.

'I don't know,' said Fintan.

# Chapter Seventy-one

The spell of good weather continued right through August. Saif started walking the Endless in the morning again, but now with the boys to give them a bit of a blow before school, and he did what Neda told him to and talked about their mother every day. They looked for the boat, of course, but more as a ritual: more of a chance for them all to be together; more as force of habit.

It was a few weeks before Lorna and Saif ran into each other.

Lorna came down later than usual with Milou that day, and Ash and Ibrahim were there, bouncing up and down delightedly as she appeared. Ash was desperate to know if she'd seen his picture that Mrs Cook had pinned up, and Ibrahim told her shyly, and to her utter delight, that he'd finished the *Horrid Henry* book she'd given him, and could he possibly have another? She was pleased to see them, but she'd managed to avoid Saif at school pick-up since the new term had started, and had absolutely no wish to see him here. She couldn't avoid him for ever, after confessing everything – but she wanted to give it a very good try. But here he was, and they were both walking in the same direction.

They stood, looking at one another, as the boys ran far away, playing with Milou, all three kicking happily in the chilly sea.

Lorna couldn't bear to look at him now. It made her tremble, with hope, with despondency, with such utter desire as she felt the reality of the two of them, alone, no other Murians for miles. It was just the feel of him on the salty air; the huge sky above them; the pale sand. And nothing for her. She opened her mouth to make small talk about Colton – nobody on Mure could talk about anything else – but then he turned round suddenly, stricken, eyes wide with his desire, his overwhelming yearning – and nothing came out.

What would it be like? he thought with a sudden shiver. He had thought of little else since the wedding. What would it be like? That red hair, coiled around his fingers, that had haunted his dreams. To count every freckle on her pale skin. He shut his eyes tightly. When he opened them she was still standing there, and the air between them felt wavy and charged, and time had stopped. Lorna realised she was holding her breath, as if there were no need to move on to the next stop, the next second, the next bit of the universe, when everything in it, everything she was and had ever wanted to be, would be changed by what was going to happen in *this* moment, in *this* instant, and after it nothing could be the same. She wanted to hold it, before she slipped and moved and changed, and she needed to bring her eyes up to meet his but she was terrified of what she might see there; the desperate desire she herself felt; the melting sense of recognition, the same wanting.

But what if it were not? Could she bear it? Could she wait? Could she not?

And she did not look into his eyes. Which was a shame because she would have seen all of those things there, and she might have tipped him over the edge, caused him to abandon everything he had planned – everything he believed and ever wanted – had she grabbed him and pulled him to her.

But Lorna was not like that. And there were children on the beach. And she did not raise her head until he started, with great difficulty, to speak.

'Lorenah …'

She closed her eyes. Trying to work out his tone.

'There is …'

He stopped. Then he took a deep breath. Because if he could not have what he wanted, he needed to explain why. He was not a man for lengthy speeches, and the phrases swirled in and out of Arabic in his head, in a more ornate and old-fashioned style, and he was reminded of the ancient formal language of the *Grimms' Fairy Tales* his mother had read to him as a child.

'There are …' he went on stiltedly, his accent making him slow down to be as clear as he could.

'There are worlds. There are so many worlds and so many times for you and me. If you were born in my village and we had been children there. If my father had moved to Britain, so long ago, and not Damascus. If I had come here to study. If you had travelled and we had met . . . '

Lorna shook her head. 'Those things would never have happened.'

'They could have happened, a million times,' insisted Saif. 'And I would have passed you in a marketplace or we would have been laughing in a coffee shop or on a train somewhere.'

Lorna smiled painfully. 'I don't think you would just have swung by Mure.'

'If I had known you would be here, I would have.'

They both stared out to sea.

'Had we but worlds enough, and time,' said Lorna ruefully. Saif glanced up.

'لذلك من حين لآخر ... إذا كان لدينا وقت,' he said softly.

'You know it!' said Lorna, the lump in her throat making it difficult to get the words out. Of course he knew it. Of course he knew poetry. Because the perfect man had walked straight into her world, shaken it up, ruined it, she felt sure, for anyone else she could ever possibly meet, especially on the quiet island.

And she had barely ever touched him, couldn't even look him in the face, had to live side by side with him, in each other's pockets – she had to look after his children – all the while knowing that they could never be together.

'Of course,' said Saif with what sounded to Lorna like kindness in his voice, although it was not.

It was the deepest of sadness, and an ocean of regret.

She wanted to take his hand, hold him, just once. But when she moved a little closer, he flinched, and she backed away, horrified, her hands at her mouth.

'I need to go,' she said, her voice sounding strange to her own ears.

'Lorenah,' he said, but she had already turned away and it was too late and he could not say to her that he had flinched because he knew the second she put her cool hands on his skin he would not be able to resist, for all his brave words, for all his love and devotion for Amena, for all that he wanted to think of himself as a good man; he would throw all of that away without a second thought; he would have grabbed her and held her and taken her home and never let her go.

Saif had been through many hardships in his life. But to watch for the second time, after first leaving his family, to watch the chance of happiness slip through his fingers, seeing somebody he loved walk away from him once again, was unbearable.

It was as raw as the bitterest of aloes, the deepest of cuts, as her footprints made a larger and larger arc away from him in the sand.

# Chapter Seventy-two

And the young knight climbed and climbed and slashed through many roses that grew up the tower of ice, and broke down the walls and fought his way inside through many hardships and much pain. And he saw the beautiful prince there. And he tried to slay the dragon that circled the tower, flapping its green decayed wings, the flesh tearing off its bones; but each time he thought the dragon must be speared, the dragon screeched once again, through its jaws that smelled of death; and escaped and circled the tower once more until the knight was exhausted.

And the prince said, 'You too cannot succeed; none can; you have failed and now you must also leave me.'

And the knight said, 'Sire. May we not fail together?'

And as the dragon screeched and roared around the castle, he crept in the slit of the window of the tower of ice from which there is no escaping, and he knelt down by the bed.

'Your mum told you some weird stories,' said Colton.

'Wherever you are I will stay with you.'

*And the prince said, 'But there is no way out.'*

Colton sleepily raised his head. 'What happens next?'

'I forget,' said Fintan, leaning his dark head against Colton's grey one. He entwined his fingers with Colton's. 'I don't think it matters. Not any more.'

➤ ➤

'I have something to tell you,' said Joel as Flora burst into the house, happy after the most successful day's takings the Seaside Kitchen had ever had. *And* there was a huge crowd of visitors from London, and they'd all made a point of remarking on how reasonable everything was, which had vindicated her decision even more. Locals made a point of brandishing their loyalty cards so vehemently that tourists, who had fallen in love with the island and Flora's food, had started asking for one too. Of course she couldn't bear to refuse, and she'd issued a couple here and there, so the problem was going to raise its thorny head again at some point, but she didn't want to think about that right now.

'Really?'

'Yes,' Joel frowned. 'I can't believe I'm making a habit of this.'

'I can't believe you made Mark go home.'

'I know,' said Joel. 'I felt guilty about Marsha. I think he'd have stayed here for ever.'

'They'll be back,' said Flora smugly. 'So, did the doc say you're cured?'

'Ha!' said Joel. 'Psychiatrists *never* say that.'

In fact, the bear hug Mark had offered and Joel had accepted at the airport had told him way more than that.

'Well, what is it then?'

'Ah, come down the Endless with me. Grab Bramble.'

'He'll be snoozing.'

'That's because he's far too fat for a dog.'

'Stop calling my dog fat, you . . . doggist. Fattist. Whatever.'

'I'm not the one overfeeding your dog.'

They picked up the lazy creature, who was snoozing at Eck's feet as usual, and headed down to the beach. Ahead, Joel spied the most ridiculous contraption: a full Bedouin tent. Nobody could remember whose idea it was, but it meant Colton could come and sit out without getting too uncomfortable or chilled, as well as proving quite the draw to people. Rare was the evening, with a fire lit on the sand, that they didn't gather round, to chat, or chew the fat, or sit with Fintan if Colton was sleeping. When Colton was awake, Fintan did the best he could to smile and look happy and chat.

When he was asleep, Fintan felt like he was teetering on the edge of a very high cliff, and it was taking an island to help him hold on.

There was a sizeable crowd tonight, and Joel paused in a quieter section of the beach. Flora looked at him curiously.

'You have to understand,' he said in his quiet, understated way, 'I have never said these words. To anyone. Ever. Out loud. Okay. You have to realise that it might not mean very much to you, but it is very difficult for me.'

Flora looked at him curiously but knew better than to say anything. Joel swallowed nervously. He opened his mouth. Started. Failed. Tried again.

'Ach,' he said.

Bramble came bouncing up, holding a ridiculously long stick. Joel looked at it, then took it off him (as a very benign creature, Bramble didn't mind at all).

'Okay,' he said. 'Give me a minute.'

And he took the stick, and gently traced

in the sand.

'Will that do?' he said, glancing up at Flora.

She looked back at him, heart bursting, grinning from ear to ear, and she saw that small, shy smile – the one only she ever saw, and even then not very often.

'Absolutely not,' said Flora. 'That "o" looks like an "a" to start with. And everyone knows it doesn't count if you don't say it. And . . .'

She realised he didn't know she was teasing. So she did the best thing she knew how, and kissed him.

'I love you,' she said.

He covered his face with his hands and looked embarrassed.

'Say it!' said Flora.

'Don't make me!'

'Okay, well, just start with . . . just say the "I".'

'"I", I can say.'

'Okay, and now try the "you" part.'

'"You".'

'See, you're already 66.666 per cent there ...'

And they made their way together down the Endless Beach hand in hand.

'How about you say, "I love strawberries" then just put "you" in at the end instead?' tried Flora.

'I'm not ... I mean, I don't really care much about strawberries either way ...'

'Okay, well pick something you really love.'

'Avocados. I love avocados.'

'You can say, "I love avocados" and you can't say you love me? What's *wrong* with you, man?'

'Also, why can't you get avocados on this island? This is a real problem with this island ...'

'I'm glad our lack of avocados is the worst thing about living here.'

'It truly is,' said Joel. 'How about I write it every day?'

'Every day?'

'Every day. Tide comes in, washes it away, tide goes out, I write it.'

'That's twice a day, you div.'

'Twice a day then.'

'I like that,' said Flora. 'Sounds committed. Low tide gets pretty late in the winter ...'

'Well, I'm a very committed person now, apparently.'

'Apparently you are,' said Flora, biting her lip and smiling.

And they wandered on, hand in hand, Bramble's huge tail wagging lazily behind them, up towards the rest of their family at the top of the Endless Beach.

# Acknowledgements

Grateful thanks to: Maddie West, David Shelley, Charlie King, Manpreet Grewal, Amanda Keats, Joanna Kramer, Jen Wilson and the sales team, Emma Williams, Steph Melrose, Felice Howden and all at Little Brown. At JULA huge thanks to Jo Unwin and Milly Reilly. Thanks also Laraine Harper-King and the Board.

# Recipes

Here are some true Scottish recipes I have collected together for you. I realise some of them have appeared in other books, but this is a proper local edition. ☺

## CHEESE SCONES

You will find these in every café in Scotland, for very good reason. Scottish cheese is among the best in the world (and I lived in *France*), and a good sharp hard cheese works wonderfully with soft warm scones. And salty butter, I insist. This should make you a dozen.

250g self-raising flour
A pinch of salt
Dried chillies *to taste* (i.e. absolutely none is also fine)

50g butter (make sure this is cold and cubed)
60g cheese (a mature Cheddar is good)
A splash of tonic water
80ml milk (or to consistency – add slowly)

Heat the oven to 200 degrees Celsius – cold butter, hot oven is always my mantra when it comes to scones.

Mix everything together, dry first, then rub in the butter and add the liquids until you have a nice sticky ball. You can roll it out if you're neat and cut out little scone shapes or just stick it into smaller random balls if you're in a hurry – trust me, they're going to get eaten really fast.

Brush the tops with a little extra milk and stick in the oven – ten to fifteen minutes should do it; they should be a lovely golden colour.

Some maniacs split them and put *more* cheese inside, but honestly, all you really need is some lovely salty butter to ooze out of them. Oh goodness, I can't even type this recipe without wanting to run off a quick batch.

# TABLET

I know, I know: Scotland has a reputation of being a country that eats a lot of sugar. And this recipe does nothing to counter that. Hey, if you like sweet things, tablet is DELISH DELISH DELISH and that is all I have to say about that. Except once, when we were living in France, I sent it in with my son for 'tastes of the world' day, and when I went to pick him up, one of his little classmates came up to me and tugged me unhappily on the sleeve, saying *'Madame! Madame! C'est trop sucré!'*

With that in mind, the recipe does start with:

    1kg granulated sugar
    1 large tin of condensed milk
    125g butter
    A drop of fresh milk to dampen the sugar

Turn the hob on to six or medium high. Butter and line a baking tray.

This is a stirring game. Put the sugar in a pot, dampen with milk, and add the butter and the condensed milk and get going. After ten minutes, it should be coming to the boil – once it is boiling, turn down the heat but keep stirring! The calories you expend doing this *totally* balance out the tablet, I promise.

When it's ready, it should be a beautiful dark gold colour, and a ball of it (use a teaspoon) will solidify in cold water.

Then take the pan off the heat and – stir faster! When it's thickened, pour into the tray and leave to cool – cut it into slices before it sets completely though. It is also nice chopped up into squares in a little tartan bag as gifts.

# SHORTBREAD

You can't make Scottish recipes without making shortbread, and this one is nice for kids to join in with as it's so simple. If you can't get your hands on Fintan's unsalted butter, buy the highest quality you can afford.

150g *very good* butter
60g caster sugar
200g plain flour

Pre-heat the oven to 180 degrees Celsius and line a baking tray.

Cream the sugar and butter well, then add the flour until you get a paste. Roll it out to about one centimetre in thickness, then cut it however you like – be creative (or lazy, like me, and just use the top of a glass ☺)!

Sprinkle some extra sugar on top, then chill the dough in the fridge for at least half an hour otherwise they won't bake nicely.

Put it in the oven for twenty minutes, or until golden brown and delicious.

# HAGGIS PAKORA

This has become so popular and widespread over the last few years that it's rapidly passing into 'classic' status. It's also ideal for kids if you're having a Burns Night supper and are a little tentative about going the whole hog (although haggis is lovely, it's just spicy sausage, just try one bite, etc., etc.).

1 haggis
150g chickpea flour (plain flour is okay if you can't find chickpea)
1 tsp turmeric
1 tsp cumin
1 tsp paprika
1 chopped-up spring onion
250ml buttermilk (again, you can use plain yoghurt if you can't find buttermilk)
2 tbsp chopped coriander
Oil for deep-frying

Cook (microwaving is fine) and cool your haggis and cut it into chunks, then mix with the other ingredients.

Deep-fry – carefully! – and place on paper towels to soak up the oil.

Serve with chilli sauce or mango chutney.

# CRANACHAN

This is so easy for pudding but delicious and really almost healthy (for Scotland).

150g raspberries
150g oatmeal
150g double cream
Drambuie to taste

Toast the oatmeal *lightly* (otherwise it will catch fire). Line the bottom of pudding glasses with the raspberries mixed in with Drambuie. Then whip up the cream and mix it and oatmeal together with, yes, more Drambuie, and pour over the top.

Leave to set in the fridge for an hour or so before serving if you can. And I like sprinkling mini meringues on top of mine but apparently that makes me a heathen, so I shan't mention it.

## Loyalty Card

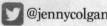

# IF YOU LIKED
## *The Endless Beach*

# YOU'LL LOVE
## *The Summer Seaside Kitchen*

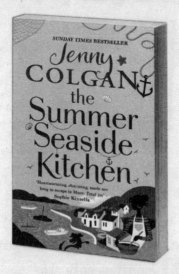

Flora is definitely, absolutely sure that escaping from the quiet Scottish island where she grew up to the noise and hustle of the big city was the right choice. In the city, she can be anonymous, ambitious and indulge herself in her hopeless crush on her gorgeous boss, Joel.

When a new client demands Flora's presence back on Mure, she's suddenly swept back into life with her brothers (all strapping, loud and seemingly incapable of basic housework) and her father. As Flora indulges her new-found love of cooking and breathes life into the dusty little pink-fronted shop on the harbour, she's also going to have to come to terms with past mistakes – and work out exactly where her future lies...

If you liked *The Endless Beach*, you'll devour Flora's first outing in *The Summer Seaside Kitchen*.

## 'Gorgeous, glorious, uplifting'
## MARIAN KEYES

### Life is sweet!

As the cobbled alleyways of Paris come to life, Anna Trent is already at work, mixing and stirring the finest chocolate. It's a huge shift from the chocolate factory she used to work in back home until an accident changed everything. With old wounds about to be uncovered and healed, Anna is set to discover more about real chocolate – and herself – than she ever dreamed.

### Can baking mend a broken heart?

Polly Waterford is recovering from a toxic relationship. Unable to afford their flat, she has to move to a quiet seaside resort in Cornwall, where she lives alone. And so Polly takes out her frustrations on her favourite hobby: making bread. With nuts and seeds, olives and chorizo, and with reserves of determination Polly never knew she had, she bakes and bakes and bakes. And people start to hear about it ...

## 'Sheer indulgence from start to finish'
### SOPHIE KINSELLA

### Meet Issy Randall, proud owner of the Cupcake Café

After a childhood spent in her beloved Grampa Joe's bakery, Issy Randall has undoubtedly inherited his talent, so when she's made redundant from her job, Issy decides to seize the moment. Armed with recipes from Grampa, the Cupcake Café opens its doors. But Issy has absolutely no idea what she's let herself in for ...

### One way or another, Issy is determined to have a merry Christmas!

Issy Randall is in love and couldn't be happier. Her new business is thriving and she is surrounded by close friends. But when her boyfriend is scouted for a possible move to New York, Issy is forced to face up to the prospect of a long-distance romance, and she must decide what she holds most dear.

### Remember the rustle of the pink and green striped paper bag?

Rosie Hopkins thinks leaving her busy London life and her boyfriend, Gerard, to sort out her elderly Aunt Lilian's sweetshop in a small country village is going to be dull. Boy, is she wrong. Lilian Hopkins has spent her life running Lipton's sweetshop, through wartime and family feuds. As she struggles with the idea that it might finally be time to settle up, she also wrestles with the secret history hidden behind the jars of beautifully coloured sweets.

### Curl up with Rosie, her friends and her family as they prepare for a very special Christmas...

Rosie is looking forward to Christmas. Her sweetshop is festooned with striped candy canes, large tempting piles of Turkish Delight, crinkling selection boxes and happy, sticky children. She's going to be spending it with her boyfriend, Stephen, and her family, flying in from Australia. She can't wait. But when a tragedy strikes at the heart of their little community, all of Rosie's plans are blown apart. Is what's best for the sweetshop also what's best for Rosie?

**There's more than one surprise in store for Rosie Hopkins this Christmas…**

Rosie Hopkins, newly engaged, is looking forward to an exciting year in the little sweetshop she owns and runs. But when fate strikes Rosie and her boyfriend, Stephen, a terrible blow, threatening everything they hold dear, it's going to take all their strength and the support of their families and their Lipton friends to hold them together.

After all, don't they say it takes a village to raise a child?

### Meet Nina

Given a back-room computer job when the beloved Birmingham library she works in turns into a downsized retail complex, Nina misses her old role terribly – dealing with people, greeting her regulars and making sure everyone gets the right books for their needs. Then a new business nobody else wants catches her eye: owning a tiny little bookshop bus up in the Scottish highlands. Out all hours in the freezing cold, driving with a tiny stock of books … can Nina really make it work?

## 'A natural, funny, warm-hearted writer'
## LISA JEWELL

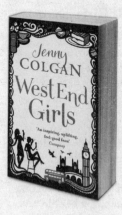

### The streets of London are the perfect place to discover your dreams...

When, out of the blue, twin sisters Lizzie and Penny learn they have a grandmother living in Chelsea, they are even more surprised when she asks them to flat-sit her King's Road pad while she is in hospital. They jump at the chance to move to London but, as they soon discover, it's not easy to become an It Girl, and West End boys aren't at all like Hugh Grant ...

### Sun, sea and laughter abound in this warm, bubbly tale

Evie is desperate for a good holiday with peaceful beaches, glorious sunshine and (fingers crossed) some much-needed sex. So when her employers invite her to attend a conference in the beautiful South of France, she can't believe her luck. At last, the chance to party under the stars with the rich and glamorous, to live life as she'd always dreamt of it. But things don't happen in quite the way Evie imagines ...

> ## 'Colgan at her warm, down-to-earth best'
> ### *COSMOPOLITAN*

### How does an It Girl survive when she loses everything?

Sophie Chesterton is a girl about town, but deep down she suspects that her superficial lifestyle doesn't amount to very much. Her father is desperate for her to make her own way in the world, and when after one shocking evening her life is turned upside down, she suddenly has no choice. Barely scraping by, living in a hovel with four smelly boys, eating baked beans from the tin, Sophie is desperate to get her life back. But does a girl really need diamonds to be happy?

### A feisty, flirty tale of one woman's quest to cure her disastrous love life

Posy is delighted when Matt proposes, but a few days later disaster strikes: he backs out of the engagement. Crushed and humiliated, Posy wonders why her love life has always ended in disaster. Determined to discover how she got to this point, Posy resolves to get online and track down her exes. Can she learn from past mistakes? And what if she has let Mr Right slip through her fingers on the way?